A CRACK IN THE ROCK

Books in this series:

A Crack in the Rock
The Warrior Prince of Berush
In Search of Magic Fire
The Throne of Cerecia
The Princess of Everywhere

A CRACK IN THE ROCK

by

Amber Gabriel

Book One in *The Edge of the Sword* Series

This is a work of fiction.
Similarities to real people, places, or events, are
completely coincidental.
It's a fantasy novel, duh.

A Crack in the Rock

Copyright © 2020 by Amber Gabriel

To everyone who, for reasons beyond their control, has had to make decisions they are not entirely comfortable with

∞∞∞

To everyone who is unloved, either by others or themselves

ACKNOWLEDGEMENTS

There were two people I interviewed while doing research for this book who must remain anonymous for privacy or safety reasons. You know who you are. Thank you!

Germaine Assi, thank you for sharing your perspective on life in Cameroon and your work with the Justice and Peace Service.

Yvonne Kay Haug, MD, your insight and experience have been invaluable in providing Sashia's adventures with a greater sense of grit and realism.

Anna Francis, RN, BS, I appreciate all the hours you spent on the phone helping me create period-accurate birthing scenes and discussing my characters. I feel like you know them as well as I do!

Thank you to Lindsey Keller for your superb editing job! Your comments, corrections, and suggestions vastly improved my manuscript and helped me create an excellent finished product.

I would like to express my gratitude to all the friends who humored me enough to read through my rough drafts and give me feedback! The story would not be what it is without you! It is a brave thing to tell someone something you think they will not want to hear.

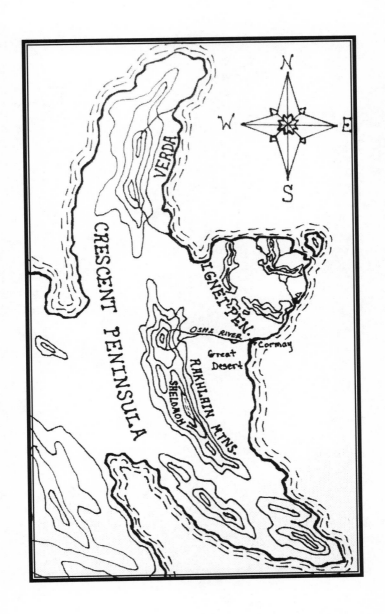

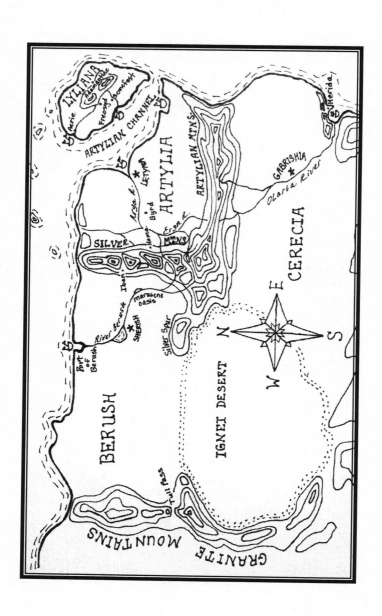

PREFACE

As soon as I wrote the first chapter of *The Warrior Prince of Berush*, I knew I would have to write this book. I didn't want to write it. In fact, I put it off by writing three other books in the series before this one. The subject matter is difficult and controversial, and I expect that it will be uncomfortable for many people. It was uncomfortable for me. However, the story practically wrote itself, and my mind couldn't ignore it. I had to let it out into print.

This story explores the subject of legal polygamy, which still occurs in many countries today. At the time of this writing, fifty-eight countries, primarily in Africa and Asia, allow polygyny, a form of polygamy where a man may have multiple wives. Approval of polygamy is currently on the rise in western society.

In some cultures, the first wife must agree to the possibility of future wives in order for the husband to acquire a second, but in some she has no say at all. In others, a man must be able to provide for each wife equally if he is to have more than one. Even in countries where women are educated, jobs are scarce and women will often agree to a polygamous marriage for economic reasons.

My goal in this book, besides entertaining the reader and providing a backstory for many characters in the rest of the series, is to raise awareness of the issues women have faced in the past and still face today. The story explores some of the reasons why women would enter into such relationships, but it should in no way be considered as an endorsement of the practice. It is also not a polyamorous sex fantasy. I have deliberately limited the perspective to only one character for that reason, and I never write anything that is sexually explicit.

I am primarily concerned with social and economic reasons for polygamy, not religious ones. That would have to be the theme of an entirely different book. In deciding how to deal with the subject, however, I did spend a lot of time praying and studying to discover what God might want me to say about it.

In the Bible it is clear monogamy is God's original design, and polygamy is neither encouraged nor prohibited. It is tolerated. We see allowances in the Mosaic law for multiple wives (Deut. 21:15-17) as well as allowances for divorce, although Jesus clarifies God allowed divorce only because of the hardness of men's hearts (Mark 10:1-12), and marriage between one man and one woman is the ideal. Kings were specifically warned against taking many wives (Deut. 17:16-17). There were also numerous prohibitions about marrying close family members, among other things. In 1 Timothy 3:2, we see that an overseer or deacon must have only one wife to qualify for the position.

In reading the stories of Sarah, Abraham, and Hagar, Jacob and his wives, and Elkanah and his wives, I came away with the impression God allowed people to learn by making mistakes, and polygamy caused conflict within the family. However, I also noticed that God answered the women's prayers, protected them when others failed them, and wanted them to be loved and fulfilled. I love the story of how God provides for Hagar in the wilderness. The Lord opened Leah's womb because she was unloved. Hannah prayed for children and was given Samuel.

Life doesn't always turn out the way we want it to. Sometimes circumstances are beyond our control, but that doesn't mean we should give up. God doesn't always miraculously intervene or rescue us from trials, but He does provide the strength to endure them. Not everyone will find their Happily Ever After here on earth, with another human being, but we can all find it in eternity with the Lord if we accept the gift of salvation through his Son.

The characters in *A Crack in the Rock*, like every human in actual history, may make some decisions you do not agree with and justify them with flawed rationales or limited information. As the author, I could have saved them from these situations or prevented them from making these decisions, but then there would be no story and no cause to consider the issues presented. Countries around the world are faced with legal and moral dilemmas about what to allow and what not to allow due to societal pressure and changing demographics, and the issue of polygamy is surprisingly relevant. I strongly encourage you to do your own research on the subject if you are interested in finding out more about it.

If you feel you are unable to extend the characters grace in this situation, or it is not something you want to dwell on, it is not necessary to read this book to understand the rest of the series. However, I believe the story is both important and entertaining, and I hope you enjoy it!

CHAPTER ONE

The Seventh Year of the Reign of King Kalin of Berush

Sashia carried the dead hare by its long ears and held it behind her back. Its feet brushed the ground as she ducked behind a horse to avoid her mother's gaze. She was supposed to skin it and take it to one of the servants to put in a stew, but this one was fresh, and it was too tempting. She ran back to the small tent she shared with her younger siblings and their great aunt. The children would be napping, and Nani usually napped with them, but they were heavy sleepers.

Sure enough, Nani was snoring away while five-year-old Cashi and baby brother Pat slept in the corner. The flaps of the tent were open to the summer breeze, so there would be light for Sashia to work. She quickly dug through her chest, found an old, stained undergarment, and spread it on the canvas floor. She laid the hare on top of it and pulled her little knife out of its sheath.

First, she cut a slit in the skin on the back, put one finger from each hand in the hole, and tugged. The skin came off the body easily. She observed the bruising and lacerations around the neck caused by its struggle against the snare. Taking the skin off the head took a little work. She left the feet and tail alone. She wasn't interested in those.

Swiftly, she sliced through the abdominal muscles and chest. Then she slid her knife under the breastbone and cut that too. The intestines and stomach had to be removed next. Those were not normally eaten, so she'd had ample opportunity to analyze the contents of a hare's stomach after previous dressings.

Most of all, she wanted to know how its heart worked. That part was eaten with the rest of the meat, so she didn't usually get to see much of it. She wanted a chance to examine it undisturbed. One at a time, she removed the organs and inspected them, all except for the head and brain. Sunen would need the brain to make his paste.

When she finally got to the heart, she took some time observing how the vessels led to it. She felt her own heartbeat and wondered what made it go. She became so absorbed in dissecting and studying the rabbit she failed to observe the passage of time.

"What is that awful smell?"

Sashia started at Nani's voice. "I'm cleaning a hare for Mother."

"In the tent?" Nani's indignation was palpable.

Sashia quickly wrapped up the offending rodent parts in the cloth and scurried away. Father's crotchety old aunt could have a nasty temper, and it was best to avoid her when she was angry. Stealthily she skirted the back of the camp and made her way to the cooking tent.

The cooking tent was really just a canopy with open sides. It kept the sun off of the workers, but allowed the air to flow. Food was prepared underneath it and cooked in a fire pit or clay oven nearby. She threw the offal onto the coals as she passed.

"Here's a hare for the stew." She plopped it down on a table before anyone could remark on its condition. Grabbing the skin, she set off to deliver it to Sunen, one of her father's servants, who would tan it. A nomad wasted nothing.

Sunen looked up as she approached and held out his hand for the skin. "Ah! This will finish Cashi's winter coat."

Sashia envied her sister the soft fur. She only had a cloak of goat hair.

Sunen took the head and prepared to remove the brain. "Finish fleshing it for me."

Sashia laid the hide flat over a log with the hair down and began scraping off the little amount of fat clinging to the animal's skin using a rock with a sharp edge. She liked working with Sunen. He didn't mind her questions and took the time to explain things to her. Carefully, so she didn't tear it, she scraped the skin until not a single filmy, white fiber remained.

"Very good," Sunen pronounced when she was finished.

"Sashia!" her mother's shrill voice made her cringe.

"Better hustle back," Sunen smiled.

"Bye, Sunen."

Sashia raced back to the main part of the camp. Hopefully her promptness would make up for her absence in the afternoon.

"Where have you been, child? There is still carding and spinning to do." Mother sounded impatient.

"I was—"

"Never mind. Kari is ready to have her baby. Everyone else is busy, so you will have to come with me."

Sashia had never helped with a human birth before. She'd watched a nanny goat give birth plenty of times. Sometimes someone had to help pull the kid out. Then the mother would lick it clean, nudge it carefully, and stand by encouragingly as it wobbled to its feet. It was the most exciting thing she had ever seen.

Mother carried her bag of clean cloths, olive oil, and a sharp knife. Sashia had peeked in the bag once, so she knew what was inside. Mother walked quickly, with long, firm strides down the rocky path to the encampment of their nearest neighbors. To keep up, Sashia had to trot. Trembling with anticipation, she almost tripped several times. Her sandals were getting too small, and she stubbed one of her toes. Mother had sturdy boots, but children didn't need boots, according to her, especially in the summer. Their feet grew too fast.

"You are not to talk, Sashia," Mother instructed. "You must do exactly as I say. Some girls, particularly those who have not had their own children yet, cannot handle being present for a birthing, but I don't expect you will feel faint or sick."

Sashia didn't expect she would either. Her eldest brother, Zarin, had turned green and emptied the contents of his stomach the first time he had helped butcher a goat, but she hadn't. Watching from a nearby rock, she was fascinated by the entire process.

Mother stopped and turned to look her in the eye. "You must not ask any questions. I can talk to you afterwards, but not during. Do you understand?"

"Yes, Mother." Sashia wasn't about to do anything to jeopardize this experience.

When they reached the small circle of tents, Sashia was hot and dusty. All feelings of discomfort were swiftly set aside when they entered Kari's tent. Kari was a young bride with only one maidservant. Mother had promised to come and help her when her time came.

The maidservant had a tub and a bucket of water ready. Kari was lying down on her pallet and moaning, wearing only her long, split tunic. A stained pair of billowy trousers lay crumpled in the corner. Mother dipped a rag in the water and pressed it to Kari's forehead.

"I'm here, Kari. Everything's going to be fine." She canted her head to Sashia to take over with the rag. Sashia took it and dabbed at the sweat dripping down Kari's face. As she watched, Mother pulled Kari's tunic back and helped her bend her knees and spread her legs.

"Sashia, hand me the oil."

Sashia laid the rag over Kari's forehead, retrieved the oil from the bag, took out the stopper, and handed the flask to her mother. Mother dribbled some on her hand and handed it back to Sashia who replaced the stopper and laid the flask within her mother's reach. She was dying to ask a thousand questions, but she had to be content with merely observing while mother spread the oil around the area from which the baby would emerge.

"You're doing wonderfully, Kari," Mother encouraged soothingly. "Soon it will be time to push."

"Ooooh," Kari moaned, and her breathing quickened.

"One, two, three . . ." Mother counted until Kari relaxed.

Nothing happened for a while, and then the process was repeated. Mother helped Kari to her feet and had her walk around. Sashia waited patiently and tried not to draw attention to herself as the tent grew warmer.

"Aaah!" cried Kari. "Now?"

"Yes, squat down," Mother replied. She directed the maidservant to stand in front of the laboring mother. "Hug your maid for support, Kari. Push, and gravity will do most of the work. Good. Push again." Kari rested and pushed, rested and pushed, over and over. "There's the head!" Mother handed Sashia the thread and knife and readied herself to catch the baby.

Sashia peeked around Mother's shoulder and saw the wet, pale, oddly-shaped head sticking out of the woman's body. Kari cried out as she pushed again, and the rest of the baby emerged, slipping into Mother's waiting arms.

"You have a boy, Kari!" Mother exclaimed. "You can rest for a moment, and then we'll deal with the afterbirth."

The maidservant lowered Kari to a kneeling position and went to help with the baby. Mother tied off the cord with a string and then cut it with the knife. Sashia felt a few drops of blood spray out of it. Mother made sure the infant was breathing correctly and handed the boy off to the maidservant to wash and swaddle.

"Sashia, you will have to help Kari now. Let her hold onto you while she kneels."

Sashia stood in front of Kari and let her put her hands on her shoulders.

Kari's cry increased in intensity and was now a full-fledged scream.

"Push once more, Kari, and it'll be over," Mother instructed with a worried expression.

Kari just shrieked. Sashia wondered what was happening. One glance at her mother's face told her this wasn't normal. Kari was obviously still pushing, but nothing was coming out. She was bearing down on Sashia so hard, she could barely stay upright.

"Finally," her mother breathed in relief. But almost immediately, Sashia heard her hiss, "Oh no."

"What is it?" asked the maidservant, gratifying Sashia immensely, since she was forbidden from asking questions.

"Her womb is delivering also. It's coming out with the placenta," she replied curtly over Kari's screams. "When I remove the placenta, she may bleed."

Sashia knew her mother well enough to know this was an understatement. Her lips were pressed into a thin, grim line. Whatever it was, this was bad.

"Let's lay her down." They eased Kari onto her back. "Sit right here, Sashia, and use your body to keep this leg bent and out of the way. You're not strong enough to hold it otherwise."

Sashia obediently braced herself against the bottom of Kari's foot and laced her fingers together around the woman's knee. Mother bent Kari's other leg and moved it to the side. Then she worked carefully, slowly separating the placenta from the red blob of tissue protruding from Kari's body. Sashia tuned out the young woman's cries, and she watched her mother intently.

In spite of how cautious she was, when she pulled the placenta free, Kari bled. Mother sat back on her heels and sighed. She looked wearily at her daughter.

"Go home, Sashia. Tell your father I'll be along soon."

Sashia shook her head. "I'm fine, Mother." She stared at her mother, willing her to let her stay.

Mother studied her daughter appraisingly. "Very well." Her tone was ominous, and Sashia shuddered, knowing Mother struggled with allowing her to be present for a death.

"Kari!"

Kari's husband's voice cut through the tension in the tent, and Mother leapt to her feet and rushed to prevent him from entering. The maidservant followed, still carrying the newborn.

"Shazar, Shazar . . ."

Sashia could no longer hear her mother's soothing voice above the wails of the stricken woman. Slowly, she lowered the leg she had been holding and studied the bleeding tissue. Why couldn't the bleeding be stopped? If the womb was outside, when it was supposed to be in, couldn't it be put back? If Kari was going to die anyway, what harm could there be in trying to fix it?

Hardly knowing what she was doing, she bent down and pushed the womb back inside where it belonged. Ignoring Kari's cries of pain and flailing legs, she tried to smooth out the warm, gushy organ and pat it into the cavity where she imagined it fit.

Kari's screams died down to a whimper. She was breathing shallowly, and it appeared she had exhausted herself.

"You must be strong, Shazar . . ."

Sashia retracted her hand and scrambled to the side just as Mother ducked back into the tent with the new father. Shazar rushed to his wife's bed and took her hand, speaking to her softly and lovingly. Mother looked at Kari, observed Sashia's bloody hand, and frowned.

Sashia edged over to the water bucket and rinsed off. Mother took the baby from the maidservant, carried him to his mother, and put him to her breast. Hoping Mother would forget about her, Sashia did her best to melt into the background.

After a while, the maidservant fetched some broth for Kari, and she was able to swallow a few spoonfuls.

Sashia watched her closely; though some time had passed, she was still alive. Mother examined Kari, and then regarded Sashia. Leaning forward on her tiptoes, Sashia could see why Mother was perplexed: Kari was no longer bleeding.

By now, it was after dark, so they stayed the night. Mother checked Kari constantly to make sure she was comfortable and didn't become feverish. Shazar had been relegated to another tent.

"Do you want to hold the baby?" Mother surprised Sashia by asking.

She nodded. She'd been lying down, but wasn't asleep. Sitting up, she crossed her legs, and Mother laid the little bundle in her lap. The tiny, wrinkled face appeared so innocent and peaceful. Bringing life into the world was incredibly thrilling. Saving it from death was even more so. Sashia had never felt so powerful. It made her feel big and small at the same time. The complexity of her feelings left her without the words to describe them. With shining eyes, she looked up at her mother, hoping to see her smile in understanding, but Mother's eyes narrowed. She didn't understand. Not at all.

CHAPTER TWO

"What did you do?" Mother asked the next morning as they walked back to their camp.

"I put it back in."

"How did you make it stay?"

Sashia shrugged uncomfortably. "Things stay when they're in the right place." That was the most logical answer she could think of. She felt defensive. Was Mother mad at her? Why was she interrogating her? Kari was alive. She should be happy.

They trudged silently back to their own camp. Sashia scuffed her feet in the dirt. Cashi ran up to them as they came within sight.

"Where were you? I missed you!"

She hugged Sashia, who picked Cashi up, though the girl was more than half of her own scrawny size.

"Do your chores, Sashia, and try to stay out of trouble." Mother stalked off. "Where is Haban?" She asked one of the servants. Father's horse was grazing nearby, so he must have returned from the tribal meeting.

"May I come with you, Sashia?" asked Cashi.

"Sure."

Nani appreciated it whenever Sashia could watch her sister and give her a break. Sashia and Cashi washed their clothes in the nearby creek and laid them out to dry. They checked the snares but found nothing.

"Sashia, your father wants to see you," called Nani when they returned. She held out her hand to Cashi to take her for her nap.

Sashia shuffled over to her father's tent and lifted the flap.

"Sashia." Her father's kind, rumbling voice made the top of her head tingle. "Come and sit down."

She sat down cross-legged on the floor in front of him. It wasn't often her father spoke to her directly. She glanced nervously at her mother, who sat to his right, for a clue as to what was in store, but her face was impassive.

"Sashia, why aren't you obeying your mother?"

Sashia frowned. "I don't understand, Father. How did I disobey?"

"You were told to be quiet and follow directions," he reminded sternly, an edge to his voice now.

"But—"

"Following directions means doing what you are told to do, and only that. Instead, you took things into your own hands. While the immediate result was good, there are other, unintended consequences. You undermined your mother. You could draw unwanted attention to yourself. People will think you have special powers. You will have to stay at home until everyone forgets about this, and you must speak to no one about it. Understand?"

"Yes, father." But she didn't. She didn't have any special powers. She'd only done what seemed like the obvious thing to do. Why wouldn't people understand?

"You also cannot play with a dead animal like a toy."

"I was just—"

"Stop talking back to me!" Father's voice hardened without becoming loud or angry. "Now you are adding disrespect to your list of shortcomings. Disrespect to me and to the animal. We need animals to live, to eat, and to clothe ourselves, but we respect them. You will remember what I say, or I will make you remember."

Sashia had only been whipped once before, but it wasn't an experience she wanted to repeat. Her voice was a whisper, "Yes, Father." She blinked back tears, struggling against the desire to flee the tent.

"Haban, you have a visitor." One of the servants stuck his head inside.

"Show him in. You are dismissed, Sashia."

She forced herself to walk until she was out of sight. Then she bolted out of the camp to the empty goat fold, the only place where she could be alone, and cried bitterly.

∞∞∞

The next morning, Sashia was told she would have to help mind the goats. There were more animals than her brothers and the servants could keep track of since her father's flocks had increased. Zarin would teach her how to herd them, and then she would have her own small flock to care for. Sashia thought it must be her father's idea of how to keep her out of trouble.

"You're lucky, Sashia. I had to start herding goats when I was eight. You got to stay at home three extra years."

"Humph." She leaned on her staff and used it to pull herself up the steep path into the rocky hills.

They had been camped here for several weeks. When the goats ran out of food, they would have to move on.

"We have even more goats today. Shazar gave Mother several for helping Kari with her baby."

She had heard this from one of the servants at breakfast. Sashia felt betrayed. It was she who had saved Kari, but Mother took all the credit, supposedly to save her from scrutiny.

A billy goat strayed off the path and Zarin picked up some loose stones. He threw them on the far side of the goat and it jumped back onto the trail. "You have to keep an eye on that one. He likes to cause trouble." Zarin used his staff to keep the rest of the herd in line, guiding them where he wanted them to go, sometimes gently, sometimes not. "You have to let them know you're in charge. You are the leader of the herd. Once they know that, they'll follow you."

When they reached an area with enough forage, Zarin directed Sashia to sit on a large rock where they had a good view of the flock. She accidentally sat on her thick, black braid and tugged it free.

"Make sure they stay where you can see them all," cautioned Zarin as he took his slingshot out and began practicing. When he got tired of that, he came back to his sister. "Now you try. Father says you must be able to use one before you can come out by yourself." He slipped the loop off his finger and slid it over the middle finger of her right hand. "Find a few round stones. You should always carry a few around in your pocket anyway."

"Like this one?"

"Yeah, that's good."

Sashia put it in the little pocket in the middle of the sling. Zarin showed her how to hold the other end of the string so the stone stayed in place.

"Now spin it around and let go when it is pointed at the ground."

Her first few attempts were pitiful. It took her several tries to coordinate her movements to let go at the proper time. After a morning of practice, the stones were at least headed in the general direction she wanted them to go.

"Have you ever had to use it?" she asked as they ate the lunch they had packed.

"No." He sounded disappointed. "Estan's used his to scare off a bobcat though."

Estan was between Zarin and Sashia in age, but he was the most skilled with a slingshot.

Sashia practiced a little more after lunch, but soon she and Zarin sought relief from the sun in the shade of a juniper. Zarin knew exactly how long it would take them to get back to camp, and he started moving the herd in time to return by sunset. Sashia was more tired than she'd ever been before and could barely chew a few mouthfuls of dinner before she dragged herself into her tent and fell asleep.

∞∞∞

It wasn't until over a month later, when they broke camp and moved farther south, that Zarin finally decided Sashia was ready to go out on her own. She'd enjoyed spending time with him. He was usually too busy to talk to her. Now it was Cashi who complained Sashia had no time to play.

Father watched her closely as she helped herd their flocks along the edge of the sandy plains. The summer grasses were nearly dry, but they were still edible. "When you're in charge of your own flock, you must be vigilant, Sashia. No daydreaming. You are responsible for every animal in your care, and you must bring them all back."

"Yes, Father."

"You'll take over my flock," interjected Zarin. "Father's going to teach me to read and write, keep records, trade, and other important things," he boasted, making Sashia jealous of everything he was going to learn.

Surprisingly, she liked being alone with the goats. "It's much better than carding wool in a stuffy tent while Mother spins it into yarn, isn't it, Billy?" she asked the nearby goat. "There's no one to nag us or order us around."

"Maa," he replied.

To keep her mind from wandering, she gave each goat a name, counted them constantly, and surveyed her surroundings. Watching the kids play entertained her all day. The way they jumped around and chased each other was so funny! Nimbly, they bounced off rocks and cliffs, occasionally butting into their elders who were usually tolerant of their antics. She held imaginary conversations with the nannies, and they never berated her for her questions.

Since she was the youngest goatherd, she was assigned the shortest distance to travel. They always camped near a water source, so the first task was to take them to the spring. The other flocks got to drink first, because they had a longer way to go. After their drink, she headed them up a narrow gorge into a shady little valley still green from the spring rains. Water dripped down the rocks in a crevasse in the wall that blocked the end.

Following her brother's instructions, she found a high spot on a boulder where she could see the goats and they could see her. She talked to them often enough that they responded to her voice alone, so she didn't have to throw rocks. Even the old billy listened to her after she'd bravely grabbed him by the horns and steered him back to the path. He'd butted Zarin before but didn't try it with her.

This morning the kids climbed the nearly sheer rock face at the back of the valley and chased each other from one ledge to the next. One young kid, a doeling named Lupine, leapt to a small outcropping of rock. The rock broke loose and the kid fell to the ground below in a shower of rubble. She bleated loudly, and Sashia rushed over to her. When she struggled to her feet, one front leg was hanging limply at an unnatural angle, obviously broken.

Sashia started to panic. *What do I do? Zarin didn't give directions for anything like this!* She picked Lupine up and carefully carried her back to the large boulder, away from the other goats, and tried to think. *Father had to kill a horse with a broken leg last winter. Will we have to kill Lupine? She's too little to give much meat.* Now that they all had names, it was harder to think about butchering any of them.

Sunen broke an arm once, and it healed! Sashia remembered. *An arm is easier to get by without using, though. Legs you have to stand on. How can I take care of Lupine while her leg heals?* It seemed like the leg would need to be protected somehow. It also had to heal straight, so it would have to be kept from moving.

Sashia didn't have much to work with, so she set the kid down and pulled off her trousers. Her tunic was long enough to keep her modest without them. She folded them with the legs on top of each other and set them aside. Then, as gently as she could, she felt the kid's leg for the location of the break. When she found it, she could tell it wasn't lined up right.

"Hold still, Lupine," she pleaded as the kid squirmed.

Sashia pinned Lupine between her legs. Oddly, the kid's bleating was harder to take than Kari's screams had been, but Sashia took a deep breath, gently pulled at the leg on either side of the break, and adjusted it until it felt smooth, without any bumps.

Taking her trousers, she started at one end of the kid's leg and wrapped them round and round until they made one big roll around it. She removed her rope belt and used her slingshot to hang her knife around her neck. Then she used the belt to secure the wrap, making sure it wasn't too tight. *Now how will I keep her from bumping it out of place?* The only thing she could think of was to carry Lupine around her shoulders.

The rest of the afternoon, she carried the kid around her neck with its legs dangling in front of her. Sashia held her by her back legs and good front leg so she didn't wiggle and fall off. Up in the hills it was cooler than down in the plains, but even in the shade, the added warmth and weight of the small goat made her sweat profusely.

Before heading home, she took Lupine to her mother and stood her up to let her nurse. She looked so funny with one leg wrapped up that Sashia would have giggled if she hadn't known how badly it hurt. Having only three good legs didn't deter the kid from nursing, and Sashia let her hobble around until she'd had a chance to relieve herself before picking her up again.

She didn't factor in the extra weight slowing her down, and the sun had dipped below the horizon before she herded her goats into the ancient stone folds they used when they visited the summer campground. The goats could easily climb out of them if they wanted, but they knew they were safer inside them at night.

"You'd better hurry and get your dinner before Father comes looking for you," Estan admonished. "I already had mine." The kid over her shoulders caught his eye. "What happened to that one?"

"Leg broke. What do I do with it?"

"Dunno." He shrugged and ran off.

Sashia sighed. She might as well face Father now. She couldn't leave the kid in the pen with the rest of the goats. The ornery animals would pull off the trousers and chew on them. Trousers! Should she run and put some on before dinner and risk missing it entirely, or hurry to dinner and be chastised for being inappropriately dressed?

Her stomach growled, and she opted for the latter, hustling over to the cook tent.

"Sashia, what on earth?"

"Sorry I am late, Mother." She grabbed a wooden bowl and spoon and peered into the shadows at the bottom of the pot. There was a small scraping of stew left. Hurish, the cook, ladled it out for her. She sat down and started shoveling it into her mouth before anyone could decide to send her to bed without dinner.

"What happened?" asked Mother accusingly.

Father came out of his tent at the sound of Mother's voice and glared at Sashia.

"A kid broke its leg. I carried it back."

Mother saw Father and looked to him to continue the questioning. Father observed Sashia's legs and the bandage around the kid.

Father sat down. "Tell me."

Sashia told him everything. Father thought quietly while Sashia waited with her stomach in knots. No longer hungry, she dipped her finger in the stew and let Lupine lick it. Then Father nodded.

"If her leg will mend, she will be worth more to us

than if we butchered her now. Don't let her become sick and weak. She must keep up her strength. Don't neglect the rest of your flock or your other chores."

"Yes, Father!" She jumped up, ignoring Mother's scowl and careful not to let the kid fall off her shoulders. She handed her bowl to Hurish, and he slipped her a slice of bread as she hurried off to bed.

Nani wasn't pleased to see a baby goat in her tent. She already had Pat down to sleep and was singing to Cashi.

"Father let me," Sashia asserted, which he had in a roundabout way.

Sashia ate a couple bites of the bread, and then fed the rest to Lupine. The food kept her quiet while Cashi petted her and Sashia made a place for her to sleep. In spite of the pain in her leg, the kid was worn out enough to go right to sleep, and Sashia wasn't far behind.

∞∞∞

The next two weeks, Sashia carried Lupine up and down the mountainside. Once they reached the valley, she set her down to graze, away from the other goats and made sure she had plenty of chances to nurse. By the end of that time, she'd nearly doubled her weight and was becoming too heavy for Sashia to carry. The herd travelled more slowly so the kid could keep up.

Sunen had given her an ointment made of comfrey root powder to rub on the outside of the leg. Nani had grudgingly found a few spare rags, so she'd used those to pad the leg instead of her trousers, checking it regularly to make sure it was still set properly. Two thin strips of rawhide helped to stabilize it. Lupine hobbled around and grazed, and didn't stray far from Sashia, but she gained strength daily.

In a little over a month, Lupine was running around without the splint and was able to resume sleeping with the herd. Nani was relieved there would no longer be goat droppings in the tent. Sashia had gained muscle carrying around the kid, but had worn herself out keeping up with her other chores. She was still required to wash her clothes and help Mother whenever she could.

With the extra food Sashia slipped her, Lupine wasn't far behind her peers in weight. Five weeks after the incident, Father met her as she returned the flock to the fold. Lupine stood right next to her wanting attention.

"This is the doeling?"

"Yes, Father."

He knelt and felt the goat's leg. Seemingly satisfied, he nodded and walked away.

CHAPTER THREE

The Eighth Year of the Reign of King Kalin of Berush

The following spring, when the clan prepared to leave their winter pasture, Father made a final count of the herd with Zarin taking notes. Zarin was now old enough to wear a sword and Father had begun teaching him how to use it.

Sashia was proud of her little flock. She hadn't lost any kids during birthing, and most of the nannies had given birth to twins. Lupine even had her first healthy kid.

Estan showed his flock, the servants presented theirs, and then Father counted Sashia's. His expression showed surprise as he listed the numbers for Zarin to record. He dismissed the goatherds and left, but Zarin lingered.

"Your flock showed the greatest percentage of increase!" he whispered with a twinkle in his eye. "Estan and the others will be envious."

That evening, Father called the goatherds in individually to give an accounting. Estan glared at Sashia on his way out. She entered the tent and stood before Father.

"So, Zarin's flock did well this year. To what do you attribute that success?"

Sashia frowned. It was her flock now, not Zarin's. "I did exactly as Zarin showed me to do and went where I was told."

"Hmm. Perhaps your goats benefitted from not having to travel as far as the other flocks."

Inwardly, Sashia grumbled. Father seemed unwilling to acknowledge her effort. She was nice to her goats! She spoke to them instead of being lazy and throwing rocks. She had missed sleep, staying with any doe in labor to ensure there were no difficulties birthing. Some credit should be given for her dedication!

"You didn't go where you were directed to go yesterday."

Father's comment broke into her thoughts, catching her by surprise. Estan was the only one she had run into the previous day. He must have told on her.

"I saw the prints of a mountain lion on the path, so I took them to another area. It would be too easy for a lion to carry off one of the young kids."

"That is not your decision. That's what you have a slingshot for."

Sashia bit back her arguments. It was almost as if Father would rather she had less goats and followed directions regardless of the cost. Her aim had greatly improved, but it wasn't that good.

"The canyon you went into is prone to flooding. If the rain hadn't held off, you could've been caught in a flash flood and been unable to get the flock out in time. There is a reason you were not told to go there."

Sashia had a sinking feeling in the pit of her stomach. It had rained heavily all night, beginning immediately after she'd returned. Could she have lost her goats, possibly herself, if it had started while she was still in the canyon?

"You must learn to follow directions, Sashia. You have good instincts and initiative, but you lack experience. You are twelve years old now, nearly a young woman, and no young man will come asking for a girl who has not learned obedience."

Sashia felt her cheeks flood with heat and shame. She'd thought she had done well, but no matter what she did, it always seemed to be the wrong thing.

"This week we will shear the goats, and then we will head south again. Sashia," he said more gently, "you must trust me. Goats are not the only thing I am raising around here." He rose, took her face in his hands, and kissed the top of her head. It was the most affection he ever bestowed.

∞∞∞

Sashia stood next to a goat and held it by the horns while Sunen sheared it. Everyone helped with the shearing, even Nani. Only Mother stayed behind with Pat. They'd driven the full-grown goats through a ford in the river to clean them beforehand. Dirty fleece was harder to shear.

On the far side of the valley, a huge boulder named Ram Rock marked the entrance. When she saw it every fall, it meant they were home for the winter. Two strangers in bright blue robes slowly wended their way past it toward the encampment, and Sashia eyed their progress with curiosity.

Suddenly, Estan screamed. Sashia turned to where Hurish was helping him shear a goat, and saw Estan with his hand over his forearm, blood dripping through his fingers. Hurish was frozen stiffer than an icicle.

"Go get help!" Sunen yelled to Hurish, who ran back to the camp to get Mother. Sunen tore away Estan's sleeve to get a better look at the injury. There was too much blood to see anything. "What happened?"

"The goat bucked and I stabbed myself with the shears," Estan spat through gritted teeth. "Aaah!"

The blood was still dripping from the wound, and all Sashia could think about was stopping it. When they butchered a goat, they hung it up and drained the blood into a bucket. The blood came from the heart. When your heart stopped, you were dead.

"Lie down!" Sashia told him.

Estan looked like he was getting too dizzy to stand anyway, so he lay down without argument.

Sashia tore her scarf from her head and pressed it into the wound. She heard footsteps, and someone tied a rope around Estan's upper arm.

"You can let go now," said a strangely accented voice.

Sashia glanced up and saw a pair of concerned green eyes in a wrinkled, brown face. The man smiled. An elderly woman stood calmly behind him.

"That was just the right thing to do, to apply pressure. Now we must carry him back to your camp so I can tend to him better."

Hurish returned with Mother.

"What happened? Who are you?" she snapped.

The stranger answered evenly. "I am a healer from the Rakhlain Mountains. This boy has a grave injury. I can treat it."

"No stranger is going to meddle with a son of mine!"

"If I do not treat him, he will lose his arm," he replied with firm conviction.

Father came running over with the other goatherds and everything had to be repeated.

"You can save the arm?"

"I believe so, but I must act quickly."

"Do it."

The man stood up and took over. "Carry him back to the camp and lay him on a table in the sun where there is light."

Sunen and Hurish picked Estan up and carried him quickly back to camp.

"Keep his arm up!"

Running alongside, Sashia reached for Estan's dangling arm and held it as high as she could. Only a few drops of blood ran from it now.

They headed toward the kitchen tent where Father and Zarin pulled out the table. With one sweep of her arm, Mother shoved everything on it to the ground, and they laid the boy down.

The stranger's wife had opened her pack and was setting out several odd-looking tools. One of them, a thin metal rod with a wooden handle, she balanced on the fire ring with the tip in the coals. Next, she handed the man a flask, and he sprinkled the wound with the contents. Sashia thought it was wine, but she wasn't sure. She'd never had any. Then, he rinsed it clean with water.

Almost everyone backed off, though the man hadn't asked them to. Mother watched him like a bird of prey waiting to snatch him up in her claws if he made a mistake. Sashia stood behind her, observing everything closely.

"It will not take long, but he cannot move."

Sunen and Father stepped forward to help hold him down. The man took a tiny blade with a shiny, sharp tip and widened the opening in the skin slightly.

"I am going to use heat to burn your blood vessel closed," he explained to Estan. He put a thick, leather strap between Estan's teeth. "Bite on this."

The man held his hand out to the old woman who handed him the tool she had set in the fire. The end of it was red. He poked it into the wound and held it there for several heartbeats. It made a tiny sizzling sound. Estan groaned. The man removed the tool and untied the rope. Sashia watched closely, but no blood gushed out. Finally, he covered the area with a salve and wrapped a clean bandage around it.

"Fortunately, the vessel that was cut was returning blood to the heart, not taking it away. That makes his chance of recovery much greater. However, I will still need to keep a close eye on him for several days to make sure the muscle does not swell and the wound remains clean."

"May we move him to his tent?" asked Mother.

The man nodded, and Mother directed the men to take Estan where he could be more comfortable.

"Give him some water to drink," the man called after them.

Father held out his hand to the man. "What is your name?"

"My name is Beyorn." He put both of his hands around Father's and gave a slight bow. Then he gestured to the woman, "This is my wife, Dorthi."

"Thank you, Beyorn, for helping my son. You are welcome to stay as long as you wish."

Beyorn bowed again, and Father gathered the men to return to the shearing. Beyorn started to put his tools away, but Sashia was overcome by curiosity and stepped closer without realizing it.

Beyorn smiled at her. "And what is your name?"

"Sashia," she replied shyly and looked back at the tools.

The man followed her gaze. "That is an awl. It is meant to pierce holes in leather, but it works well for cauterizing smaller vessels."

"How did you know it was taking blood back to the heart?" She asked the question before she could stop herself.

"Because of the volume of blood and the direction it was moving."

"Why does it go there?"

"No one really knows. We know the blood brings life, but why or how it works is still being studied. You are interested in the workings of the body?"

Sashia nodded.

"What do you know about it?" His tone, unlike Mother's, was open and interested, not accusatory.

She told him how she had studied the heart and organs of the rabbit and noted the blood vessels. She described what she knew of the skeletal system and how she had set Lupine's leg. Bracing for the man to react as Father had and tell her that her interest was morbid and disrespectful, she looked at his face and was surprised to see delight there. Beyorn was grinning.

"Do you want to learn more?"

Sashia's head bobbed up and down vigorously. "There is a place where people study these things?"

"Yes, there is. Would you want to go?"

"Oh, yes!" she replied without hesitation, though she doubted Father would let her leave. Could there really be a place where she could learn how her insides worked and where people would answer her questions? Though she would hate to leave Cashi, she would love to see it.

"Well," Beyorn glanced at Dorthi, whose eyes were shining, "we will see what we can do."

After a week of careful treatment, Estan's muscles had not swollen and the wound hadn't suppurated. Beyorn made sure to dress it whenever Sashia was available to watch and soon had her changing the bandages and cleaning the affected area herself, in spite of Estan's disapproving frown. Sashia quickly lost her shyness and constantly plied Beyorn with questions.

The shearing was finished and all the fleeces were dry and bundled for sale except those they would use for themselves. Several other clans had gathered in the valley to shear their goats, and there was going to be a great feast. She was rounding the corner of a tent when someone grabbed her ear and yanked her back, bringing tears to her eyes.

"How dare you waste your time when there is so much work to do!" remonstrated her Mother. "You weren't given permission to assist the healer. He has his wife to help him. Go prepare your things to leave, and don't let me catch you bothering Estan again!"

With a shove, she sent Sashia toward her tent without waiting for a reply. Sashia ran blindly toward her tent in a rage. Mother was so unfair!

"There you are!" Nani threw some clothes at her. "Fold these and put them in your sister's pack."

Fuming, Sashia folded them. Nani kept her busy until dinnertime. Fortunately, Nani didn't want to miss any of the feast, so they finished early, headed toward the center of camp, and joined the rest of the family in carrying food to the large, open space where the clans would come together. The leader of their tribe was supposed to give a speech.

Estan was feeling well enough to attend, and Sashia was proud and pleased Beyorn had been able to heal him, though another compartment in her mind was furious at her brother for his meanness in continuing to report her doings to their parents.

Once the festivities began, Sashia forgot her anger completely. The day the tribe gathered to celebrate the kidding and shearing was one of the most exciting days of the year. The surplus fleeces and yearling bucks would be taken to Sherish and sold to buy grain and other foods, and everything they had left was cooked to lighten their loads before travelling. There would be no shortage of delicacies that evening.

Platters of meat, cheese, beans, bread and dried fruits were passed around, along with wild onions and herbs. There were several types of bread and cooked grains she had never seen before.

Zarin surreptitiously passed Sashia a flask of wine and cautioned her, "Just a sip."

She dribbled a few drops on her tongue and tried not to cough. It was sweet, but it burned.

When everyone had eaten nearly to the point of bursting, flutes and other instruments were brought out, and there was dancing. Men and women danced separately, but they watched each other. Sashia noticed Zarin watching a pretty, young girl from another clan. The girl's movements were lithe and graceful, and she had a sweet smile. It surprised her to think Zarin would be old enough to marry soon.

A brash young boy waved at Sashia to join the dancers, but she only raised her eyebrow at him and turned her head. She wasn't interested in silly boys. Her friend Vani, a couple years older and already betrothed to the chief's son, beckoned to her, but she shook her head.

Beyorn addressed Father, and Sashia perked up her ears and scooted closer so she could hear them.

"My wife and I will be leaving tomorrow, as well," began Beyorn, "but we will be travelling in a different direction."

"We are indebted to you for healing our son. Tell me your price, and I will pay it."

"It is my pleasure to use my skill to benefit others."

"Nevertheless, there must be something we can do to show our appreciation."

"There is one thing."

"Name it."

"I would like to take your daughter, Sashia, on as my apprentice."

Father was silent. Sashia held her breath.

Beyorn continued, "My wife and I have no children. Sashia has shown great aptitude for the healing arts. She is a keen observer with a sharp mind who learns quickly. I can train her to become a healer like myself."

Father put his hand over his mouth in thought. He had told Beyorn to ask whatever he wanted. It appeared to Sashia that Beyorn had manipulated the conversation deliberately to make it difficult for Father to say no. She dug her fingers into her palms so deeply she nearly broke the skin.

Mother looked at Father and took the opportunity to speak. "Sashia is a great help to me. I don't know if I can do without her."

Sashia's chest tightened in fear. Would her mother keep her from following her dream? Why did she continue to prevent her from pursuing an interest in healing?

Father cleared his throat. "In a few years, she will marry and leave us. If you need more help, I can marry a second wife."

Father's sarcastic rebuke surprised Sashia. Mother

pursed her lips but was wisely silent.

"Is this what you wish?"

It took a moment for Sashia to realize Father had spoken to her. "Oh yes, Father. More than anything!" She looked at Cashi, asleep in Nani's lap, and felt a pang, but her resolve didn't weaken.

"And when her training is complete?" Father questioned Beyorn.

"She will be free to do as she wishes. Her skill will be more than great enough to earn a living as a healer for any chief or village."

"You will understand if I am reluctant to hand my daughter over to a stranger."

"Not having a daughter, I can only imagine. However, I do have a writ of safe passage from King Kalin himself, if you would like to see it." Beyorn extracted a document from a purse around his waist and handed it to Father who held it up to catch the light of a torch. "I can write the terms of the apprenticeship into a contract, if you wish."

Father nodded. "Do that. If everything is satisfactory, I will agree, with the understanding she is to be treated as your own daughter, not as a wife."

Sashia blanched as the meaning of his words sank in. Father continued to surprise her, looking out for her and thinking of things she would never have thought of. What he had said was true: there were many things she had no experience with.

"If I find out it has been otherwise, you will wish you were a goat because I will shear your skin from your body." Father rarely changed the timbre of his voice. He had an even way of speaking. However, no one was ever in doubt as to the sincerity of his words.

"It will be as you say," Beyorn bowed his head gravely.

The next morning, Mother woke Sashia early. Her bag was packed, ready to go if Father gave his approval. Cashi had cried half the night and held onto Sashia tightly. Sashia slipped out from under her arm and dressed quickly. Before leaving, she knelt down next to her sister and kissed her forehead.

When she stepped out into the dim morning, Mother grabbed her arm.

"You think you're so smart! Well, you cannot save everyone. One day you will fail. You will lose someone, and you will be sorry you ever learned healing!" She hissed.

Sashia knew better than to reply, but she didn't see how she could ever be sorry for learning how to help people.

"Go on," Mother said bitterly. "They are waiting for you."

Beyorn brought three sheets of paper to Father's tent. Father perused the documents, and to Sashia's relief, he dipped a pen in the inkwell and affixed his signature. He kept one copy and handed the other two to Beyorn who handed one to Sashia.

"This one is yours. We will teach you how to read it."

Dorthi put her arm around Sashia and smiled at her. Sashia grinned back.

CHAPTER FOUR

The Fifteenth Year of the Reign of King Kalin of Berush

"So what did he die of?"

"Besides his heart stopping?" Sashia quipped. Mother would be shocked to hear her speak of death so flippantly.

"Yes, besides that. What made it stop?"

"It appears he had a cancer in the lungs."

Beyorn looked where Sashia was pointing. He observed how expertly she had cut and peeled back the skin over the chest and sawed through and removed the ribs. The cancer was clearly visible.

"I told Aerick it was not consumption. He was worried about contagion, that Lorn might spread it to the others. I am glad I was right."

"Lorn's hoarse voice was your clue?"

"One of them." Beyorn tsked. "I told him he smoked too much."

"Does that cause cancer?"

"Sometimes. We think." He sighed. "There is still so much we do not know."

Sashia regarded the corpse of their friend. He had

agreed before he died to let them study his body. Here in Shelomoh, a remote community in the Rakhlain Mountains dedicated to seeking peace and truth, there were no laws or taboos preventing them from conducting an investigation of this sort. As always, she was thankful her parents hadn't known this would be part of her training. They would never have allowed it.

Beyorn and Dorthi had taught her death is a part of life. True, you couldn't save everyone. They hadn't been able to save Lorn from the cancer. But they had been able to ease his passing. He'd been at peace.

When Sashia first set foot in Shelomoh, with its vast educational resources and freedom of thought, she felt like she was walking into a fantasy world. It couldn't be real. But it was. A place where everyone asked questions and everyone wanted to know the answers. They would even help you find them. A place where you could learn everything available to learn.

One of the most important things she had learned was to direct her anger into proper channels and let it go. No longer stuffing her emotions down inside of herself, she was able to speak her mind, but at the same time, she had to learn to accept and validate the feelings of others, and learn to admit when she was wrong. Communication between Magi, or the wise, had to be kept open.

Sashia was not officially a Mage. Those born in Shelomoh, or who came there as children, had until they were twenty to decide if they wanted to say the vows to become a permanent member of the community.

"It is time for lunch," called Dorthi from the warm kitchen. It was a cold, spring day with snow still covering the ground, and there was no fire in the examining room, so the interruption was welcome.

"Wash your hands," Dorthi reminded them. "Life and death are intertwined, but not at dinner."

Sashia complied with a smile. Dorthi maintained that washing impurities away from the body helped relieve the mind of its burdens. This had yet to be put to a wider test, but Sashia had no desire to eat with bloody hands anyway.

The three of them sat down around the kitchen table and ate companionably. They had done this nearly every day for the past seven years, but today there was an undercurrent of tension, and Sashia waited expectantly for someone to break the silence.

"You will be twenty this year." Beyorn's statement reverberated through the room like the felling of a giant tree. Dorthi put down her spoon.

"We don't have to speak of that yet." Dorthi's eyes begged Beyorn to stop time.

"We must."

Two pairs of eyes turned to Sashia, and she forced herself to swallow her mouthful of stew. Their sad but understanding expressions showed they knew her decision already. She was not going to stay.

Tears trickled down her cheeks.

"Oh, my dear!" Dorthi jumped up and threw her arms around Sashia.

Beyorn patted her hand. "It is alright. You must take your knowledge home."

It was true. She had learned much from the scholars on the mountain as well as from her adoptive parents. But theirs was such a small community, and the level of education was so high, that she wasn't needed here. She was needed in Berush. With her newly acquired skills, she could save so many lives.

"I love you both!" she choked out.

"We know."

∞∞∞

Over the next few weeks, Beyorn and Dorthi helped Sashia plan for her journey back to Berush. There were Magi stationed in strategic places all over the Crescent Peninsula. With the help of Aerick, the Mage chosen by lot to oversee Shelomoh for the current term, they planned the safest route for her to travel. In order to avoid the unrest in Cerecia, she would have to cross the desert and approach Berush from the west. Her people lived west of Sherish, on the eastern side of the Granite Mountains, so that would be the fastest way to get home, though it was not an easy trip.

Dorthi made sure she would have all the clothing she needed, while Beyorn had all her notes and diagrams bound into a book.

"I've had the scribes copy all the important scrolls we have on healing and anatomy available in Berushese. There are also several works in Rakhli." Rakhli was the primary language spoken in Shelomoh. Sashia's first task on arrival had been to learn it.

Sashia inspected the writings with awe. "This must have taken longer than a few weeks."

Beyorn nodded. "In our hearts, we have known you would not be with us forever. It has been a work of years."

"Thank you!" sobbed Sashia as she threw her arms around him.

Sashia spent many hours in the examining room finishing up several projects and experiments, but still made sure she had time to say goodbye to all her friends. One important farewell was a young orphan she had been mentoring.

"Why are you leaving?" asked Farouk petulantly.

The precocious and intelligent youngster reminded her of herself. Like her, he had insatiable curiosity, but his particular gift seemed to be language. He'd overheard her and Dorthi speaking Berushese one day and wanted to learn it, so she had taught it to him, spending time with him in the evenings and keeping him out of trouble—usually.

"I want to teach others what I know and use my knowledge to heal them."

"You can teach me."

"You have many teachers here. But I will write to you in Berushese, so you don't forget it."

His eyes lit up. "A letter? Oooo! Only Aerick gets letters! That will be pretty special."

Sashia smiled. She was sure she would hear interesting things about Farouk in the years to come.

As Farouk skipped away, a young man burst into the room.

"I heard you are leaving! You're not taking the vows of a Mage?"

"No, Pa'tryk, I am not."

He frowned in confusion. "Which?"

"I *am* leaving. I am *not* taking the vows."

"But," Pa'tryk pouted, "I thought you were going to marry me!"

"That might be what *you* want, but it's not what *I* want."

"Why not?"

"My people need my medical skills," she stated firmly as she stood and straightened the papers on her desk. "Did Aerick give you permission to ask me?"

"No, you are not yet twenty, but—"

"Then you know the rules, Pa'tryk. This conversation is over."

"I could come with you," he persisted wistfully.

Sashia put her hand on his arm and gazed at him compassionately. "You would be miserable. You belong here. Search your heart and you will find it is true. Here you have peace. I don't."

He looked away. He shrugged off her hand and stomped out the door, mumbling.

"He will be alright," said Dorthi as she hobbled into the examining room. She suffered from rheumatism, and it flared up in cold weather. "He just needs a little time."

"He's not really in love with me. He only thinks he is."

"And how do you know what he is thinking?" Dorthi smiled.

Sashia opened her mouth but immediately closed it. She took a moment to reflect before speaking. "You are right. I only know my own thoughts, and I am not interested in Pa'tryk. At all. Quite the opposite. Is that better?"

Dorthi cupped her face and kissed her forehead. "Much better. You must be honest with yourself before you can be honest with others."

Sashia sighed and plopped back into her chair. "I don't know if I even have the capacity to love in that way."

"Whatever makes you say that?" Dorthi raised an eyebrow.

"Such sentiments are illogical and transitory. I prefer things I can see, things that are solid and reliable."

"Have we been so remiss in your training you have missed the importance of the will and emotions in healing? Remember our discussions on care by a mother versus care by a stranger?"

"Yes, those treated by their mother, or a spouse,

healed faster and were more likely to survive. But all mothers are not equal. Besides," Sashia rushed on, "healers are around all kinds of different illnesses. We still don't know how they are spread. That could also affect the outcome."

Dorthi looked at her quizzically and was silent for a few moments. "Is it possible," she asked finally, "you have put up a wall in your mind in this area? No one is incapable of loving or being loved, but bitterness can prevent it from being shared. It will cause you grief if you do not deal with it, child."

Sashia's jaw tensed, and she sat in sullen silence, not wanting to acknowledge Dorthi's words.

"Promise me you will meditate on this, Sashia. Do not let it fester."

"I will," she relented. But she didn't say when.

∞∞∞

Finally there came a morning when the passes were clear. It was best to cross the desert as early in the spring as possible, so Sashia had to leave at the first opportunity. She had her essential belongings stuffed into a pack she could carry on her back. It was heavier than she would've liked, but there wasn't one scroll she felt she could leave behind. There were also small quantities of basic herbs, salves, and ointments to help start off her career on her own.

"Do you still have your copy of your apprenticeship paper?" asked Dorthi anxiously.

"Yes."

Beyorn had written it in such a way that she was dependent on no one once the apprenticeship was finished. Her parents no longer had any sway over her. She needed no one's permission to go where she wished, employ herself where she wished, or marry whom she wished. Not that she was interested in the latter, but she couldn't be pressured into it, which was reassuring. He signed it to indicate her training was complete.

"Take this also." Beyorn held out a yellowed sheet of paper, folded into quarters.

"What is it?"

"It is the writ of safe passage from King Kalin. Because it is written to the bearer, anyone may use it."

Sashia took it reverently and placed it in her oilskin pouch next to her apprenticeship contract.

Beyorn put his hands on her shoulders. "You have been the best student I ever had, but this is not the end of your education. It is just the beginning. Remember to keep peace and seek truth, and you will not go astray."

"I cannot think what my life would be if the two of you hadn't appeared that day." Sashia wiped tears from her eyes. They had originally been in Berush to visit Dorthi's family and deliver some scrolls to the royal library in Sherish, the country's capital.

"You have enriched our lives more than we can say." Dorthi's voice wobbled, and she dabbed a handkerchief at her tears.

"I will write to you." Sashia hugged the elderly woman and squeezed her gently.

Arm in arm, they accompanied her down to the edge of the lake where a boat waited to take her to the opposite shore. The large body of water on one side, and steep cliffs on the other, protected the long strip of land and sheltered it from the outside world. She intended to leave this beautiful, peaceful haven and return to a harsher, more difficult life. It was the right thing to do, but that didn't mean it was going to be easy. The hardest part was leaving these wonderful people who had given her so much.

An herbalist named Bram met her at the dock. He and his wife, who was already in the boat, were going to guide her as far as the Cormay River. There she would join a reputable caravan headed across the Great Desert and through the eastern badlands to Berush.

Sashia hugged her mentors one last time and stepped into the boat. Sitting in the stern, she twisted her body so she could see them wave as the shore receded. She waved back until they disappeared from view. Then she turned toward the bow of the boat and whatever new adventures waited.

CHAPTER FIVE

Weeks later, after crossing the Great Desert by camel, Sashia left the caravan and walked alone across the Berushese countryside. She turned northward, planning to cross the mountains and visit her family at one of their usual summer campsites.

Travelling alone didn't bother her. Part of her training had included instruction in wrestling techniques and self-defense. Already she had been able to put it to use with a camel driver who was too forward. Though she was considerably smaller than the man, her superior knowledge of anatomy enabled her to bring him to his knees, causing him some severe, albeit temporary, pain—not to mention humiliation.

As she descended a gravelly path into a ravine she heard a groan. She left the trail and skirted a boulder to investigate. A man writhed on the ground; his torso was covered in blood. Sashia stepped forward but immediately felt a hand clap over her mouth and a knife press against her throat.

"You had best run along, girly, and forget what you've seen, or else I'll have to slice open your pretty neck."

Sashia bit one of the man's fingers, pulled down on the wrist holding the knife, and pushed up on his elbow. He dropped the knife and howled, and she twisted his arm as she stepped around him, bracing her leg behind his thigh and toppling him onto his back. Still twisting his arm nearly to the breaking point, she kept him pinned to the ground while she grabbed the knife and pointed it toward him with her other hand.

"Now we will start over. Are you this man's friend," she canted her head toward the injured man, "or his enemy?"

"Friend," he gasped out.

"If you can leave off threatening me, I can help him."

The man nodded. "Why would you help us?"

"I am a healer. That is what I do." She let the man up, but kept his knife, and walked over to the wounded man. "What happened?"

"He got stabbed in the gut."

"How long ago?"

"Couple o' days."

The man was evidently not much of a talker.

"Well, since he is still alive, likely no major blood vessels were severed. Help me get his shirt off and I will take a look."

Both men appeared middle-aged and were unkempt and unshaven. Fortunately, smells didn't bother Sashia at all. They got the shirt open, and Sashia saw what looked like a knife wound to the upper right abdomen. Technically, not the 'gut.' It wasn't actively bleeding, but the man was filthy, and risk of festering was considerable.

She had just refilled her flask in a cool, mountain stream, so she poured water over the wound and used a rag to clean it off. The man resumed writhing and moaning.

"Hold him still for me." Her former attacker held down his friend's arms. Then she addressed the patient. "My name is Sashia. I'm going to clean and treat your wound and try to prevent it from festering. What is your name?"

"Lang," he managed to say before moaning again. It was not a Berushese name.

"Alright, Lang, try to lie still."

Now that the area was clean, she could see a narrow stab wound penetrating the skin and entering the liver. Fortunately, this type of wound often healed itself, especially if it was a clean, sharp knife. She poured some wine on it from another flask and let it sit.

"If you are able to stay here without moving for a few days, it would be better to leave the wound to close on its own. The longer you can rest, the better. If you must move on immediately, I can stitch it up for you, but it will scar, and there will be greater chance of infection."

"Stitch it up," decided the first man gruffly, and Lang nodded in agreement.

Sashia took out a copper needle and some thread. "This will hurt." She heard Lang suck in his breath as she made the first stitch, but she was quick and was soon done. Then she smeared a salve over it. "You really should rest now. At least until tomorrow."

The first man shook his head. "We have to keep moving." He hefted a pack onto his shoulder and pulled Lang to his feet. Lang barely stood taller than Sashia herself.

"Hold!" shouted a new voice.

Suddenly, archers appeared atop the walls of the ravine, their arrows trained on the three people below. Sashia instinctively took a step back from the two men so they wouldn't be tempted to use her as a shield.

"Drop your weapons and raise your hands!"

Sashia had the other man's dagger in her belt, so she pulled it out and dropped it to the ground. She left her own knife hidden in her boot.

Lang sagged against the boulder and raised his hands, but the other man attempted to run up the ravine only to stop short when he encountered several men with drawn swords. He raised his hands. The soldiers, most of whom wore armor, bound his hands tightly behind his back. Several advanced toward Sashia and Lang.

"Be careful, he is wounded," she cautioned the men who approached her patient. "You should tie his hands in front or it will strain his stitches."

Most of the soldiers wore a leather cuirass and bracers, but one of them, evidently their captain, wore a shiny metal breastplate. He seemed young for the job, not much older than she. He stopped in front of her and studied her. "And who are you?"

"My name is Sashia, and I am a healer. Please tell them to tie his hands in the front," she insisted as the guards ignored her.

"Do as she says."

The captain leaned forward and inspected Sashia's handiwork. Lang, if he even owned one, hadn't had time to put on a clean shirt. The captain looked back at Sashia. "What are you doing out here? Were you travelling with these men?"

"I was on my way home to visit my family when I ran across them," she answered without giving any details.

"Who is your family?"

"My father is Haban, of the Granum tribe." That

was as close to an address as a nomad could give.

Another man, who looked to be in his late twenties or early thirties, came and stood behind the captain as the archers began filing into the ravine. The captain spoke to the other man over his shoulder without taking his eyes from Sashia. "Topec, was there any report of a woman with the thieves?"

"No, my lord, not that I heard, but we had better take her with us for questioning."

Two things struck Sashia at once and she tried to process them swiftly. First, she was most definitely not a thief, but it was no surprise if the two men were. Second, there were no lords in Berush. That title was used informally for royalty only. The man in front of her was too young to be King Kalin, so he had to be the eldest son, Cyrus. That explained why he was the one in charge instead of Topec, who must be an advisor.

The prince was more than a head taller than she was, and she had to tilt her head back to gaze up at him. When she did, she saw a pair of intelligent hazel eyes and a mouth that looked eager to smile. He was clean shaven, and his face, though deeply tanned, appeared young and healthy. Energy and vitality radiated from him. She tried not to feel awed and stood as straight as she could. She didn't let herself think 'handsome' either; it wasn't a clinical term.

"F-forgive me, my lord," she stammered and bowed as she tried to calm her nerves. "I did not know who you were."

"You must have been absent from your family for some time not to know your prince," Topec upbraided her sternly. "We were in Haban's camp last month, and you weren't there, nor was there any mention of you."

"You will need to come with us until we can verify

your identity," affirmed Cyrus. "Restus—"

"Actually, my lord," she summoned the courage to contradict him, "I do not need to go anywhere with you. If you will allow me, I will remove a paper from my purse which verifies my statement."

"By all means."

Sashia took the oilskin packet out of her purse and retrieved the writ. She held it out to the prince and watched his expression change as he read it.

"Where did you get this?"

"How I acquired it is of no consequence. It only matters that I possess it."

"She could have stolen it, my lord," cautioned Topec.

"She is right; it makes no difference. We have to let her go." He handed the paper back, seeming almost regretful.

"I will travel with you freely if you will allow me to see to my patient."

"Your 'patient'?"

"The man, Lang, has a stab wound to the abdomen. It will fester if I cannot treat it."

"I think he will soon have worse things to worry about," Cyrus said with a hint of sarcasm, "but you are welcome to come along."

"She may be hoping for an opportunity to free the prisoners," Topec grumbled. "How do we know she is really a healer?"

"You are awfully suspicious today, Topec, though I appreciate your caution. You have only to look at her sutures to see." He waved at Lang.

"I have a document to prove my qualifications as well." She dug out her apprenticeship contract.

"That is not necessary," protested Cyrus, but she continued to hold it out, so he took them. "You studied with the Magi?" His tone was incredulous.

The contract said nothing of the Magi; it merely stated she had studied under Beyorn of Rakhlain. "You know of them?"

"A little." He turned to Topec, "Before you tell me she is a forger also, I will say that if she were such a master criminal, it would be best to keep her close where we can watch her."

He handed the contract back with a grin that made her feel warm all over. Sashia couldn't help smiling back.

"Walk with me, O Wise One, and tell me of the Magi."

Sashia raised an eyebrow, and his eyes twinkled back at her. He had told her, not asked her, but she couldn't resent him for it. The soldiers started moving the prisoners down the ravine, and she and the prince followed them, walking side-by-side.

When Cyrus and his men had suspected her of being one of the thieves, she had felt defensive and wanted to prove herself, but the prince's easy-going manner soon disarmed her. He showed genuine interest in her, in the Magi, and in her training. She soon found herself telling him everything.

Like a lodestone attracting iron, he had a magnetism that drew her in and made her open up. Though she knew it was happening, she was powerless to stop it.

The ravine opened onto a rocky hillside where two soldiers stood guarding a score of horses.

"We have no extra mounts. The prisoners will have to walk. Will you walk, or ride with me?"

For no logical reason, Sashia's heart leapt into her throat, but she responded automatically with what she knew was the right answer: "The wounded man should ride. I will walk."

"Then I will walk with you." He directed his men

to help Lang onto his own beautiful, black gelding, took the reins, and led the horse toward the nearest village. There was one large, permanent settlement on this side of the Granite Mountains where the western tribes came regularly to trade. It was there the men would be tried.

"Why are you so far from Sherish, my lord?"

"My patrol has been stationed here for the summer. My father likes to keep a close eye on our borders, and I can give him a firsthand report. The village we passed through yesterday warned us to be on the lookout for a pair of thieves. I am more than a decoration in the palace, you know."

"I didn't mean to imply—"

"I am teasing you."

"Oh." Her cheeks began to burn. Had anyone ever teased her before? She glanced back to check on Lang to break the strange connection she was beginning to feel. The prisoner's face looked strained, but the stitches seemed to be holding.

As they drew closer to the village, people came out to greet them, and Sashia observed more evidence of the prince's magnetism, that it didn't affect just her. Children ran along next to them, and he smiled and nodded at them. A young boy shyly admired his shining armor, and he took off his helmet and set it on the boy's head. Without his helmet, he looked more boyish himself.

Astronomy had not been a focus of Sashia's study. She didn't care whether the sun went around the earth, or the earth went around the sun, though many of the Magi enjoyed debating such subjects. If it had no practical application, she wasn't really interested in it. What was obvious, however, was everything revolved around Cyrus wherever he went.

When the slower adults caught up to the more

exuberant children, there was still evident respect and admiration for the prince, and they offered thanks and gratitude for the capture of the thieves. But then the people began jeering at the prisoners.

"Not so tough now, are you?"

"You cannot get away with robbery in Berush!"

"We'll see how much you can steal with only one hand!"

Sashia had seen a man flogged before for beating his wife, but she'd only heard of amputation being used as a form of punishment. Nomads had little of value to steal, other than their animals, which were their entire livelihood. If someone stole a horse, goat, or a herd of goats, they didn't usually live long enough to make it to a trial.

Disputes over pastureland or ownership of unmarked flocks were solved by the chief of the tribe. Occasionally they resulted in open warfare between clans, but usually the leaders were able to achieve a peaceful solution. The current situation was different from anything she had previously encountered, but she couldn't see how losing an appendage could be helpful to anyone.

"They will lose a hand?" she looked at Cyrus.

He pressed his lips into a grim line. "They will be tried, and if it's not their first offense, then that is the punishment."

Before she could say more, Lang was yanked from his horse, and the two prisoners were dragged roughly into the center of the village green where the people formed a large circle around them. Cyrus' men led the horses away, and someone brought him a stool. He took the seat of judge, as the person of highest rank, with the village elders standing on either side of him.

"State your names," Cyrus instructed the accused

men.

Lang shifted his weight and stared at the ground, mumbling.

"Speak up." Cyrus' voice rang out authoritatively but not without sympathy.

"Lang."

Cyrus looked expectantly at the other man. One of Cyrus' soldiers knocked him on the side of the head.

"Thitus." He glared at Cyrus angrily, but Cyrus was unaffected.

"Let their accusers step forward."

Several men lined up. Cyrus signaled to the first man to begin his statement.

"These two men attacked my wife and me on the road three days ago. We were returning home after selling some rugs my wife had woven to one of the merchants here. They hit me over the head and took the coins from my purse. My wife was thrown to the ground. She was with child and miscarried as a result!"

This information was new to some in the crowd, and gasps of indignation were heard. Cyrus held up his hand for quiet.

"Do you know which one shoved her?"

"That one, my lord." He pointed at Thitus.

"How do you know it was he if you were hit over the head?"

Sashia was impressed with Cyrus' line of questioning. He didn't miss anything. It sounded like the men would at least have a fair hearing.

"They rushed at us, one from each side of the road as we passed through a stand of junipers. That man shoved my wife, and then the other hit me over the head."

"How many coins did you lose?"

The man stated a number and listed the value of

each coin.

"Search the men and inventory their belongings."

This took a little time, as Thitus had carried a pack. They brought the coins to Cyrus and he counted them. The coins the villager had described were there, along with a few more.

"Do you have anything to say in your defense?"

"Those coins are our own," growled Thitus. "He lies."

The man rushed at Thitus, and Cyrus' men had to hold him back before he could tackle the prisoner.

"Say that to my wife!" he cried. "Shall I send for her to accuse you also?"

Other people began yelling curses at the two men and Cyrus' soldiers had to push back the crowd.

When everyone had settled down sufficiently, Cyrus asked the victim, "How is it you are back in the village?"

"I took my wife home, and then I came to report the robbery to the town elders and heard we were not the only victims."

The next man in line was given permission to speak.

"Two nights ago, these men came to our inn. They slept in the common room with myself and two others." He gestured to the other men in line. "I wasn't sleeping well and woke to find them rifling through my belongings. I keep a dagger in my boot, which they hadn't thought to check for, and I stuck that fellow in the side. At his cry, the others awoke and the thieves ran off. We pursued them, but it was dark, and we lost them."

"Can you testify these were the two men in question?" Cyrus asked the remaining witnesses who replied in the affirmative.

"Do you live here in the village?"

"I do," replied the first man.

The other two, a man and his son, were in town to finalize a marriage agreement.

"Why were you staying at the inn?" Cyrus asked the first man.

Sashia wondered why he bothered to ask since it didn't seem pertinent to the case. He must have a curious mind like she did.

The man shuffled his feet in embarrassment. "I was there at the request of my wife."

The crowd tittered.

Cyrus looked amused but raised his hand again and turned to the prisoners. "What do you have to say in response to this second accusation?"

Lang hung his head and was silent.

"He fell and punctured himself on a tree stump," asserted Thitus.

Sashia's mouth fell open at this ridiculous lie. Cyrus turned to her.

"You treated his wound. Could he have received it in that fashion?"

She shook her head. "The wound was made by a thin, sharp blade. A knife or small dagger. An injury such as Thitus described would be jagged and leave splinters. There were none."

"Let me see your dagger," Cyrus told the man from the inn. He handed it to the prince who inspected it and held it out to Sashia, hilt first. "Could the cut have been made by this weapon?"

She measured the width of it against her pinky finger. "Yes, this is exactly the width of the wound and is sufficiently sharp." She was glad to see it was clean and rust free. She handed it back.

Thitus lunged in her direction, but the guards on either side of him held him securely. His shirt tore and exposed a scar on his shoulder.

"Look, my lord!" cried Topec. He pointed to the scar. "He has been branded."

The scar was similar to markings some people made on their cattle. Goats were not branded that way because of their fleece. Cyrus rose from his seat to examine the symbol.

"Where did you receive this?"

Thitus didn't answer.

"It is the mark given to thieves in Cerecia," explained Topec.

Sashia caught her breath. This man was a hardened criminal. She was lucky, even with her knowledge of self-defense, he hadn't killed her as she finished treating his companion. She'd been vulnerable then. However, the idea that her testimony would contribute to the severe punishment awaiting him made her uncomfortable.

"Evidence this is not the first time he has been caught," stated Cyrus solemnly. He resumed his seat. "Do either of you have anything further to say?"

Both men were now silent. Sashia wondered briefly how Thitus had gotten out of Cerecia. The two countries had been enemies for many years. Fortunately, an impassable desert and steep mountains separated them, and travelers of any kind, friend or foe, were prevented by nature itself from passing through easily. It would have been an arduous journey.

"Lang, have you nothing to add?"

He lifted his head enough to look the prince in the eye. His entire countenance expressed remorse. "I am guilty, my lord," he whispered hoarsely and returned his gaze to the ground.

"Then I must now pronounce your sentence," Cyrus declared gravely. He stood and conferred briefly with the town elders who listened and nodded their heads. "Thitus and Lang, you have both been found guilty of thievery and assault. You will each lose your left hand as punishment for these crimes and as a deterrent to others, to be carried out immediately."

CHAPTER SIX

"Wait!" cried Sashia as Lang drooped and Thitus struggled against his captors.

Cyrus turned to Sashia, his eyes telling her to be cautious. But caution wasn't in her nature, and she stepped forward.

"The removal of a hand is a consequence reserved for a second offense. It hasn't been proven the man Lang has committed any previous crimes."

"There is sufficient evidence he has participated in at least two robberies." Cyrus frowned at her.

"This woman is no advocate of the law," waved one of the elders dismissively. "It's not her place to speak in this matter."

The prince turned to Lang. "Do you grant this woman permission to plead your cause?"

The man nodded, hope alight in his eyes.

"Now she may speak," declared Cyrus crisply. "Make it quick."

"He may have been party to two robberies, but he has not been tried or punished before."

"That we know of," interrupted the elder.

Sashia ignored him. "It should be treated as a first

offense since this is the first time he has been sentenced."

Cyrus hesitated, and he appeared troubled as he considered her words. He motioned Topec over. "How do you interpret the law in this case?"

"It is not the law that matters as much to me as the safety of the rest of our citizens," he answered gruffly. "If we let him off easy, and he commits another crime, maybe a worse one, it will be on our heads."

Cyrus opened his mouth to speak, but Sashia forestalled him.

"A man cannot be judged on his future actions! I propose he be indentured to me."

"What?"

Disregarding his towering glare, she rushed on, "He will owe me the next seven years in exchange for retaining his hand. I could use an assistant, and I can keep an eye on him."

"This is nonsense!" interjected the elder. "You are practically a child! You will find yourself deflowered and dead in a ditch within a day. Where is your father? He needs to come and take you home!"

"I answer to myself alone," was her only response to the elder's insults. Cyrus knew this already as he had read her papers. "What do you say, my lord?"

Cyrus deferred to Topec.

"The idea is not without precedent, my lord. Indentureship is more common in Artylia than here, I have heard, but I would not advise it."

"I prefer to err on the side of mercy whenever possible. I hope I don't regret it. Bring Lang forward."

Two guards brought him before the prince.

"Do you wish to accept indentureship to the healer, Sashia, in exchange for your hand?"

He nodded vigorously. "Yes, my lord."

"So be it. Untie his bonds."

One of the soldiers untied the rope from his hands, and he fell at their feet. "Thank you, thank you!" he sobbed.

"Get up."

Lang stood shakily.

"I am still counting this as a second offense. If you are found guilty of a third, it will mean your life. Do you understand?"

"Yes, my lord."

Cyrus turned to the town elders. "You may proceed with carrying out the sentence on the thief, Thitus."

"My lord, may I be permitted to perform the removal?" Sashia was afraid she was pushing the prince too far, but she ventured to ask anyway.

"No, you may not!" This was the first time he had been short with her. "But you may tend to him afterwards if you wish," he conceded.

Sashia grabbed her pack, which she had set down during the trial, and rushed to prepare. The soldiers already had Thitus' right hand and feet tied together behind his back so he knelt on the ground. His left arm was stretched out on a block of wood while another guard tied it down.

"Go stick these in the fire," Sashia held out a couple of awls to Lang. "Bring one to me when I call you."

He hastened to do her bidding, though he walked unsteadily.

"Watch him," Topec told one of the soldiers. "The villagers won't be comfortable with him walking around freely."

Sashia nodded in acknowledgment, knowing he was probably right, but continued laying out her instruments. A man approached with an axe, and the guards held Thitus down. Sashia dug desperately in her pack and removed another tool.

"Here, use this." She held out a surgical saw to the man with the axe. "It won't splinter the bone."

"It'll take longer," he viewed it skeptically, but she extended it insistently, and he shrugged and took it.

Sashia spied a short length of rope on the ground and grabbed it. "Excuse me." She leaned between the men holding Thitus and tied the rope around his forearm. It was just in time. As she stepped back, the saw tore into the flesh.

Thitus strained against his bonds, but the men holding him down were stronger, and he was tied in such a way that movement was almost impossible. The saw met bone, and he began to scream. At his piercing shrieks, many of the women and children in the crowd fled indoors. Sashia tensed, ready to step in as soon as it was finished.

It only took a few moments, and the deed was done.

"Move!" she ordered the man who'd used the saw. "Keep him still," she told the guards. "Lang!"

He hustled over with a red-hot awl.

"Set it down." She couldn't pick it up by the metal rod.

As soon as he laid it down, she grasped the handle, bent over the stump of Thitus' arm, and began to cauterize the dripping blood vessels over his continued screams. While she worked, some in the crowd grumbled.

"Let him bleed! Why care for such a dog?"

"He deserves no pity!"

She paid them no heed. Everyone was entitled to their opinion, but she was a healer. She couldn't stand by and not do her job, no matter who she was healing. This was what she was trained to do.

One of the vessels gave her quite a bit of trouble,

so she sent Lang to switch the awl for a hot one. She wished she could tie it off, but the only thread she had was made of plant fibers, which couldn't be used under the skin because it would eventually have to be removed.

After an amputation, the muscles temporarily contracted, putting pressure on the vessels to prevent them from bleeding severely. She had to finish before they relaxed. It took longer than she would have liked, but she finally got them all closed.

Next, she had to sew up the end. The problem with this type of careless amputation was a lack of extra skin to pull over the stump. She would have to stretch it tightly. Fortunately, the cut was right above the wrist, where it was narrowest.

Deftly, she stitched it up, trimmed the thread, and spread salve over the area. Then she bound it up with clean strips of cloth, removed the tourniquet, and stepped back with a sigh. She noted, as she rinsed her hands in a nearby bucket of water, that someone had already removed the hand. The soldiers began to untie him.

Cyrus appeared at her side with a cup of watery wine, and she drank it gratefully. She felt a little shaky. She'd never had to perform a surgery under such pressure or with so much scrutiny.

Thitus got to his feet with difficulty. He was dripping with sweat and panting heavily.

"Leave here and never set foot in this village again!" ordered one of the town elders.

Thitus lurched forward, clutching his left arm to his chest.

"He cannot travel in his condition! He needs several days of bedrest!" Sashia objected, and she started forward.

Cyrus grabbed her arm. "Leave it be," he spoke

gently. "You have done what you can for him."

"But he will die!" She was amazed he hadn't passed out from the pain and gone into shock already.

"Perhaps. My men will see he has water and food."

As he spoke, Topec slung a pouch of food and a flask of water over Thitus' shoulder. The man staggered onward without a word.

"How is such a man expected to earn a living?"

"He has a chance to start over, Sashia. What he chooses to do with that chance is up to him. A man is capable of almost anything if he puts his mind to it. We could have taken his life for causing a woman to lose her child."

Sashia was too angry to think clearly, though part of her supposed Cyrus could be right. However, anyone who saw Thitus would know what he'd done. Would anyone else give him a chance? Then she remembered the brand. That hadn't stopped him either. Had anyone ever shown him mercy? What made a man go wrong like that? She closed her eyes. There were some questions that would never have answers.

"A woman is capable of anything she puts her mind to as well. You were amazing, Sashia, not just with your skill as a healer, but with your arguments."

She opened her eyes to see Cyrus' hazel orbs gazing intensely into hers, pulling her in. She gulped, her anger dissipating at the compassion she saw in them.

"I am afraid I was too bold in putting myself forward. If I was disrespectful in any way, my lord, I apologize. It's a fault of mine."

"You may be forward with me anytime." Cyrus smiled, his eyes mischievous.

She was suddenly aware of the soft pressure of his

hand still on her arm. He seemed to realize it at the same time and dropped his hand, brushing her fingers as he returned it to his side. Words escaped her. She couldn't think of a response. She could barely breathe.

"My lord." Topec came to their rescue. "We are ready to move out."

"You and Lang will camp with us tonight. It would not be safe for you to stay in the inn."

Sashia opened her mouth to protest, but she looked at Lang and changed her mind. "Very well. Thank you."

"I will borrow an extra horse for your new manservant, so you can ride behind me," he grinned.

∞∞∞

It was a warm, clear night, and the soldiers camped out on the ground rather than set up tents. With Cyrus' men taking turns on watch, Sashia slept soundly. She woke to see Topec assisting Cyrus with his armor. While she was still rubbing the sleep from her eyes, Lang brought her breakfast. Though fatigued from his own trauma, he seemed anxious to appear useful.

She was scraping the last bit of porridge from a tin cup when Cyrus approached.

"May I speak with you?"

He held out his hand to help her up. She took it, but once she was up, he didn't let go. He led her to the edge of the camp, out of earshot from his men.

"I want to see you again."

Heat crept up Sashia's neck, and she stared at her toes. When she managed to look up at him, she saw worry in his eyes. She didn't know what to say. She definitely felt the attraction between them, but she wasn't sure what she wanted to do about it.

"Sashia, I am so nervous," he laughed anxiously. "I could hardly sleep last night. I've never felt this way before. But I have no idea what you feel. Please say something."

"I—I don't know how I feel, my lord."

"Call me Cyrus."

She shook her head. "You are going to be king one day."

He winced. "Don't think of that. I am just a man. Right now I feel like a little boy, both excited and scared out of my wits. Give me a chance, Sashia. Let me call on you when my patrol passes through your area."

Only two days ago, she'd thought she had her life planned out. She should've known better. Though he'd administered a harsh sentence on Thitus, the prince had been merciful to Lang against the advice of every other man present. He'd listened to her. Now, he was asking for her permission without assurance of consent, something he'd probably never done in his life. How could she tell him no?

"You may call," she gave in.

Cyrus' face was suffused with delight. "Thank you! I'll think of nothing else in the meantime." He motioned to two of his men. "I'm sending two soldiers to accompany you home—no, don't argue with me. I insist."

Sashia pressed her lips into a thin line. Was this what it would be like to belong to a prince? To be constantly under guard?

As if reading her thoughts, he continued, "Thitus is still out there, the villagers are on edge, and I would perish of worry if I let you go alone."

"I can take care of myself. Plus, I have Lang." Not that she fully trusted Lang, either.

"They are partly for his protection as well. Both Thitus and those they robbed have reason to wish him ill." His eyes darkened. "It's unseemly for you to travel with only Lang as a companion, especially as he is still a stranger to you."

"You are right, thank you," she agreed reluctantly, believing his mind was set.

"I will see you soon," he promised.

Sashia nodded shyly and headed over the pass toward home.

∞∞∞

The two soldiers, Deppan and Restus, alternated watches at night, not letting Lang take a turn. It took three days of steady walking to reach her father's camp. The herders they met along the way assured Sashia he was in the normal summer grazing site. The closer they came, the more anxious she felt. Her stomach tied itself into knots.

"Are you alright, my lady?"

"For the tenth time, Lang, I am not a lady. Just call me Sashia."

"But you are my lady," he asserted. "I am indebted to you. I am your servant. You must allow me to show you . . . serving. What is a good word?"

"I must not do anything!" she declared, ignoring his lack of vocabulary. "If you are my servant, you must listen to me and do as I say!"

"I have tried, my lady, but I cannot call you otherwise. I will obey you in all else."

Sashia rolled her eyes. After only three days, this was already an old argument.

"Something seems to be bothering you, my lady," he persisted. "How can I help?"

"I'm only anxious about seeing my family. I haven't

been home in many years."

"I understand. I have not been home in many years either."

"Where are you from, Lang?"

"From very far away, on the continent. Lalowoiya."

"I have never heard of it."

"As I said, very far away."

They stopped to eat in the shade of a pine grove. Cyrus had provisioned them well, and they'd foraged for wild herbs and roots along the way. The streams were still flowing out of the mountains, so they had not wanted for fresh water. Before sitting down, she checked Lang's stitches again and was pleased to see he was healing well. He grimaced, and held his side occasionally, but didn't complain. She knew it had to be painful.

Once they started again, they only had a couple of hours left to travel. Finally, they crested a hill and beheld a sheltered valley nestled between two mountain spurs. A ring of tents sat in the middle.

Sashia turned to the soldiers. "You're welcome to stay in my Father's camp tonight. You deserve a good rest."

"Thank you, 'Lady Sashia'," replied Deppan, grinning.

"Not you too!"

Restus snickered.

Sashia made an exaggerated sigh, but she couldn't help smiling to herself. The banter helped distract her from the butterflies in her stomach.

Halfway down the hillside they ran into a young girl herding a flock of goats. Sashia stared at the girl. The girl glanced at Sashia, turned away, and then looked back.

"Sashia?" she exclaimed.

"Cashi!"

The two sisters ran to each other and embraced.

"I can't believe you're really here! I thought I would never see you again!"

"I am here, Cashi." She held her sister at arm's length and took a good look at her. "How old are you now, twelve?"

"Uh-huh. Same age you were when you went away." Cashi peered around Sashia and noticed her companions. "Which of those men is your husband?"

Sashia laughed. "None of them! Come along. I will tell you all about it."

CHAPTER SEVEN

Sashia's reunion with her parents was both better and worse than she had feared.

"You are not to speak, Lang."

"Yes, my lady."

"Even if my father speaks to you, let me answer for you. Understand?"

"Oh, yes. I will be silent."

"Speak only if I tell you to speak."

He pressed his lips together with his fingers and mimed sewing them shut.

Sashia was glad she had encountered Cashi first. When they reached the camp, her sister quickly herded her goats into a pen and ran ahead to announce Sashia's return. Many goatherds took their flocks higher into the mountains during the summer and stayed with them in the hills rather than return daily to camp, but Father had never asked Sashia to do that, and it appeared he was keeping Cashi close as well.

By the time Sashia and her companions reached the camp, Father and Mother were rushing out to meet them. Father greeted her with open arms. He seemed genuinely happy to see her.

"Daughter, you look well. I am anxious to hear everything you have learned."

"What are you doing here?" asked Mother, with barely veiled antagonism.

Though Sashia had expected it, Mother's frigid manner still riled her. After a seven-year absence, this was the welcome she received? It took a great effort to keep her voice even. "I'm here for a visit before I search for a place to practice healing. This is my manservant, Lang." He made an exaggerated bow as she introduced him, and she cringed inwardly. She hadn't told him how to act. "And these are two of Prince Cyrus' soldiers, Deppan and Restus. I was a witness in a trial, and he lent them to me as an escort home." She'd thought long and hard about how best to describe the three men without telling an untruth. "This is my father, Haban, and my mother, Yania."

"You are most welcome," said Father graciously. "I would be interested to hear news from the east. Come and join us for dinner."

One good thing about being from a family of goat herders was there was always plenty of meat, even when unexpected visitors arrived. Cheese and milk could also be served in abundance, along with whatever fruit was in season. Grains and legumes were rationed, but this went unnoticed as long as everyone's belly was filled.

"Can I get you anything else, my lady?" Lang was as attentive as ever during the meal.

"A brief brush with the prince and now you fancy yourself royalty?" Mother gibed scathingly.

"Lang is from the continent," Sashia shrugged as if that explained everything. "I have told him I am not of royal birth, but I cannot get him to stop." Her eyes lit up with humor. "Perhaps you will have more success." She could hardly keep herself from giggling. That would be a conversation she would pay to hear.

Mother turned up her nose but made no further comment.

Deppan was giving Father the latest news from Sherish, since he'd only recently been assigned to Cyrus' patrol, and Sashia was happy not to be the center of attention. Pat came up to give her a shy greeting and ran off to play with the servants' children.

"Where is Nani?" Sashia asked Cashi.

"Nani passed away last winter," replied Cashi sadly.

Sashia received the news with a pang in her heart. Though she'd been crotchety, Nani had always been there. It didn't feel the same without her.

"Zarin and Estan took the fleeces to market and are due back in a week. That's Zarin's wife over there," Cashi nodded in the direction of a pretty young woman with two small children. Somehow, Sashia had expected everyone to be the same as she'd left them, but they'd moved on without her.

∞∞∞

The next morning, Deppan and Restus set out to rejoin Cyrus' patrol. Sashia and Lang helped around the camp while trying to ignore Mother's grumbling. Despite her mother's attitude, Sashia enjoyed being able to stay in one place for a while. The journey across the desert and then the mountains had been strenuous and more physically demanding than she was used to.

The fourth day home, a messenger came from Shazar's household asking for Sashia.

"My master has heard you are home and requests

you attend his wife as she gives birth."

"Certainly! Is Kari already in labor?"

"It is Janith, his second wife, and yes, she started this morning."

Sashia fetched her pack and told Lang firmly to stay and help Hurish in the cooking tent. No one had told her Shazar had taken a second wife.

"Janith is not a Berushese name, is it?" she asked the manservant as they headed toward Shazar's camp.

"No. Her mother is Cerecian," he said deprecatingly.

That attitude could be why Janith consented to be a second wife. Though the two countries hadn't traded openly in years, a lot of animosity towards Cerecia remained. It may have been difficult for Janith to find a husband.

Kari nodded curtly to Sashia as she entered the camp. She had her hands full with a squirming toddler. A boy played with some carved wooden animals at her feet, and Sashia noticed he was about the right age to be the boy she helped bring into the world.

"Thank you for coming!" Shazar greeted her gratefully. "I heard you had returned. We are lucky to have a trained healer present."

"Shazar," she nodded. "Where is Janith?"

Shazar indicated a nearby tent. Sashia entered to find Janith nearly ready to deliver with a maidservant attending her. Barely had she introduced herself before Janith began to push. The baby emerged shortly thereafter. There were no complications, and Sashia quickly did everything that needed to be done.

"Shazar, you have a healthy son, and Janith is doing well," she announced as she stepped out of the tent.

He thanked her profusely and entered the tent to meet his new child.

Sashia sucked in a breath of fresh air and went over to chat with Kari. "How are you doing, Kari?"

"I am barren, thanks to you!"

"What?"

"Do you think I am unaware of what you did? Shazar thinks it was your mother, but I know it was you!"

The anger in Kari's voice unnerved Sashia. "I—I don't understand," she stammered.

"After Halem," Kari nodded toward her son, "I have been unable to bear any more children. Shazar took a second wife. Now I have to tend her daughter as she bears him a second child."

"Why did you agree?" In Berush, a man's first wife had to give permission for him to take a second.

"If a woman is barren, her husband doesn't need her consent to remarry."

"But you are not childless," Sashia argued. It was an unusual circumstance.

"We could have taken the issue to tribal council, but I knew if they ruled in my favor, he would only take a mistress, maybe more than one. The situation would be little different."

"But you still have your son. You are alive."

"I would rather be dead! Leave me alone!" She turned her back on Sashia.

Sashia stood quietly and walked away. Her heart ached for Kari. This was what her father had meant about 'unintended consequences'. Was Kari's current grief her fault? How could she have known what would happen? She kicked at a rock in frustration and wiped at the hot tears trickling down her cheeks. She sped up her pace, and the exercise helped to ease the tightening in her chest.

No matter how she looked at it, she didn't see how she could have acted otherwise. It was not for her to choose who lived or died, or what they did with their lives afterwards. She couldn't regret saving Kari, but she would give anything to make her happy again.

∞∞∞

A few days later, Sashia sat on a stool in the center of camp removing Lang's stitches. As she pulled them out, she took the opportunity to ask him a few more questions.

"How did you get mixed up with Thitus?"

Lang shook his head sorrowfully. "I was a slave in Cerecia. Thitus was being held prisoner in the house where I belonged. My master had caught him stealing a . . . bird?—I don't know the name in Berushese."

"Chicken?"

"Oh yes, I think that's it. He'd already been branded, and this time he would've been sold as a slave. He told me if I helped him escape, he could get me to Berush where I would be free. I got him out of the house, when my master was working in the fields, and we took the long way around the desert to these mountains," he gestured to the land around them. "He taught me Berushese on the way."

"Why did you help him with the robberies?"

"He threatened to kill me if I refused," Lang hung his head.

Sashia decided to move on from a traumatic topic and asked another question. "How did you get to Cerecia from the continent?"

"When I was a young boy, a man tricked me into joining his train—or is it caravan?—saying he would pay me good money to help with his camels. He took me to the slave market in Herida and sold me to a farmer."

"I'm so sorry, Lang! You've suffered many hardships. Now you're little more than a slave still."

"You are a much better master to serve, my lady," he grinned. "You use kind words, and you don't beat me. I could have chosen to live without a hand," his grin fled as he continued, "but I was afraid. I know no one here. How else could I earn a living?"

Sashia was about to say more when another messenger came looking for her. Her friend Vani was preparing to give birth, and there was some difficulty.

"Pack us a lunch, Lang."

He hustled to obey.

"We must hurry," urged the messenger. "Master Rolind is away, and my mistress is worried about the baby."

Sashia gathered her things as quickly as she could, and Lang carried them as they followed the servant into the hills. Rolind's camp was farther away than Shazar's, and they didn't arrive until nearly evening. Lang went to sit by the fire while Sashia hurried into Vani's tent.

"Sashia, I am so glad to see you!" Vani greeted her cheerfully as she lay resting on a pile of plump cushions. A maidservant sat next to her with a fan while another rubbed her feet.

"Hello, Vani!" Sashia went and kissed her friend on the cheek. "You're looking well."

"I've begun having pains, but they're still far apart."

"The messenger said you were worried?"

"Yes, the baby hasn't turned." She pressed on different places on her belly. "I can feel its head here, and the feet kicking here."

Sashia felt in the areas to check. The baby kicked against her hand, leaving her in no doubt as to the location of its feet.

"I can turn it for you Vani. It will be painful, but not as painful as trying to give birth with the baby in this position. Do you want me to try?"

"Have you done it before?"

"Several times."

"Yes, turn it, please."

"One of your maids must help. It will take two of us."

Vani beckoned to the maid at her feet.

"You'll need to push right here," instructed Sashia. "Don't stop until I tell you to or until the baby moves, even if she cries out. Ready?"

She nodded.

"Push."

Vani groaned and tried not to scream.

"You can yell if you need to Vani," Sashia grunted as she pushed, and Vani took her at her word.

It took time and effort, but together, she and the maid manipulated the baby into the proper position. Sashia's arms hurt afterwards, and she shook them out.

"I will stay here until you deliver to make sure the baby keeps its head down."

"Thank you," panted Vani.

"Let's get you up and walking. Is this your first pregnancy?"

Vani shook her head and grinned as Sashia helped her to her feet. "I had twins two years ago."

"Twins! Oh, my. They must keep you busy!"

"They are a handful, but I love them. Wait until you have some of your own! Or do you already have children?"

"Not yet!"

Vani dismissed one of her maids, and the other curled up to take a nap. "Tell me everything you've been up to! I want to hear all your adventures!"

Sashia readily complied. When she got to the part where she met Cyrus, Vani pressed her for details.

"You met Prince Cyrus? Isn't he your own age?"

"Maybe a little older. He behaves like someone much older." Except when he asked if he could call on her.

"So do you. You've always seemed like an old woman in a girl's body." Vani giggled. "I suppose responsibility will do that to a person. I have never been very responsible." She glanced at Sashia slyly. "Prince Cyrus is still unmarried. Is he handsome?"

"He's not bad looking. Very tall. His eyes are his best feature."

"Ooh, you gazed into his eyes?"

"I had to talk to him. We're not slaves in Berush who cannot look at their masters."

Sashia quickly moved on to the trial and refrained from mentioning Cyrus' planned visit. She would believe it when she saw it. Cyrus might change his mind when he realized there were no political or economic advantages to their union. Sure, Father was prosperous, as far as goat-herders went, but Sashia's legal status was unprecedented. Father had no further obligation to her, and she had nothing of her own.

"It was thoughtful of him to send you back with an escort." Vani viewed her appraisingly when she had finished. "I know better than to ask if you flirted with him. Unless you've greatly changed, you're not the type. Too bad. You would make an admirable queen. You'd go quietly behind the scenes, arranging everything, letting everyone else think they were in charge."

Sashia laughed. "Is that what you would do?"

"Oh no, I would lie lazily in bed, growing fat and

letting everyone wait on me."

They giggled at the picture, but then Sashia turned serious. She peeked over at Vani's maid, who was snoring peacefully. The temptation to confide in someone was too strong. "He said he would come and see me, Vani," she whispered.

Vani gasped. "No! Did he really?"

Sashia nodded.

"Why do you look like someone died? You should be excited!"

"Because . . . I am a healer. I want to help people. I want to train others in the techniques I've learned. I cannot do that if I'm stuck in a palace caring for children of my own."

Vani sighed and rubbed her swollen belly as another contraction seized her. After it passed, she surveyed Sashia critically. "Not everyone has your freedom, you know. In some ways, I'm glad the choice was out of my hands. Your mother is going to strangle you if you reject him."

"I don't care in the least what my mother thinks. I just don't look forward to hearing it."

"But you told him you would see him?"

"I couldn't bring myself to refuse, which, I suppose, means I am uncertain," Sashia admitted as she tried to honestly analyze her feelings.

"You like him!"

Sashia rolled her eyes and shrugged. "I was only with him for two days—not much time to form an opinion."

"But that's more than enough time to feel an *attraction*. Many women never see their betrothed before their wedding day. Rolind and I only saw each other once a year, at the spring festival, before our fathers arranged our marriage."

"And are you happy?"

"Very! Rolind dotes on me. I am quite spoiled, really."

"I knew that already," Sashia grinned as Vani gave her a playful shove.

They talked late into the night, and Vani's contractions intensified and became more frequent. Early in the morning, she went into active labor and delivered a healthy baby boy. Spent as she was, Vani gushed over her new child, and Sashia was happy for her. Helping bring a baby into the world was still her favorite part of being a healer.

∞∞∞

After catching a few hours of sleep, Sashia and Lang headed back to her parents' camp. As they reached the point where the trail joined the main path, Sashia heard someone coming and looked up. It was Thitus, a few horse-lengths away.

"There you are!" he roared. "You did this to me!" he was panting heavily and his eyes were wide and heat-crazed. He picked up a rock and lunged forward as if he intended to bash in their skulls. Some loose rocks rolled down the hillside, but Sashia was focused on Thitus.

Lang tried to step in front of her as his former accomplice barreled toward them, but she blocked him with her left arm and spun her slingshot with her right. As soon as she'd seen Thitus, she had snatched it from her belt where she always carried it. Even in Shelomoh, she had practiced with it. Before he'd taken three steps, she released the string and a small, round object hit him in the center of his forehead. There was no way she could miss from that distance.

Thitus fell forward and lay still. Sashia stared silently as what she'd done sank in. Suddenly, two men came sliding down the talus slope next to them. One of them held a bow. It was Deppan and Restus.

They stopped beside Thitus and rolled him over. Sashia managed to tell her feet to move and walked forward to meet them.

"Dead," pronounced Restus. He inspected the wound and then stared at Sashia. "What did you hit him with?"

Silently she drew another of the objects out of her pocket and held it out to him. He took it and studied it. It was an oblong ball of lead. He handed it to Deppan who rolled it around in his hand.

"Where did you get this?" he asked in awe.

"I made it." She held out her hand and he gave it back.

"Well, we can definitely report to Prince Cyrus you can take care of yourself."

"How did you happen to be here?" she asked, numb and shaking now the encounter was over.

"When we returned, Cyrus sent us to find Thitus and keep an eye on him. We followed him here. Restus was about to stick an arrow in him when you loosed your slingshot." He motioned to the bow the guard had set on the ground.

"We can dispose of the body," offered Restus. "You don't need to worry about it."

Sashia shook her head. "No, bring him to my Father's camp. He will have a proper funeral pyre."

"He doesn't deserve such consideration," scoffed Deppan. "He was going to kill you."

"It's not for him," she put her hand on Lang's arm. "It's for us."

∞∞∞

Mother was incensed at the thought of holding a

funeral for a thief and went and sulked in her tent, but Father allowed it to proceed.

"If his body is buried in the hills, he will remain with us. If the fire consumes him, he is gone. Watching the smoke rising in the air helps us to let go. It would be indecent of us to refuse a man a funeral."

As Sashia watched the flames devour Thitus' body, she shed a few tears of her own. In a way, this was the first patient she had 'lost,' and she'd killed him on purpose. She didn't know what to make of that. The slingshot on her belt seemed to burn her skin as she fingered it. For a brief moment she considered throwing it into the fire with Thitus. She'd claimed it wasn't her place to decide who lived and who died, but defending your life, or that of a friend, was another matter, wasn't it? Could she have done anything differently that would have changed the outcome? Could Cyrus?

From what Lang said, Thitus had been cruel and manipulative. He had shown no remorse at the trial. If they had shown him more mercy, would he have changed? What would mercy have looked like? They couldn't have let him go free.

Cyrus had felt like he was showing mercy by letting him live at all. He'd given him a chance to change, but not the tools. However, you couldn't force a man to change if he didn't want to. Even the Magi in Shelomoh might not have been able to change him. Students had to go there voluntarily. Perhaps Mother was right: she couldn't save everyone.

"Are you alright, daughter?"

The gentle pressure of Father's hand on her shoulder gave Sashia a small measure of comfort.

"No." Her voice broke, and the single word was all she could utter.

"Sometimes it is acceptable not to be alright."

Father gave her a look of sympathy and walked away, but Sashia breathed a little easier. Lang let out a sob, and Sashia followed his example. She allowed herself to be overcome by grief and tried not to think at all.

CHAPTER EIGHT

The next couple of days Sashia spent time meditating in her tent. Dorthi had taught her to do this whenever she was troubled. It would be so nice to be able to talk to her mentor right now! Dorthi's gentle and sympathetic counsel had brought her through homesickness, frustration with her studies, and the perilous transformation from a girl to a woman. Writing a letter was not the same as having her present, and it would take weeks or months to receive an answer.

"I miss you, Dorthi!" she cried as she wiped the tears from her face and despised herself for being weak. After a few racked sobs, she steadied her breathing and tried to recognize and validate her feelings. Meditation was not as easy away from the sheltered peace of Shelomoh, but she couldn't put it off any longer.

She needed to sort through her turbulent emotions and decide what she was going to do next. Thitus' angry face haunted her dreams, and she could only hope the memory would diminish with time. All she could do about that problem was acknowledge it and set it aside.

Mother complained about the fact she wasn't working, but Shazar and Rolind had each sent a bred doe as payment for her services, and she'd given them to her father in exchange for her board as long as she needed it. It was not her original plan to work out of her parents' camp. She'd thought she might be an itinerant healer rather than be based in one place. That way, she could spread her knowledge over a greater area.

However, Cyrus expected to find her with her parents. How long would she have to wait before he came calling? And did she want to be found? What would be waiting for her if she went down that road? Could she continue practicing healing? She wouldn't want to become a prisoner in a palace, to be kept safe and look pretty.

Then she remembered, though he had been jesting, Cyrus indicated people thought the same of him, and he resented it. She realized she'd been imagining a scenario in her head without any real information. Until she knew him better, knew what he would expect from her, she couldn't make any decisions about him. Feeling much better, she resolved to stay where she was for now and take one day at a time.

∞∞∞

"Prince Cyrus is coming!"

Cashi rushed into their tent and made the announcement Sashia had anticipated with both apprehension and excitement. Her throat constricted, and she was stricken dumb with panic.

"Mother says we must all be there to greet him. Come on!"

Somehow Sashia managed to get to her feet and

follow her sister to the center of the camp. *He has been here before. A visit will not seem unusual to everyone. Act normal!*

She arrived at her father's tent to see him conversing with Deppan, who had the audacity to wink at her. She took a place behind Cashi and Pat, whose eager, smiling faces made a sharp contrast to her drawn cheeks and uncharacteristic shyness. She held her hands behind her back to keep from wringing them nervously. She'd never felt so unsure of herself.

Lang came and stood next to her. His presence buoyed her a little—but only a little.

They didn't have to wait long before Cyrus' patrol came thundering into the camp. Cyrus dismounted, and his men led away the horses while he strode confidently up to her father.

"Greetings, Haban. May my men and I impose on your hospitality for the night?"

"Of course, my lord. You are most welcome."

These were merely polite formalities, as Father could hardly refuse, though it meant he'd have to feed all of Cyrus' men, but it was commendable Cyrus didn't feel himself above such things.

Cyrus' eyes sought her out, and she tried her best to return his gaze unflustered.

The prince turned back to Haban. "I am aware of your daughter Sashia's unique legal status, but I feel it only right to ask your permission, in your own camp, to speak privately with her."

"If she wishes." Father's even voice gave no hint of surprise.

Cashi pulled Pat to the side as Cyrus walked over and stood in front of Sashia. Every head turned to watch, and Sashia kept her eyes on the prince, if only to avoid looking at her mother. She did not want to see her expression. So much for acting normal.

"Will you walk with me?" His earlier assurance was replaced by doubt.

Sashia nodded mutely, and when he turned, she took her place next to him. She motioned for Lang to stay when he started to follow. Together, they walked out of the camp and up a trail into the hills. For every step Cyrus took, she had to take two in order to keep up, though he walked slowly for her sake.

"Are you well? I heard what happened with Thitus," he remarked with concern.

"I am fine, thank you." Sashia tried to soften her voice, but her words came out strained and tense.

"It is not an easy thing, to take a life, especially when you have devoted yourself to doing the opposite."

"No."

"I am sorry you had to do that. I was hoping to prevent anything like that from happening." The prince sounded genuinely concerned and sympathetic.

"It wasn't your fault, my lord. You did your best." She attempted to assuage his worry, but felt like she was being trite.

"It would be reasonable to be affected by what happened," he persisted. "You seem upset. Are you sure you are alright? You can tell me."

"I am fine," she repeated. "Although I would've handled things differently, I don't blame you. It's not that. At least not primarily." She was anxious to clarify Cyrus' intentions, but didn't know how to bring it up.

Cyrus turned to face her. "Then what is it? Are you angry with me about something, Sashia? You don't seem glad to see me."

"What is it you want?" Sashia blurted out less

tactfully than she'd meant to.

Cyrus was taken aback. "What do I want?" he repeated. "I'd have thought it would be obvious."

"Still, I need to hear it out loud."

"Very well." He hesitated a moment and took a breath before plunging ahead. "As the heir to the throne, I am expected to marry and . . . and produce heirs of my own. I could wait for my father to arrange something, or I could marry one of the many chieftains' daughters who are constantly being paraded in front of me, or . . ." he paused for emphasis and held her gaze, "or, I could find a wife on my own. One who would stand by my side as I lead the country, stand up for me, and to me, if necessary. Someone I could love, and who would love me. That is what I want."

"Oh," was all she could say as he took her hand. He was a persuasive speaker, and she felt herself being drawn into his vision of the future, although it was the stark opposite of hers. He would be able to talk her into almost anything if she wasn't careful.

"I feared such a thing would be impossible," continued Cyrus, "and then I met you. You're unlike any girl I've ever known. I had to see you again." He rubbed his thumb against her palm, making concentration a challenge. "What do you want, Sashia?"

"I am a healer." She focused her thoughts with effort. "I've trained for years to become one. I am free to make my own decisions. If I marry, I would have to give that up."

"I see. And you don't want to give it up, even for something greater?"

"Who is to say which calling is greater?" She bristled at the implication that healing was lesser than bearing royal children.

"You don't think shaping the future of the country is the greater calling?"

"Anyone can do the type of shaping you are thinking of."

"Not anyone, Sashia. Your strength, wit, and courage are part of what drew me to you. Those traits are not going to disappear if you take a different path. I need someone like you at my side. What are you really afraid of losing? Your occupation or your independence?"

"Both!"

Cyrus chuckled and combed his fingers through his wavy, black hair.

"You think that's funny?"

"No, I am laughing at myself. While hoping to marry for love, my heart has led me to the one woman with the power and the will to refuse me."

Sashia softened at his words. A prince might never know if his wife truly loved him for himself or not.

"Would I have to give it up? Healing, I mean."

"Yes, at least, to a certain extent. You couldn't wander all over the country, but you could practice in the palace, perhaps in the city. You could be wherever I am."

"The writ allows me to travel as I please."

"Yes, but if you were to become my wife, you wouldn't need the writ. Instead, we would have to come to an understanding. We must agree on where you go and what you do. My duty to my country must come first, and your duty would be to support me."

Sashia's hand slipped out of his, and she walked away from him to sit on a rock. The sun was already hidden by the mountains, and the land before them was shrouded in shadow. Cyrus came and sank down onto the rock next to her.

"You know," he bumped his knee against hers

playfully, "I had imagined this conversation progressing rather differently."

"If you were interested in any other woman, you'd be talking to her father. You could have any woman you want."

"Except you. No one can give you to me. You have to choose me."

"You have no idea what you're asking."

"I'm not asking you anything yet. I'm just trying to get to know you better."

Sashia stood up and paced. Cyrus sat and watched her. "Your father would have to approve of me, for your sake, even though my family has no say?"

"He would." Cyrus squirmed a little.

"Is he likely to approve of someone like me?"

"He's not excited about the idea of me choosing my own wife, but he's not forbidden it."

Sashia narrowed her eyes at him. "You've talked to him about it?"

"I have." Cyrus' mouth was a firm line. "Not about you specifically."

When he didn't elaborate, she continued, "I am sorry to ask so many questions, but I have to know the full situation." She studied him to observe his response.

Cyrus nodded. "I understand."

It was a good sign that he wasn't impatient with her. Sashia tried to appraise Cyrus impartially. He was strong, intelligent, handsome—yes, she finally admitted it—and already a respected leader. Any other girl would accept him without a thought. In fact, looking at him seemed to render her incapable of thought. She felt dizzy and had to look away.

Cyrus stood to his feet. He closed the distance between them with two steps and placed his hands on her shoulders. They were shaking. If the physical connection affected him as greatly as it did her, it was no wonder.

"Sashia, please don't make a decision today. I'm afraid it would be 'no'. Let me come and see you again. There's no reason to rush into anything. I understand this would take your life in an entirely different direction, and you would have to trust me with your happiness, where now you only have to worry about yourself. Let's take some time and see what happens."

She gazed into his eyes and found herself unable to do anything but agree.

∞∞∞

Cyrus conversed politely with Father during dinner. Everyone looked at Sashia curiously, expecting an announcement or explanation, but she couldn't give them satisfaction. The ease with which Cyrus spoke was admirable. Sashia couldn't say a word and only stared at her food. Mother's frown barely even registered.

When the sun rose the next morning, Sashia was already awake and dressed. Knowing someone would come to fetch her if she wasn't there, she went to say farewell to Cyrus.

His men were already mounted, and Cyrus was speaking with Father, who bowed and backed away as she approached. The prince smiled at her, and she felt tingly all over.

"It takes about fifteen days for my patrol to make a complete circuit, depending on what issues come up." He held the reins of his horse in one hand, and the animal's body shielded them partially from the eyes of his soldiers. He reached up with his free hand and gently brushed her cheek with his fingers.

Her lips parted and she exhaled slowly.

"I will be counting the days," vowed Cyrus.

Sashia's mouth felt dry and wooly. "So will I," she managed to reply.

He swung himself easily into the saddle, gave her a grin, and rode away.

∞∞∞

Cyrus did not return. Instead, Topec arrived after two weeks had passed, and he asked Haban to call everyone together. Zarin and Estan had returned successfully from their venture and were present as well. When the entire camp was gathered, Topec gave them a message.

"I have dire news to convey. Our western border is under attack. An unknown army has encamped in the plain on the other side of the mountains, razed several camps and villages, and appropriated all their livestock. Prince Cyrus has asked that you send everyone who can fight to gather at the Tull Pass in three days."

Topec looked at Sashia. "He also asks that you join them, Sashia. We will need healers if we go to battle." He turned back to the rest of the group. "He has sent messengers to Sherish and the eastern tribes, but it will take several days for them to reach us with reinforcements. If we can keep the enemy from crossing the pass until they arrive, then we can defeat them and minimize our losses. Otherwise, they will do the same here as they have done on the other side."

"How many are they?" asked Father.

"Hundreds, if not thousands, Haban. Reports vary. Captain Kritus' patrol sent us warning as soon as they were spotted but without giving an accurate count.

Cyrus has sent scouts, but they haven't returned yet."

"That's why you're not ordering us to flank them?"

"Yes." Topec sighed. "Our numbers are too few. If we divide our forces, we won't have enough to hold the pass."

"Lang," Sashia began.

"I am already packing, my lady." He hustled to the tent he shared with the other single menservants.

"Tell Prince Cyrus he can count on us," assured Haban.

"We will see you at the pass." Topec gave a slight bow of respect and took his leave, but not before managing to surreptitiously pass Sashia a sealed letter which she quickly shoved in her pocket.

Then everyone started talking at once.

"Quiet!" ordered Father. "Zarin, Estan, Sunen, and I will go. The rest will stay here to protect the women, children, and livestock. You may use some of the winter forage so the flocks won't have to range far."

"Haban," Mother's voice cracked as tears ran down her face.

"Yania," he put an arm around her waist and kissed her cheek, "you are in charge while I am gone." He looked at his sons, who stood by solemnly. "It will take us nearly three days to get there. We must leave immediately. Get ready!"

Sashia ran to her tent to grab the necessary belongings and her healing supplies. Father and the others would have horses, but she and Lang would have to walk. In only a few moments, she had everything she needed and was lined up with her brothers at the cook tent to receive provisions.

"You're not going! Your father didn't list your name," declared Mother.

"Because he no longer has authority over me. I thought you would be glad to be rid of me, Mother."

"Is that what you think? I'm only trying to protect you!"

"Thank you, Mother, but I will make my own decisions." She held out her pack to Hurish who placed in it a loaf of bread and a lump of cheese wrapped in a cloth, along with a packet of dried fruit and one of dried meat. Lang came up behind her to receive his.

Zarin's wife stood crying with their youngest child in her arms as he kissed her goodbye. Estan's betrothed lived a day's ride away. He wouldn't be able to say goodbye to her.

"Zarin," Sashia caught up with him as he mounted his horse. "Take a few of these," she held out some of her lead projectiles. "Use them in your sling. They will fly farther than a stone with deadly accuracy."

He picked one up and inspected it. "This is what you used on the thief?"

"Yes."

"Thanks. Too bad we don't have time to make more."

"I have a mold. Maybe Sunen can make some more when we catch up with you."

Zarin nodded. "Take care, sis."

"You too."

The others rode up to join him, all armed with swords and slingshots, and they galloped north toward the Tull Pass.

Sashia and Lang walked after them.

"Have you ever seen a battle, my lady?"

"No. Have you?"

"When I was a boy. That was why I so readily accepted the merchant's offer of a job elsewhere. There was much fighting in my country."

"This is the first such call in my lifetime. Hopefully the last."

"As long as there are people, there will be fighting," he said sorrowfully.

"Well, our job is healing."

"We will be busy."

Sashia sighed. "Let's not talk of it. It will come soon enough."

"Yes, my lady. You are right." He was silent for a moment. "Was it my fault—what happened to Thitus?"

"Of course not. You were his victim, not the other way around. He forced you into thievery."

"But he got me out of Cerecia."

"For his own purposes. He used you to help him escape."

"Why did he say I did it to him?"

"He could just as easily have been talking about me giving evidence about the knife. He was out of his mind from heat and exhaustion."

"My punishment should have been the same as his."

Sashia shook her head. "You would never have committed those crimes if he hadn't forced you to. You admitted your guilt." She stopped and put a hand on his shoulder. "We cannot change the past. What's done is done. Let's focus on how we can make a difference in the future. Alright?"

Lang nodded and seemed to receive her words. He'd appeared depressed ever since the incident, although he'd been more in awe of her than ever. Hopefully, he would soon get past both feelings.

Before he could get started on another subject, they were joined by other foot soldiers on their way to the pass. Sashia was surprised to see Kari among them.

"I can sling a stone as well as anyone," she stated with her head held high. A long dagger hung from the belt around her waist. Neither Shazar nor anyone else from his camp had come. They had few servants, and Kari, sadly, was the one who would be least missed.

The farther they travelled, the more people joined their ranks. A wide range of ages were represented, from boys in their early teens to men in their fifties. Most of those answering the call to fight were male, but a few were female. Wives who came with their husbands or servants from the same household stuck together, but the few single women, like Kari, gravitated to each other and formed their own group.

Every male in Berush was encouraged to learn to use a sword, and even females could learn with permission from a father or husband, but not everyone owned such a weapon. Most members of Sashia's tribe, those who lived in the mountains, were proficient with the slingshot. Stones were plentiful and slingshots easy to make. The materials for a bow and arrows were tougher to find, and fletching was not a skill learned by many in the west.

It wasn't until evening that Sashia had the time, and the privacy, to bring out the letter Topec had slipped to her. After most of the others had gone to sleep, she held it up to the flickering light of a dying fire and tried to decipher Cyrus' handwriting.

Sashia,

These past two weeks since I saw you, I have thought of nothing else. Faced with the possibility of leading my people into battle against an unknown foe, I feel alone and afraid. Yes, I am afraid, but your memory sustains me.

I cannot command you to come to me, but I ask it. Please. Please come, Sashia. From your enthusiasm for healing, I surmise you would come

anyway, but I want you to know I ask you for myself,
not just Berush.

Cyrus

Sashia felt tears welling in her eyes, and she wiped them away with her sleeve. Why must she be faced with such a dilemma? On one hand she had the dream of becoming a healer, helping others, saving lives. On the other was Cyrus, prince of Berush, so perfect it was hard to believe he was real. Certainly, he was a little full of himself, believing he and his destiny were more important than anyone else, but his letter showed a vulnerable side.

He needed her, or at least, he needed someone. Did she want it to be her? Could she trade a future of heroism and independence for childrearing and semi-seclusion? Would love be enough of a reason, if she came to love him?

And if he, a prince, was afraid, how could she possibly help him? The odds must be even worse than Topec had intimated if Cyrus was that worried. She started to be a little scared herself. What should she say when she saw him again?

Her questions echoed in a mind empty of answers. She curled up on her pallet and cried herself to sleep.

CHAPTER NINE

On the third day, as they drew near to the pass, the little army had swelled to nearly three hundred. When they reached the location of Cyrus' camp, sentries met them and directed them to the areas where they would be needed. By the size and number of tents in the camp, Sashia estimated at least another five hundred volunteers had already arrived.

At the base of the mountain was a small fort. It was the only such structure in the Granite Mountains and was used to store shields and swords for the express purpose of defending the pass. Riders on patrol couldn't carry around the heavy shields needed to protect fighters forming a human barrier against an enemy army.

As soon as there was an opportunity, Sashia spoke to one of the soldiers. "I am a healer. Where do I go?"

"The infirmary is being set up over there," he motioned to a group of large tents at the far end of the camp.

Sashia and Lang wove their way through the bustling camp to the indicated tents. Several women sat tearing cloths into strips, and a man grimly sharpened knives at a small table. In the tent behind them, a few cots had been set up, and a platform large enough for a surgical table sat in the center. A stack of pallets was piled to one side to be used if needed.

Sashia went over to the man. He was thin and wiry, with graying temples, but he exuded energy and competence. "My name is Sashia. I am a healer. I was sent to help you."

The man looked her over and grunted. "What experience do you have?"

"I apprenticed under Beyorn of Rakhlain for seven years. I have performed amputations, cauterized blood vessels, treated fevers, and I can suture. I can assist with surgeries—whatever you need."

He sat back and raised his eyebrow. "How old are you?"

"I have seven years of experience," she repeated firmly. "Prince Cyrus himself can vouch for my skills."

"Well, I cannot afford to be choosy." He stood up. "My name is Kassius. We will need plenty of water. You can take buckets to the stream and start filling up that barrel." He pointed to a barrel standing outside the tent.

Sashia nodded, and she and Lang went back and forth to the stream until the barrel was full. It was a good sign Kassius was intent on keeping things clean, or at least keeping patients hydrated. When they finished that task, Kassius was nowhere to be found.

"I don't see anywhere for a fire, Lang," observed Sashia. "Dig a pit and build a ring of stones while I gather some fuel."

The camp had been set up in a flat, grassy area, and she had to venture some distance into the hills to find any dry wood. When her arms were full with all she could carry, she headed back to camp. It was close to sunset, so this would be all she could do for the day. As she reached the first row of tents, someone called her name, nearly startling her into dropping her bundle of firewood.

"Sashia!" It was Cyrus. He rode up on his black gelding and quickly dismounted, letting the reins trail as he walked over to her. He removed his helmet and put it under his arm. "You came." He stood so close the firewood was the only thing between them.

"I am here to help in whatever way I can, but you should know, I did not come for you." It might hurt his feelings, but she felt like it needed to be said. She wasn't ready to commit to anything yet.

Cyrus' expression became more solemn. "Whatever your reasons, I am relieved to see you." He glanced back toward the pass. "I fear we will have need of your skills."

"You think they will attempt to push further into Berush? Do we know who they are yet?"

He shook his head, answering her second question first. "We've stalled for time, trying to communicate with them, but none of their number speak any of the Ignei languages."

"Have you tried Rakhli? I speak that."

"Yes, to no avail." He sighed and ran his fingers through his hair.

Sashia was beginning to recognize it as a symptom of frustration or exasperation. It was endearing. She tried not to think about it. "You said in your letter you were afraid. Why? If anyone can defeat them, I'm sure you can."

"The scouting reports are grim. They slaughtered every man, woman, and child camped on the western side of the pass, including the village where we held the trial." His voice shook. "A few in the northernmost regions escaped, mostly those ranging higher up in the mountains and those warned by Kritus' patrol before they perished attempting to defend evacuees fleeing toward the pass. None of them lived other than the messenger sent to warn us. The enemy is heavily armed, skilled with a type of long dart I've not seen before."

Cyrus stepped to the side so she could resume walking. He looked down at her burden, as if only now noticing it, and replaced his helmet. "May I carry that for you?" He held out his arms.

Feeling she should maintain her image of self-sufficiency, she refused. "No, thank you, my lord."

His shoulders sagged, and she was immediately sorry. He was already discouraged, carrying the burden of leading an informal, undisciplined army against a ruthless, unknown opponent. How could she help without letting things get too personal? A sudden inspiration brought an exclamation to her lips.

"Oh! Lang! He is from the continent! He may speak a language they could understand."

Cyrus' eyes lit up, and he stood up straighter. "That would be extremely helpful."

They hurried back to the infirmary to find him.

"Oh yes, my lady, I speak Lalowoy, a very common language on the continent," was Lang's response to their query.

"Would you be willing to interpret for Prince Cyrus if someone in the opposing army speaks it also?"

"Oh, my. Oh, my." He wrung his hands. "I have never done anything like that before."

"You don't even need to do a good job of it, Lang," explained Cyrus. "If we can get nothing out of them, at least we can buy more time for my father to arrive with more men. So far, they've been willing to try talking with us."

"I will go if you go with me, my lady."

The corner of Cyrus' mouth curled up in amusement.

"Don't ask," she muttered. "I'll go."

"We'll set out at dawn, then. You'd best get some sleep." Cyrus looked deeply into Sashia's eyes, the last rays of the sun painting his face golden. "I am glad you are here," he said softly, "even if it's not for me."

∞∞∞

Early the next morning, they headed up the pass. Sashia didn't have much experience riding horses, so she consented to ride behind Cyrus again. Luckily, his armor kept her from being too comfortable, so she didn't get sucked further into an emotional state she couldn't get out of. She couldn't understand why he seemed attracted to her. Sashia had always considered herself rather plain.

Lang had ridden horses and camels in his youth and took it up again easily. He seemed fond of animals and navigated his horse along the mountain path without any trouble.

Several warriors rode with them, including Topec. When they reached the top of the pass, a troop of soldiers stood guarding the gap. Cyrus helped Sashia down, dismounted, and went to speak to one of his lieutenants. Sashia didn't recognize him and assumed he belonged to another patrol.

"Any change, Orlin?"

"They continue to enjoy the spoils of their previous raids. We estimate they've already eaten a quarter of the goats they captured."

"So they won't be content with what they have for long. Are our archers in position?"

"Yes, my lord. They are strategically placed on either side of the pass." The lieutenant whistled, and dozens of men emerged out of their hiding places to give a salute before melting back into the landscape. "I only wish there were more."

"We'll have Granum slingers to support them. Signal the enemy's lookout. We want to try and talk with them again."

A soldier went forward with a banner and waved it back and forth. In the valley below, a horn sounded, and a banner waved in reply.

"How long will it take for a delegation from the enemy camp to arrive?" asked Sashia.

"About an hour. Lang, let me acquaint you with what I want to say so you can practice translating it in your mind."

Lang was so nervous, Sashia doubted he heard anything the prince said.

"They come," announced Topec when the representatives from the opposing army approached within hailing distance.

Cyrus motioned for Lang and Topec to follow him as he went forward to meet them. Sashia kept close to Lang and patted his shoulder reassuringly. A few of the archers showed themselves and trained arrows on the visitors. The rest of Cyrus' men spread out behind him.

The warriors who approached were intimidating. Their heads were shaved; they wore leather armor and carried wooden shields covered in animal skins. They were armed with long darts, dart throwers, and either heavy spears or swords. Their tunics were sleeveless, and their biceps bulged on their bare arms. There were half a dozen of them. At least one of them appeared to be female. Sashia found it impossible to tell for sure.

"First, ask if any of them speak Lalowoy."

Lang's voice shook as he complied.

One muscular young fighter who looked a little older than Cyrus replied.

"This man speaks it, my lord," interpreted Lang.

Cyrus took a step forward. "My name is Cyrus, son of King Kalin and commander of his army. Who are you and why have you carried out this unprovoked attack on our lands?"

Lang addressed the young man who turned and spoke to the older man next to him. Then a message was relayed back.

"They call themselves the Breakers, my lord. Their leader is Viper; the one who speaks is his son, Gar. He says they took what they needed."

"It is customary to pay or trade for what one needs."

More translating.

"Not when you can take it," was their smug reply. Viper crossed his arms and Gar smirked.

"We require you to pay for the livestock you've stolen, rebuild the villages you destroyed, and you will be indebted to us for the lives you have taken."

The Breakers laughed derisively when Gar interpreted Cyrus' demands.

"Who will make us?"

"Berush would prefer to avoid any further bloodshed, but if necessary, we will annihilate you."

Lang hesitated and leaned over to Cyrus. "Excuse me, my lord, what is 'annihilate'?"

"Destroy. Wipe them out. Kill them all."

"Ah." He continued translating.

Viper only grunted, and Gar replied with a grin.

"We know you have no standing army. If you wish to avoid bloodshed, give us one thousand more goats, two hundred young men and women to use as slaves, and we will leave you in peace."

Sashia didn't know how Cyrus could keep calm

during the exchange. She was infuriated. How could they stand there and laugh when they had wantonly massacred hundreds of people without warning?

"We do not give in to bribery or threats," Cyrus continued, his voice firm and steady. "I repeat, you must reimburse us for our losses or suffer the consequences."

"You are dooming yourselves into—I don't know the word," interjected Lang, "—nothingness? We will give you one more chance to save yourselves. Send your best warrior to fight ours in single combat. If you win, we will go away. If we win, you give us the goats and slaves."

"Give us until this time tomorrow to think it over."

The Breakers agreed and the negotiation ended. Both delegations prepared to return to their respective headquarters. Lang gave a huge sigh of relief and wiped drops of sweat from his forehead.

"You did very well, Lang," soothed Sashia.

Cyrus didn't mount his horse right away and instead turned to Topec.

"Do we have an accurate count yet?"

"They appear to number near a thousand warriors, my lord. Their children and elderly are in a separate section near the back. Their tents are smaller than ours, so it was difficult to estimate at first."

"Have they sent any scouts across the mountains?"

"It does not appear so. They are unfamiliar with this range, which is an advantage for us. We have the high ground."

"So they're either arrogant and overconfident or untrained in military strategy."

"Let's hope for both."

"We can plan on an attack tomorrow afternoon. Boulders, archers, slingers, and swordsmen, in that order. You know how to arrange it."

"Yes, my lord." Topec mounted his horse and rode off.

Cyrus remained gazing down at the enemy tents. Sashia approached him tentatively.

"So you're not really considering single combat?"

"Why, were you worried about me?" he flashed her a rakish grin.

She scoffed good-naturedly. "You and all the rest of us."

"Would you trust them to keep their word?" He shook his head. "I don't. And no Berushese would willingly become a slave just because their prince lost a fight. I refuse to let the fate of that many ride on the skill of my own blade, or any other single person's."

Sashia considered his words. It was true; if he won, and killed whoever they sent to fight him, there was nothing to stop them from attacking anyway. Without knowing anything about the Breakers' history, the Berushese could make no judgments about their future behavior. What little they did know did not inspire confidence.

"You spoke well, my lord," she said quietly.

"Thank you. That means a lot coming from you."

He turned his intense gaze on her again, and her throat went dry.

"Excuse me, but has anyone brought anything to eat? All that interpreting has made me hungry. It was hard work!"

Cyrus laughed. "Yes, Lang. I brought rations for all of us." He went to his saddlebags and retrieved some dried meat and fruit along with half a loaf of bread and portioned it out. After eating, they headed back down to the Berushese camp, and Cyrus returned Sashia and Lang to the infirmary.

"I will need you both again tomorrow." He

dismounted and walked with Sashia to the tent. "If you hadn't intervened in Lang's trial the way you did, Sashia, we would have no interpreter, and we might not have had this extra day. It could make all the difference."

"When will King Kalin arrive?"

"In two days, perhaps." He paused, looking as if he wanted to say more, but decided against it. "I will see you in the morning."

Sashia watched him ride off and then went in search of Kassius. She found him in the tent rolling bandages. Picking up a strip of cloth, she started to roll it up.

"Kassius, how will they bring the wounded soldiers down the mountain?"

"However they can. There are litters available. It depends on how heated the battle is. Sometimes it's not possible to treat all the wounded until the battle is over."

"What if I took my tools and a supply of bandages up to the pass? I could treat those who might otherwise be seen too late."

"That is a noble idea, but if the pass is overrun and you are killed, then who will treat the wounded?"

"If the pass is overrun, we are all lost. I can save you trouble if I can treat and assess injuries as they occur, caring for those unable to be moved and sending you those with the best chance of recovery."

Kassius contemplated her and took time before replying. "Very well. Two more healers showed up today. I will have enough help. What you propose is dangerous, for you, but could be extremely helpful."

Sashia rolled bandages until there were no more. Then she stuffed her pack with them and set it by the door of the tent where she could grab it in the morning.

That evening, Cyrus ordered the rag-tag militia making up his army to gather together at the foot of the mountain. When everyone was assembled, he addressed the crowd.

"Berush is facing a daunting foe. Our very existence is threatened by this new enemy. They have already massacred hundreds of our people without mercy, without provocation, and without warning. The enemy tried to threaten us into becoming their slaves. We do not own slaves in Berush. Nor will we allow any of our people to be enslaved. We will fight for our freedom!"

He paused as the crowd roared in response.

"They think they are better than we are. They think they are stronger. In might, perhaps they are, but not in heart. We will defend these mountains because they are ours! I ask each one of you to fight for yourselves, for your families, for Berush!"

"Berush!" The cry echoed off the hills. "Berush!"

CHAPTER TEN

Cyrus arrived at dawn. "What is that for?" he asked when Sashia hefted her pack onto her back.

As she told him her plan, several different emotions played across his face.

"My first instinct is to tell you to stay put, but that would be selfish." He bent down, held out his hand to help her onto the horse, and moved his foot out of the stirrup. "You are a brave woman, Sashia. Promise me you won't put yourself in unnecessary danger."

"I promise to put myself in necessary danger only."

Her arms encircled his waist, and she leaned against his polished, steel cuirass as he urged his horse into a canter. He put his free hand over hers and held it there. Sashia felt a strange burning in her chest. Getting used to riding with Cyrus wasn't a good thing. Was it? Suddenly, she realized she was starting to enjoy it.

They rode silently, with Lang following. Hundreds of soldiers marched up the pass with them. Some branched off into the trees and climbed higher into the mountains. Others would be used as reserves in the gap. Every man and woman was strategically placed.

The Breakers were correct that Berush had no standing army, but they had enough career soldiers to patrol the borders and defend the capital. The warriors spread across the pass itself were highly trained and well-armored.

Like the people of the mountains, the rest of the country would answer the call to arms and arrive as soon as they could. They had a greater army than the enemy realized.

They dismounted once they reached the top and stood waiting with the rest of the soldiers for the Breakers to appear.

When the Breakers came, they were greater in number. There were at least fifty of them. Sashia wondered if they were expecting Cyrus to agree to single combat.

"What is your decision?" asked Viper through the relay.

"Our demands are the same. Reparation for our damages."

Viper replied in a particularly nasty tone and spit on the ground, and his son interpreted with a sneer.

"'Forget it.' That is the gist of it, anyway," Lang summarized. "I would rather not repeat everything he said."

Gar pointed at Cyrus and gave some parting words, and the Breakers retreated down the mountainside.

"What did he say, Lang?"

"He said, 'you are dead,' my lord."

Cyrus nodded. "Topec, prepare for an attack. We hold the pass."

Soldiers with heavy shields began lining up to form a wall. Sashia gestured for Lang to follow her, and they began weaving their way to the rear of the defenders.

"Sashia!"

She turned to see Cyrus running after them. When he reached her, he slid his arms around her waist and lifted her so close to him she was on her tiptoes.

He bent down and murmured, "In case we do not see each other again." And he kissed her.

A shiver ran through her small frame, and she closed her eyes involuntarily. She was taken by surprise, unable to react. His lips were warm and tender, and he gently pressed her body against his. When he released her, she opened her eyes to see him studying her face.

"Be careful," he whispered hoarsely. Then he was gone.

Her subconscious barely registered the grinning soldiers on either side of her. It dawned on her Cyrus had been hoping to see some hint of reciprocation in her expression. Did he see enough to sustain him in the coming battle? How had it happened she was the one he turned to? She should have said something to him! Encouraged him in some way. Sashia's own emotions were uncertain enough to cause her some anxiety over his state of mind.

She shook herself back to reality. Chanting voices and rhythmic drumbeats began echoing off the rocky, western slopes.

"Come on, Lang."

Sashia led her manservant behind the line of warriors and found a small, flat area sheltered from falling rocks by a thicket of junipers and brush. On the opposite side of the clearing, a couple of large rock formations provided some shade. The first thing to do, as always, was build a fire. Then she arranged the rest of their supplies.

Lang had carried several flasks of water and wine

and a couple of pallets. They unrolled these and sat on them, prepared to wait until they were needed.

Sashia took the opportunity to calm herself and mentally prepare for what lay ahead. This would be more taxing than anything she had previously experienced. People would die. Depending on how the battle went, she wouldn't be able to treat everyone. She had to remain detached, or she wouldn't be any good at all.

Beyorn had told her of an experience he'd had treating wounded after a clash between two rival desert clans. She'd also read accounts of the aftermath of large battles, so she had some idea what to expect. But she was still scared. She didn't know how she was going to handle failure, which would be inevitable.

Lang, thankfully, was uncharacteristically silent. He imitated her and sat quietly on his mat, occasionally getting up to stir the fire or add a few sticks to it. Figuring the best way to help him was by example, she left him alone.

The shadows under the trees stretched slowly toward them. Out of the direct line of the pass, the noise from the opposing army continued but was barely audible. Every time her heart started to speed up and give in to the strain of waiting, she forced herself to breathe calmly and evenly. The Breakers were building up the tension deliberately, and she would not give in.

When the battle finally started, the yells and clash of steel blades jarred her into instant awareness. Though she'd been expecting it every moment, it was still startling. She stood to her feet, as did Lang, who began fidgeting with the hem of his tunic.

The first man who was brought to her was a slinger whose shoulder had been pierced by one of the Breakers' long darts. No sooner had she finished treating him than an archer was carried in with a similar injury. The rest of the afternoon, she and Lang worked non-stop. Sashia divided the clearing into sections for different types and severity of injuries and had Lang direct the wounded into the proper area so she could prioritize treatment. Runners from the main camp came to carry patients to the larger infirmary, but it wasn't fast enough.

"Where do I put this man, my lady?"

"What's wrong with him?"

"I cannot find a heartbeat."

Sashia glanced over at Lang. The poor man looked strained and exhausted. He didn't want to say the man was dead.

"Put him over there," she nodded toward the other end of the clearing. She wished they had blankets to put over the deceased, but that was an unheard-of luxury on the battlefield. Neither did she have anything to relieve the pain of the living. The wine was needed for cleansing the wounds. The Magi had discovered it helped prevent suppuration.

She didn't have a chance to ask any of the patients how the battle was going. As long as the enemy hadn't broken through the pass, they were meeting their objective.

Restus was brought in with a deep spear wound to the leg. "One of your mountain slingers saved my life," he informed Sashia while she treated his injury. She stopped the bleeding, but it wasn't likely she could save the leg. That information would keep for later, however. She didn't have time or space to do an amputation on the spot. As soon as a stretcher was available, she would send him to Kassius to monitor.

"They broke through the front line, and one of those cursed Breakers stuck me in the thigh before we pushed them back. He would have skewered me through the heart if I hadn't deflected his thrust, but he pulled it back and was poised to strike again when a stone hit him in the head and he fell, dead."

That explained why the leg wound was as jagged as it was. "Try not to talk, Restus. Save your strength."

"I could have kept fighting, but the prince ordered me back."

"A good thing. You would have bled to death otherwise. Since your arms are working and you're alert, you can help bandage incoming patients." Maybe giving him an occupation would help him feel useful instead of harboring misplaced guilt for leaving his comrades.

During a lull, she double-checked those who'd been declared dead. Sometimes a heartbeat could be too faint to find easily. Those carrying the stretchers knew their jobs, however, and she found no one in that section who still breathed.

Closing her eyes, Sashia inhaled slowly, but all she could smell was the tangy scent of fresh blood. All she could hear were groans of suffering and cries of intense pain. The horror of it all pressed in on her and made her want to scream. She stiffened her spine. She couldn't let herself fall apart.

"Here's another with a dart to the chest." The litter-bearers laid a woman down at the edge of a row. It was Kari.

Sashia had instructed everyone not to remove projectiles from the wounds. Otherwise, the patient would bleed out before she could help them. Kari still had the dart protruding from her torso. The end of the dart had been broken off so she could be transported more easily. Bandages had been placed around the bottom of the shaft, and her hand held them in place, but she didn't appear to have the strength to apply pressure. She rasped and struggled for breath.

"Kari!"

"Let . . . me . . . die!"

"I cannot do that, Kari."

Kari reached up with a bloody hand and grabbed the collar of Sashia's already soiled tunic.

"You kept . . . me alive . . . when I should have died . . . once before," she wheezed. "You owe me . . . death!"

Sashia removed the bandages from around the dart and studied the injury. It was bad. The slim weapon had entered between two ribs, piercing a lung. Even if she lived through the day, she would likely die from infection. She grasped Kari's hand and gazed into her dark brown eyes. How strange that Kari's fate was in her hands for a second time.

"I will treat the others first," she choked out.

Kari closed her eyes and nodded. Somehow, she knew Sashia probably wouldn't get back to her in time and was satisfied.

Sashia replaced the bandages and laid Kari's hand back over them. She was going to respect her wish, but she couldn't stop to think about it or she would lose control. She steeled herself to move on.

Sashia looked around for Lang. He'd worked unceasingly without complaint and showed no sign of becoming ill at the sight of blood. Though he had a sensitive and sympathetic nature, he exhibited toughness when the situation required it. Everything he'd been through had conspired to make him the ideal assistant. She held out a flask of wine to him.

"Take a drink, Lang. There are still two hours of daylight left."

He pushed it away. "We must save it for those in worse need, my lady."

"We cannot help them if we do not take care of ourselves. Take a sip, Lang. I order you."

He took a small swallow and handed it back. Sashia drank some herself.

"Give two or three swallows of water to everyone who is able to drink."

Lang took a flask and began to make rounds.

Runners from the base camp returned with an empty litter. Sashia looked for Restus, but his place was empty. She didn't remember sending him down, but someone must have already taken him. She sent another man with a severely slashed forearm instead.

It wasn't until she had finished stitching up a head wound that she discovered Restus had not been transferred below. He had dragged himself down the row of injured fighters and now lay next to Kari. Propped on one elbow, his other hand held the dying woman's.

"Do you have family?"

"A . . . son." She was so weak her reply was barely audible.

"I will tell your son how you saved my life," he promised with tears running down his cheeks.

As Sashia watched, Kari exhaled her last breath with a shudder and was still. Restus pressed his trembling lips against her forehead. Sashia turned away with tears in her own eyes.

The entire eastern side of the mountains was now covered in shadow. The sky was still bright, and the Breakers would have light for another hour yet. Then even more patients would begin pouring in when it was safe to remove them. They would be the ones with sword and spear wounds instead of darts. Most of them would already be dead. Restus had only been brought because he was mobile enough to make it to the rear of the fighting with minimal assistance.

Once the darkness took over, Sashia heard horns sounding.

"If I were the Breaker commander, I would keep pushing," muttered Restus.

"Are they ceasing hostility for the night? You think they are retreating?"

"Sounds like it."

"Could it be a ploy of some sort?"

Restus shrugged. "Cyrus will leave plenty of men on guard in case it is."

They soon heard the sound of hundreds of feet as the bulk of the army retreated down the mountain. Torches were lit and every able-bodied fighter helped carry down the dead and wounded. Soon Sashia was staring at an empty clearing. Empty except for Lang, who had collapsed against a rock. He was shaking uncontrollably and sobbing softly.

"Lang," she put a hand on his shoulder. "You did an amazing job today. Thank you."

"So much death and pain! So—terrible!" he shuddered.

Sashia had wondered how he was coping. Normally, he cried easily. With a flash of insight, she realized it was because he did cry he was able to do what needed to be done—how he had kept slavery from breaking him entirely. He gave way to his emotions whenever he could so they didn't build up. That was something she could learn from him.

One drop of salty liquid trickled from her eye, followed by a torrent of tears. She sank against the boulder and gulped for air. Once she got started, it was hard to stop.

"Lady Sashia!"

Sashia blinked as Deppan rode into the clearing leading an extra horse.

"Prince Cyrus sent me back to fetch you."

Lang wiped his nose with his sleeve and mounted the second horse while Sashia stomped out the remains of the fire and climbed up behind Deppan. She was barely able to stay awake enough to hold on. At least they were riding downhill.

When the horse stopped, Sashia swung her leg over and slid off. Exhausted, she would have collapsed if a pair of strong arms hadn't caught her.

"I need to get to the infirmary." Why wouldn't her eyelids open?

"You will do no such thing! You are nearly dead on your feet. Sleeping is the only thing you will be doing."

"Kassius—"

"Kassius hardly had anything to do until the fighting ceased since you kept all the patients to yourself. He has everything under control for now."

Sashia felt her feet being lifted off the ground. She noticed Prince Cyrus was much softer to lean on without his armor, and then she lost consciousness.

∞∞∞

"Hey, Sis! Time to wake up!"

Sashia blinked and saw only darkness. She rubbed her eyes and squinted in the direction of the voice. Her eyes adjusted, and she saw firelight in the distance.

"We expect the Breakers to attack again at dawn, so we have to march out early to relieve the night watch," explained Zarin. "Come get some breakfast before it's all gone."

Sashia sat up and pushed away a blanket. She wondered whose pallet she had slept on since hers was left bloodied in the clearing. It probably belonged to someone who didn't need it anymore, she thought grimly. She followed Zarin to where Lang and the rest of her family sat eating porridge.

"Here, my lady." Lang handed her a bowl.

"How did the battle go?"

"Our clan was stationed on a ridge overlooking the pass. The first thing we did was send as many boulders down into the enemy's midst as we could. Then we focused on making sure none of them tried to climb around the edges of the pass. I think we had over twenty kills between the four of us," Zarin boasted proudly. "Your lead shot was extremely effective."

Sashia felt a sick feeling in her stomach. No one should be so happy about ending a life. She tried to focus on the fact all her family was alive.

"We just had to try and avoid their darts," continued Zarin. "Aiming downhill is much easier than aiming up, though, so their darts weren't much of a threat where we were. Cyrus' archers were able to discourage them from throwing many. They couldn't hold a shield and place their darts in the throwers at the same time."

"How does the thrower work?"

Zarin mimicked the motion of the dart throwers. "It is a wooden tool with an indentation in one end that holds the end of the dart. The tool is used as an extension of the thrower's arm and makes it go faster and farther."

"Like a lever," put in Sunen.

"They didn't climb the mountain?"

"Nope. They came nowhere close to us. My sword stayed in its sheath."

"Many fell in the pass," Sunen commented soberly.

Zarin nodded. "The shield wall was pushed back and collapsed at one point, but Prince Cyrus fought like a madman, and we soon regained the ground. I wish I was that good."

"It was the prince who brought you here last night." Sunen's somber mood disappeared and his mouth twitched. "Is there anything you want to tell us?"

"No, there is not." She hoped they hadn't heard about the kiss. She'd forgotten about it until now.

Father and Estan had been silent up to this point. Sashia glanced at Estan and saw his face was drawn and his hands shaking. She looked at Father, but Father shook his head slightly. She left it alone.

"Was Kari with you yesterday?"

"No, I never saw her," replied Zarin.

Kari must have deliberately put herself in harm's way instead of staying with the clan. She would be unhappy no longer.

A horn sounded.

"That's the signal to move out." Zarin jumped to his feet.

Sashia bid farewell to her family and went to check in at the infirmary. Kassius was washing his hands outside the tent when she arrived. He stared at her incredulously.

"I thought you were going to send some of the patients to me. I had less than a score of them until well past sunset."

"Really? I thought I sent more."

"And considering the ferocity of the fighting," he continued without acknowledging her reply, "I would have expected more casualties and less wounded. I believe more of them survived due to being treated sooner. I am sending two more healers with you today, and more supplies."

Sashia gaped at him. She wasn't used to people other than the Magi accepting her innovations, but Kassius seemed open and excited about change if it showed improvement.

"Take whatever you need," he urged.

Sashia refilled her pack with bandages and took a turn around the infirmary to check on the patients. Kassius walked with her. Restus was still sleeping when she stopped by his cot.

"I think he may be able to keep his leg."

"Oh, good! I was worried about that."

"There's not much swelling, and the rest of his leg is maintaining the proper color."

They stopped beside each patient's pallet and discussed his or her injuries and prognosis. Kassius treated her like an equal, and they were able to share some valuable insights. Not since she left Shelomoh had she had a conversation like this.

The healers who were to accompany her arrived, and they set out for the battlefront on foot. The sun was sending its first rays over the eastern horizon, and they picked up the pace.

"Do you know what our total losses were yesterday?" Sashia asked a healer named Joran.

"I heard it was near two hundred."

There were less than fifty patients in the infirmary, most of whom she had treated the previous day. Sashia was sure less than twenty casualties had passed through her clearing. That meant most of the injured were dying in the field, whether they were killed outright or died before they could be treated or moved. Would it be possible to save more if they could be reached more quickly?

When they finally arrived at the clearing, a patient with a dart injury awaited them on a stretcher. Joran and Madia, the other healer, hurried to help him while Sashia and Lang set up the temporary infirmary.

"Follow me, Lang. We're going to take a closer

look," directed Sashia once everything was ready. Her muscles were sore, and she was still tired, but the prospect of saving more lives gave her energy and propelled her onward. The clash of metal in the gap grew louder and louder the closer they came. Finally, they reached the spot where the reserves were waiting.

"You don't have to go with me," offered Sashia. "It is your choice."

"If you are going, I will go." Lang was quaking with fear, but he was determined.

A company of soldiers received an order to move forward and marched into the gap, swords drawn. Hugging the rock wall that formed one side of the pass, Sashia followed.

CHAPTER ELEVEN

When she rounded the corner, Sashia was overwhelmed by the press of soldiers in the gap. They were so close together it was no wonder no one was able to get the wounded behind the lines. They defended the gap at its narrowest point, where it was about twenty men across, and the shield wall was a dozen men deep. She climbed up on a rock where she could see over their heads.

The Breakers had shields as well, but theirs were smaller, so they had to stand closer together. Arrows and stones pelted the enemy from above, but the arrows stuck in their wooden shields and most of the stones bounced off. Occasionally a well-slung stone broke through a shield.

The Breakers were using their spears to thrust between and around the larger Berushese shields. Many of the injuries in the infirmary were to the feet, head, and neck which were the body parts most exposed.

What worried her most was the lack of armor on the volunteers waiting in reserve. Cyrus' men were on the front lines and had no doubt sustained the most casualties. Less experienced fighters would have to take a shield from a fallen comrade if ordered into the gap.

A thunderous roar reached Sashia's ears. The soldiers waiting for their turn gripped their weapons more tightly. From her vantage point, Sashia could see movement through the opposing ranks.

"Part and let them through on my command! Now!" Topec ordered over the chaotic noise of battle.

A group of enemy soldiers rushed forward but were surprised to find no resistance. They ran right through the shield wall which closed behind them before the rest realized what was happening and tried to follow. They carried the trunk of a tall pine tree to use as a battering ram. The branches had been stripped with only a few shortened limbs left as handles. The reserves rushed forward and attacked them. All but one, who dropped his sword in fear and ran in the opposite direction.

The Breaker warriors dropped the tree and took out their swords, but the delay was costly. Most of them were run through before they unsheathed their blades. One of them got a sword loose and hacked away at the Berushese fighters. He was a large, burly man with greater skill and strength than his opponents. He stabbed one man through the stomach and hacked off another's hand before he was overcome by sheer numbers and met his demise.

"Lang!" Sashia rushed to action. This was the hardest part. She had to make a choice between the two wounded men. Leaving the one with the stab wound, she tied a tourniquet around the arm of the other and lifted his legs while Lang put his hands under the man's shoulders, and they carried him away from the fighting. There was no point in trying to get him to walk on his own. All he could do was stare at the place where his hand had been. A young man standing nearby vomited.

Once they got him around the corner, they found a stretcher and placed him on it. Then they carried him back to the clearing.

"Joran, see to this one. We're going back," ordered Sashia as she and Lang moved the man onto a pallet and grabbed up the empty stretcher. On the way, they passed the other litter bearers picking their way carefully down the mountainside carrying an injured archer.

The soldier pierced in the gut had been moved out of the way of the fighting. He was already dead. The width of the sword made too great of a wound, and he had bled out. Sashia was grieved, but she knew she couldn't have helped him.

The warriors forming the shield wall still strained against each other, jabbing with swords and spears anywhere they could find an opening, but the Berushese were slowly being pushed back. Warning cries from those in the hills echoed through the pass. The sky darkened, and hundreds of deadly darts rained down on the defenders. The first three rows of men had their shields forward, forming the barrier, but the rest held them over their heads. Most of the darts harmlessly struck the shields, a few found weak spots and splintered them, and a few slipped in between and injured the men underneath. If any were hurt badly enough to need attention, Sashia was unable to reach them.

Then the Breakers let out a mighty roar. Using the Berushese shields as stepping stones, they broke formation and began to overrun their opponents. Arrows flew from the cliffs and pierced many of the enemy. Others were impaled on swords or spears as they fell between the shields before Cyrus' army finally lowered them and began fighting hand-to-hand. The reserves entered the fray, but the Breakers were so many it appeared they would soon be obliterated.

"My lady, we must get out of here!" Lang grabbed her wrist and dragged her back.

Sashia was still trying to find a way to rescue some of the injured, but she wasn't a fighter and had no way to defend herself, so she turned and ran with Lang back to the clearing with the other healers to await the outcome.

"What is happening?" asked Madia.

Before Sashia could reply, high, clear blasts from multiple trumpets cut through the air. She scrambled onto a nearby boulder, scraping a knee and putting a hole in her trousers in her haste. When she scanned the plain, she gasped in relief.

"It's King Kalin!"

The Berushese royal banner was clearly visible at the front of a vast column of horsemen. As she watched, they began galloping full speed toward the pass. The reinforcements had arrived just in time!

∞∞∞

The rest of the day, Sashia and the other healers worked furiously, trying to save as many as they could. There were far more than they were able to care for. Sashia had to force herself to focus only on the patient immediately before her. Once, she stood to move on to the next wounded soldier and saw Madia staring vacantly and unmoving.

"Madia!" Sashia went over and shook her by the shoulders. "Madia! Clean this man's wound and stitch it up. Now!"

Madia blinked and moved mechanically toward the indicated patient.

To her relief, Kassius and several other healers arrived to help.

"We received word the battle was over, so we decided to move up here."

"Who is tending to the wounded in the infirmary?"

"Don't worry," Kassius patted her arm. "It's under control."

Litter bearers continued to bring in more wounded on stretchers. Sashia stopped them before they could return to the field.

"Find Cyrus or Topec and tell them we need more help. Any of the volunteers from the mountain tribes will have enough basic knowledge to assist us." Nomads and herders had to know how to treat common injuries as trained healers were rare.

It wasn't nearly soon enough for Sashia, but a dozen extra men and women eventually came to their aid. As she was working, Sashia heard bits and pieces of news from the battlefront.

"I never thought we could hold out as long as we did. If the king had arrived any later, none of us would have survived."

"Those cocky invaders are wishing they had never set foot in Berush."

"Last I saw, we were setting fire to their camp and slaughtering every last one of them."

"I wish I could have been there to see that."

"You did your part. We were all needed."

A groan of pain recalled her to her task. She kept her ears open for any mention of Cyrus.

"I thought I saw the younger prince, Darius, riding with the king," said one of the assistants, a woman Sashia had seen with the slingers. "Did you see him?" she asked the man she was tending. Talking to the patients was one of the only ways they had to distract them from their pain.

"Yes, he came. This is his first battle."

"How did he do?"

"He is well-trained. Aaah!" The man gritted his teeth as she cleaned out the wound. "But he is very different from his brother."

Sashia wanted to hear more, but she had to move on to another patient. She wanted to hear Cyrus was alive and uninjured but couldn't bring herself to ask anyone. Since he hadn't been brought in on a stretcher, she had to hope he'd survived.

"Sashia, we need Lang to interpret again."

She turned around to see Deppan beckoning to her. He was haggard and covered in blood, but it didn't appear to be his own. "Lang!"

The clearing had more patients than it could hold, and the treatment area had spread into the surrounding terrain. When she found Lang, his eyes were hollow and his expression shadowed, but he nodded and followed her to where Deppan waited with two horses.

Deppan mounted the first one and held out his hand, but Sashia hesitated to leave the clearing. She didn't want to leave while there were still injured soldiers to treat. Torn, she considered Lang, and he was silent, knowing the dilemma that faced her, but he looked so worn and frail she knew she couldn't send him alone. He needed her moral support.

"Go," encouraged Kassius from the side of an amputee. "The work will still be here when you return."

Reluctantly, Sashia got up behind Deppan, and they turned toward the pass. She was glad Kassius was there. If he hadn't been, she knew she couldn't have left.

At the top of the pass, the sun shone directly into her eyes as it prepared to sink below the horizon. A haze of smoke obscured much of the western plain, and the stench of burning flesh filled her nostrils. As Deppan guided the horse down the path, it had to step around the piles of dead bodies littering the trail. The light was dimming, and it was hard to tell if they were Breakers or Berushese. Shields of both types were stacked on either side.

When they finally stopped, night had fallen, and before them was a ring of torches. The first person Sashia recognized was Cyrus. Her relief at seeing him made her knees momentarily weak. Two middle-aged men stood next to him, one obviously King Kalin. Though she'd never seen him before, his air of authority clearly labeled him as the sovereign of the realm. His helmet, though still eminently practical, was overlaid with gold.

To the king's left was another man whose scars and armor declared him to be a career soldier, probably a general. Behind them was a fourth man, a boy really, though nearly as tall as Cyrus, who she thought must be Darius. On the ground in front of them, a man knelt with his hands bound behind his back. It was the Breaker, Gar.

"Here is the interpreter, my lord." Deppan bowed and backed out of the circle.

"Bow," whispered Sashia in Lang's ear. Her manservant was quaking. He managed a bow as the king impatiently waved him forward.

"Tell this vermin the lives of his remaining followers depend on how he responds to our demands, so he must weigh his words carefully."

Lang stuttered a little, but he translated the king's warning. Gar replied with a stare of venomous hatred.

"We have spared your children and elderly, which is more than you did for us. If you desire any of your people to survive the night, you must swear neither you, your people, nor your descendants will set foot in Berush again."

Gar snarled. "You have killed my father, the mother of my child, and nearly all of my warriors. Just kill me too and get it over with."

"Your father doomed you all when he chose to attack us. I am showing you mercy, against my better judgment. Do you accept it or not?"

"I swear to leave Berush and never return."

"Your people are also not to return."

"Nor will my people or their descendants return to Berush."

"Now, so we will recognize you if you do return. . ." King Kalin took out his dagger and carved a long gash across the left side of Gar's face, from temple to chin.

Gar stared at the king without flinching.

"Now gather what remains of your people and get out."

A soldier cut Gar loose, and he stomped off into the night. Sashia knew better than to ask to treat his cut.

"I fear we haven't seen the last of them, Cyrus." The king remarked to his elder son. "We should have killed them all."

"It would have ensured our future safety but blackened our hearts, father."

Kalin sighed and put his hand on his son's shoulder. "You are so like your mother," he said in a soft tone that implied it wasn't derogatory. "Topec!"

Topec stepped forward and bowed.

"Take a company and follow them. Make sure they leave."

"Yes, my lord."

The young man Sashia assumed was Darius stepped forward. "How many are left, Father?"

"Too many."

"There were three hundred children and youths too young for battle. Around a hundred warriors surrendered once we had them surrounded. We captured Gar early on, and his father was killed in the first charge, so they were leaderless," Cyrus explained.

"Fools," muttered the general. "If they had continued through the gap when they first arrived, they could have defeated us."

"I do not think that was their aim, Uncle Mathis."

"What was it?" asked Darius.

"Only to feed themselves, not to conquer a nation."

"It sounds like you are sorry for them, Cyrus," chided his brother.

Cyrus shook his head. "I am sorry they would not negotiate. Sorry for their arrogance. Sorry for the loss of my men."

"Do not become bitter, son. We won the day. Be content with that. There will be plenty of work and worry tomorrow." Kalin turned to the general. "Mathis, take Darius and supervise the clean-up. It will be good for him to understand the consequences of warfare. Cyrus, go get some rest. You have earned it."

Cyrus bowed to his father, but instead of leaving, he approached Sashia and drew her aside. "I am so glad you're safe. I heard what you did today." His voice held both admiration and exasperation.

"I am glad to see you as well," she confessed softly.

Cyrus sucked in his breath and took a step closer.

"No one mentioned you, and—and I was afraid to ask . . ." Words failed her. Her hand moved of its own accord to rest on his chest. The air went out of his lungs in a whoosh as he wrapped his arms around her and held her. The beating of his heart was loud enough she could hear it through his armor.

"Sashia," he whispered into her hair. "Are you starting to care for me?"

She let out a sob, squinted her eyes against the tears, and leaned into him in reply.

"Never mind. Now is not the time to speak of it." He rested his cheek against the top of her head. "Knowing you were back there, behind the lines, fighting for the lives of the wounded, helped me somehow. I was able to fight more boldly. I cannot explain it—but your presence lent me strength. I am happy to give some of it back. You can lean on me as long as you like."

It wasn't long enough. They'd only stood there a moment before someone called for a healer.

"I am a healer," Sashia replied as they stepped apart.

"We've set up an infirmary on this side of the gap," explained a soldier, "but no healers have arrived yet. They are busy with the injured they have. We need you to take over the care of the wounded here in the plain."

Sashia looked back at Cyrus and he nodded gravely. "We will talk later."

Already near the point of exhaustion, she and Lang stumbled along behind the soldier. When she saw the number of wounded, Sashia instantly sobered and leapt into action. "Lang, build a fire. You there, fetch fresh water, buckets of it. Take down one of those tents and cut it into strips for bandages," she ordered another soldier who had been assigned to tend the wounded.

Dozens of men lay groaning on the ground untreated. A few women lay in a separate section. All that had been done for them was to remove them from the battlefield and gather them conveniently in one place. Methodically, she began to assess injuries and prioritize treatment, barking directions to anyone who came within range.

Frantically, she cleaned and bandaged wounds with the help of Lang and several others she conscripted into service. They worked all night. She barely looked up when young Prince Darius entered followed by a guard.

"Gain!" the prince rushed to the side of a severely injured young man. "Gain, I heard you were hurt and I came right away! Are you alright? Gain!"

Sashia quickly finished treating her current patient and hurried to the prince's side. He was more likely to cause harm and agitate the wounded than help his friend with his voluble concern.

"My lord, we are doing what we can. Please, speak calmly. He is resting."

"Will he recover? Will he live?"

Darius' eyes were swimming with tears, and he choked on his words. War was all too real for him now. For all of them.

Sashia grimaced. "He has lost a great deal of blood. In addition, his wounds are at high risk of festering. We are doing the best we can, but only time will tell."

Darius drew his sword and began waving it wildly. "Fix him! Heal him! He is my friend!"

Sashia put up her hands and spoke in a hushed voice. "Please don't disturb him. Everything that can be done will be done."

She sympathized with the prince's feelings, but she was losing her patience with him. She also feared what he might do. Then she remembered he had lost his mother, the queen, a few years back. The sad news had reached her in Shelomoh. The queen had succumbed to injuries during a difficult childbirth, not violence like this, but the loss might make her young son afraid of losing others he cared about.

"Put it down, Darius!"

Sashia heard Cyrus' firm voice from the edge of the tent, and she threw a grateful glance in his direction. The guard that had been with Darius now stood next to Cyrus. He must have gone to fetch him.

Darius let out a roar of rage, dropped his sword, ran at Cyrus, and began pummeling him with his fists. Cyrus wrapped his long arms around his brother and tied him up in a bear hug. Darius began sobbing.

"It's my fault! I should have stayed with him!"

"Come, Darius. Let's go talk to Father. There is nothing you can do here."

Cyrus calmed his brother and led him away. Though several years apart, they were clearly close. Sashia let out the breath she had been holding and went back to work, but she found focusing a struggle.

When everything calmed down, Cyrus would come to see her again. Eventually, he would want an answer. She had to decide what to say to him. Her feelings for him had intensified over the last few days, but she'd also seen how valuable her skills were. What was one person's life compared to hundreds? The choice wasn't any clearer to her than it was before.

∞∞∞

Sashia tried to move, but she couldn't. All she could see was the faces of the dead, the ones she couldn't save. The fallen soldier from the gap stared at her unblinking. Everything turned red, and she cried out. Her eyes flew open.

"Are you alright, my lady?" called Lang from outside the tent.

"Yes, fine."

She'd had a nightmare. Sashia sat up and took a sip of water from her nearly empty flask. She crawled out of the tent on her hands and knees, stood up slowly, and blinked at the morning sun. A few hours of sleep weren't enough to make up for two straight days without it. She was stiff and sore, and she hadn't changed or bathed in days. Her clothes were smeared with blood that wasn't hers.

Sashia sighed and stretched, but then she trudged to the infirmary with determined steps. Healing was what she lived for. It invigorated her, challenged her, gave her purpose. Gave life to those who might die otherwise. What could be better than that? Maybe a bath and a soft bed? The thought broke in, and she chuckled. Maybe Cyrus' strong arms around her? She shook the picture from her head.

Madia and Joran had arrived the night before, allowing her a short respite, but there was still much to do, and she threw herself back into the work wholeheartedly.

∞∞∞

Gain died. So did many others. The smoke of funeral pyres filled the air for days, both Breakers and Berushese. There were no Breaker wounded to care for. Sashia didn't inquire why. The Berushese were thorough in their warfare. Any of the enemy who lived had fled the country.

Sashia attended as many funerals of her own tribe as she could. The sheer number of them was draining. After the first half-dozen, she felt completely numb.

It was customary to speak a few words over someone you knew. Sashia felt like she repeated herself over and over. When it was Kari's turn, there was no immediate family present, so Restus spoke

137

over her.

"This woman represents everything that is Berush: courage in the face of the enemy, selfless defense of her people, bravery in death. I was proud to have met her, and I owe her my life. May her memory live forever."

Darius choked out a few words for his friend. "Goodbye, Gain. I will miss you."

A week after the battle, most of the local volunteers had returned home. The few patients still recovering were removed with the rest of Cyrus' patrol back to the eastern side of the mountains. Sashia's family, positioned in the heights on one side of the gap, had all survived.

"I am proud of you, daughter," Haban acknowledged before he left. "I heard of all you did. Many are indebted to you."

"I still feel I could have done better. The care could have been organized more efficiently, especially on the western side."

"There is always room for improvement. Not all of it is your responsibility." He paused. "I hope we will see you again soon?"

"You will, Father."

He smiled and joined her brothers and Sunen as they headed home.

Sashia stayed to tend to the injured until they were all well enough to leave. Kassius was ecstatic at the survival rate.

"You must come to Sherish and work with me! I have a small group of students I train in the healing arts. Your assistance would be greatly appreciated."

"I will consider it. How did you get here in time for the battle if you came from Sherish?"

"Ah, luckily I was already in the area on a consultation. I am interested in cancers."

"I have some scrolls on the subject. I will bring them when I visit, but first I must spend some time with my family."

"Come as soon as you can!"

∞∞∞

Before King Kalin and Prince Darius returned to Sherish, the king summoned Lang and Sashia.

"Lang, for your great service to the people of Berush, you are hereby pardoned of any and all crimes and released from your servitude."

Lang bowed low. "Th-thank you, my lord, but no thank you."

"Excuse me?" Kalin was perplexed.

"I do not wish to be released from my service."

"Why not?"

"I have been happier with Lady Sashia than at any other time in my life. I wish to continue serving her."

"Well, you now have permission to do as you choose," Kalin turned to Sashia with amusement. Heat flooded her face. "You have brought honor to your country and your tribe with your skill. I expect to hear great things of you in the future."

The king bowed to her, which was the greatest honor he could bestow, and he and his men departed. Fortunately, Sashia was not required to reply. Between Lang's expression of devotion and the king's commendation, she was completely tongue-tied.

CHAPTER TWELVE

Sashia stayed in the camp until the last patients were able to return home or to active duty. Many of those she had treated came to thank her before they left.

"I owe you my life, healer. If there is ever anything I can do for you, please ask," was something she heard more than once.

All the other healers, including Kassius, had left for their homes and families. The day before she planned to leave, Deppan rode up to the infirmary.

"Prince Cyrus would like to see you." One corner of his mouth was turned up in a hint of a smile.

"Would he? Well, he knows where I am," she teased.

"Don't make it difficult for me, 'Lady Sashia.' You know I must persist until you agree to come with me."

"What did he say, exactly? You haven't asked me anything."

Deppan cleared his throat. "Prince Cyrus humbly requests the honor of your presence. Is that better?"

"Sort of. So, it is a request? He knows he cannot order me."

Deppan sighed. "Fine. I'll be mucking the stalls for

a week for telling you, but here is what he really said: 'Bring her to me, Deppan. Don't let her say no. I need her.'"

That sounded more like Cyrus. However, knowing his words didn't help her decide how to respond. Her mind wanted to rebel against this use of authority, but her heart was utterly helpless.

"No need to worry, Deppan. I'm coming."

The relief on his face would've been hilarious if her pulse wasn't pounding in her ears. She checked her clothing to see if she was presentable. At least there was no blood on it today.

"If I know my prince at all, he couldn't care less about what you are wearing."

Sashia made a face at his impertinence, but she took his outstretched hand and climbed onto the horse behind him.

It didn't take long to ride across the camp, and in moments, Deppan deposited her at the entrance to the fort. He rode off again immediately, and Sashia felt momentarily lost. Then a maidservant hurried over to her.

"You are Sashia?" she inquired eagerly.

"Yes."

"I am Halah. Follow me."

The woman led her across a small courtyard to a room on the far side. Sashia felt the eyes of every soldier on her, though there were few remaining in the fort now the battle was over. Halah ushered her into a private room, and all thought fled Sashia's mind at the sight of a tub of steaming water in the middle of the floor. A bath!

The maidservant had barely lit a lamp and closed the shutters before Sashia had shed her clothing and sunk into the metal basin. She was small enough that most of her body was able to fit inside the portable tub. The warm water relaxed her tired muscles and made her feel sleepy. Halah washed and brushed her hair and worked scented oils into it. Sashia sighed in contentment.

Only when she got out of the bath and Halah helped her dry off did she have a thought about why Cyrus had provided it.

"Are you employed here regularly, Halah?"

"Oh, no. Only for today."

Sashia became even more nervous about what Cyrus might have in mind. She glanced around, almost expecting to see a fancy dress or silk tunic set out for her to wear, but there was none. Good thing. She would have refused to wear it. She wasn't about to let Cyrus turn her into someone else. Maybe he knew that.

When she put her own plain clothing back on, she didn't feel quite as comforted as she had anticipated. But her skin felt soft, her hair smelled like jasmine, and her body and her heart were her own, for now.

Halah led her across the courtyard to another room. Sashia could hear muffled voices inside.

". . . are well away from our borders and headed back toward the continent."

When the maidservant knocked, she heard Cyrus reply, "Enter."

Halah opened the door, and Sashia walked in nervously. Out of the corner of her eye, she saw Topec bow to the prince and exit the room. She could only look at Cyrus. And he was looking at her. His face was full of boyish delight, and his hazel eyes were bright with appreciation. Suddenly, she realized her long, wavy hair was hanging loosely over her shoulders. Halah hadn't braided it. How could she not have noticed?

"Sashia, you—" his voice broke and he couldn't

finish.

"You wanted to see me?" she asked softly.

"I—yes."

Cyrus' words were heavy with emotion. He took two steps with his long legs and stood in front of her. Sashia felt her chest rise and fall with each breath, and she forced herself to inhale slowly.

"You see, I stole something from you. Before the battle. I admit my guilt, and I need you to pronounce my sentence."

"Is this your first offense?" She held back a smile.

"It is. Therefore, I am required to make restitution." He moved within a hair's breadth of her but didn't touch her.

"And how do you propose to do that?"

"I suggest you take back what I stole."

The air caught in Sashia's throat. "I could reject your offer of restitution. I could banish you from my presence instead."

"You would not be so cruel. I know you prefer mercy, as I do." His words were confident, but his eyes showed apprehension. "You wouldn't do that, would you?"

"No," she whispered. She cast her eyes down at the floor and back up at him. "If I accept your offer, you understand I am only taking back what is mine? I make no other concessions or promises."

"I understand."

Sashia looked around for something to stand on and decided the simple chairs didn't appear very stable. "Sit on the edge of the table." Bringing him down to her height would be better anyway.

Cyrus obeyed with alacrity. Sashia hesitated. What was she doing? This was crazy.

"Look, I will keep my hands on the table." Cyrus gripped the edge of the tabletop.

Sashia stepped forward and stood between his knees, putting her hands on his shoulders. Cyrus' eyes turned darker as his pupils dilated. She gazed into his eager face and was mesmerized. He was beautiful. Perfect. More than anything in that moment, she wanted to kiss him. She leaned forward, closed her eyes, and stopped resisting.

As she kissed him, a thrill passed through her entire body, from the top of her head to the tips of her toes. She slid one hand around the back of his neck and rested the other against his cheek. He kept his hands off her, as promised, but his mouth moved in response to hers. For a moment, it felt like they were a single person, and she forgot everything except her desire.

Then she remembered: he was going to be king. She would have to give up all her dreams and plans in order to be with him. She would have to live for him. That wasn't something she was sure she could do. But if it meant kissing him every day, loving him, belonging to him, would it be worth it? Her heart screamed, "Yes!" Her body echoed the same sentiment.

She pressed into him, and he moaned. It dawned on her she had him under her power. Could she have more influence as a queen than a healer? The idea went to her head, and she kissed him harder.

"Sashia, stop. I cannot take any more!" Cyrus cried in anguish. Sashia leaned back, startled. His knuckles were white where he held onto the table as if his life depended on it. "How can you act like this means nothing to you, when you mean everything to me?"

"It's not nothing. I—I do care for you!"

"But it's not the same as what I feel for you." He let go of the table and stood up, taking her gently by the shoulders and holding her at arm's length. "You must know, Sashia. I am in love with you." He took a ragged breath. "But you do not love me back."

Sashia's lips parted to form an argument, but she could not give it voice. The attraction she felt was intense, but that wasn't the same. The kind of love he wanted would require great sacrifice on her part, and she wasn't ready to give it. Her mind refused to let her tongue speak the words, knowing it would change her future completely. "Cyrus . . ." She couldn't finish. Her eyes pleaded for him to understand.

Cyrus studied her face intently and then turned away. His chin sunk to his chest. "You said you would make no promises, and I thought I would be alright with that, but I'm not."

"I'm sorry, my lord. I didn't mean to hurt you." His pain caused her immediate remorse. She should have said no. She should have just forgiven him and told him it was no good. It had been selfish to kiss him if there was no future for them.

Cyrus snorted cynically. "You say that whenever you're trying to distance yourself from me."

"Say what?"

"'My lord'." He sighed. "It's not your fault. I set myself up for this. I wished so hard for you to love me, I ignored the signals you were giving me. I hoped your concern for me after the battle meant you had decided in my favor. That you would choose me."

He straightened and faced her again. His hand reached out and stroked her hair, letting the silky strands fall through his fingers. Sashia trembled. His touch nearly drove her wild. Why, oh why, did he have to be a prince? If only he were an ordinary citizen, free to wander as she was, without the fate of an entire country on his shoulders.

"If the circumstances were different . . ."

"But they won't be. Not for me. My path is

predetermined. Yours is open to you. I won't stand in your way. Goodbye, Sashia."

He fled from the room and left her standing there alone.

∞∞∞

The next morning Sashia's eyes were red and puffy from crying and lack of sleep. Cyrus didn't make an appearance. Sashia looked over her shoulder frequently, hoping to catch a last glimpse of him as she rode away, and then scolded herself. Of course he wouldn't want to see her again after yesterday. It would only make it harder. Her heart was heavy as she and Lang left the plain and headed home.

Restus accompanied them. He was determined to deliver the account of Kari's death to her son firsthand.

"You really shouldn't do a full day of riding in your condition," Sashia chided him.

"As it is, I won't be the first one to tell him the news. I want to make sure he knows all the details. He should know how heroic she was, that her death was not in vain."

Sashia let it be. At least she was there to keep an eye on him. And riding was better than walking. Cyrus had sent Restus with a gift of two horses for Sashia and Lang in gratitude for their service.

"I don't know how to ride," she had protested.

"This horse is very gentle. Too gentle for a war horse. Her name is Favor. She'll be perfect for an itinerant healer."

Sashia had accepted the mare without further argument. It would be better than always having to ride with someone else. Was this a message from Cyrus that he was respecting her independence?

Restus gave her a short lesson on the control of the animal, and she picked it up easily. Her horse contentedly followed the other two with hardly any effort on her part.

The trip passed quickly. All three travelers had plenty to think about. Sashia wasn't sure which was worse, remembering Cyrus' heartbroken expression, the agony of the wounded and dying, or the pain in her chest that seemed to worsen with every step she took away from him.

When they rode into her father's camp, Sashia felt the weight of her worries begin to diminish. Until she saw her mother's dour expression.

"There you are! You took plenty of time returning home."

"Hello, Mother." Sashia didn't bother to argue with her.

Father came up and surprised Sashia by enveloping her in a hug. "Daughter. I'm glad you are back."

"I'm glad to be home." They did not speak aloud their relief that they were *all* home safe. "You remember Restus? He is here to speak to Kari's son."

Father nodded. "That is good. Pat, help Lang with the horses. Restus, you are our guest. Come and refresh yourself in my tent."

Restus was still favoring his injured leg. Father, as always, was observant and hospitable. Sashia watched her youngest brother hurry to obey. He seemed like a good boy, and she felt a pang as she realized she would probably never really get to know him.

"How is Estan?" Sashia took the moment to inquire privately as everyone returned to their work.

"Not good. Not yet, at least. But he will be. No one returns from battle the same. His mind needs time to adjust." Haban surveyed his daughter perceptively. "How are you?"

Sashia sighed and looked at her father. Her eyes began to sting. Haban grimaced in understanding and squeezed her arm.

In her tent that night, with her sister and younger brother sleeping next to her, Sashia knew she should be planning what to do next, but couldn't bring herself to think about it. Her mind needed time to recover from what she had seen as well.

However, when she closed her eyes, all she could see was Cyrus. Even from the other end of the mountain range, he managed to pull her thoughts toward him. Had she made the right decision? Would she ever find another man who affected her the same way? Her original plans had not included a man. Had that changed? No other woman in Berush had the freedom she had. Berush had no slaves, but being unable to make important life decisions for yourself was a form of slavery.

Sitting up slowly, she settled herself into a more meditative position and tried to arrange her thoughts. There was no way she was going to sleep productively otherwise. What was most important to her? Being a healer. The answer came quickly and unquestioningly. But after that? Cyrus. What would he do now? Would he be alright?

Worrying about him would do no good. He was not her responsibility. Then her Magi training kicked in. In some way, everyone was connected, and everyone was responsible for everyone else, but to what degree? *Everyone must make their own choices,* she argued. His happiness couldn't be dependent on her. That wasn't reasonable.

However, no amount of reason could explain away how she felt when he touched her. His eyes, his smile, his genuine interest and concern for her well-being were going to be impossible to forget. But her choice was already made, wasn't it? Did she want to change her mind? No, she'd made the best decision she could, given the alternatives. Tomorrow she would make more decisions. Hopefully they would be the right ones.

∞∞∞

"Will you guide me to the campground of Kari's family?" Restus asked her early the next morning.

"Certainly."

Sashia directed Lang to assist Hurish while she was gone. Hopefully that would forestall any complaints from her mother.

"Tell me about her family," Restus prodded once they started out.

"Kari had one son. He is about eight years old now. Her husband, Shazar, has a second wife, Janith. Janith has one daughter and one son."

"Ah. I see."

It sounded like he really did see.

When they reached Shazar's camp, he and his son had already taken the flocks into the hills. A servant told them where they were headed, and they set out after them. It didn't take long to catch up to the herd on horseback. Sashia wondered how she had gotten along without Favor before.

"Shazar!" She waved at him and he came to greet them. "Shazar, this is Restus, a soldier in Prince Cyrus' patrol. He wants to talk to you and Halem."

She and Restus dismounted as the boy ran to join them.

"I owe my life to your wife, to your mother," he began. "I wish to tell you of her last moments."

150

He told them of the battle, how Kari had saved him, and how she had died bravely. When he finished, the boy's eyes were swimming, and he sniffled. He clutched his own slingshot tightly.

"Mother showed me how to sling stones. I will practice to be the best slinger ever!"

Restus ruffled the boy's hair. "Good for you!"

Halem looked up at his father. "May I be a soldier, father?"

"We are goat herders, son." Shazar put his hand firmly on his son's shoulder.

"But I want to be a soldier like Mother and Restus."

Shazar shot Restus and Sashia an aggrieved expression.

"Right now, you have a responsibility to your family, Halem. You must obey your father and work hard. Every soldier must first learn to follow orders. When you are old enough, if you still wish it, I will recommend you for training as a soldier."

"Alright!"

Shazar glared at Restus, but Restus ignored him.

"I will check in on you whenever I pass this way and see how you are doing, both with the slingshot and following orders!"

They waved goodbye and headed back the way they came. Restus shook his head. "I wish I could take him now, but he's too young. That boy is going to miss his mother."

Sashia agreed. Janith wouldn't love Halem like Kari had. She would likely show preference to her own children.

Sashia also reflected she would not have made a good soldier. She would have questioned everything. Obedience had never been one of her strengths.

It was barely midday when they returned, and

Restus decided to start back right away. That evening during dinner, Sashia passed on his thanks to her parents for their accommodation.

"How will he manage three horses by himself?" Cashi asked.

"Oh, the other two horses are mine. Mine, and Lang's. They were given to us in gratitude for our service to the wounded."

"Are you sure that is the only service you rendered?" remarked Mother snidely.

"Mother!" Sashia was aghast at the implication. Her hackles rose as understanding dawned on everyone present. She stood to her feet, shaking with anger. "How dare you say such a thing!"

"Vani told me Rolind saw the prince kiss you. I assume that's not all he did."

"Yania!" Haban's voice thundered over the gathering. "Yania, this has gone far enough. You must no longer take out your own shortcomings on your daughter! Much less malign the heir to the throne. You will tell Sashia the truth, tonight!"

"Haban, no!"

Sashia watched in wonder as her mother shrank back in fear.

"Tonight, or your punishment will be what it should have been twenty years ago!" Haban resumed eating, emphasizing his words were final.

Yania turned and stomped out of the camp.

"Go with your mother, Sashia," Father urged gently.

Sashia followed apprehensively. What dark secret was her mother harboring? Mother's longer legs made it hard for Sashia to catch up, but fortunately the moon was bright and the path was easy to see. When Mother finally stopped, Sashia was out of breath. She waited in silent suspense, wondering if she was going to volunteer an explanation, or if she would have to ask for one.

"You are not Haban's daughter."

"What?" Everything she'd ever believed was completely upended by this unexpected statement.

Mother sniffed and hugged herself, and Sashia noticed she was crying.

"When I was a girl, I loved a boy named Arius. His family was poor, so he was sent to Sherish to find work. I thought I would never see him again. My family arranged for me to marry Haban. He already had a large herd of his own, and it was a good match, so I agreed.

"Several years later, while Haban was taking the fleece to market, Arius appeared. He had completed his apprenticeship with a weaver and had come back to find me. He talked me into running away with him." Mother sobbed but rushed ahead with her story.

"I left Zarin and Estan sleeping in their tent with Nani, and we raced off into the hills. I betrayed my husband. That night, as if all of nature conspired to punish us, there was a thunderstorm. Rain poured down, and the overhang where we slept was washed away in a landslide. Arius was buried in a pile of rubble. He was still alive when I found him, but it was too late. He died in my arms.

"I returned home, clothing torn and covered in mud. I hid in my tent for over three weeks, afraid of what everyone would say. I hardly ate. When Haban returned, he looked at me and asked if it was true. I just nodded. By then, I was late, and I told him. He said we would never speak of it again. He made sure no one else ever spoke of it." Mother put her head in her hands and wept.

"He is a good man, better than I deserve. But I

knew what I did. So did Nani and all the servants, though they said nothing. I could see it in their faces. I can see it in your face every time I look at you."

Sashia listened in shock to her mother's confession. She didn't know what to feel: outrage at her mother's actions, sorrow for a father she never knew, or loss of the one she had. The experiences of the past week had drained her thoroughly, and she didn't even have the strength to cry. On top of everything else, this seemed so absurd she almost wanted to laugh. She could hardly imagine her bitter, uptight mother being carried away by her passions. But so many things made sense now. She no longer felt weighed down by Mother's disapproval. Suddenly, she felt angry.

"All this time, you have been punishing me for your own failings!"

"I wanted you to avoid my mistakes!"

Mother stretched a hand out toward Sashia, but she swatted it away.

"Don't touch me! Your past mistakes have no bearing on my future. I will blaze my own path. You no longer have the right to worry about me."

"I cannot help it," Mother cried desperately.

Sashia realized her mother truly was worried about her. Her guilt kept it from taking a healthy form. She remembered Beyorn's admonition to seek peace and truth. Her training had never been put to a greater test.

"Do Zarin and Estan know?"

"No, we kept it from them."

"Thank you for telling me the truth." Now was her chance to make peace with her mother. Sashia couldn't add the weight of this tragedy to her heart. It carried too much already. She set her anger aside and spoke the words, "I forgive you."

Mother sniffed. "My offense was not against you."

Peace, peace, peace. Sashia ground her teeth. What could she say that wouldn't make things worse? Though it was the last thing in the world she felt like doing, she wrapped her arms around her mother and kissed her cheek. "I love you, Mother."

Yania burst into tears.

∞∞∞

"Father?"

Haban sat in the glow of a few remaining hot coals. Everyone else had gone to bed.

"Sashia."

She sat down next to him, unsure of what to do or say. Tears streamed down her cheeks. Haban put his arm around her and kissed the top of her head like she was a child. "You were my daughter from the moment you were born. Nothing has changed."

"Everything has changed! The whole world has changed. I feel like I know nothing anymore."

"Ram Rock is gone."

"What?" Sashia was as shocked at the sudden change of subject as the loss of the landmark. "How could it be gone?"

"It has had a crack for many years. Two winters ago, we had a very hard freeze. Colder than I remembered in a long time. Water froze in the crack and caused the rock to split in two. But, Daughter, we will still find our way home."

"Because there are other landmarks?"

"There are, but that is not how."

"How then?"

"Just as birds migrate to an ancestral home they have never seen, our hearts guide us home. We will know when we are there."

"I don't know what my heart is telling me. I have left pieces of it in too many places."

"You will know when the time comes. Until then, you keep looking."

"Mother's heart guided her the wrong way."

"Yes." Haban stiffened briefly and then relaxed. "Perhaps because she ignored it in the first place."

"How could you live with her after?" Sashia asked angrily. Her peace of mind vanished in indignation as she brushed the tears off her face.

"Because I love her."

"Even though she didn't love you?"

"Yes. Love is not dependent on reciprocation. But, it is strengthened by determination. I promised her when we married I would care for her. I could still keep my promise even though she broke hers. She grew to love me afterwards."

Sashia's respect for her father deepened with this new insight into his character. Gratitude for his acceptance overwhelmed her. He had always treated her like his own daughter. In his mind, she was.

"You know," he continued, "It's good to come to a place where you feel you know nothing. Only then will you have the humility to learn the most important lessons in life."

"Like what?"

"All the knowledge in the world is worthless without love to temper it. You've learned a great deal, Daughter, but you have not loved greatly. Someday you will."

CHAPTER THIRTEEN

Over the next several weeks, Sashia travelled up and down the Granite Mountains treating the sick and wounded. She also gave instructions on more modern methods of cleansing, bandaging, and managing injuries and illness. Some people were receptive to her ideas, others were not. Changing the habits of ages would not be accomplished in a season.

Every day, she was worn out from travel and exertion, but she felt content what she was doing was important. The constant occupation kept her from dwelling too long on Cyrus and how she missed him. So did Lang's prattling. Lang was an invaluable companion and assistant, though his conversation tired her.

"My lady, if it is not impolite to ask, why did you refuse Prince Cyrus?"

"It is very impolite to ask."

"Oh, forgive me, my lady."

Lang's penitent silence was even more irritating than his blabbering.

"What makes you think he even asked me anything?"

"Oh, well, I just assumed, but maybe I shouldn't

have, I mean, because he, you know, in front of everyone, and then he was always around. Then he summoned you to the fort, but that could have been for anything. Sorry."

Sashia sighed. "It's fine, Lang. If Prince Cyrus offered anything, I wouldn't accept it because I have no wish to be confined to a palace. There is too much work to do, and I have too much knowledge to pass it by." The words carried nearly enough conviction to convince herself.

Lang frowned. "But couldn't you do as you do here, go out when someone needs you?"

She smiled. "Do you want to live in the palace, Lang?"

"Oh, no, at least, not especially, not if you weren't there. But I imagine it would be very comfortable, though still as exciting as this life, just in a different way."

"Let's not talk anymore. I have a headache." She didn't really have a headache, but he was going to give her one. They'd had a long day, assisting at a birth, setting a broken arm, and treating a child who had been kicked by a horse. The child would require looking in on.

By the time they reached her parents' camp, she was exhausted, even with the use of Favor's legs. Briefly, she considered visiting Kassius in Sherish. It might be nice to have people come to her for a change. The possibility of encountering Cyrus in the capital couldn't be any higher than the chance of running into him on patrol.

"How was your day?" Mother asked when she had taken care of the horse. Things had been awkward between them for a while, but slowly their relationship became less strained.

"Good, but challenging." Sashia recounted her

adventures and described the child's injury. "It's serious. I will have to check on him tomorrow."

Mother's face reflected grim concern.

Dinner that night was the most enjoyable Sashia had had with her family in a long time. Mother seemed relaxed and happy. She laughed at her grandchildren and smiled at everyone. It must have been freeing to unburden herself of her guilt and share her secret. The mood of the entire camp seemed lighter.

Sashia heard hoof beats and everyone turned to stare as a man galloped right up to the campfire.

"I need the healer!"

"I am here, Battus. What is it?"

"You need to come with me right away! It's Lanin! He's worse."

"Tell me what happened."

"He vomited, started shaking, and lost consciousness."

"His brain is swelling," Sashia muttered to herself. "Mother, will you come with me?"

Mother glanced at Sashia, surprised. "Of course!" She jumped to her feet. "Let me fetch my bag."

"Lang, get the horses ready again, and then you may rest tonight. I may need you tomorrow."

Sashia gathered her surgical tools and mounted her horse. "Sorry you haven't had much time to rest, girl." She patted Favor's neck, sat forward, and dug in her heels.

Sashia still felt insecure on horseback, and it was night, but Battus didn't push his horse more than was reasonable despite his anxious state. They didn't speak but concentrated on their riding.

When they arrived at Battus' camp, Sashia rushed into Lanin's tent with Mother right behind her. The boy was semi-conscious and moaning, his fists balled in pain.

She didn't have to explain what they were going to do. Trepanning had been a common practice for centuries. However, it was usually done by scraping away at the scull with a sharpened piece of flint or similar tool until the brain was exposed. This took valuable time, depending on the age of the patient and hardness of the skull, but made sure the hole wasn't too deep.

The Magi had designed a special gimlet that tapered into a flat shield to prevent penetration into the brain. When Sashia removed the tool from her pack, Mother's eyes widened with comprehension, but she didn't speak as she straddled the boy, locking his arms to his side with her knees. Carefully, Mother leaned forward and held Lanin's head still. They couldn't risk him moving during the procedure and thrashing around.

"Ready?" Sashia glanced at her mother as she moved a nearby lamp closer.

"Ready."

Sashia positioned the gimlet and quickly created a hole in the back of the top of the boy's skull. When she removed the drill, fluid squirted out. Lanin's body went limp as the pressure eased, and his breathing became normal.

Sashia's shoulders relaxed, and she tried not to feel jittery. She placed a rag under the boy's head to absorb further drainage and checked his pulse. Mother released her hold on the boy and moved to the side.

"I should have done this earlier," Sashia upbraided herself.

"There's bruising, but the skull is not depressed," observed Mother as she examined the wound more closely. "It's hard to know if trepanning is necessary without clear symptoms." She paused. "You did very well, Sashia. I'm proud of you."

"Thank you, Mother." Sashia's eyes teared up, and she felt suddenly vulnerable and raw.

Mother took a deep breath. "I'm sorry, daughter. Sorry I discouraged you from studying healing. Haban was right. I was letting my own failures muddy my judgement."

"It's alright, Mother. I understand now. You were trying to protect me."

"I was silly. It's not possible to protect your child from everything. Look at this boy. Anything can happen, right in your own camp." She sighed and gazed at her daughter with love and concern. "You're stronger than I ever was. I doubt you will repeat my mistakes."

"I am sure I will make plenty of my own." Sashia squeezed her mother's hand.

Lanin stirred and slowly opened his eyes. The two women smiled at each other.

∞∞∞

When her family began heading northward for the winter, Sashia determined she would go to Sherish to visit Kassius. She felt an irresistible, inexplicable pull toward the capital city. It had to be she was missing interaction with her intellectual peers. After being in a learning community for seven years, she missed the mental stimulation.

It couldn't be because of Cyrus. He was on patrol, not in Sherish. She constantly had to guard her thoughts to keep them from turning his direction. How pleasant it would be to come home to his comforting arms after treating a traumatic injury. He was so patient and considerate, strong and determined, yet sensitive and honorable—*Argh*! She had to stop thinking about him!

"Sashia," cried her mother as she hugged her tightly, "I just got you back, and now you're leaving again!"

"I love you, Mother," she whispered in Mother's ear. "That won't change no matter where I go."

"Farewell, Daughter." Haban smiled at her. His words were simple and straightforward, like he was, but heartfelt. They meant more now than ever.

"Have fun in the capital! I wish I was going too!"

"I wish you were, also, Cashi, but Mother cannot do without you. Maybe once I am finally settled somewhere you can visit me."

While Sashia climbed up on her mare and waved goodbye to her brothers, Father steered Lang aside and spoke a few words to him. Lang nodded vigorously in response.

"What did my father say?" Sashia asked once they were far enough away.

"He told me I should guard you with my life, which I told him I had already decided to do."

Sashia's heart warmed at her father's concern and Lang's sincerity, though she felt it more likely she would protect Lang than the other way around. "Thank you, Lang. Thank you also for staying with me even though you were pardoned. We only earn enough for our keep, and I wish I could pay you more, but I cannot put a price on your devotion. You're a great help."

"Oh, I wouldn't want to do anything else, my lady. Not anything. I am happy, very happy, to be helpful, even more now that I do it freely."

They caught up to a small wagon train of traders headed toward Sherish and joined them, more for companionship than for safety. Thitus and his ilk were the exception rather than the rule. Highway robbery was a rare occurrence in Berush.

One of the traders was suffering from congestion, and Sashia made him a poultice that helped to clear it up. In exchange, they were invited to partake from the communal stew pot.

On the fourth day, while Sashia was enjoying the scenery, she observed all the changes in the landscape. She'd never been this far into Berush before. Rolling hills of dry grass waved in the breeze, dotted with occasional shrubs. Once, they spotted a herd of antelope, and she saw a doe and fawn drinking from a brook. Several times they saw men herding cattle.

"Someone's coming," shouted one of the traders.

Sashia turned in the saddle and saw a pair of horsemen galloping toward them. Some of the traders readied their weapons, but most merely stared in curiosity.

The horses cantered up to the wagons while the riders looked the group over, searching for someone.

"Sashia!"

It was Restus and another one of Cyrus' soldiers. The merchants relaxed when they saw the pair was not a threat and gathered around to find out what they wanted with the healer.

"Sashia, finally we found you!"

"You were looking for me? What is it?"

"We've been searching everywhere for you!" Restus paused to catch his breath. "Your family told us you were on your way to Sherish."

"What's wrong?" prodded Sashia.

"It's Cyrus."

Sashia felt like a giant hand was squeezing her heart. Blackness encroached on the edges of her vision, and she shook it away. She was not going to faint. How ridiculous. "What about him?"

"He's dying."

"What do you mean, 'he's dying'? He cannot be!" The idea was ludicrous. Cyrus was perfectly fine. He had to be. Someone like Cyrus didn't just die!

Restus shook his head. "He is terribly sick. Kassius has been tending to him, but he's tried everything, and the prince is only slipping further away. King Kalin sent us to find you. I only hope we don't return too late."

"Take me to him."

They rode ahead of the wagon train, and Sashia pushed the mare as fast as she would go. The chilly autumn wind stung her eyes and made a good excuse for her tears. They pressed on through the night, stopping only to water the horses. Late the next morning, they saw the city of Sherish. The golden turrets of the palace reflected into the shimmering blue water of Sherish Lake. It was a spectacular view, but Sashia didn't notice any of it. She was focused on the tail of Restus' horse, which was galloping toward the city gates.

The guards at the gate recognized Restus and didn't hinder them. They clattered as quickly as they could through the crowded city streets and into the palace courtyard. Grooms came forward to see to the sweaty, tired horses, and Sashia followed Restus and the other guard through a maze of corridors until they reached Cyrus' room.

"Only you are to enter," Restus informed her.

"Go find a place to rest," she directed Lang. "I will send for you if I need you."

Kassius opened the door to Restus' quiet knock, and Sashia rushed past them into the room. Cyrus lay limp in the bed with his eyes closed, breathing shallowly. He looked gaunt and wasted, a shadow of his former self.

"Oh!" Sashia flung herself to his side and clutched his hand. It was cold and clammy. His face was beaded with perspiration and hot to the touch. She dampened a cloth with cool water from a nearby pitcher and laid it on his forehead. "Cyrus! Cyrus, can you hear me? It's Sashia."

Cyrus' eyes fluttered and half-opened. "Sashia!" he wheezed. "I dreamed of you."

"This isn't a dream. I'm here."

"You came?" He was overcome by a sudden fit of coughing. Kassius held a cloth in front of his mouth. It came away covered in phlegm.

"Of course I came, my darling," she choked out. "And this time I came for you."

Cyrus smiled and closed his eyes. In a few moments he was sleeping peacefully.

A figure rose from a chair in a dark corner. In her concern for Cyrus, Sashia hadn't noticed anyone else in the room. It was King Kalin.

Sashia was flustered, but she didn't let go of Cyrus' hand.

"So, you care for my son after all?"

Sashia swallowed and nodded as she held Cyrus' hand against her cheek.

"He rode three horses to the ground before I called him home. Topec sent word he neither slept nor ate, and I was concerned. When he returned, he had already developed a cough and could barely stand. He has been here ever since." Kalin walked around the bed and picked up a pile of letters from a side table. "I found these in his dispatch case."

Sashia took the letters he held out, and the king quietly exited the room. They were not sealed, and they were all addressed to her. She let go of Cyrus' hand and opened the first letter with trembling fingers.

Dear Sashia,

Though you will never receive this letter, I must have some vent for my feelings. You consume my thoughts as though no one and nothing else exists in the world. All I want is to hold you, to feel your lips against mine.

You are everything I could wish for. You are strong, in heart and body, despite your stature. You stand up for what you believe is right. You have compassion for others and champion the disadvantaged. In terms of selflessness you are taller than I am. You are the bravest woman I know. I could not find a more perfect partner if I searched for a thousand lifetimes.

I love you with my entire being. I wish I could stop. Being without you is killing me.

Sashia fumbled for the next letter.

Sashia, my love,

We rode back through the gap today, and instead of the fighting and the bloodshed, all I could remember was the kiss I stole from you . . .

Sashia quickly devoured the letters. In some of them he recounted the events of his day, in some of them he reminisced about their brief encounters, but in all of them he told her he loved her. He loved her too much. It wasn't healthy for a person to love this intensely. He was heartsick.

What was she to do? Marry him to keep him alive? She cared for him deeply, more than she thought she did. The shock of his illness had affected her more than she would have expected. If he should die . . . She couldn't think of that. It hurt too much.

"Tell me everything you have tried," she demanded desperately.

"I have bled him, I have applied poultices to aid his breathing, and I have tried to keep him hydrated, but without much success. Perhaps you will be able to persuade him to take in more fluids. I tried to draw the fever into his feet by warming them, but he still burns."

"The Winter Fever is more common among the elderly, especially in the mountains," mused Sashia.

"Or those in an already weakened state."

Sashia made a strangled cry that sounded more like a gurgle. She took out a scrap of paper and a charcoal pencil and scribbled a few words on it. "Can you brew me a tea with these herbs?"

Kassius took the paper and nodded. "I will prepare it."

"You've done most everything that can be done. I don't know what else to do."

"Just stay by his side. You are the best medicine we can give him."

Kassius left, and Sashia was alone with Cyrus. His black, wavy hair was plastered to his forehead, and his normally tan cheeks were pallid, but he still drew her. That he loved her so greatly was both awesome and frightening. And how did she feel? Whenever he needed her, she would come. She couldn't help it. But what if he needed her by his side always? When he became king, he would need someone to support him. But that couldn't be her reason for marrying him, could it? Being a healer didn't mean she had to offer herself as a remedy. He had to recover on his own before she could tell him how she felt, once she decided it for herself.

She reached over and gently stroked the side of

his face. Her eyes closed as she felt the familiar tremor run through her fingers. The two of them were connected. It was undeniable. Separation had not weakened the bond but thrown it into sharp relief. She would do whatever she could to keep Cyrus alive. She had to.

The air in the room was stifling, almost as much as the weight of her inner conflict, so Sashia stood up and walked around. The large apartment was furnished with solid, well-made furniture, but it was simple and serviceable. Everything was of high quality, but only what was necessary. Nothing ornate or opulent.

She checked the fireplace and saw it was well-ventilated. No smoke was entering the room. The outside air was too cold to open the window, so she walked over to the door and opened it.

Cyrus' brother, Darius, was sitting on the floor of the passage. When he saw her, he jumped up eagerly. "May I see him? Please?" he begged. "Father and Kassius refuse to let me in. They say I will excite him, but I promise to behave."

Sashia studied him appraisingly. She had seen herself how emotional he could be, but he was Cyrus' only brother. However it would affect Cyrus, Darius needed to see his brother for his own sake. Maybe it would help them both.

"You must keep your voice low, and your comments encouraging."

"I will!" He bounced on his toes.

"Slowly! Quietly!" she hissed as he flew past her.

The draft from the corridor was not too cold, and the stale air in the room needed to be replaced, so she left the door open and followed Darius back to the sick bed.

Darius stopped short at the edge of the bed in

shock at his brother's condition. He turned to Sashia in alarm. "Is it bad?"

"I am afraid so."

Darius knelt by Cyrus' side and buried his head in the blankets, twisting fistfuls of fabric in his large hands.

"Darius?" Cyrus rasped.

"Cyrus!" Darius' head snapped up and he grabbed his brother's arm.

"Gently," murmured Sashia.

"They wouldn't let me see you, but I have waited outside your door for hours every day!"

"I," Cyrus coughed several times, "I missed you."

Cyrus tried to lift his hand but didn't have the strength, and it fell back on the bed. Darius took the limp hand, set it on top of his own head, and moved it around, ruffling his hair.

"Cyrus," Darius' tone became solemn, "you have to get better. You have to. I cannot be king. I wouldn't be able to do without you at all. Please, Cyrus!" he begged.

"Alright."

Cyrus' voice was full of love for his brother, but it was barely audible. He was tired and weak. Sashia put her hand on Darius' shoulder.

"That's enough for now."

Darius stood up shakily, and his tall, gangly frame towered over her just like his brother's. "I love you, Cyrus."

Cyrus' eyes were closed again.

Darius walked slowly to the doorway, took one last glance at his brother, and turned to Sashia. "Thank you."

It was all he could choke out, but his gratitude was sincere.

Sashia returned to her seat by Cyrus' side.

"I must . . . get better." He half-opened one eye. "But . . . I am not doing it . . . for you."

"Good!" Sashia grinned.

CHAPTER FOURTEEN

Kassius returned with the tea and Sashia didn't mention Darius' visit, though she was sure it had done Cyrus good. Probably as much good as her own presence. If Cyrus had lacked the will to fight, he had it now.

Sashia and Kassius propped him up and put an extra pillow behind his back so he could sit up slightly.

"Drink this." She held the cup of warm liquid carefully to his lips.

He swallowed dutifully. It took some effort, but eventually, between coughs, he drank over half of the tea. Later, he ate a few spoonfuls of porridge. Sashia's heart soared unreasonably at this small amount of progress.

Kassius was also hopeful. "Now perhaps he will begin to regain some strength."

That night, Cyrus began shaking. His teeth chattered. Kassius wrapped hot stones and placed them by his feet. They stoked the fire, closed the door, and put on another blanket. Nothing would take away the prince's chill, and his fever still raged. He moaned and tried to speak, but his words were unintelligible.

"I have tried everything I know to do," Kassius lamented. "We must watch and hope."

"There is one more thing."

Sashia took off her boots and socks. She walked around to the other side of the bed where there was more room and climbed under the covers. She scooted right up against Cyrus, draped herself over his body, and laid her head against his chest. Her mass was probably half his, but this seemed like the simplest and most efficient way to warm him. Perhaps it would bring him comfort as well. The physical proximity certainly affected *her*. As her entire body began to tingle, she started to cry.

You are being silly! Get ahold of yourself! To keep her mind on more rational things, she focused on the medical aspects of the situation. She listened to his breathing and heard the wetness in his lungs. She felt the dampness of his clothing. It was uncomfortably warm for a healthy person, and she began to sweat also.

Kassius shifted his weight uneasily, as if unsure what to do or think, but finally he sat in a chair in the corner. "I suppose I should remain as chaperone so no one can say you took advantage of the prince's weakened state to put him in a compromising position."

"If you wish," replied Sashia dismissively. She didn't care what anyone thought at this point. She was not going to lose Cyrus!

"You run a great risk of catching the fever yourself," observed Kassius.

"He matters more than I do."

"The king might agree, but I do not."

Sashia couldn't make out Kassius' features in the dim light, but his tone conveyed a depth of feeling that surprised her. Was his interest in her more than academic, or was he concerned about her as a healer who didn't want another patient on his hands?

"Every life matters, regardless of the circumstances into which it is born. I only consider the likelihood of survival when deciding who to treat first and how to treat them, not their social or political position. Even then, people will defy the odds if the will is strong enough," he explained.

"Have you lost someone? Someone who others considered unimportant?" asked Sashia, suddenly enlightened.

"I have been asked to leave caring for some patients in order to treat those who are considered more valuable. It is not something I am comfortable with."

Kassius didn't sound like he wanted to discuss it any further.

Sashia didn't feel like talking either, and her eyelids felt heavy. She had gone nearly two days without sleep, and she was exhausted. Before she could reflect on the impropriety of the situation, she fell asleep in the prince's bed with her arms around him.

∞∞∞

". . . warming him, my lord. I have been here the whole time."

"Yes, yes, I have no objection to a woman being in my son's bed. It is something I would hope for, eventually, just not under these circumstances. How is he?"

The king's voice penetrated Sashia's consciousness, but she kept her eyes closed as she pushed the fog from her brain. The inevitability of

173

King Kalin's return was not something she'd considered when she climbed under the covers. The awkward circumstances weren't as important to any of them as Cyrus' condition. She noticed he was not shaking.

Sashia opened her eyes and reached up to feel his brow.

"His fever has broken!" Somehow, she managed to keep her excitement and relief to a whisper. "Kassius."

Kassius was already at Cyrus' side, and he leaned over to confirm Sashia's assessment. He exhaled audibly. "He is no longer fevered, my lord."

"Is he over the illness?"

"Not yet," Kassius cautioned. "The fever could return. We need to rebuild his strength. His lungs will be weak."

"But this is good! He will recover?"

"If his fever had not broken soon, there would've been little hope. Now . . . now complete recovery is more likely."

Kalin walked over to his son's bed, and Sashia started to slither away.

"Stay," he held out his hand to motion her back. She stilled, and he looked at Cyrus. "Be well, son." He turned and left.

"I will go and brew more tea and send for some food. When he wakes, we must make him eat." Kassius followed Kalin out the door. His sensibilities were no longer offended now that Kalin consented to Sashia's tactics.

Cyrus shifted and began to wake. Sashia scooted away so she wouldn't startle him. He started coughing violently. She jumped out of the bed and grabbed a rag. Cyrus coughed up a large amount of phlegm and fell back, spent from the effort, but Sashia noticed his breathing was less labored.

"I dreamed—" he closed his eyes.

"Hush. Do not try to talk. You must rest."

"—so happy."

Sashia was glad when Kassius returned with the tea. She wasn't ready to discuss her feelings with Cyrus. She wasn't ready to think about them.

∞∞∞

The next several days, Sashia and Kassius carefully nursed Cyrus, and he slowly began to regain his health. Kassius returned to his students during the day and resumed visiting his patients. Sashia remained with Cyrus. Kassius had agreed he could have visitors, and Cyrus spent a few hours every day listening to reports from Topec and others. Darius visited routinely, and Cyrus always seemed energized by his brother's presence.

After everyone left, Sashia transcribed letters for him. She read to him from her scrolls. While he slept, she considered how close he had come to death and how relieved she was he lived. Somehow, she had to come to terms with the fact she wanted him in her life. Forgetting him was impossible.

"What are those papers on the table?" he asked one afternoon when he and Sashia were alone.

Sashia hesitated to answer.

Cyrus' expression became solemn. "Are those the letters I wrote?"

"Yes." She hadn't thought to give them back to King Kalin.

"Did you read them?"

"Yes," she answered honestly.

"I did not wish for you to read them. You'll think me even more of a desperate lunatic than before."

Sashia walked slowly to his side to give herself time to formulate a response. If she was going to say anything, now was the time. She sat next to his bed and took his hand. His eyes followed her every movement.

"You're not a lunatic. You are a good man."

"Humph. A good man." He closed his eyes and sank back onto his pillow. "Why did you come, Sashia?"

"You don't remember what I said before?"

"I remember little during that time other than some pleasant dreams." He smiled wistfully.

"I came because you needed me."

"Because your prince needed you, or because a man named Cyrus needed you?"

Sashia's chin quivered and she blinked back tears. She swallowed hard and acknowledged the truth, what she had known in her heart the moment she heard he was sick. "I came because I love you."

Cyrus raised his head and blinked. "You what?"

"I love you, Cyrus."

"Sashia! Do you mean it?" He cried joyfully and clutched her hand.

She nodded, grinning foolishly, too overcome to say more.

"You're not just saying it because I've been ill? I'll have more sense than to wear myself down like this again. I have other things, other people to live for besides you. You are not responsible for me."

"Your illness made me admit it, but I loved you already. I should've known it by how I felt when we parted at the fort."

"Then . . ."

"That does not mean I am ready to marry you."

"What? You tell me you love me, but you won't marry me? Why not?"

She took a deep breath as she prepared to answer

176

him. As a healer, she was used to making decisions based on facts and physical evidence. Her mind was what she used to determine a course of action, not her heart. How would she know if it was leading her the right way? She had to use her head.

"We need to clear some things up first. One is that I will not agree with you about everything."

"I'm counting on it," he smiled. "We must agree on the important things, but I fully expect you to challenge me on others."

"That's the second thing. Healing is important to me. I want to come to an understanding about that before I make a promise."

"Practicing in the palace would not be enough?" he frowned.

"I just don't want any limitations." The words sounded cold and selfish as she uttered them.

"If you loved me enough, it wouldn't matter." Cyrus sighed and closed his eyes.

Sashia jumped up and felt his forehead. "I'm sorry. You need to rest. We can discuss it another time."

"Mmm." He started to drift off. "I love you enough."

"Enough for what?"

Sashia waited for a reply, but Cyrus was asleep. The conversation had drained her as well, and after watching him breathe for a while, she got up and paced the room. Was Cyrus right? Didn't she love him enough? It *felt* all-consuming. He was all she thought about. Did love mean you had to be willing to give everything up? Was it selfish to insist on the freedom to help others?

Father had loved Mother in spite of everything. She frowned. Her thinking was muddied. She had been cooped up in this room too long.

She heard muffled voices in the passage and turned and walked out the open door, pulling it closed automatically. As soon as it shut, a hand grabbed her arm painfully hard, dragged her down the corridor, and shoved her into the wall.

"We need to talk!" It was King Kalin. "You must tell my son you will marry him!"

"Wha-what?" Had the guards overheard their conversation and reported it to the king?

"I will not lose him! He nearly died because you denied him. He needs to get you out of his system. If you will not marry him, then seduce him! Lie with him until he tires of you."

"I most certainly will not!" Sashia replied, outraged. She tried to yank herself free, but he only tightened his grip.

"Obstinate woman! I will pay you."

"No!"

"Don't think I'll spare you because of your healing skills! I have no qualms about employing more serious methods of persuasion," he warned sinisterly. "Perhaps that will change your mind. Guard!"

A soldier hovering nearby closed in, and the other at the end of the hall advanced toward her. Fear gripped her, and she froze. She might be able to get away from one of them, but not two, and not unless she was willing to become a fugitive in her own country.

"Father! Let her go!"

Sashia and Kalin turned and saw Cyrus standing outside his room in his dressing gown with disheveled hair and bare feet.

"Get back in bed, son. You are not well," Kalin commanded with an edge of panic.

Cyrus walked forward unsteadily. He had been up a couple of times, but only around the room.

"Let her go," he repeated.

"No. She must remain here until you get what you

want out of her."

Sashia winced as Kalin's nails dug into her skin.

"You cannot hold her against her will, Father. She has a writ of safe passage in your own hand."

"What?" Kalin let go of her instantly, as if she burned him. Sashia sagged against the wall and rubbed her arm. "I have only written one of those. Let me see it!"

Sashia fumbled in her purse, found the paper, and held it out to him with shaking fingers. In her shock, she'd momentarily forgotten about it, but Cyrus hadn't. She longed to run down the corridor and throw herself into his arms, but her legs refused to move.

Kalin perused the document and threw it back in her face in disgust. "I don't know how you acquired this, but it is genuine. I knew I would regret writing it. Stay out of my sight!" He spat the words spitefully at her and stalked out of the corridor.

"Are you alright?" Cyrus asked softly as the guards retreated to their posts.

Sashia grasped his outstretched hand and he easily pulled her to her feet, even in his weakened state. She nodded numbly.

"A sound woke me, and I looked around the room, and you were gone. I panicked, thinking you might have left me."

"Oh, Cyrus!" She flung herself at him and buried her head in his chest.

"I also realized I was ungrateful," he spoke gently into her ear. "Thank you. Thank you for coming when I needed you. I—I will always love you, whether you marry me or not. If you ever need me, I will come to you."

"I cannot leave you! I was trying to be logical, but I was lying to myself. I don't know what to do." she sobbed. She hadn't been trained for this. How did one decide when the rewards outweighed the losses without numbers or a formula? But as she basked in the comfort of his embrace, she acknowledged continuing to love him at a distance, without marrying him, was unthinkable.

"Trust me, Sashia. Whatever happens, we can get through it. I know it is difficult for you to give up control, but if you put your future in my hands, I will prove myself worthy of your trust. We can work out a way for you to continue using your skills."

"What about the writ?"

Suddenly, he wavered, and Sashia barely held him steady.

"Whew. I feel lightheaded. Help me back to my room before you have to carry me."

He leaned on her as they walked back to his chamber, but as soon as they were through the door, he closed it and straightened again.

"Cyrus, what—"

He led her to a chair and pulled her into his lap. "I don't want the guards to overhear the rest of our conversation, but I am not so weak I cannot hold you." He wrapped his arms around her and bent his head to breathe in the scent of her hair. "In light of Father's behavior today, I think you should keep the writ. I love you enough to trust you with it. It is a powerful document, more powerful than you may know. The king is bound by few laws, but that is one of them. He cannot violate his signed words."

Sashia snuggled into his shoulder. Her heart was beating so hard she thought it would rupture any moment.

"The laws of our country are straightforward and fair, but the king is still the judge. It is he who interprets and enforces the law. As you have seen, he can be heavy-handed and is used to getting what he wants."

Cyrus let his hands slide up and down her back. The rhythm of her pulse was deafening.

"Father hates it when people defy him. He could make life very disagreeable for us if he wanted, but I will never let him hurt you."

"I know." She gazed up into Cyrus' fiery eyes. "I also know he cares about you. That's why he acted the way he did."

"You are very generous," Cyrus chuckled cynically. "Since you've already rejected his offer once, we will have to approach him with our request to marry in such a way he is unable to leverage anything out of us in exchange for his approval." He gently caressed her jawline with his fingertips. "You *will* marry me, my love?"

"Yes." As she spoke the word a weight seemed to lift from her shoulders, and everything felt right, for the first time since she'd met him.

Cyrus' voice was low, and thick with emotion. "Say that again."

"I will marry you, Cyrus."

"You have no idea how I've been longing to hear you speak those words."

He bent down and kissed her hungrily—with such intensity it made her feel faint. Her arms encircled his neck, and she kissed him back, losing herself completely in the rapture of the moment.

The feeling she had fought against for so long of being pulled into his orbit was finally given freedom to follow its course, and she no longer existed as a separate entity. Like a meteor, she was burning away into nothing and becoming part of his atmosphere. But she didn't care. It felt wonderful.

As she let go of her fears, Sashia couldn't believe

how at peace she felt. If Cyrus trusted her enough to allow her to keep the freedom the writ offered, the least she could do was trust him in return. That didn't mean nothing bad would happen, but she was sure he was right, and they would get through it somehow if it did.

A plan began to form in her mind.

"I think I know how we can persuade the king to agree to our marriage, but you won't like it."

"Why not?"

She gasped as he kissed her neck and ran his hand along her thigh. "Uh, it will require us to be apart for several weeks, for one thing," she panted, "long enough for you to fully recover and return to your patrol while I work with Kassius."

"No, I do not like that at all."

CHAPTER FIFTEEN

Six weeks later

"I will marry him on one condition."

"Name it," growled Kalin.

"You must send ten of your best horses to my father, and he is to be exempt from taxes for the rest of his life."

"That is two things. I will do only one or the other!"

Sashia shrugged. "It is a small price to guarantee your son's peace of mind." Playing the mercenary went against everything she had been taught, and part of her was scared to death, but part of her was enjoying it.

"You said you didn't need your father's approval."

"No, but I want my family provided for, regardless."

Kalin rose from his throne and loomed over her menacingly. Only the thought of Cyrus kept her from withering under his gaze.

"I will agree to your requests if you surrender the writ."

"No, I will not do that."

Cyrus was adamant she must not give it up. It was the one concession he was able to make toward maintaining her independence.

She spun on her heel and started to walk away. It was the height of disrespect to turn her back on the king. He took a step after her, and she heard an angry exclamation, but he couldn't touch her. She got all the way to the door before he called her back.

"Wait! Twenty horses, but he pays the taxes."

Sashia stopped, but still faced the exit. "And I keep the writ?"

"Yes," he hissed through clenched teeth. "Now will you go to my son?"

"I want a copy of the marriage contract in writing first."

Kalin cursed at her, went to the door, and called for a scribe. When she'd answered Kalin's summons, Sashia had asked for a private audience, and the hall had been cleared. It was not a conversation either of them would desire witnesses to.

Sashia listened closely while the king dictated the details of the contract. When it was finished, he looked it over and stood aside for Sashia to do the same. It appeared to be exactly as he had stated, simple and straightforward with no ambiguity, until she reached the last paragraph.

"I am familiar with barrenness as grounds for multiple wives, but what is a 'Bridge Bride'? It says the king cannot refuse one."

"A traditional way of sealing a peace agreement between warring tribes. It hasn't been used for generations."

"I want it left out."

Kalin shook his head. "I lack the power to remove it. It can only be removed by a tribal council."

Sashia glanced questioningly at the scribe.

"It is true. The Verdans requested a tribal council before the union of then Prince Kalin and Princess Valanai to adopt the current law giving wives veto power over a second marriage. They wished to ensure she would not be supplanted. The chiefs agreed only if we included the clause for barrenness and remained open to the possibility of a Bridge Bride. Verda agreed only because it occurs so rarely."

"How rarely?"

"Of a king, it has only been required once. The first king of Berush married one wife from each tribe. The tribes have required it of their chiefs several times over the centuries," the scribe explained.

"I see." After a moment of consideration, she took the pen and affixed her name to the document under the king's signature. It would likely be many years before Cyrus would be the one called on to fulfill such an obligation, if ever. She loved him enough to take the risk.

"It's not valid until the prince signs it," informed the scribe.

King Kalin gave him a nasty look.

"I will sign it now." Cyrus' clear voice carried across the hall as he entered.

"Cyrus! Topec's message claimed you were at death's door!"

"Topec didn't write the message, I did, and the messenger was unaware of the contents."

"You didn't relapse?" Kalin's voice was shaky.

"No, father."

Kalin's shoulders relaxed in relief. But only for a moment. Then he became angry.

"You lied to me!"

He reached for the contract, but it was no longer on the table. Sashia had quietly removed it and held it out to Cyrus.

"And now I ask you to forgive me."

Cyrus took the parchment from Sashia, tore it into pieces, and dropped them on the floor.

Kalin gaped at the scraps of paper. "I don't understand."

"I didn't want to deceive you, but I needed you to know I am serious. I will not build my marriage on a lie, and I don't want us to be at odds. Forgive me, father. Forgive us both and let us start out with your blessing."

Sashia held her breath as Kalin contemplated his son with a stony expression. This was the crucial moment. He could have Cyrus killed for lying to him if he wanted, but Cyrus spoke for them both when he said they didn't want to continue the lie. They only wanted to make a point. Kalin's hand gripped his sword tightly.

"You could have signed the paper in secret, kept up the deception, and returned after a suitable time, yet you desire my approval enough to risk it all," he drew out his words slowly. The king directed a piercing gaze at Sashia. "You could have married him when I suggested it the first time, but you refused. Why accept him now?"

"I want to marry him because I love him, not because I am being forced into it. We'd not yet come to an understanding. Now we have." She glanced at Cyrus, and his eyes shone with adoration. He held his hand out to her, and she took it.

Kalin shook his head. "I knew you had some sort of conference before you parted ways. There is little that goes on in this palace I am not informed of, but I didn't know the result of that meeting. The guards reported you had an argument. I am disappointed, Cyrus, you did not come to me yourself. Did you think I would refuse you?"

"I was afraid you would impose conditions, Father."

Kalin regarded Sashia darkly. "Perhaps I would," he muttered. Then he straightened his back and lifted his chin regally. "I will forgive you, this time. In the future, I will not take such behavior lightly. Write it again," he commanded the scribe, "but leave out the horses."

∞∞∞

Sashia stood in front of a sheet of polished silver and studied her reflection.

"You look beautiful, daughter," said her mother softly.

"Thank you, Mother." The woman staring back at her was a stranger. "I hardly recognize myself."

"You have always been your own person, different from everyone else. You are still the same on the inside. This new responsibility you are taking on will challenge you. Don't let it change you."

Sashia nodded uncertainly. "I am glad you are here, Mother. I don't know if I could do this alone."

"Nothing could keep me from it! Who would have thought my daughter would be marrying a prince?" Mother laughed nervously. "I would never have believed it."

"I try not to think of that part." Sashia shivered. "To me, I am just marrying Cyrus."

"Everyone out," boomed Kalin's voice from the door to her chamber. "I would speak with my future daughter-in-law alone."

Mother squeezed Sashia's hand and bowed deeply on her way out. Sashia hoped the king would not make a habit of entering her room unannounced. Wishful thinking, she was afraid.

Kalin looked her up and down and nodded his approval. Then his eyes turned to steel, and he stared at her malevolently. Sashia gripped the back of a chair for support as his gaze threatened to bring her to her knees.

"You gambled my son's life against my love for him and won. You will not always have that leverage. If you oppose me, though I cannot touch you, I can destroy everything you hold dear. That paper you hold does not extend protection to your family. Remember that."

He turned and stalked out of the room before Sashia could reply. She filled her empty lungs with air and stood shaking.

"It is time," proclaimed a maid from the doorway.

Mother returned and draped a shimmering veil over Sashia's head, securing it to her long, wavy hair with strategically placed pins. Cashi came and stood on her other side, and they proceeded to the hall flanked by dozens of girls waving streamers.

Father met them at the double doors, smiling widely.

"I'm proud and happy for you, daughter."

His words warmed her and momentarily chased away some of her worries.

"I'm following my heart, Father, as you suggested, but I'm afraid."

"If you were not afraid, you would be foolish."

"What do you mean?"

"You like to study, to know how things work, to know the likely outcomes. No one can tell what will happen tomorrow. No matter how well we plan, too much is out of our hands. 'The wind blows where it will, the rain falls where it may, my home is in my heart, and no one can take that away'."

Sashia smiled at the familiar saying. Those who

depended on nature for their livelihood lived by those words. "Thank you, Father."

The guards opened the heavy wooden doors, and Sashia saw Cyrus waiting for her in front of the dais. King Kalin stood imperiously in the center, but she hardly noticed him. If the future was out of her hands, it was also out of his. The love in her husband's eyes was all she needed.

CHAPTER SIXTEEN

The Sixteenth Year of the Reign of King Kalin of Berush

"Aieeee!"

"There is the head! Push again!"

Sashia panted, took a deep breath, and pushed. "Umph!" Once the shoulders were through, the rest of the baby slid into Mother's waiting hands.

"A boy!" exclaimed her mother proudly. She tied off and cut the umbilical cord and passed the child to Madia to clean him up.

Men were not allowed in the birthing chamber during the delivery, so Kassius had suggested Madia assist, just in case. Madia had proved herself in the aftermath of the Battle of Tull Pass, but she had lost most of her family and relocated to Sherish. Sashia could walk her mother through anything unusual that came up, as long as she was conscious, but it never hurt to be prepared. She could have had a dozen midwives in attendance, but she insisted her mother and Madia would be enough.

"Now the afterbirth," Mother reminded her.

Giving birth herself was vastly different than assisting in the delivery. It was much more intense. She pushed again.

"Excellent. Are you going to eat it?"

"Actually, oof, our research shows—"

"A simple 'yes' or 'no' will do, dear. I know it's not the custom in the city."

Sashia held out her arms as Madia brought her the infant. Right away, she could see he would take after Cyrus. His limbs were long, and he looked strong and healthy. She put him to her breast and encouraged him to suckle.

"Shall I call in the father?" Mother smiled.

Sashia nodded, not taking her eyes away from her beautiful baby. Hers. Hers and Cyrus'.

Cyrus rushed to her side and fell to his knees beside the bed, his eyes brimming with tears of joy and happiness. He stretched out a timid finger and brushed his son's soft tuft of hair. "He is amazing, Sashia." He kissed her forehead. "You are well?"

"Everything is fine. I am wonderful." She smiled at their son. Tarin, they had agreed, if it was a boy. The baby fell asleep, and she turned for Cyrus to take him.

"I won't wake him?"

She shook her head. "He's more worn out than I am."

Cyrus took the tightly swaddled bundle from her and engulfed it in his own strong arms. He gazed at his son and laughed with delight. Then he sat down next to Sashia, and she leaned on his shoulder and fell asleep.

∞∞∞

"I have to leave tomorrow."

"So soon?" Sashia protested in dismay. "You only

returned from the port three days ago. Your son is a month old, and you've hardly seen him."

"Father has asked me to take Darius on a tour of the eastern mountain range. He is to take over Uncle Mathis' patrol." The general's horse had thrown him, and he'd died of his injuries.

"But Darius is so young! He's only what? Sixteen? Seventeen?"

"He needs the activity, the purpose. He's not like me. Already he has seen battle, much earlier than I."

"But I want you here," she whimpered.

Cyrus looked down at her and whispered softly, "It is not my choice. You know I would rather stay."

Sashia leaned into him, and he held her head against his chest. They stood together without speaking.

Tarin's cry broke the silence, and Sashia picked him up. Gaia, Cyrus' old nurse, was hovering nearby and handed Sashia a small flask. She held it to the infant's tiny mouth, but he continued to cry. She bit her lip in frustration.

"What's wrong?" asked Cyrus.

"My milk is drying up, and he refuses to drink goat's milk. Madia is looking for a wet nurse."

"Let me hold him."

Cyrus took Tarin from her gently and sprinkled some milk on his little finger. Tarin sucked at it frantically and wailed louder when he discovered there was no more.

"I think he dislikes the flask."

"Try this," exclaimed Sashia, suddenly inspired. She soaked a clean cloth with milk and twisted it to a point.

Cyrus rubbed it on his son's lips, and the baby began to drink.

Sashia sighed in relief. "I should have thought of

that before. It's what we do with orphaned goats."

"Go and rest. You are tired. I won't see him for a few weeks."

"You're tired also. You and your father have been closeted in his study with his advisors for hours." She tried to suppress a yawn.

Cyrus laughed. "But I don't have to nurse a baby. Your mother is resting, and Gaia has already had a turn. Let me help you. He is my son too."

Sashia smiled. His laughter made her tingle from the top of her head down to her toes. "Alright, just for a little bit." She could barely keep her eyes open long enough to make it to her bed.

∞∞∞

Hours later, Sashia woke and reached out to find the sheets next to her cold and empty. She thrashed around in a panic trying to find whatever was missing, though she couldn't remember what it was.

"He's right here, daughter."

Sashia focused on a dark corner of the room where her mother sat with a small bundle. Her baby! She threw off the covers and rushed to retrieve him. The soft light of a single candle illuminated his sweet, sleeping face.

Mother chuckled. "At least there is one way you are like everyone else."

"Where is Cyrus?"

"He woke me before he left. He and his brother had to leave before dawn."

Sashia glanced out the window and saw a tinge of orange on the horizon. Her shoulders slumped.

"I told him I could stay until he returns. He left a letter for you."

Mother pointed to a folded sheet of paper on the

table. Sashia set Tarin on the bed and snatched up the letter.

> *My darling Sashia,*
>
> *When you told me you loved me, I was the happiest man alive. When I looked into the face of my son, my joy exceeded even that. I love you both more than I could ever express. Thank you for this wonderful gift. My thoughts will be with you every moment I am gone.*
>
> *I sign this "your husband," the greatest title I could hold.*
>
> *Cyrus*

When Sashia finished reading the letter, she broke down and sobbed. She cried until she began to hiccup. Mother came over and put her arm around her shoulder.

"What's wrong with me?"

"You have borne a child, that's what's wrong with you. Your reactions are perfectly normal."

"It's not (hic) normal (hic) for me!"

Tarin started to cry, and Sashia began to nurse him. He wanted more than she had to give him, and when there was no more, he bawled again. With Mother's help, she coaxed him into drinking enough goat milk to satisfy him temporarily.

"Why aren't I producing enough for him?" Sashia moaned.

"Sometimes a woman dries up early. Other women never produce enough milk. It just happens."

"But why me? I'm doing everything right!"

Mother shrugged and took Tarin from her to burp. Somehow, they struggled through the day. Even with Mother and Gaia taking turns, it seemed like Tarin cried constantly, and Sashia hardly got any sleep.

Early the next morning, Sashia had just dozed off when someone knocked on the door.

"Who is it?" Mother asked as Sashia rolled over.

Lang's muffled voice answered. "The wet nurse has arrived."

"At last!" exclaimed Sashia as she rushed to the door, now fully awake.

"My name is Pannai, my lady," the woman introduced herself. "My daughter is old enough to be weaned, but I have plenty of milk left. I only ask that I be allowed to bring her with me to the castle."

"Absolutely!" Sashia was so exhausted from Tarin's crying and the effort it took to get him to eat she would agree to anything. "What about your husband?"

"He's on a voyage to Verda and won't return for six weeks. After that, we can arrange something. Perhaps I could come up during the day only."

"Excellent. Can you start right now, or must you go collect your daughter?"

"If you send a message to my sister-in-law, she will deliver her."

Sashia directed Lang to take the message while Pannai walked over to the bed and picked up Tarin. Mother gave up her seat, and Pannai sat with the baby who immediately began to nurse. Sashia's nerves were jittery and she began to quiver like jelly.

"You have that look, dear," observed Mother. "You need to take a walk. Get a change of scenery."

"What look?" frowned Sashia.

"The look all mothers get when they have had enough. Go. Everything is under control." Mother practically shoved her out the door and shut it behind her.

Sashia sagged against the wall and inhaled deeply. All her studying was nothing to the actual experience of motherhood. Mother was right. She needed to refocus or she would break down. It had been a long time since she had meditated.

She made her way up to the roof and sat to watch the sunrise. The morning breeze off of the lake was cool and soothing. The early spring sun soon warmed the air and Sashia grew hungry. She made her way back inside the palace, but then thought she might like something to read as a distraction, so she headed toward the study.

As she approached, she heard King Kalin's voice, so she determined to pass by without entering.

"Ah, daughter! Come in!"

Sashia winced at the familiarity. She had not tried to be stealthy, thinking he would have no more wish to see her than she did to see him.

The king stood around a table cluttered with papers. Yarin, one of his closest advisors, hovered nearby, and a harried scribe sat ready to take dictation.

"Leave us," he commanded.

The scribe scurried away, glad for the break, but Yarin glanced at Sashia thoughtfully on his way out. He had a calming presence and often tempered the king's extreme reactions by suggesting moderation. Sashia wished he'd stayed.

"How is my grandson?"

"He is well, my lord."

Kalin relaxed into a chair and motioned Sashia to do the same. He put his fingers together and contemplated her. Sashia tried not to show her discomfort. She hadn't meditated long enough for this.

"My son is very happy."

He straightened some papers, and Sashia waited for him to continue.

"All parents want their children to be happy, but what makes them happy in one moment is not always good for them." He stared at her pointedly. "I didn't think you would be good for him."

He paused again, wanting his statement to sink in. Sashia did not rise to the bait. He wanted to rile her. She wasn't sure herself if she was good for Cyrus, but she wasn't going to say it.

"But," Kalin said in a resigned voice, "we both know what he was like without you. And you have proved me wrong, so far. I thought you would be conniving and scheming behind my back, but, as far as I am aware, you have not done so."

"There's been no occasion to." *Oops*. Sashia chastised herself. The thought popped out before she could rein it in. "I prefer to be direct. I have been taught to seek peace, not to build walls."

Kalin chuckled. "You are physically unremarkable, strong-willed, and too smart for your own good. But for whatever inexplicable reason, Cyrus loves you. He loves you too much. I propose we join forces, for his benefit."

"What are you suggesting?" She bristled at his description, but she was also worried. If King Kalin had the same thoughts she did, maybe they were true.

"Right now, he's teaching Darius how to lead a patrol. I told him a month, but Darius is . . . going to need more time than that. I have good men riding with him, but Cyrus has always had a way with him. The longer they can work together, the better."

Sashia was disheartened at the idea of a prolonged absence. "What do you want me to do?"

"Go out there with him for a couple of weeks. Stay in one of the mountain villages so he can come and see you. Then he won't be as anxious to return home."

"What about Tarin? He's a month old. I can neither take him nor leave him."

"There are many here who can care for a child, but Cyrus only has one wife. I know you're not ready to travel yet. Take some time to prepare and think about it. Spend two or three weeks with him and then return. He should be able to manage the rest of the time without you."

Sashia's brain was foggy. She tried to figure out why Kalin might want her out of the way. Was he going to do something she would disapprove of and didn't want her to interfere? "I will think about it," she said finally.

Kalin nodded. "You might find it will be good for you as well. You are used to more activity and purpose."

Sashia nodded mutely and excused herself. She couldn't fathom why Kalin was being so congenial. He must have an ulterior motive, but try as she might, she couldn't figure out what it was.

Sashia fretted and worried, first over Tarin, and then over Cyrus. She missed her husband but couldn't abandon her son. It was a letter from Cyrus that finally convinced her.

My love,

I have heard when two people marry, they become one in body, one in heart, and one in purpose. It must be true, because I do not feel whole without you. I miss your warmth beside me at night, your kisses in the morning, and your insightful thoughts during the day.

Darius has great skill with the blade. He will soon surpass me in that area, but he is headstrong and quick-tempered. It will take him time to acquire the skills necessary to become a great leader, though he is perfectly capable of becoming one someday. I do not feel I can leave him to his own devices, even with the years of experience of the soldiers assigned to his company. Their opinions on some things are not the same as mine.

I will come home as soon as I can, but I fear it will be longer than expected. There is some discontent among the tribes of this region that must also be dealt with.

Write to me, my love. Write to me every day and tell how you are. Tell me how Tarin fares. There is nothing so mundane I would not wish to hear it. It will help me feel closer to you.

Your husband,
Cyrus

How could she stay away when he obviously needed her? Pannai and her daughter were settled in, and Tarin was growing at a healthy rate. Mother promised to remain as long as necessary to help Gaia. The old nurse was happy to be of use again, but she didn't have the energy for night feedings. Sashia hinted at some of her concerns about King Kalin to her mother before she left.

"Nothing will get past me, daughter, never fear."

No one's mind was sharper than her mother's, and no one knew better how to protect her family's interests. She was also an experienced healer and child-rearer in her own right. They snapped at each other occasionally, but their relationship had improved. Sashia's anxiety eased slightly, but she felt guilty about leaving Tarin. She was still trying to nurse him twice a day. However, a few days before she planned to leave, her milk dried up entirely, leaving her without that excuse.

On the morning Tarin was six weeks old, Sashia set out with Lang and a score of guards to join Cyrus on the eastern border. Sashia rode Favor, the same mare Cyrus had given her.

"Good morning, Lady Sashia," grinned Deppan as he rode up next to her.

"Deppan! How good to see you!"

"Cyrus reassigned me to the palace since he has to be gone so often. I am to look after you. Although I know," he added, "you can look after yourself."

Sashia grinned back. "I'm glad to have you along."

He nodded and rode to the front of the column, and Lang took his place beside her.

"This is like old times, my lady! Out on the road. Off to find adventure."

"It's not been so very long, Lang, since we were on a journey. You make it sound like we are old and gray."

"I have some gray, my lady. See," he pointed to his sideburns, "right here!" He sighed. "It's easy to become old and gray inside of an old, gray palace."

"The palace is actually quite bright compared to most stone buildings." It had white walls and gleaming, golden turrets. The walls were decorated with tapestries, and the furniture used rich, vibrant colors.

"It feels gray, my lady."

"If you say so." There was no reasoning with Lang once he took hold of an idea. In a way, he was right. The atmosphere was strained and oppressive at times.

Spring in Berush was a beautiful season. There was plenty of rain, but it swept through in short bursts and the sun quickly reappeared. Sashia's company was doused by a brief shower as they rode through the city, but she was invigorated by it. Kalin was right; this trip would be good for her also.

Lang's chatter sometimes wore on her, but today it buoyed her up. Besides, he was one person she couldn't leave alone with Kalin. He would get himself into trouble one way or another.

People stopped to bow and wave at her as the procession passed through the city streets. Many shouted congratulations on Tarin's birth, and Sashia waved and smiled back. As they approached the eastern gate, a man hailed the riders.

"Lady Sashia!" He waved frantically. His face seemed familiar.

Her guards closed in around her protectively, but she urged the mare forward. "Let me through," she ordered, and the men made way for her. "I am Lady Sashia." She now held the title legitimately, but the words still sounded strange on her tongue. "What is it?"

The man's eyes swept over the soldiers accompanying her. "I merely desire to wish you peace of body, peace of mind, and peace of heart on your journey, my lady."

The Magi greeting triggered her memory, and she recognized him as a frequent visitor to Shelomoh, though he hadn't introduced himself as a Mage. This caution on his part made her instantly alert. "The same to you," she replied warily.

"May you always choose the true and right road." He bowed and backed away.

"Thank you," she called after him, and the company continued forward.

"That was nice of him," observed Lang cheerfully.

"Yeees."

"You think not?"

"Of course it was nice," Sashia snapped.

Lang subsided, thankfully. She needed to think.

That last part was not a Magi saying. What did it mean? Was it a warning? She could think of no other reason for them to contact her. She knew they had safe houses all over the Crescent, but since she wasn't actually a Mage, she wasn't privy to their locations. They must feel some responsibility to look after her.

When they left the palace, the freedom of the outdoors had lulled her into complacency. She must stay on her guard.

CHAPTER SEVENTEEN

Nothing unusual happened the first day. Sashia was so on edge she could hardly sleep. Lang felt her anxiety, though she shared none of it aloud, and took it upon himself to sleep outside the entrance to her tent. She hoped he wouldn't get rained on, but she was glad he was there.

She had just drifted off to sleep when she was awoken by a scream.

"Aaah!"

It was Lang. She crawled out of the tent to see him grasping a writhing rattlesnake. He threw it to the ground and stomped on it. Deppan ran up, drew his sword, and cut off the snake's head.

"Were you bitten?" Sashia rushed over to Lang with a sinking heart. Treatment for snakebite was rarely successful.

"Yes, my lady, but don't worry. It cannot hurt me."

"What?" she grabbed at his wrist frantically and saw two small puncture marks. "Lang, this snake's poison is deadly!"

He shook his head. "Did I never tell you? The camel driver who brought me to Cerecia also kept snakes as an amusement. He pricked my skin with their poison until I was immune to it. Then he would make me handle them to entertain in the villages we passed."

"You have been bitten before?"

"Many times."

"By this type of snake?" She pointed to its rattle.

"Oh, yes. It is a desert snake. Very common on the route we took." He put a hand on Sashia's shoulder as her nerves got the better of her and she began to shake. "Sit down, my lady."

She sank to the ground and put her head between her knees, breathing in and out slowly.

"That was lucky," declared Deppan, sheathing his sword.

The other men on guard gathered around to gawk at the rattler. Soon the entire company was awake. It was nearly dawn, so they ate a quick breakfast and broke camp early.

Sashia kept a close eye on Lang all morning, but he suffered no ill effects from the serpent's bite other than a slight inflammation around the fang marks. She treated them with an ointment to ensure they wouldn't fester.

Early in the afternoon they approached a fork in the road. The right-hand fork continued along the river, and the left headed straight toward the mountains. Without pausing, the company rode down the left fork. Sashia pulled back on the reins, and Favor shifted her weight nervously. The mare wanted to follow the others.

"What is it, my lady?" asked Lang.

"'May you always choose the true and right road'," she muttered. "Lang, we must go right."

"But everyone else is going left," he pointed after them.

She shook her head.

Deppan turned around and saw her hesitating. "What's wrong?"

"I am not going that way."

The captain, a man named Sorin, rode back to investigate the hold-up.

"What is the reason for this delay?"

"Lady Sashia wishes to follow the river," Deppan explained more calmly than Sashia could have.

"Our orders are to travel along the foothills," Sorin replied sternly.

"Orders from whom?" asked Deppan. "I received no such orders."

"From King Kalin himself. We ride directly toward the mountains."

Sorin reached for Sashia's reins, but Deppan rode between them.

"You dare to defy me!" Sorin drew his sword.

"In the desert, a man and his horse are one entity. You cannot touch the lady; therefore, you cannot touch her horse."

Sashia was amazed at Deppan's presence of mind.

Sorin howled in rage. Everyone in Sherish knew about Sashia's writ by now.

"Your protection does not extend to your manservant," he signaled to the men on her other side. They surrounded Lang and took hold of his mount's bridle. "You will come with us, or he dies!"

The soldier closest to Lang drew his sword. Lang swallowed, and his eyes were glassy, but he was silent.

"Kill him and Cyrus will have your head," stated Sashia with conviction, staring directly into Sorin's eyes.

Sorin glared at her, and when she refused to back down, he relented. "Fine. Do as you please, but my soldiers and I are taking the mountain road. You too," he ordered Deppan.

"Captain, our orders are to escort Lady Sashia to Prince Cyrus' camp."

"By way of the mountains! If she refuses our escort, that is not my fault. You know the penalty if you disobey me." Sorin raised his blade menacingly.

"Go, Deppan," Sashia softly urged. "Your death would accomplish nothing. We'll be alright."

"My lady," his voice broke.

Sashia saw his distress, but he was a soldier, and the captain could execute him on the spot for insubordination without repercussion. She feared for him on the road, but his death would be certain if he disobeyed the captain's orders now.

For a long, tense moment, Deppan debated where his duty lay. Then he slowly backed his horse away from her. Sashia let out a long breath as Sorin sheathed his sword. He gave the sign to move out, and the company rode away. Deppan glanced over his shoulder at her and followed the captain reluctantly.

"Hoo," sighed Lang. "That was something."

Sashia fought back tears as she dug in her heels and turned her mare to the right. They walked their horses slowly and silently at first. Then Sashia felt the need to put some distance between them and Sorin, and she urged her horse into a lope.

Near sunset, they arrived at the Marusene Oasis and found several families and caravans camped there.

"Don't tell them who I am, Lang. If you cannot refrain from calling me 'my lady,' then do not speak at all." It was hopeless, but she had to say it anyway.

They rode up to the largest tent, and a boy ran to greet them.

"I will see to your horses," he offered, and Sashia gratefully slid out of the saddle and handed him the reins. The nomadic people of Berush were renowned for their hospitality. A stranger could always count on a hearty welcome.

She approached the fire and directed herself to the man sitting in the entrance of an enormous tent. "May a weary traveler join your circle?" she bowed slightly.

"You are most welcome," the man gestured to a place next to him. "I am Udin. My uncle is chief of the Augers."

Sashia recognized the name. His tribe oversaw the silver mines. Though technically not nomads, they were one of the most affluent tribes in the country.

"I am Yania, a healer from the Granite Mountains. This is my manservant, Lang."

"A healer. How fortuitous. Perhaps you can do something about this lesion on my arm. None of our own healers have been able to rid me of it."

Sashia examined the indicated irritation and recognized the fungus. "I do have something that will cure it, but you must apply the salve daily for at least a month until it disappears." She retrieved a pot of ointment from the saddlebags the boy had thoughtfully placed next to her and offered it to Udin. She always carried a supply of her most useful medicines.

"I am indebted to you."

"The warmth of your fire for the night is all I require."

"Nevertheless, if there is anything you need, I will supply it."

"Perhaps some rations for our journey tomorrow?"

"Done. Tell me the news of the west."

They talked well into the night, discussing everything from the succession to the best methods for shearing goats. When he retired, Udin insisted she take a space on the floor in the tent of his head wife, Iona, which she did gratefully. Though they were from opposite sides of the country, Sashia felt at home among the Augers. Their tents felt safe and familiar. Knowing Lang was sleeping outside the entrance, she was able to drift off to sleep.

∞∞∞

The next morning, Udin personally filled her saddlebags with bread and dried meat. "My lesion already feels relief due to your treatment. I thank you."

"You are quite welcome."

"Prince Cyrus' camp is in a valley northeast of here, but you may wish to follow the river another day and circle back," he advised.

"How do you know that's where I'm headed?"

"We do a great deal of business in Sherish, my lady. We hear things," he smiled. "Everyone knows of the skilled healer from the west. But no one will hear of your location from me, for whatever reason you wish to keep it secret."

"Now it is I who am indebted to you."

"My lady," he bowed.

Sashia followed his advice and did not head straight for Cyrus' camp. They slept a night in the open before heading north. Sashia scanned the horizon constantly, but it did not appear they had been followed.

Around midday, she saw smoke coming from a valley like Udin had described and noticed evidence of many horsemen passing that way. At the entrance to the valley they were stopped by a sentry.

"My lady," the sentry exclaimed when he recognized her. It was one of Cyrus' men. "We received word you were dead!"

"What?" That was the last thing she expected to hear.

"A messenger arrived only this morning saying you and your party were killed in a rock slide."

"I am most certainly not dead. Take me to Cyrus immediately!"

"He's two hours north of here. Follow me."

The sentry signaled another soldier to take his place, mounted a horse, and led Sashia up the northern road. Her heart clenched when she saw the destruction on the mountainside and the enormous mound of rock extending far across the road. Someone saw her and gave a shout. Restus, and several others whom she knew, rushed up to her and surrounded her horse, all expressing their relief to see her, touching her to make sure she was real.

"Cyrus! Cyrus, she's alive!" Restus dashed toward a group of workers yelling at the top of his lungs.

Tears sprang to her eyes as she watched her grief-stricken husband set down a rock and turn her way. His hair stood on end, and his eyes were wild and red. When he saw her, he was so overcome he sank to his knees with his head in his hands. She rushed over to him and threw her arms around him.

"I am here, Cyrus, my love, I am here."

"Sashia," he sobbed into her shoulder and wept uncontrollably.

Sashia felt everyone melt into the background and give them space. "My poor darling!" She kissed the top of his head and held him tightly. His shoulders shook and his large frame shuddered as he struggled to regain command of himself.

"I thought I lost you," he rasped.

"I would've come straight here if I'd known."

"What happened?"

211

Sashia nodded toward a row of tents erected a safe distance from the debris. "Let's go inside."

Sitting inside the canvas shelter, Sashia related the entire adventure from start to finish. Cyrus' jaw tightened, and he didn't speak for several moments.

"Father is clever. We have no proof of anything other than his order to ride directly for the mountains. That and the fact Sorin is, or was, an obstinate fool."

"You think both the snake and the rock slide were deliberate? The one could be easily done, but the other?"

Cyrus shook his head. "Recent rains have weakened the mountainside; that will be Father's explanation. Darius and I set out immediately to investigate and search for survivors." The tortured look returned briefly to his eyes, and Sashia could only imagine what he felt when he thought she was buried with the rest. "We sent riders to rouse the countryside to render assistance."

"How is it a messenger arrived from Sherish so soon? There hasn't been time for news to reach the capital."

"He said he came upon it early this morning and rode straight to my camp."

"His message must have been important to follow only two days behind us."

"The first thing he told me was you and your company had been buried by the mountain. I heard nothing after that." He stood and opened the flap of the tent. "Find Lotus and bring him to me," he told Restus who was hovering outside. Cyrus jerked his head at Sashia, indicating she should follow him out.

Restus and another man returned dragging a third man along with them.

"What are you doing? I've done nothing!" he

protested.

They threw him at Cyrus' feet. He looked up at Cyrus, then Sashia, and blanched.

"The truth," demanded Cyrus.

"I—I came upon the scene early this morning, my lord," he stammered. "The company had camped at the foot of the mountains. I knew, or thought I knew, Lady Sashia was with them and came to report it to you right away."

"What was your original mission? How did you know where Sorin would be?"

"Sorin's orders had changed, and I was to overtake him and report to you afterward."

"Let me see the new orders."

Lotus retrieved an oilskin from his satchel and handed it to Cyrus. Cyrus opened it and removed a folded paper. Sashia peered over his elbow as he opened it. It was blank.

"Who gave this to you?"

"Nerod, one of the king's guards."

"What exactly did he say when he handed it to you? This is important."

Lotus appeared to be thinking hard. "He said, 'Captain Sorin has new orders. Ride due east toward the Silver Mountains and catch up with him. He will be camped in the foothills.'"

"He didn't say who the orders were from?"

"No. Were they not from the king?"

Cyrus dismissed him without answering. He turned and walked a short distance away from all the activity. Sashia put her hand in his as he stood staring grimly into the distance.

Cyrus didn't say it in front of his men, but Sashia knew he was thinking it: Kalin had sent the messenger, knowing what was supposed to happen, so someone would be able to give Cyrus the news.

Otherwise, she might not have been missed for weeks.

"Cyrus, Deppan was with Sorin," she reminded him.

For a moment, Cyrus fought to keep his composure, but he maintained it. "I must continue with the search."

"I'm staying with you."

"Of course you are. If you think I'll let you out of my sight, you're crazy."

∞∞∞

"Say nothing of what we suspect to Darius. He needs his father's image intact. I will explain," Cyrus instructed as they picked their way carefully around the debris to the area where Darius and his men were working.

Sashia nodded. She trusted Cyrus to know best how to deal with his brother.

"Sashia!" Darius' eyes widened when he saw her. "We thought you were with the others!"

"The messenger was mistaken. What have you found? Are there any survivors?"

"There are so many rocks to move that we haven't found any bodies yet. There is one curiosity though." He motioned for them to follow him as he picked his way cautiously along the mountainside. "Careful, the ground is still unstable. Here," he pointed. "There is hewn timber amongst the rubble."

Cyrus took Sashia's arm to guide her safely to where Darius stood. There was indeed worked wood, like what might be used to shore up an excavation or build a retaining wall. They stood and observed it solemnly.

"Thank you, Darius. Keep working, but send some

men farther up the slope to look for footprints."

Darius studied his brother's face but knew better than to question him. When the younger prince was out of earshot, Sashia turned to Cyrus.

"Could it have been rigged to collapse while they were camped below?" From this distance, it would have been difficult for the sharpest observer to determine if she were among the riders. If she hadn't received the Mage's warning, she would've been buried with them. The air rushed out of her lungs as the full weight of what had happened caught up with her.

Cyrus put his arms around her. "It's not your fault."

"Why does he hate me so?"

"It's not you he hates, it's the writ. It's his lack of power over you. He views you as a threat."

"Maybe I should just give it to him."

"No. Then you would be completely at his mercy."

"But if he no longer viewed me as a threat . . ."

"We will find another way out of this," Cyrus said firmly.

"What about Tarin? Mother? They're still with him in the palace!"

"He would never harm my son."

"But he could hide him from us! He could—"

"Hush." Cyrus held a finger to her lips as she threatened to become hysterical. "There's nothing we can do at this moment. We must consider our next steps carefully and do nothing in haste."

Sashia tried to calm herself and reason clearly. He was right. Much as she wanted to rush back to the palace, that would accomplish nothing other than to anger the king further. Whatever plans he had laid would already be in place. The first thing they must do is find Deppan.

"Let's get to work."

∞∞∞

Hundreds of people from the surrounding hills joined in the recovery effort. Darius' men discovered footprints farther up the mountainside, but lost them in the rubble. There were goat-prints as well, so no conclusions could be drawn from them.

On the fourth day of digging, Deppan's body was found. Both Cyrus and Sashia wept over him. Restus stood vigil with them.

"If he hadn't intervened, Sorin might have prevailed in taking me with him, or at the least, left me stranded without a horse, or killed Lang."

Cyrus held her hand tightly and could find no words.

Deppan's funeral pyre was nearly as tall as Favor. It was the least they could do for him.

That night, back at the main camp, Restus roused Cyrus and Sashia from sleep.

"What is it?" Cyrus asked groggily.

"It has occurred to me, my lord, we have a short window of time where we are the only ones who know Lady Sashia is alive. Somehow, we must be able to use that to our advantage."

Cyrus rubbed the sleep from his eyes. "You are right. We must work out a plan." He opened the flap of the tent so Restus could enter.

Before he could close it, Topec approached. He'd been assisting Darius in the clean-up and therefore absent when Cyrus questioned Lotus.

"My lord, I must insist you inform me as to what is going on. How is it Lady Sashia is here when Lotus said she was dead? Why are you meeting secretly in the night? Don't keep me in the dark."

216

"Topec, let me remind you I do not report to you. I am under no obligation to explain anything."

"My lord," he bowed respectfully, "I have been charged by the king to advise and protect you. I cannot do my job if I do not know everything."

"That is the very reason why I cannot tell you, Topec."

Topec looked at each of their faces. "You're not plotting against the king?"

"No, Topec," said Cyrus softly. "It is the other way around."

"What? Why would he do that? What evidence do you have? Tell me, so I may advise you," he pleaded.

Sashia laid a hand on Cyrus' arm. "Tell him. His knowing can hardly make anything worse."

"Very well. You must promise to surrender yourself to me if we cannot agree on a course of action."

"I swear it."

The four of them moved their conversation to warmer seats around the fire. Restus built it up while Cyrus related everything that had happened.

"It's thin," was Topec's assessment. "It's also a lot of trouble over one woman. No offense, my lady."

"None taken," she replied dryly.

"What do you advise, Topec?" asked Cyrus impatiently.

"First, let me say I have known your father longer than you have, and while he can be vindictive, he has never made tactical errors nor regarded the lives of his men lightly. The lady says he has threatened to use her family as leverage, but I find it hard to believe he would sacrifice an entire company to be rid of her."

"You think someone other than my father is behind this? Who else could possibly have a motive?"

"That brings me to my second point. I saw the evidence of the shoring on the slope as well as you. Have you considered who worked it? It was not done by soldiers. You and Prince Darius can account for all your men. It was done secretly and was well-coordinated, which shows careful planning."

"Father could've hired other workers to do it. He planned it and waited until after Sashia had given me an heir before implementing his plot. He's the only one in a position to do it."

"He also knows how much Lady Sashia means to you. Would he be willing to cause you so much pain to achieve his ends?"

"He might think I'm over her now."

Sashia shook her head, doubt entering her mind for the first time. "No, he knows that's not true. The reason he gave for sending me was that you couldn't be without me."

"He was right," Cyrus squeezed her hand, "whether he believed it or not." He turned to Topec. "Nothing would make me happier than to believe my father innocent, but who else could be behind it? It would have to be someone with a great deal of influence. Nerod indicated to Lotus that he knew Sorin would still be there two days later."

"Is there anyone else who would want Lady Sashia out of the way?"

"I can think of no one."

"Nor I," asserted Sashia. Topec himself had harbored doubts about her in the beginning, but he'd just been doing his job.

"Let me put it this way. Is there anyone who would want you to be without a wife?"

Cyrus frowned. "What do you mean?"

"If Lady Sashia was eliminated, who would benefit from it, besides your father?"

"Everywhere I go, men throw their daughters in my way, but I was never interested in any of them—"

"They still do? You never told me that."

"It was not relevant. Besides, I could take another wife without getting rid of the first, so what would be the point?"

"Everyone who knows you and Lady Sashia knows that would never happen. Even if you wanted another wife, she would have to agree, and she has the writ, so no one can make her," argued Topec.

"This is even thinner than our first explanation," protested Cyrus. "Restus, what do you think? Have you anything to add?"

"I am a man of action, my lord, not politics. I judge by results only. And what has actually been achieved? Men are dead, and you suspect your father. Who would want to pit you against the king?"

Cyrus sat straight up, and Sashia gaped.

"I hadn't thought of it that way, but that is the result!" exclaimed Cyrus.

"But why wouldn't they take you or the king himself out of the way? Why go to all this effort?" wondered Sashia.

"Because," explained Topec, warming to Restus' idea, "then we would be on the lookout for an assassin instead of fighting amongst ourselves. Get your enemies to remove each other, and you can swoop in and save the day. Take them out yourself, and you are branded a traitor."

"Or take advantage of their distraction to attack," put in Restus.

"This brings us no closer to knowing who they are," Cyrus maintained.

"I suggest you lay all this before the king, gauge his reaction, and see what explanation he offers," advised Topec.

"And if he is the one behind it after all?" pressed Cyrus.

Topec's reply was cut short by a commotion at the entrance to the valley. By now, the sun had risen, and they saw two guards escorting a man into the camp.

"The healer," he cried. "I need the healer!"

Sashia started to rise, but Cyrus grabbed her arm. "Wait. It could be another ruse to separate us." She remained seated.

Topec took charge. "Who are you, and what do you need a healer for?"

"I come from Udin's camp. One of his daughters was attacked by a mountain lion early this morning when she got up to relieve herself. She is in grave condition. I was told to ask for 'the healer from the Granite Mountains'."

"That's what I told Udin. I must go."

"Then I am going too," insisted Cyrus.

Sashia didn't argue.

CHAPTER EIGHTEEN

Topec stayed behind with Darius while Cyrus took Restus and a score of others to guard Sashia and Lang. It took an hour for them to reach Udin's tents. He had returned from his trip to Sherish and rejoined his family.

Udin met them when they rode into his camp. He raised an eyebrow at the number of guards, but immediately led Sashia to his injured daughter. "This way."

Sashia handed Lang several of her tools to heat and entered a tent large enough she did not have to stoop over. A woman sat crying next to a moaning girl of around sixteen years. Sashia lifted the blanket covering the girl and grimaced. It had been a while since she had seen anything so gruesome.

"I removed her clothing and washed the wounds, but I'm afraid anything more is beyond me," explained the woman.

Sashia quickly assessed the injuries. The girl's torso was almost completely flayed. The cat had clawed the skin over her ribs to shreds, some of the marks reaching down past her naval. Her hands and arms were covered in bites and tears where she had tried to fend it off. She was lucky to have gotten her arms up before it got to her neck.

"Are you her mother?"

"Yes," the woman sobbed. "I am Baria. This is Marthi. Can you help her?"

"It appears her internal organs are intact, but there is great risk of festering. The wounds must remain clean until the skin regrows. She won't be able to move for some weeks."

Sashia removed a flask of wine from her bag. "Hello Marthi. My name is Sashia. I am going to help you, but this is going to sting. Hold her down by her shoulders, Baria."

Marthi screamed as Sashia poured the wine over her torn body and hands. Sashia put in stitches wherever she could, covered the affected areas with ointment, and wrapped the girl up in clean bandages. She used everything she had with her. When she was finished, Baria covered her daughter up with a blanket.

"I will need to send for more ointment. It will have to be applied every time you change the bandages."

Sashia gave Baria detailed instructions on cleaning and dressing the wounds and went to find Cyrus. When she exited the tent, a young man waylaid her.

"How is she?"

"Her injuries are not deep, but they are extensive. She will recover with time if the wounds don't fester."

The young man frowned as if he didn't understand. "I heard she was all torn up."

"Her hands and chest are," Sashia said somewhat impatiently. She looked around for Cyrus.

"I may have to break our betrothal then."

"Whatever for?" her attention snapped back to the youth in front of her.

"I am my father's oldest son. I must marry

someone who can give me heirs."

"Her reproductive organs are unaffected. She'll have no problem bearing children if she survives."

The boy stuck up his nose. "I cannot take the risk."

"Then you are a foolish child, and she is well rid of you," Sashia spied Cyrus sitting with Udin in front of a fire. She left the fickle fiancé gaping behind her and sat down next to her husband.

"Well, how is my daughter?"

Sashia told him.

Udin nodded. "We will feed her the lion's heart so she can absorb its strength."

Sashia was proud of herself. Her nostrils only flared slightly at this absurd statement. It wouldn't hurt anything for Marthi to eat it, but the meat would be no more nourishing than any other.

"Thank you for coming," Udin continued, "especially during such a catastrophe."

"You can repay us by telling us anything you know about the activity on the slope where my father's men were killed," proposed Cyrus.

"Killed? You imply intent?"

"There was evidence of shoring on the slope above. Who would have done that, and why?"

"Well, no silver has been found in that area so there would've been no mining, but, excuse me, my lord, for speaking bluntly, your men were fools if they camped beneath those cliffs."

"What do you mean?"

"That slope is notoriously unstable. Even the goatherds avoid it. No one familiar with the area would have camped there."

"What about the shoring?" prodded Cyrus.

"A retaining wall along the mountainside might help prevent it from deteriorating, but it would've been noticed by everyone."

"Not a wall, but a trap. A pile of large boulders triggered to start a rock slide."

"I suppose it's possible, but who would do such a thing?" He shook his head. "It seems unlikely."

"Then how is it twenty-one soldiers are dead?"

"Bad luck?" Udin sighed at Cyrus' dark expression. "I can do nothing but guess without seeing it for myself, and if your men have removed most of the debris, it will be difficult for me to determine anything even then, but I will try if you wish."

"Any input you can give us will be welcome. Can you return with us now?"

"I'll get my horse."

While they waited for Udin, Sashia whispered to Cyrus, "I notice you didn't mention the goat prints."

"No," he replied as Udin rejoined them.

The ride to the site of the disaster took three hours, since Udin's camp was in the opposite direction. Udin pointed out many things as they passed, the extent of his tribe's grazing lands, which was limited only to what they needed to feed themselves, and the different types of rocks and soils where various ores might be found. Most of the silver was mined further south.

When they arrived at the scene, Darius and Topec were supervising the removal of the remaining debris. Sorin and all his men had been found. Now they just needed to clear the road.

"Well, there's nothing to learn down here," declared Udin. "Let's go farther up and see if we can discover where the slide began."

Cyrus led him up the slope to the spot where they had seen the goat prints. Udin frowned when he saw them.

"This is strange. I don't know of anyone who grazes these hills. But this is not my tribe's territory.

You'll have to ask Iban, or one of the other members of the Pastura tribe." Udin walked around a little more. "The ground above us is undisturbed. You're right; this must be where it started. If they cut any trees for timber, they must have been further down, so the falling rocks would have obscured the evidence." He looked below and sighed.

"What is it?"

"This is what I meant. Your brother and his men are working in the same location where your father's soldiers were camped. It is so far down, we cannot distinguish them, but you can see they are in a depressed area, with the sides of the mountain curled around them. Any rocks that rolled down the hill would be funneled right onto that spot. Your own camp is only a couple hours away. Whatever possessed them to stop here for the night?"

Cyrus and Sashia looked where he waved and saw exactly the same thing. It was a death trap.

∞∞∞

"Cyrus!" yelled Darius when they returned to the road. "Cyrus, we found another body!"

"You did? I thought we'd found everyone already."

"This one's not dressed like a soldier."

Cyrus went over to investigate, and Sashia followed. Udin had already headed home.

"He looks like a goatherd," observed Sashia.

Darius nodded. "We also found half a dozen dead goats."

"Can you tell what tribe or clan he's from?" asked Cyrus.

"The Pasturas use a dye similar to this yellow color," Darius indicated the man's clothing.

"Sashia, can you learn anything from him that can

225

help us identify him?"

Sashia bent down to examine the crumpled form. "He appears to be in his late teens. No beard, and he has most of his teeth, but his wisdom teeth haven't come in yet. He was probably about the height of Restus."

Restus had just rejoined them after conferring with Topec.

"That should help narrow it down. Darius, send riders out to all the nearby villages and encampments. Find out if anyone with that description is missing."

"The remains of a fire and some bones were found near him. That could be how the company was enticed to camp here. The boy may have killed a goat and cooked it," Darius added before leaving to relay Cyrus' order.

"That's what a goatherd would've done if a full-grown goat had broken a leg this far from home," Sashia explained. "But Sorin was adamant he must follow orders. I find it hard to believe, if he wasn't in on the plot, that he would have stopped. Since he is dead, it seems unlikely he was part of it."

"We may never know now," murmured Cyrus. "Topec!"

The captain came striding quickly toward the prince. "Yes, my lord?"

"Where were Sorin's sentries found? Were there any men farther away from the others?"

"No, they were all approximately in the same place. The sentries would've rushed back to the camp as soon as it started and tried to wake the others."

"Were the soldiers in their bedrolls, or did it look like they were attempting to flee?"

"Now that you mention it, most of them were still wrapped in their blankets. Why didn't they run?"

Cyrus looked at Sashia. She nodded back at him somberly. "Hemlock is plentiful along the roadside this time of year."

"Is there any way to tell if the soldiers had been poisoned to prevent them from fleeing in time?"

Sashia returned to the corpse of the goatherd. She examined his hands more closely and noticed some redness and blistering around the fingers. "This man handled something that irritated his skin. Hemlock can do that. Anyone who ingested it would have been unconscious or paralyzed by the time the rock slide started. The sentries might've returned to camp as soon as they began to feel ill. That could also be why they decided not to continue their journey that night."

"This brings up more questions than it answers," complained Topec. "If the goatherd poisoned them, why stay and be crushed by the rocks? If Lady Sashia was the primary target, why continue with the plan?"

"I don't believe we were meant to think of poison. If Sashia had—" Cyrus choked, and Sashia took a step closer and held his hand, "—if Sashia had been among them, I would not have kept a clear head. I would've run right back to my father and—I don't know what I might've done."

"If the aim was to alienate Cyrus and King Kalin, they achieved it, just by making it look like he wanted me dead."

"The poison also ensured no one would be left to explain what really happened. Sorin cannot be questioned. Neither can the goatherd, which makes me think he was used as well," mused Restus.

"Hemlock has leaves similar to several other edible plants. Someone could have given them to the Pastura and told him they were something else." The last rays of sun were sinking over the plains. Sashia shivered as the air began to turn colder.

Cyrus laced his fingers through hers. "There's nothing more we can do here tonight. Let's get a good night's sleep and hope Darius' messengers will tell us something useful tomorrow."

CHAPTER NINETEEN

The next morning, Cyrus reluctantly allowed Sashia to return to Udin's camp to check on Marthi. Since the clean-up was complete, plenty of soldiers were available to accompany her, and she and Lang found themselves riding with a large escort. Cyrus had sent a rider to Kassius to collect more ointments with strict instructions to avoid the palace and tell no one, even Kassius, what had transpired. Sashia gathered what she could from the supplies she'd insisted Cyrus send with every patrol and found enough to last until the messenger returned.

Baria met her when she entered the camp. "Marthi is in a great deal of pain, my lady."

"I will do what I can for her," assured Sashia.

Baria lowered her voice. "Her betrothal has been broken off. Hanin, Udin's cousin, came to tell us this morning his son will not marry her. She is quite distressed."

Sashia tsked. Baria left her at the entrance to the tent. Another girl was sitting with Marthi.

"Are you the healer?"

"I am."

"Do you need my help?" the girl asked nervously.

Sashia shook her head. "Run along if you do not wish to see." She had no use for squeamish assistants. "How are you, Marthi?"

The stricken youth turned piercing dark eyes toward her. "Is it true I cannot have children?"

"Certainly not," Sashia replied forcefully. "The scratches on your abdomen parted the skin, but your organs are intact." She took a breath and prepared to explain everything in detail, but more gently. She began unwrapping the bandages and used her words to distract Marthi from the pain.

"The worst injuries are far above the womb. It's too early to tell if the damage to your breasts will affect your ability to produce milk. That's never guaranteed anyway," she said somewhat bitterly.

"My betrothed refuses to marry me now," Marthi's eyes teared up. She gritted her teeth as Sashia began to treat the wounds. "Father doesn't want to insist, so he released him from his promise. If everyone thinks I cannot have children, no one will want to marry me."

"Perhaps he's too shallow to desire anyone as scarred as you will be. That may be your biggest obstacle."

Marthi stared at her mangled hands as Sashia rebandaged them. "What about my hands?"

"You may lose the use of these two fingers," Sashia pointed to the index and middle fingers of her left hand. "The tendons were severed. They will have scars, but you should not be hampered more than that. You are lucky someone came along before the lion killed you."

"It was my brother, Jairus. He was on guard duty. He's an excellent shot with an arrow. Aaah!"

"Sorry. That's the last one." Sashia studied Marthi. "You fought back admirably. I imagine it was very painful. You must have great strength of mind to have kept your arms up in spite of it."

"It happened so fast. All I could think about was living to bear children and raise a family. It's all I've ever wanted to do."

"And you will. Someone will want a strong, brave woman like you. I'll give your mother some herbs to steep for your pain." Sashia smiled and took her leave. After repeating the instructions for the girl's care and giving Baria the remaining salve, she and her escort headed back to Cyrus' camp.

"How is the girl?" asked Lang.

"She has a strong will. I believe she will recover."

"Ah, good."

"I don't suppose you're looking for a wife, are you Lang?"

Lang was horrified. "Oh, no, my lady! I'm perfectly content as I am."

"Pity," Sashia smiled.

Lang had been helping Darius clear the rubble the last few days. Sashia glanced over at him and saw his hands were full of scrapes and cuts. He was no longer used to manual labor.

"Lang, have you treated your hands?"

"What? Oh, this is nothing, my lady. Your ointments were needed elsewhere."

"No, Lang. You must take care of yourself if you expect to be able to help others. Clean them and rinse them with some wine, if nothing else."

"Yes, my lady."

As they rode into the camp, two riders joined them from the north. They nodded at Sashia but did not slow their pace. The messengers rode directly up to Cyrus and dismounted. Sashia followed suit.

"My lord, one of the Pastura encampments was missing a young man. His father rode with us to view the body, and he confirms it is his son," one of them reported.

"Was he able to provide us with any useful information?"

The messenger shook her head. "Only that his son had a simple mind, was anxious to please, and was easily persuaded by others."

"Someone could've given him the hemlock and asked him to put it in a stew," Sashia interjected.

The messenger nodded. "He would have happily complied without asking what it was."

"That puts us no closer to finding the one responsible," Cyrus stated with frustration. "You felt the man was telling the truth?"

"We did, my lord. His grief was profound. He cursed anyone who would take advantage of such a good, kind boy. He did mention he'd been in the area himself two weeks ago and noticed nothing out of the ordinary."

Cyrus thanked the messengers and dismissed them.

"Cyrus," Sashia pulled him aside. "As intriguing as this mystery is, I feel I'm needed at home. I must see how Tarin is for myself and make sure he's unharmed. There's nothing more I can do here."

"You do much for me by your presence alone," he said with feeling. "I cannot leave here yet."

"I know, but I must go," she insisted.

Cyrus drew her into his arms and held her tightly. "I've not completely cleared my father from connection to these events in my mind. You could face more danger on your return."

"Have you sent any messengers to him?"

"No, and he will find that suspicious, especially if he's heard reports from other sources."

"Then it's even more urgent I return and set the

facts before him myself, as Topec suggested. Let me hear what he has to say and send a message back to you."

"There is something else you must do, Sashia."

"What?"

He looked at her seriously. "You must find out how the Magi knew of this plot. They must know more than we do. Why haven't they told us everything they know?"

Sashia quailed. "They cannot have anything to do with this!"

"But they knew, Sashia."

She nodded. "I will see what I can find out, but I don't know how to contact the safe-house in Sherish. I may have to write to Beyorn in Shelomoh and wait for an answer. That could take weeks, or months."

"Do whatever you can. I'm sure Topec will bring it up to me as soon as you leave."

"He still doesn't trust me?"

"It's just his nature to be protective." He kissed the top of her head. "And it's my nature to be protective of you. I can never tell you too many times how much I love you. Be careful."

"I will."

∞∞∞

The return journey was uneventful. Cyrus sent Restus to accompany her and Lang, along with as many soldiers as he could spare.

"Restus, find the king and let him know I wish to speak to him," Sashia ordered as soon as they rode through the palace gates. "I must find Mother and Tarin."

After interrogating the first servant she came across, Sashia was informed Tarin was with her mother and Pannai in her rooms.

"Tarin!" She cried when she saw him.

Mother quickly handed the baby to Sashia. "You're back earlier than expected. Is everything alright?"

Sashia gave her mother a quick summary of what had occurred. "Has nothing unusual happened here?"

"No, nothing," Mother assured her with a worried expression.

Sashia sank into a chair and nuzzled her son's head. She sighed and her eyes stung with tears of relief. Before she could gather her thoughts, a fist pounded on the door, and it was thrown open to admit King Kalin.

He stomped into the apartment with his bushy eyebrows furrowed and a scowl on his craggy face. Pannai scooped up her daughter and fled to an adjoining room. Mother glanced at Sashia, who nodded at her, and she slipped out the door after the other woman.

"You are well?" he demanded.

Sashia opened her mouth to reply, but he launched a barrage of questions at her.

"What has happened to my men? They should have returned by now. Why hasn't Cyrus sent a report? Why did you refuse the escort? I am hearing conflicting reports, and I insist you explain!"

Sashia set the facts before him as clearly and concisely as she could. The king paced up and down the room in fury.

"What nonsense! Who is behind this?"

"You didn't order Sorin to camp in that spot?"

"Of course not!" He bellowed. "I merely told him to take the quickest route."

"I think, my lord, it may be very important to note what you have heard already, and who you have heard it from."

Kalin stopped pacing and frowned even deeper. He tugged on his beard in concentration. "The first news I heard was that you were seen at the Marusene Oasis."

Sashia was surprised. "Who told you that?"

"I don't remember." He paused. "It was at a forum of merchants and tribal leaders. I spoke with many people."

"Was Yarin there? Maybe he heard something."

Kalin went to the door and ordered one of the guards to find Yarin.

"Who told us Sashia was at the oasis?" the king barked when his advisor arrived.

"Let me think. A young man named Rolind was there representing the consolidated tribes from the Granite Mountains. Not many came from the west since so many of them were wiped out by the Breakers. The harbor master from the port, representatives from the guilds, Aloysius and Udin from the Augers, several of our more prominent tradesmen. Iban, of the Pastura."

"No one but the Augers would have come from that direction, so one of them must have said something," interjected Kalin.

"I believe the person who said it was standing behind me. It cannot have been Udin. I was speaking to him at the time, and I specifically remember him frowning when Lady Sashia's name was mentioned," recalled Yarin.

"One of my captains repeated it to me later when we were discussing that I'd heard nothing from either Sorin or Cyrus."

"Which captain?" queried Sashia.

"Javan," Kalin replied tersely. Javan was Kalin's spymaster. He knew everything that went on. "I will find out how he knew. I will also track down the guard who gave Lotus the letter and interrogate him. Let me handle it from here." He started to leave and turned back. "Why did you say you parted from Captain Sorin?"

She hadn't said why. She had left out everything to do with the Magi. "Sorin was being extremely provoking and obtuse. He wouldn't explain why we had to leave the river so early. After the episode with the snake, I was already touchy and disinclined to indulge him. You know I can be obstinate, my lord."

"Well I do." He nodded curtly at her, the only indication he gave he was glad she was still alive, and stalked swiftly out of the room.

Yarin wasn't in a hurry to depart and raised an eyebrow at Sashia quizzically.

"Is there something else, Yarin?"

"I would like to hear the rest of the story, my lady."

"Would you? Do you know of any Magi in the city, Yarin?"

Yarin clasped his hands behind his back and frowned slightly. "That is not something I can discuss with you, my lady."

"Whyever not?"

"You evidently don't wish to tell me anything either."

Sashia sighed. "You know I studied with the Magi?"

"I know."

She told him about her encounter at the city gate.

"So the Magi must have discovered something about the plot and knew you were in danger."

"But why speak in riddles? Why all the secrecy?"

"From what I understand, the Magi never reveal themselves unless required to do so. It depends on their specific mission. If the source of the threat was unknown, the Mage might not have felt able to speak freely."

Sashia looked at Yarin with new eyes. "You seem to know a great deal about the Magi."

Yarin shifted his feet. "I believe if there was anything you needed to know, they would find a way to communicate it to you."

"Uh-huh."

"If you will excuse me, my lady, I must return to my duties." Yarin bowed and left.

Sashia considered what she'd learned. It was very little, but it was important. First and foremost, she was convinced King Kalin had *not* orchestrated the trap that killed Sorin and his men. His outrage appeared quite sincere. Second, Yarin knew something about the Magi, but wouldn't say what. However, she instinctively trusted Yarin.

She sent for Restus and made him memorize a message to deliver to Cyrus. She didn't trust anyone else to relay it, and if Kalin was not the threat, she should be safe in the palace.

"I will leave first thing in the morning, Lady Sashia."

When he left, Gaia returned from a nap followed by Mother, Pannai, and Marri, and the rest of the day was spent with the women and children. Sashia wished there was something else she could do to help, but it seemed she'd done all that could be done. Now she would enjoy time with her son.

∞∞∞

In the middle of the night, Sashia was startled awake by the sound of yelling in the passage. She shrugged on a robe and opened the door to find Lang and Javan standing over the body of a guard. Lang's mouth hung open and his eyes were as big as

237

coconuts, so Sashia turned to the spymaster whose bloodstained sword was still extended. He was focused on something behind Lang, so she pivoted and saw Restus running through the arch at the opposite end of the passage.

"Excuse me, my lady," Javan apologized, breathing heavily, as he wiped off his blade and returned it to its scabbard. "This is Nerod, the guard who gave Lotus the blank message. The king asked me to find him, and I've been searching for him all day."

Sashia bent down and felt for a pulse, but the man was clearly dead. It appeared he'd been stabbed in the back and had fallen forward.

"Why did you kill him? We wanted to question him."

Lang found his voice. "I woke at the sound of footsteps and saw the guard run around the corner. He—he was running at me with a dagger in his hand."

"I believe he was planning to assassinate you, my lady," explained Javan, "but as you can see, I have eliminated the threat."

"Indeed. Thank you."

Lang had been sleeping outside her door and would've been the first killed if Javan hadn't been there.

Restus picked up a dagger that had fallen not far from the body.

"I'll get someone to clean this up," Javan waved at the corpse and walked away jauntily.

Sashia turned to Restus. "I expected you to be sleeping since you are leaving in the morning."

"After all that's taken place, Lady Sashia, sleep was impossible. I've been pacing the corridors restlessly waiting for dawn. I happened to see Javan chasing the guard and thought I might head them off."

"Thank you for your vigilance, my friend. Go and

get some sleep."

Restus nodded wearily and headed back to the barracks. Sashia checked on Tarin and found him sleeping soundly. Then she sat down next to Lang to wait for the body to be removed. She couldn't allow him to sleep *inside* the room. There were enough raised eyebrows at the fact she had a manservant instead of a maidservant already. So, she stayed with him in the passage instead. Restus was right. Sleep was impossible.

∞∞∞

It was over a month before Cyrus returned. Sashia wrote to him every day, if only to let him know all was well. Sashia wrote letters to Shelomoh, but she knew it would be several weeks before she could hear anything.

King Kalin sent messengers all over the country with alarming frequency. Mother returned home.

Sashia loved her son, but she chaffed at the inaction. She was also getting annoyed with Pannai's daughter, Marri. The toddler was into everything, and Pannai rarely disciplined her.

"No, Marri, that's Tarin's." Sashia remonstrated when Marri pulled away the blanket he was lying on. The girl cried and pouted when Sashia took it back.

"Here, baby. Have a sweet," Pannai handed her a piece of candied date.

The girl took the sweet and sucked on it sullenly, getting her fingers, and subsequently everything else she touched, sticky. Sashia felt unable to rebuke Pannai for her parenting technique. She needed Pannai, and the woman knew it. They danced around each other all day in a semblance of politeness that strained Sashia's nerves.

It didn't help that the palace wasn't Pannai's home. She and Marri took walks when the weather was nice, played in the garden while Tarin was sleeping, and Pannai brought her mending, but there was only so much to do. The palace servants did everything else.

At least Pannai was only there during the day now. The rest of the time, Sashia and Gaia had to coax Tarin to drink the goat's milk.

When Cyrus rode through the gate, Sashia was there to meet him, and she fell into his arms. "Oh, Sashia, I missed you!" He whispered tender, intimate words of love into her ear. "Where is Tarin?"

Pannai had finished nursing him by the time they returned, and she took Marri and went home for the evening.

"I will give you some privacy," smiled Gaia, and she left as well.

Tarin was sleepy, and he yawned and stretched his little arms.

"He's grown so much already!"

"He smiles now," Sashia grinned.

"I've missed too much." Cyrus held his son close and gazed at him in wonder.

"How is Darius? Have you discovered anything further about the rock slide?"

Cyrus shook his head. "There are no new leads. Every trail ended in death." The hint of frustration in his voice was tempered by the love he felt for Tarin.

So many questions waited on the tip of her tongue, but she didn't want to badger her husband when he'd just arrived home. Cyrus went over to the bed and lay down with Tarin asleep on his chest. Sashia went around the other side and snuggled up next to him.

"Everything at the border appears to be under control. A band of Artylians stole some goats near one of the passes, but King Ilytan has promised to deal with them. The Augers are worried about the security of their silver shipments, so we'll provide them additional escorts. The Pastura wanted to graze the hills near the mines, and that was causing some discord, but it's been resolved. Father has sanctioned them for being implicated in the rock slide."

"Sanctioned them? Why?"

"It happened on their land, and one of their people was clearly involved, knowingly or not. They'll have to pay higher taxes and give up some of their land to the Augers for mining."

Cyrus closed his eyes.

"Darius will be able to handle the patrol on his own now?"

"I left Topec with him."

"Ah."

Cyrus grunted. "I demoted his previous captain after I saw a female scout leaving his tent early in the morning. That's not the kind of influence someone Darius' age needs."

"What about the woman?"

"She was sent home. She was with child." Cyrus sighed. "Before the battle of Tull Pass, we had no women on patrols, but several wanted to join afterwards. We accepted a few of them, orphans or young widows with no children, as slingers or scouts if the heads of their families permitted it, but we're going to have to think seriously about how it will work going forward."

Sashia could see how easily it could become an issue, especially between members of the same unit. "Will they marry?"

"I don't know. It's up to her father. If he refuses to let them marry, he can require a bride price."

Sashia knew how difficult it was to fight a strong

attraction to someone. "Would you have taken me into your 'tent' that day at the Tull Pass, if I had told you I loved you?" Slowly, she traced the strong, calloused fingers holding their small son.

"I wanted to, but it wouldn't have been wise without first gaining my father's approval to marry you. If we'd been intimate then, it would've been impossible for me to let you go. It's impossible now." He turned his head to meet her eyes.

Sashia leaned over and kissed him.

"I am happy with how things worked out," he said softly.

"As am I." Sashia carefully lifted Tarin, placed him in his cradle, and returned to the bed.

CHAPTER TWENTY

The Seventeenth Year of the Reign of King Kalin of Berush

"Are you going to eat the after-birth this time?"

"I'll do anything anyone tells me will have the slightest chance of enabling me to nurse longer," Sashia huffed. "Just tell them to cook it. I doubt I could manage it raw."

Mother handed over her lovely new granddaughter and carried out Sashia's instructions. They had already collected a vast array of herbs reputed to increase milk production. If a woman was nursing, she was less likely to become pregnant, at least in the first few months. Sashia's monthly cycle had never been regular, so she had little hope of being able to manage it that way. At least barrenness wasn't an issue.

Only a week after Tarin's first birthday, Onia was born. Cyrus was as pleased with his first daughter as he'd been with his son.

"She's gorgeous, Sashia! She'll be the most beautiful princess in Berushese history!"

Sashia smiled. Cyrus was an incredible father.

"I was so excited when Darius was born," he continued. "I wanted a brother so badly, but we were so far apart in age. And I hardly ever see my sister."

"We should send for her. Now that I'm here, she should be with us."

Cyrus' eyes lit up. "Are you sure? Now that Uncle Mathis is gone, my aunt is going to live with a daughter and can no longer care for her, so we would have to make new arrangements anyway."

"Absolutely."

Fashima had been living with her aunt and uncle since the queen died shortly after her birth six years ago.

"I'll speak to Father about it," he said with satisfaction. "Will you need someone besides Gaia to help with so many little ones around?"

"From what I hear, Fashima is a very responsible, serious child. She shouldn't be much trouble and may be able to help. After Pannai, I am going to be more careful whom I employ."

Pannai had been dismissed when Tarin was six months old. Gaia had been down with a cold, and Sashia had returned from a walk to find Marri stuffing a cloth into Tarin's mouth to keep him quiet while Pannai slept. After that, he drank goat's milk.

"Have you found a new wet-nurse?"

"Yes. Madia had several for me to choose from, since we thought we'd probably need one. This one is a widow who can stay in the palace as long as necessary. Her son is Tarin's age."

"That sounds perfect."

∞∞∞

The new wet nurse lasted a month before Sashia dismissed her for fooling around with the guards. She

244

was an incorrigible flirt who even tried to seduce Cyrus. Sashia only produced enough milk to nurse twice a day and supplemented with goat milk. No matter what she tried, that was all she could do, and when Onia was four months old, she dried up.

"No more wet nurses!" Sashia declared when Cyrus asked her about it. Fortunately, both her children were flourishing with the goat milk. Tarin was already eating solid food. "Fashima adores her niece and nephew. She is better help than any adult. Plus, Lang loves to play with Tarin now that he's a little older."

Cyrus had spent most of the previous year in Sherish, for which Sashia was grateful. The majority of his day was occupied with correspondence, meetings, and sitting as judge for the local citizens. With Sashia's input, he also created guidelines for female soldiers.

"I know this has been hard on you, to have two children so close together, to have difficulty nursing. If we—if we need to sleep in separate rooms for a while, we can do that. Tell me what you need."

"I want you beside me," Sashia hugged him, "but I don't want any more children! At least not for a couple of years. We'll just have to be more careful."

Cyrus chuckled. "That's easier said than done. You tried counting days the last time."

"There are other things we can do."

"No herbs that could harm you or a child," he admonished sternly.

"Oh no, nothing like that." She explained to him what she meant.

"I will do whatever you say. I love you." He kissed her amorously. "Let's try some of your suggestions right now." He winked.

"How are your lessons going, Fashima?" Sashia had found a tutor who was teaching her reading and sums.

"Good, but I would rather play with Tarin and Onia."

"You are a great helper, but you must not neglect your own learning."

Fashima nodded absently and joined her nephew and niece on the floor. Having other children around had helped her adjust to her new life. Lang let Tarin ride around on his back, pretending to be a horse, while Gaia snoozed in a chair. Tarin squealed and giggled. Fashima dangled a toy above Onia for her to bat at.

Sashia smiled. A messenger brought in some letters for her along with a small package. A quick glance showed they were from Shelomoh. One from Farouk, one from Beyorn and Dorthi, and one, surprisingly, from Aerick. Their replies took much longer to arrive than anticipated. She perused them quickly. The first two were full of news of friends, updates on medical procedures and other mundane matters. Aerick's was different.

Lady Sashia, Princess of Berush:

As you are aware, the mission of the Magi is to promote peace through knowledge and understanding. When asked, we attempt to promote reconciliation and mediate disagreements. If we can prevent harm to anyone, we will.

To this end, I have authorized certain persons to communicate with you if they deem it necessary. You are in a unique position, and you may have opportunities in the future to promote peace within

*the country of Berush. Already you have helped your
people by sharing with them what you have learned
about healing.*

*There are always those who do not wish for
peace and strive for their own ends. Seek to
understand the motives driving those around you.*

*I have sent several scrolls to you which you
might find useful. Keep* The Heredity and Breeding
of the Goat *handy.*

Aerick

Sashia laid the letter down, puzzled by its
contents. Why was he so cryptic? The Magi must
believe it was not safe to communicate by letter. She
opened the package and found several scrolls,
including the one mentioned. The scroll was written
in Berushese, and it detailed the lineage of various
breeds of goats going back centuries. It also listed the
names of prominent breeders and their tribes.

Over the next few days, she familiarized herself
with the text, but gained no particular insight. Cyrus
was concerned when she showed him Aerick's letter,
but he agreed there seemed to be no action to take.

"My lady, there is a woman here to see you," Lang
announced one morning.

"Show her in."

A well-endowed young woman with a worried
expression entered the room. "My lady, my name is
Coria. I heard you might need a wet-nurse. My own
child died of a fever, and I have no husband or family.
I hoped you might be able to employ me?" she asked
hopefully.

"Well, I had pretty much decided to do without
one." Sashia looked the woman over. "I'm sorry for
the loss of your child. How long has it been?"

"Three days. I helped out a woman with twins on

the journey to the palace."

"You've had no fever yourself?"

"No, my lady."

"Describe to me your child's symptoms."

The woman described typical symptoms of fever. Sashia didn't want to expose her children to anything, but it was probably something to which the woman had already developed resistance. "Can you give me the name of the woman with the twins?"

Coria gave Sashia the information, and Sashia sent Lang to the house in the city where the mother was staying to find out if the twins were well and verify the woman's story. When he returned, he reported everything was fine.

"We will try it out and see how it goes," decided Sashia. "This is Onia, my youngest. She's the one who needs nursing."

Fortunately, Onia was not a fussy baby, and she easily took to the new nurse. Coria seemed to dote on her. A week later, everything seemed to be running smoothly, and Sashia started to relax.

"My lady, a runner from the town sent you a message," Lang handed her a scrap of paper.

Sashia unfolded it and saw a list of numbers in sets of three. The format was familiar, but she had to think for a moment. Then it came to her. When she left Shelomoh, the Magi had been working on ways to communicate with coded messages. This one only worked if two people had copies of the same scroll. The copies had to be meticulously done, so every line, every word was the same, but the Magi were experts at this. And Aerick had given her the key.

Sashia unrolled *The Heredity and Breeding of the Goat* and studied the first set of numbers.

"Here is your lunch, my lady." Coria set a tray in front of her. Fashima was eating with her tutor, and the other children had already been fed.

"Thank you," she replied absently. The first set of numbers was five, eleven, and three. She picked up a spoon with her right hand and moved her left finger down the fifth column, to the eleventh line, and found the third word. Then she froze. The first word in the message was *Coria*, a common name in the Pastura tribe.

Sashia put the spoon down and turned to scrutinize the wet-nurse. Coria was looking at her anxiously, wringing her apron. Sashia acted quickly. She scooped up Tarin and handed him to Lang, then she stood between Coria and the cradle where Gaia was rocking Onia.

"Coria, what have you done?"

Coria's lower lip trembled and she started to cry. "I—I had to!" she cried and bolted out of the door.

Sashia ran after her. "Stop her!" she yelled.

A guard farther down the corridor attempted to block Coria's way, but she turned into a side room. A room with a balcony.

Sashia and the guard rushed in after her and arrived just in time to see her throw herself over the railing. A sickening thud soon followed. Sashia made her way to the courtyard as quickly as she could and pushed the bystanders aside.

It didn't take a healer to know the woman was dead. Sashia inspected her pockets but found nothing. Then she saw her hands. They had red blotches. She sped back to her own room and arrived out of breath.

"Did anyone touch my food?"

"Of course not, my lady. I wouldn't eat your meal." Lang still stood exactly where she had left him holding her squirming son.

"No one went near it," affirmed Gaia.

Cautiously, Sashia inspected the stew with her spoon. There were several chunks of white vegetable that could be hemlock root. She deciphered the rest of the message.

Coria met man from east.

The man must have given her the poison and the instructions. At least they were narrowing down the source of the threat. Cyrus was gone for two weeks to meet with Darius, so Sashia took the stew and reluctantly set off in search of her father-in-law. She encountered him in the passage.

"What is going on?" he roared.

"My lord, I was just coming to find you. May we speak in your study?"

He motioned her in, and she told him what had happened, minus the note from the Magi.

"So, you saw her hands, called her on it, and she lost her head?"

"Yes, and it unfortunately prevents us from questioning her."

Kalin frowned. "So, it appears someone still wants to eliminate you. You suspect the stew is poisoned?"

"I fear so. She must have added the hemlock root when no one was looking."

Kalin called a guard. "Feed this to one of the dogs. We will find out for sure."

"Coria said she came from the eastern mountains, but that's all I know about her." Sashia gave Kalin the name of the woman with twins who recommended Coria.

"I will find out everything there is to find out, I assure you. Whoever is behind this is undermining my authority and scheming behind my back! I will not have it! I will not have people attempting murder under my very nose! No matter how pestilential the object of their plot." He turned up the corner of his mouth at her.

Sashia raised her eyebrow. Over the last two years they had come to grudgingly tolerate and respect one another. His jabs at her now were more good-natured than resentful.

"At least it seems unlikely the originator of this plot has any more spies inside the castle."

"Why do you say that, my lord?"

"We've had no incidents since Nerod was killed, and Coria was brought in from outside."

That made sense. "Did you find out who mentioned I'd been at the oasis during the forum last year?"

"I did. It led nowhere."

"But who was it?"

"It was Aloysius, chief of the Augers."

"His nephew must have told him, though he said he wouldn't."

Kalin waved his hand. "As I said, not helpful. In the meantime, I will get you a food-taster."

"I don't—"

"No argument! The culprit is trying to remain nameless. Undiscovered. Make it look like an accident, poison by mistake, rock slide, snake bite. To what end I don't know, but I will find out! Leave it to me."

∞∞∞

If Kalin found anything out, he didn't tell Sashia. When Cyrus returned, he and his father spent several hours in the study in heated discussion. Sashia prodded Yarin into mediating so they wouldn't lose their tempers. Raised voices were heard anytime anyone ventured near the room.

When Cyrus entered their apartment that night,

he was in a sour mood. However, as soon as he saw Sashia, he gathered her in his arms and kissed her, his anger dissipating into relief.

"I'm so glad you're alright."

"Was the stew poisoned?"

"Yes," he replied darkly.

"What are we going to do?"

"I suggested offering a reward for information, letting everyone know the king condemns these actions and will not tolerate it, but father believes that would show weakness and not inspire confidence in his rule. He seems to think the Pasturas are behind it again. He's going to give in to the Auger's request to mine further into the mountains and place greater restrictions on the Pasturas. Iban will be furious. He denies any involvement."

Onia began to cry and Sashia went to pick her up. "To think, I let that woman suckle my daughter!"

"There was no way you could've known."

Sashia told him about the coded message. "I cannot trust anyone anymore."

"You must persuade the Magi to tell you everything they know."

Sashia shook her head. "They have their own way of doing things. They may not know any more than we do. If I needed to know anything else, they would tell me."

"I can at least hunt down the traveler Coria spoke to."

Sashia doubted he would find anything. She still couldn't believe anyone wanted to kill her. *Seek to understand the motives driving those around you*, Aerick had said. *Look at results*, had been Restus' advice. Her thoughts swirled around in her head, almost forming an answer and then fading into nothing. The solution was so close, but she couldn't grasp it. She felt the strength of Cyrus next to her and leaned into him. She was safe here, for now.

CHAPTER TWENTY-ONE

The Nineteenth Year of the Reign of King Kalin of Berush

"Push!" Madia instructed.

Mother had been unable to attend her for this birthing, and Madia had found another midwife to help her. However, Cyrus insisted on being in the room. At this point, Sashia didn't care who was there. She only wanted the baby out!

Her first two pregnancies had been easy compared to this one. She'd been sick every day for the first three months. Madia had been afraid she'd lost too much weight, but she'd gained it all back and then some. Her feet had swollen, and she'd spent the last month in bed. At least her body had had two years to recover since her last pregnancy.

"Squeeze my hand," encouraged Cyrus.

Sashia pushed. "Eeeah!"

"Another healthy boy!" declared Madia.

Sashia cried.

Cyrus washed his new son himself and handed him to his wife. She took him and cried some more.

"He's perfect, darling," Cyrus told her, not

understanding her tears.

She didn't want to hold him. She didn't want him at all, and it made her feel terrible.

The worst part was that Varus couldn't tolerate goat's milk. The third time he threw it up, Sashia wanted to throw him in frustration and had to lay him down and take a walk. She cried in vexation at the thought of having to hire another wet nurse. As with the previous two, she had a little milk, but it wasn't nearly enough.

Cyrus fretted and worried over her. "I've sent for a few camels. Perhaps Varus will be able to drink their milk."

Cyrus stayed with Sashia the first two weeks to help her with the children. He played and laughed with Tarin, now three, and Onia, who was two and into everything. Sashia watched them but didn't participate. She felt listless and hollow, barely able to manage a smile.

Finally, one morning, Cyrus was called away.

"The king requests that you look into a situation at the city garrison," relayed a guard.

"Will you be alright without me?" Cyrus asked Sashia.

"I'll be fine."

"Do you want to come with me?" he asked hopefully.

She shook her head. "I don't feel very well."

"Promise me you'll let Gaia watch the children for a while and take a walk."

"I suppose."

Cyrus kissed her and left.

Tarin and Onia made a terrible mess at lunch. For some reason, they decided today was a perfect day to throw all their food on the floor. Fashima came to the rescue and cleaned up Onia while Sashia gave Tarin a quick bath. Gaia fed Varus his camel's milk, which he was better able to digest, and Fashima coaxed Onia to lie down for a nap before returning to her tutor.

Onia fell asleep, but Tarin refused to lie down. Sashia hated to call a maid to help with the children. After Coria, she didn't trust anyone other than Lang and Gaia, who had served the royal family her whole life. Sashia felt she should be able to do more herself, but she was so tired! Right now all she wanted to do was scream.

"I can take him, my lady," offered Lang.

"Thank you. I'll take Cyrus' advice and go for a walk. Perhaps up to the roof."

Sashia wandered the halls as if in a trance and finally made it to the rooftop garden. She hadn't left the palace in months. Her difficult pregnancy, combined with the fact Kalin and Cyrus had never discovered who was behind the plot to kill her, had kept her confined—just as she'd feared when Cyrus first expressed an interest in her.

She took several slow, deep breaths of fresh air. There was a cool breeze, and the sun was shining brightly. She strolled over to the wall and peered over the edge. This side of the palace overlooked the lake. There was a thin strip of rocks along the bottom of the wall, and then sparkling, blue water.

The sun went behind a cloud, and Sashia felt a chill. The water called to her. It looked peaceful and calm. She climbed up on the wall for a better view. It was a long way down. She felt a strange urge to jump, to escape. Why did she want to escape?

"Sashia!"

She heard someone calling her name. The voice sounded far away, as if at the other end of a tunnel. Who was it?

"Sashia!" the voice called desperately.

She turned to look. She knew who that was. It was Cyrus.

"Sashia, give me your hand!" He was holding his hand out to her. Why did he seem so upset?

Her hand went out involuntarily, and he grabbed it and pulled her off the parapet. He caught her and crushed her against his chest.

"Sashia, what were you thinking?" He gave her a shake. "You cannot leave me! I need you!"

The fog in her brain started to clear. She grabbed at the folds of his tunic. "Help me, Cyrus. I don't know what's wrong with me."

He carried her back to their room and laid her on the bed. "Go get Madia or Kassius," he ordered Lang, "Whoever you can find first! Now!"

Lang jumped up from his vigil by Tarin, who had fallen asleep on the floor, and rushed to comply.

"I'll take Varus to my room," offered Gaia, and she crept softly out of the door.

Cyrus sat next to Sashia and held her hand.

"Sashia, tell me what to do! I love you! You know that. I'll do anything for you."

Sashia could only shake her head. She didn't know what to do. She couldn't think. She felt nothing. Except she was tired. Very tired.

Lang returned shortly with Kassius.. Cyrus told the healer how he'd found her.

"Lang told me she went for a walk on the roof, and I went to join her. She was—standing on top of the wall, looking down. She hasn't been herself."

Kassius examined her carefully, finding nothing. "How do you feel?" he asked.

"Tired."

"What have you eaten today?"

Sashia frowned. Had she eaten? "I don't remember."

"She ate a bite of her porridge, but that's all," put in Lang.

"How has her appetite been lately?" the healer looked at Cyrus.

"Now that you mention it, she hasn't been eating very much. What does that mean?"

"She is suffering from a malaise."

Sashia closed her eyes. *Malaise*. A word that meant no one knew what was wrong.

"What do we do?" asked Cyrus urgently.

"She shouldn't be left alone. Let her rest but try and coax her to eat and exercise. Move the older children to a room of their own."

"Will she be alright?"

"She's a strong woman. She'll come out of it, but only when she's ready."

Kassius sounded confident, but Sashia was skeptical. How could she come out of 'it' when she didn't even know what, or where, 'it' was?

The next several days all blurred together. Cyrus tried to get her to eat, but she wasn't interested. She sipped some broth to make him happy, but that was all she could do. Cyrus or Gaia would hand Varus to her twice a day to nurse, but he was still hungry afterward and cried incessantly. Fashima was better with him than anyone. She was able to get him to drink the camel's milk from a flask.

Sashia began to feel irritated by Cyrus' constant hovering.

"Darling, you must eat something."

"I'm not hungry."

Cyrus dipped some bread in a bowl of broth and held it in front of her. "You need to regain your strength. Please."

She pushed it away.

"Sashia, just a bite!"

"Leave me alone!"

Sashia knew in the back of her mind she was hurting her husband, and she felt guilty but powerless to do anything about it. The idea of food was repulsive.

"Come for a walk then."

Sashia turned away from him. He scooped her up, blankets and all, and walked toward the door. Tangled in the sheets, Sashia struggled in vain to squirm away. Cyrus carried her to an inner courtyard and set her on a bench in the sun.

"The fresh air will do you good." He sounded like he was trying to convince himself as much as her.

Sashia obstinately shrouded herself with the blanket.

"Come now, you're being childish," declared Cyrus with exasperation.

When she didn't respond, he got up and paced around the garden. After a while, he picked her up, carried her back to the room, and left her with Gaia and Lang.

"I'm going riding," he muttered.

"I will stay with her, my lord, never fear," Lang assured him.

"Give me the bread, Lang," Sashia relented as soon as he left.

Lang happily handed it to her. He'd taken on the task of tasting her food himself after King Kalin's suggestion. "That's it, my lady. That will help. Soon you will feel better."

Sashia wasn't so sure. Her stomach tied itself into knots as soon as the food touched her tongue. She forced herself to eat as much as she could. Then she fell asleep.

∞∞∞

Sashia heard voices, but she kept her eyes firmly closed. Kassius checked in on her and left a packet of herb for a tea. King Kalin even came to visit.

"Perk yourself up, woman! You cannot survive multiple assassination attempts and then allow yourself to waste away. You're doing their work for them."

She threw a pillow at him.

"Ha! I knew I could get a rise out of you!"

Cyrus resumed his normal routine but made sure she was never alone. Gaia and Fashima cared for the children with occasional help from the maids. Sashia remained indifferent and made no protest over additional servants in the room. She didn't care anymore.

When she heard Cyrus' anguished voice in the passage one afternoon, she felt a pain in her heart.

"She's never needed me the way I need her," he bemoaned.

She heard a muffled reply. Who was he talking to?

The door creaked open.

"Daughter."

"Mother!" Sashia burst into tears and held out her arms.

Mother crawled into the bed next to Sashia and embraced her tightly. "My baby."

Sashia hadn't cried since the day Varus was born. She'd felt empty and emotionless. Now she wept with abandon.

Mother stroked her hair and spoke soothingly to her. "Poor dear. I'm sorry I couldn't be here right away. Cyrus sent for me and told me I had to come, so I came as soon as I could."

"Mother, I have been awful!"

Mother tsked. "I can well believe that!"

"What's wrong with me?"

"Nothing, dear. Absolutely nothing."

∞∞∞

Dorthi had been right. There was no better nurse than a mother. Sashia gradually regained her appetite and began to feel like her normal self. Within a week, she was up and about, although she still felt random waves of unreasonable sadness.

"I am so sorry, Cyrus," she told him as they walked together in the inner courtyard.

"You had me worried, my love." He put his hand to her cheek. She leaned into him.

"Mother says many women feel like this after childbirth. I'd read about it before, but I never thought it would happen to me. Reading about it isn't the same as experiencing it. I am a healer, and I was not able to heal myself."

"No one can do everything. That's why you have family."

"And you were wrong, Cyrus."

"How so?"

"I may not always show it, but I do need you. Very much. Thank you for being there for me." She looked into his hazel eyes, and they affected her as powerfully as they ever had. The depth of emotion they revealed melted her heart, but they held more worry than normal.

"Sashia, I—I feel like I've failed you. I promised to take care of you, and I've done nothing but put you in all sorts of dangerous situations."

"Oh, Cyrus! You haven't failed me. You promised whatever happened, we would get through it, and we have."

"You don't regret giving up healing to be stuck in a

palace surrounded by children?"

"Not when they are *our* children. Not when I have *you*."

"You will always have me," he vowed fervently and followed it up with a kiss just as ardent.

CHAPTER TWENTY-TWO

"There's trouble with the Augers. I must ride out immediately with as many soldiers as I can muster."

"Trouble within the tribe, or with the Artylians? Or the Pasturas?"

"Within the tribe." Cyrus grimaced. "Two clan leaders involved in a dispute over a watering hole. Darius went to mediate and was taken hostage."

"What?"

Cyrus grimaced. "By our own people. Such a thing is unheard of. I must rescue Darius, and then I will ensure something like this will never happen again."

Sashia was about to ask how he would ensure that, but he continued.

"You are coming with me."

"I am?"

"There's always a need for healers after a battle. Darius may need attention. There's no telling what condition he's in, and I am not going to leave you."

Sashia knew he meant it. She turned to Mother.

"I will stay with the children. Gaia and I can handle it. With Fashima's help." Mother smiled down at the girl. "I told your father I would be gone at least a month, so I don't have to leave for another week."

"Alright. Let me gather my things." A trip like this meant she would no longer be able to nurse Varus twice a day.

"And Lang can stay and help your mother," Cyrus declared imperiously. "I'm taking care of you this time."

It had been three years since she'd taken her bag outside of the palace. Kassius came occasionally to consult, but she hadn't treated anyone but her own children since the last time she'd been east. Though she was anxious about Darius, she found herself looking forward to an adventure.

In under an hour, she was riding her little mare through the city gates next to Cyrus with nearly two hundred mounted warriors following behind them. Although Kalin and Cyrus had slowly been expanding their active military, less than half of them were career soldiers. Most of them were volunteers with a sword and a horse. The Berushese were extremely loyal to their king, which made the current situation all the more inexplicable.

As they rode, Sashia's morale rose and fell with the rolling of the landscape. One moment she was thrilled to be on a mission, the next she was missing her children. The sunshine would fill her with happiness, and the cool breeze would produce unfounded feelings of despair and hopelessness. Now that she knew the source of the changefulness, she could discount it and not give in to it, but it frustrated her to be so out of control of her own body.

"Where exactly are we going?"

Topec was riding next to her now. He'd been promoted and returned to Sherish to start a family.

"Almost due south toward the Silver Spur. Darius is being held by a man named Hanin. He wants the king to award him control of the spring there."

"Hanin. The name sounds familiar."

"He's the son of Aloysius, chief of the Augers."

"Ah, yes. What does this mean for the clan?"

"We have our orders."

Topec was being tight-lipped.

"What about Darius' men?"

"According to the messenger, everyone he took with him was killed, along with Faban, the head of the other clan disputing rights to the water."

Sashia tried to think who in Darius' current company she might have known. Restus had been given command of the western border. Most of Darius' soldiers were unknown to her.

That night, Cyrus, Topec, and several other men conferred together in the royal tent. Cyrus had told her she could not take part in it, and after much arguing, Sashia repaired to the campfire.

"I've been present for other planning sessions of this sort. Why can I not be present for this?"

"This is different, Sashia. It's going to be challenging enough without you there, trust me. I'll tell you about it afterwards."

Sashia fumed by the fire until the meeting was over. Her muscles were sore and aching after riding all day, adding to her perturbed mood. As soon as the others left the tent, Cyrus came looking for her.

"Come with me."

He took her arm and led her away from the camp, and they walked along the grassy dunes in the twilight.

"Hanin expects us to meet him tomorrow evening at the spring. We are not going to do that. We are going to attack his camp at midday."

Sashia digested this information and waited for him to elaborate, but he didn't. *Attack the camp . . .* "Why the camp?"

"Our first objective is to rescue Darius. According to our reports, he is being held there. The second objective," Cyrus took a deep breath, "is to eliminate Hanin and his clan. All of them."

"What? Wait—all of them? You mean . . ."

"All of them, Sashia."

Now she knew why he hadn't wanted her there for the discussion. She would have protested vigorously. Her eyes stung with tears, and she clenched her fists.

Cyrus took her by the shoulders and turned her to face him. "I know what you would say, Sashia, and on one side, you are correct. There are innocent people among them. There are children. But they have attacked and taken prisoner a member of the royal family. A prince of Berush."

"But these are our people! You were not this harsh on the Breakers!"

"Exactly. Our own people should know better. They should be loyal. This is treason, Sashia."

"Then just execute Hanin and those responsible!"

"That is not enough. We have to make an example of them."

Sashia wrenched herself out of his grasp and took a step away from him. She hugged herself tightly and ground her teeth.

"Darius took only half of his men. The rest went to look for him when he failed to return. That's how we know where he's being held. Hanin sent a messenger to my father with a list of demands."

"He doesn't know the king!" she scoffed.

"No." Cyrus was silent for a moment. "I will need you to be ready to see to Darius and attend to any wounded among my warriors, but there will be no wounded to care for among Hanin's people. Do you understand?"

"Oh, I understand well enough. I just cannot

believe it! I cannot believe it of you!"

"It's not something I want to do, but it must be done."

"It does not!"

"Sashia, it is *going* to be done, whether you like it or not. I must carry out the king's orders. I need you to accept that. I need you on my side."

"This is not a matter of sides. It's a matter of right and wrong!" She knew the consequences of defying Kalin would be dire, but they had risked his wrath before. They could do it again.

"Right and wrong, in this case, is determined by the king, and this time I agree with him."

Cyrus' words fell like blows of a hammer on Sashia's ears. She couldn't believe he could be so cold-hearted. He'd told his father executing the remaining Breakers would leave a black stain on the country. What would this do?

"Cyrus, think of Tarin."

"I am thinking of him. His future safety is foremost in my mind. I hope to hand him a country that is stable, prosperous, and peaceful. It will not be so if we allow people to get away with things like this."

Sashia could think of no other arguments. If the thought of his own son didn't sway him, nothing would.

"I will be ready to treat the wounded, but I do not accept this!" she declared and stomped back to their tent with tears blurring her vison. Her breasts were sore, reminding her of a missed feeding, little as it would have been. There were too many things happening at once, and her emotions threatened to overwhelm her again. She took several slow breaths in an attempt to get ahold of herself, trying unsuccessfully to focus her fury on the situation instead of her husband.

Cyrus followed a few moments later. Silently, she helped him remove his armor. She would save them both the embarrassment of asking one of the other soldiers to do it, but her hands trembled with rage. In spite of distress, his nearness made it difficult to think. His breaths were ragged, and she knew their disagreement was upsetting him. It was almost impossible to stay angry at him, though she tried.

She turned away from him, but her feet refused to go any farther. He slipped his arms around her waist and held her without speaking. Sashia turned and hugged him and cried.

∞∞∞

Early the next morning, the company broke camp and headed toward the Spur. Cyrus sent soldiers ahead to surround Hanin's base and make sure no one escaped. Darius' remaining men had been watching the camp, and a scout met them on the way with a report. Hanin was still there, and Darius had not been moved.

"Sashia, you will go with Viola and approach the camp from the rear. She is leading the squad that will fight through to Darius. As soon as the way is clear, go to him and assess his condition."

An archer a few years younger than herself nodded to her. Sashia had noticed her when they left Sherish and had thought she looked particularly anxious. Today, she was grim, but determined, as was everyone else. Her bow was already strung, and her quiver was full.

"Follow Viola's orders," he admonished and rode off with the rest of the company.

Sashia guided her horse into line behind Viola's little band. They took a wide circuit around the back of Hanin's camp. They left their horses a safe distance away and took up positions behind a group of boulders. One of Darius' men met them.

"That's where they're holding him." He pointed to a tent guarded by two armed men.

Viola peered at the sun. "Cyrus and Topec are waiting for our signal." She glanced at Sashia and explained, "They won't attack until they know we are ready to rescue him. Jacobus will stay with you until it is safe for you to join us. Ready?"

The soldiers with her drew their swords. Viola nocked an arrow, drew back the bowstring, and aimed at one of the guards. Almost before her first arrow hit its mark, she'd loosed a second.

Jacobus raised a horn to his lips and blew a long, loud blast. Answering horns echoed off of the rocks.

"Go!" Viola ordered. Her warriors raised their swords with a yell and charged into the camp while she covered them with her bow. Soldiers swarmed out of the surrounding hills into the encampment. Screams mixed with the clash of metal and the thunder of hundreds of feet.

As soon as Darius' tent was secure, Viola drew a short sword and ran down the slope. Jacobus gripped his blade, straining to join the fray. Viola peeked inside the tent, and then waved her sword in their direction.

"All clear, my lady. Let's go."

Sashia followed Jacobus quickly down the hill and into the tent while averting her eyes from the dead Augers. Viola was kneeling by Darius' side, but she rose quickly to let Sashia approach.

"He was tied to the cot. I cut him loose," Viola pointed to the discarded rope.

One look at him told Sashia his condition was not good. "I will need clean water," she ordered.

"As soon as we can get it," Viola assured her.

"Can you look at me, Darius?"

Darius turned slowly toward her, eyes half open. He squinted against the light flooding through the open tent flap. She felt his forehead; it was hot and feverish.

Darius' head was bandaged, and she carefully removed the cloth strips to inspect his wound. He'd received a blow to the side of his head. It was scabbing over, so she cleaned it and applied new bandages. After finding no other injuries, she prepared to do what she could for his fever.

There was some commotion outside, and Viola stepped out to investigate. At the same time, a gangly young man squeezed under the canvas at the back of the tent. Sashia instinctively went for her dagger, but she wasn't quick enough. The boy threw himself at Darius.

"Save me, my lord, save me!" he cried.

Viola reentered the tent and dragged the youth off the prince. Cyrus followed right behind her, his sword dripping with blood.

"Wait!" rasped Darius, as he raised a trembling hand and tried to sit up.

Viola had raised her blade to strike, but she paused when Darius spoke.

"He . . . was kind to me. He tried . . . to help me." Darius' hand fell to his side, exhausted by the effort it took to speak.

Cyrus shook his head. "He is under sentence of death. Hanin's line is to be wiped out. Completely."

"Prince Darius!" the boy sobbed. "Please!"

Darius rolled onto his side and struggled to raise himself on one elbow. "Cyrus, surely . . ."

"I am sorry, brother." He jerked his head toward the door. "Do it outside."

"There may be another way."

All eyes turned to Sashia.

She licked her lips nervously. "Hanin's line can be ended without killing him."

One face looked at her with hope, and the rest blinked, unable to grasp her meaning.

Understanding dawned in Cyrus' eyes, and he lowered his sword. "You mean . . . castrate him?"

Viola raised an eyebrow and held the Auger at arm's length like he was diseased.

Darius gaped. "That's worse than death!"

Sashia's eyes were locked on Cyrus. "Would that satisfy the king's order?"

"The words of it, I suppose," he agreed slowly. "Father won't like it."

"I'll serve you faithfully and do whatever you say if you will only spare me!"

"Is that what you wish, brother?" Cyrus asked Darius.

Darius nodded and fell back onto the cot. "I will take . . . responsibility for him. Father cannot deny me."

"He'll throttle you in your sleep," warned Viola.

"I would never do that!" the youth protested. Everyone ignored him.

"I'll risk it." Darius' voice was so weak it was barely audible.

There was silence for a moment while Cyrus debated. "Very well. Take him away and guard him until Sashia can see to him. I suppose you'll insist on doing it yourself."

"Of course." Sashia was glad he knew better than to argue with her.

Viola took the boy away, and Cyrus went to Darius' side and grasped his hand.

"How are you?"

"I am well, now that you are here." Darius sighed, and his body relaxed as the tension and fear of the last few days dissipated.

Cyrus turned to Sashia with concern. "How is he?"

"He's concussed and feverish, but he should recover quickly with close care. His clothing is soiled, so there will be some skin irritation. I need fresh water so I can clean him up."

Someone brought in water as soon as she said the words. Cyrus found a rag and carefully cleaned his sword, and then he helped Sashia remove Darius' clothing. They bathed him, applied ointments, and dressed him in clean garments.

"Now he needs rest and fluids."

"How soon until we can move him?"

"With a head injury, it is better not to move him unless absolutely necessary. At least a week. The fever is what worries me."

"We can stay until he's better. Father is supposed to arrive this evening."

"I should see to the boy now, so it's done before he gets here."

Cyrus nodded curtly. "Now that Darius is cared for. There are a few others with minor injuries after you're finished."

The boy looked pale and scared when Sashia took him into another tent for the procedure. "Drink this," she handed him a flask of wine. "It's all I have to dull the pain. I'll brew some herbs for you afterwards."

She'd never performed the surgery on a man before, only on a billy goat, but she had seen it done with horses. She set her feelings aside and focused on the work, knowing it would save the boy's life. It was simple and soon completed.

When it was done, she left him under guard and went to assess the rest of the wounded. Cyrus' soldiers had outnumbered Hanin's people nearly two to one, and it had been over quickly. There were only head injuries and lacerations and one casualty: a soldier who hesitated. Sashia didn't blame him.

She returned to sit with Darius. She couldn't watch the disposal of the bodies. Not this time. The little she saw as she walked through the camp disturbed her greatly. Cyrus might have justified it in his own mind, but she certainly had not. Granted, he was acting under orders, but he could've at least argued with Kalin about it. Then again, maybe he had.

When King Kalin arrived, Cyrus brought him straight to Darius. "Son, how are you?"

"Hello, Father. I am better than this morning."

Darius sounded stronger and more alert already. The king looked at Sashia and she gave him her assessment.

"Tell me what happened out there," he prompted Darius.

"I went to the spring to meet Hanin and Faban. He had a tent set up so we could have our discussion out of the heat of the sun. I listened to both men's arguments, and it seemed to me Faban had the greater claim. His people had been using the spring for generations. Hanin wanted to expand his grazing area. The Augers want to increase their herds so they don't have to spend their silver to buy food. His argument was that since his herds were larger, he had greater need of it.

"I suggested Hanin and Faban agree on a fair amount of compensation so Hanin could use the spring. Faban reluctantly agreed, but Hanin signaled to two men at the door who proceeded to fall on me. At the same time, Hanin drew his dagger and stabbed Faban."

Darius closed his eyes. "I mortally wounded one

man. Another came and hit me from behind or I would have taken down more of them."

Kalin considered Darius' story. "It sounds like Hanin planned ahead of time to take matters into his own hands if things did not go his way. Out of curiosity, why did you only take half your patrol to the spring?"

"I didn't think I would need them. I'll never make that mistake again."

"You're lucky you're alive to learn that lesson," Kalin said sternly, but his eyes were softer than Sashia had ever seen them.

The king rose to leave, moving rather stiffly after a day of riding, but Darius called him back.

"Father, I asked Cyrus to spare a boy who tried to help me."

Kalin turned to Cyrus with a piercing stare. "Did you?"

"We ensured Hanin's line is ended, Father."

"And just how did you do that?" Kalin growled.

Cyrus explained.

Kalin barked a laugh. "I can guess whose idea that was," he raised an eyebrow at Sashia. "Trust you to find a way to bend my words. Let me see the boy."

Darius opened his mouth, but Cyrus quieted him with a hand gesture. Sashia followed along silently. Once he decided something, she knew she could trust Cyrus to take care of it. She was glad Darius had brought it up since he was the one Kalin was least likely to be angry with.

Kalin stormed into the boy's tent and surveyed him. Though a little thinner and sallower than when she'd first met him, Sashia couldn't imagine anything more intimidating than the king in that moment.

"What is your name, boy?"

"Effan, my lord," the youth squeaked when he

found his voice.

"How old are you?"

"Fourteen years, my lord."

Effan tried to sit up, but Kalin motioned for him to stay where he was.

"Lie down, for pity's sake. Even I am not that cruel. I'd slit your throat before making you sit up in your condition." He paused, taking the boy's measure. "Do you swear to be loyal to me and my line, to serve Prince Darius faithfully, and to forget the name of your father?"

The boy trembled. "I promise the first two, gladly, but how can I truly forget my father's name? I could say I will forget it, but it would remain in my heart."

Kalin grunted. "Good answer. You are honest, at least. I wouldn't trust anyone who said they could forget something so dear." He stood up. "This is on your head, Cyrus. I hope you don't regret it."

When they were outside the tent, Kalin asked, "What about Hanin?"

"We were going to save him for you to interrogate and execute personally, but when he saw our numbers, he fell on his sword."

Kalin made a noise of disgust. "I will question Aloysius instead. I sent for him."

The chief of the Augers arrived later that evening with fifty warriors, but they would be no match for Cyrus and Kalin's combined battle-ready forces if he tried to follow his son's example. Sashia wondered how he would proceed. Aloysius dismounted, walked confidently toward the king, and bowed humbly. The smoke of the mass funeral pyres swirled ominously in the background.

"My lord, I have come to offer my most profound apologies for the actions of my son, Hanin. What he did, he did without my knowledge or approval."

"Explain to me why you did not resolve the dispute between Hanin and Faban yourself."

"Hanin is my son. I did not want to appear biased."

"Instead you wished to appear incompetent?"

Aloysius became flustered. "Of course not."

"Faban's murder and the capture of my son was premeditated. Hanin lured them into a remote area for a peaceful meeting and attacked without provocation. He told you nothing of his plans?"

"Nothing, my lord."

"If your own son plots behind your back and acts without consulting you, it seems your position is superfluous."

"My lord?"

"You are unnecessary. You are not fulfilling your obligations as chief; therefore you are removed from your position as head of your tribe."

Aloysius gaped. "You cannot do that!" he protested.

"As part of your confirmation ceremony, all tribal chieftains are required to swear loyalty to the king. You are authorized to settle disputes and collect taxes from your people. The king has the right to revoke that authority if your results are unsatisfactory, which they most assuredly are. Your people have four days to elect a new chief and report back to me."

Kalin dismissed Aloysius with a wave of his hand, and the king's men closed in on the former chieftain and escorted him to his horse. Aloysius was furious, but he had no choice but to ride ignominiously away.

"The entire tribe could rise up and rebel against us," warned Cyrus.

"Let them try."

CHAPTER TWENTY-THREE

Four days later, a delegation from the Augers arrived.

"I have been chosen as the new chief, my lord," declared Udin as he prostrated himself before Kalin. "I pledge to guide and serve my people in loyalty to our king."

"Rise, Udin. Let us discuss a few matters."

Kalin led Udin into his tent, and Cyrus followed. Sashia entered behind him since no one told her she couldn't. They sat on cushions on the floor, Cyrus at Kalin's right, Udin before them, and Sashia in the dimness behind Cyrus.

"What is the current disposition of your people, Udin?"

"Many were discontent with my uncle's lack of leadership, my lord, but the events of this week have instilled them with fear."

"Rightfully so."

"I believe it would help solidify my position and settle the people if you were to give a show of confidence and reconcile the Augers to yourself."

"I am listening."

"I propose Prince Cyrus wed my daughter, Iesha."

Sashia's head snapped up, and Cyrus stared in

disbelief. "That is not an option," he said frostily.

"It is the obligation of the king to marry a Bridge Bride," admonished Yarin.

"Come now," Udin looked from one to the other of them. "We all know that is impossible."

"Precisely what do you mean?" Kalin's tone was frigid.

"My apologies, my lord, I assumed your advisors would be aware of your . . . condition."

Cyrus and Yarin looked at the king, whose veins were bulging with suppressed anger.

"Father?" asked Cyrus quietly, but he received no answer.

Sashia watched Kalin's reactions and was suddenly enlightened. Several random symptoms now made sense. Though she'd just done the same thing for Effan, she balked at picturing Kassius perform such a procedure on her father-in-law. Her fingers curled tightly around Cyrus'.

"You will tell me how you know," Kalin hissed through clenched teeth.

"You know the saying, 'It's easier to keep a secret in a tent than a castle'."

Kalin glared at Udin, speechless with rage, and Yarin took up the reins of the conversation.

"If it cannot be Kalin, then why Cyrus? Darius was the one offended." The advisor stroked his beard thoughtfully, projecting calm into the tense atmosphere.

"If the king is unable, then it must be the next in line for the throne. You know this." Udin said condescendingly. "Besides, Cyrus already has a wife from the west," he gestured to Sashia, "so it seems only right he have a wife from the east also. Truly, Darius was the injured party, but Cyrus is the one who carried out the sentence. It is more fitting for him to be the means of reconciling us."

"What about a betrothal to the young prince, Tarin?" proposed Yarin.

Udin laughed. "That's like offering a thirsty man an empty flask. Too much could happen before the boy is old enough to marry."

"There must be another option," Cyrus insisted. He squeezed Sashia's hand.

Udin shook his head. "A connection with the royal family through marriage will promote goodwill better than any other solution. My people will accept nothing less. This is what they have sent me to say." He folded his hands together as a signal he had finished speaking.

Cyrus started to rise, but Kalin gripped his arm and finally spoke. "Give us a moment, Udin."

The Auger rose, bowed, and backed out of the tent. As he disappeared behind the flap, he cast an inscrutable look at Sashia. Why would he look at her? She owed him nothing. If anything, it was the other way around!

"I am not taking another wife, Father! The Augers will accept Darius as an alternative if he is the only option. That east-west argument is nonsense."

"Not really. If you align with the western tribes, and Darius with the east, that sets you up for a division of loyalty. It could split the country right down the middle."

"Darius would never—"

"Right now he doesn't have the temptation. He has no one influencing him to oppose you. Do not set him up for it. Anyway, Udin is right. The bride is to marry the king, or the next in line. To change the law would require a council of the tribes. The Pasturas and the Granum would likely vote against the Augers, and we would still have a rebellion."

Cyrus got up and paced the small space inside the tent. He turned toward his father, set his mouth in a hard line, and balled his fists. "What about you, father? You are not an old man. What does Udin know that I don't?"

Kalin's jaw tensed. He glanced at Sashia, then turned away. "Let your wife tell you. I can see from her expression she has guessed it."

Cyrus turned to her. His eyes were troubled. Hurt, fear, worry, anger. The same emotions compressed Sashia's lungs.

"He—" she squeaked, and had to calm herself. "Your father most likely had a tumor in the prostate. Kassius recently borrowed some of my scrolls on tumors. He must have removed it."

"What is the prostate?" Cyrus asked, looking back at his father.

"Let's just say I understand the young Auger's pain," Kalin snapped.

Cyrus blinked. "Why did you keep this from me?"

"I didn't think there would be a reason to bring it up!"

Father and son glared at each other. Cyrus took a deep breath. "Are you well now, Father?" he asked quietly.

When Kalin didn't reply right away, Sashia answered for him, as diplomatically as she could. "If the tumors have not spread, he still has many years ahead of him. But he cannot . . . fulfill marital duties."

"What I want to know," growled Kalin, "is how Udin heard of it. Kassius was sworn to secrecy. Heads will roll when I get to the bottom of this!"

"But he does know, so we must decide what is to be done," Yarin brought them back to the issue at hand.

"There has to be something else we can offer him,"

insisted Cyrus.

The king shook his head and gazed earnestly at his son, setting aside his own embarrassment. "Marriage is a traditional method of ensuring peace without ceding any control. Anything else would require a gift of more land, or more resources, and I cannot take any more away from the Pasturas than I have already, especially since there have been no further incidents the last two years. If we deny Udin's request altogether, it will promote discontent."

"Accepting it will promote discontent in other areas."

"I know you and Sashia love each other, and this seems like an unthinkable situation, but you only have to give Iesha one child. Then you can do whatever you wish."

"We don't have to acquiesce to the Augers' demands. We wiped out Hanin and his people for their treachery. Shouldn't all Berushese be held to a high standard of loyalty on the same principle?"

"As a healer might say, we have cut out the infected limb to save the body, but the body can only stand so much trauma. Now is the time for healing. If we reject this path to peace, we open the door to civil war."

As Sashia listened to the king's words the horror of their predicament began to overwhelm her.

"Sashia, what are you thinking?" Cyrus looked at her with a hopeful expression. "Tell me you see a way out of this."

Sashia stood slowly. Her hands were shaking so badly she had to clasp them tightly to make them stop. "Your father is right," she choked out tearfully. "If I do not agree, it will be seen as a slight against the Augers. I will be setting myself and the Granum up as being above them. I can see no way of changing

283

Udin's mind that does not involve further hostility."

Cyrus shook his head as if he couldn't believe what he was hearing. "Sashia, this would change everything. *Everything!* I know you don't want this anymore than I do!"

"'It is not something I want to do, but it must be done'."

Cyrus grabbed Sashia by the shoulders and searched her expression. "Are you trying to punish me by throwing my words in my face?"

"No, my love," she whispered. "I am trying to make this easier for you, for both of us. I married you knowing this could happen. It was in the contract."

"But I never thought it would, Sashia, believe me! I never even considered it."

"I know." She shuttered her mind and closed off her emotions to prevent herself from dissolving into a blubbering fool. There was no way out of this that would mitigate the possibility of more treachery or rebellion. She had to grasp what little control of the situation she could. Sashia looked past Cyrus to Kalin. "May we impose one condition, that Cyrus will marry a girl of my choosing from among Udin's daughters?"

"That is reasonable," Kalin conceded.

"Sashia," Cyrus choked out. It was all he could say. He held her head in his hands and rested his forehead against hers.

"We can do this, Cyrus. You once told me your path was predetermined. You have to do what's right for Berush."

"This is the first time I have not wanted to do it. I love you. You are all I need."

"And I love you. You are still enough of a reason."

She slipped her arms around his waist, and he bent down and kissed her passionately.

Kalin cleared his throat. "Ahem."

Cyrus dropped his hands to his sides and stepped away. "Yarin, call Udin back in."

Udin returned and everyone resumed their seats. Sashia watched Udin closely as Kalin explained their conditional agreement. His eyes flickered at Sashia.

"Iesha is my eldest unmarried daughter, and the most suitable."

"We are not excluding her, but it will be Lady Sashia's decision."

Sashia's heart warmed at the firmness with which Kalin enforced her stipulation. She wasn't going to let anyone else choose. The wrong sort of woman could poison the minds of the entire palace. Cyrus was in no state to decide. It would have to be her.

"Very well. As long as there is an alliance, that is acceptable to me," Udin assured them.

"Then tomorrow Lady Sashia will return with you to your home to make her choice. By the time you return," Kalin looked at her, "Darius should be ready to move, and we can all go home at once. The marriage will take place in Sherish."

"By the end of the month," added Sashia. "Not right away."

"Why delay?" Udin frowned.

"It is an important ceremony. There are preparations to be made."

Udin gave in. "Until tomorrow then." He left them alone.

"Go check on Darius," Kalin told Cyrus. "I wish to speak with your wife."

Cyrus hesitated and glanced at Sashia, but she nodded and waved him away. When he was gone, Kalin turned and looked at her quizzically.

"You agreed to that more quickly than I would have expected. What is going on inside your head?"

Sashia traced the embroidered pattern on her

boots with her finger as she arranged her words. "We have spoken before of your son's feelings for me. He will not want to hurt me. If this has to happen, I want to ease his concern for my well-being. If something were to happen to me, I fear how he would react. He may not think he can love another woman, but I know he can. He won't be able to help it." Her voice faltered.

Kalin rescued her by continuing her thought, "Having someone to console him might help him through such a tragedy," he agreed with a hint of sarcasm. "But what about you? What if you live?"

"I suppose we will figure it out as we go."

Kalin shook his head. "Not good enough. You are already unhappy. This could push you over the edge. What are you planning to do?"

The king's unexpected and accurate assessment surprised her into being more open. "I don't know. I had always planned on being a healer, not a wife, certainly not the wife of a prince. I would not give him up, I love him still, but being confined to the castle, looking after the children, and I love them too, I just . . . I feel like I am dying on the inside."

"Perhaps it would do you some good to go away for a while. Spend some time with your family. Go back to Rakhlain if you wish. You would be safe there, and the Magi have methods of healing the mind beyond anything I know."

The idea appealed to Sashia. "Thank you, my lord, I will consider it." She felt the need to defend Kassius. "I am sure Kassius told no one about your procedure."

"I will get to the bottom of that, have no doubt!" Kalin's eyes flashed. "By the way, I never told you Javan found out that woman, Coria, had met with a man from the Pastura tribe the day before she tried to poison you. Cyrus told him she had seen someone but would not say how he knew. We found the man, in a private room in a tavern, dead. No correspondence or any other clues as to who he was or why he was there."

"How do you know he was Pastura then?"

"He was dressed in their colors."

"Someone could've changed his clothing."

"It's possible. No one in the tavern saw or heard anything though."

"What did he die of?"

"Javan thought it was poison."

"You should have let me examine him!" Sashia tsked. "Why are you telling me this now?"

"Because, I wonder how our assassin will view a second marriage. Though my sanctions against the Pasturas seem to have alleviated the threat, I'm still concerned. It's not just Cyrus who would miss you, you know, if something happened to you. I'm not the easiest person to get along with, but I enjoy sparring with you." His eyes twinkled. "So, what is behind your request to choose the girl yourself? You say Cyrus will love her. You don't plan on picking the most repulsive of the bunch? Do you have someone in mind? You probably know more about the family than I do."

Sashia forced a smile. "You'll have to wait and see."

∞∞∞

Sashia and Cyrus spent a silent, sleepless night on opposite sides of their tent. They were both in such turmoil they were unable to comfort each other.

Sashia's chest was tight as she tried to ignore the pain constricting her heart. One moment, she had logical, concise arguments for her actions, and the next moment she felt she had to scream or she would burst. The thought of Cyrus being with someone else made her sick to her stomach.

At dawn, she forced herself to get up and eat something. Everything tasted bitter.

"Here is the clothing you requested." Viola held out several carefully folded garments.

"Thank you." Sashia had sent her to the nearest village to purchase the finest clothing available. She'd worn a serviceable tunic and trousers suitable for setting up a field hospital, not for selecting a new bride for her husband. Still feeling dumpy and overweight after her recent pregnancy, she wanted to look formal and imperious and enter Udin's camp with as much fanfare as possible.

When she mounted her horse, Cyrus came and stood next to her. "Just so you know, I trust you implicitly. I am not in the least concerned about who you bring back with you, as long as I have you. There is nothing in the world that could keep me from loving you with all my being."

Sashia couldn't speak. She could only incline her head in acknowledgment. She knew how much it cost him to say those words. It cost her as much to hear them.

Viola rode up next to her, along with every other female warrior in the camp, a half-dozen of them. Udin regarded her curiously when he rode up with his men, but he gave the signal to move out, and she followed.

No one spoke to her during the ride. It took two days to travel to Udin's camp from the Spur. They arrived in time for the evening meal on the second day, and Udin took the opportunity to give a speech. Several other clan leaders and village headmen were still present, awaiting the outcome of Udin's appearance to Kalin.

"My fellow Augers, King Kalin has confirmed me as your choice of chief!"

The assembly cheered.

"The king has also accepted our proposal of an alliance between the Auger tribe and the house of Berush."

More cheers.

"Lady Sashia, princess of Berush, is here to select a bride for Prince Cyrus from among my daughters. A marriage finalizing the union will take place in Sherish at the end of the month."

Applause mixed with murmuring greeted this statement. Sashia knew the situation was unusual, and people wouldn't be able to help commenting on it.

"Tomorrow morning, I will formally introduce you to my daughters, and you can make your choice."

"Thank you, Chief Udin. I am looking forward to it," Sashia lied.

CHAPTER TWENTY-FOUR

As Sashia surveyed the line of young women standing with their mothers, she felt butterflies in her stomach. She wondered if the girls arrayed in front of her felt the same.

"This is my third wife, Dana, and her daughter Elina."

Dana nodded to her and Elina bowed. Dana was a beautiful woman, and her daughter was quite pretty, but she looked barely fourteen, and Sashia immediately dismissed her as too young.

"A pleasure to meet you," she said and moved on.

"This is my second wife, Baria, and her daughters, Bellai and Nadia."

Sashia recognized Bellai as the squeamish girl who was unable to remain in the tent while Sashia treated her sister's wounds. She would never do. Nadia looked around seventeen, sturdy and sensible. She was a possibility. "Pleased to meet you."

"And this is my head wife, Iona, whom you met at the oasis, and her daughter Iesha."

Iesha had striking features and silky black hair, but shrewd eyes and pouty lips.

"A pleasure to meet you. Tell me, Iesha, if your son wanted to play with a toy my son was playing with, what would you do?"

"I would tell your son to share. Selfishness is an undesirable trait."

"I see. Nadia, how would you resolve the situation?"

"What situation, my lady?"

Sashia repeated what she had asked Iesha.

"I have no son."

"Use your imagination."

"Weeeeell," she said finally, "I suppose I would just give my son another toy."

"Thank you." Sashia looked back at Udin. "Where is Marthi?"

"Marthi?" he repeated in surprise. "She is minding her younger siblings."

"Is she still unmarried?"

"She has not married."

"Then she should be included with the rest of the girls."

"Marthi is hardly a suitable wife for a prince," he frowned.

"That is up to me to decide. Take me to her."

Udin reluctantly led Sashia toward a group of more permanent structures at the back of the camp. Baria followed, along with Iona and Iesha. They headed toward the door of a long, low building made of rock. As Sashia passed an open window, she saw Marthi playing with several young children. One of the girls grabbed a rag doll from the child next to her, and the child cried in protest.

"No, Tori, you cannot grab things, it's not nice."

Marthi took the toy from her and handed it back to the other child.

"Now ask her nicely if you may have a turn."

"May I pway wid youw dowwy Anai?"

The child nodded and handed over the doll.

Sashia smiled. "I would speak with her alone, Udin," she said at the door.

Udin bowed and stepped back.

"Lady Sashia!" exclaimed Marthi as she entered. The girl, now a woman of nineteen, jumped up to greet her.

"Hello, Marthi. How are you?"

"I am very well, thank you."

"You have no lingering discomfort from your injuries?"

"My scars itch sometimes, but that's all. Some things are a little harder to do, but I get by. Please, take a seat."

Sashia sat on a nearby stool. "You know why I am here?"

"I heard the announcement last night. Father wants Prince Cyrus to marry Iesha. Do you like her?"

"I want him to marry you."

Marthi rocked back in her chair, and her mouth fell open. "You of all people know I am not—I—no one else has wanted to marry me!"

"And their reasons are entirely superficial. As I told you before, you will have no problem bearing children. The inside of a person is much more important than what they look like on the outside."

Marthi flushed and put her hands to her cheeks. "I'm not on the same level you are. I'm a nobody!"

"I was born to a family of goat herders. You are the daughter of a chief. You have more status than I had."

"But you are a healer. You are highly educated. I cannot even read."

"That is easily remedied."

Marthi stood and picked up a sleepy toddler and rocked him in her arms. "Iesha is beautiful. She has studied with a tutor. Why choose me over her?"

"We don't need someone beautiful or educated. We need someone who loves children. Someone kind and nurturing. Someone who will be a good mother, and, I hope, someone who will be my friend."

Marthi looked over at her with wet lashes. "I would love to be your friend."

Sashia smiled at Marthi, her own eyes becoming moist. "I cannot pretend this is easy for me. It won't be easy for any of us, but I believe we can work it out."

"You will have to share your husband," Marthi sympathized. "I don't want to take him from you."

"There is no one in the world like Cyrus. You won't be taking anything, we will be giving it. This alliance is beneficial for the country, and you are my choice, if you will accept it."

Marthi stared down at her left hand and then at her misshapen chest. "Prince Cyrus won't mind my appearance?"

"Not at all."

"Then I accept your offer gladly."

∞∞∞

Udin looked less than pleased when Sashia announced her decision, but there was nothing he could do about it. Instead, he made the best of it and ordered Marthi be dressed for the part. Sashia was anxious to leave and declared her intentions of returning that day, and everyone scurried around preparing for Marthi's departure.

Baria found a moment to take Sashia aside.

"Why are you doing this?"

"King Kalin has agreed an alliance with the Augers would help to stabilize the region," she answered in a clipped monotone, unsure what Baria was asking.

"I mean, why are *you* doing this? What reason do you have for agreeing to this plan? Even if you had no say, why are you doing the choosing?"

"You agreed to become a second wife, and then you agreed to allow a third. Why?"

"My family had endured a rough winter. My father could no longer work in the mines, and they couldn't support me. I had to marry."

"And Dana?"

"Iona and I would agree to any number of wives," Baria looked around to make sure no one could overhear. "It means less time we have to spend with Udin ourselves."

"I see," said Sashia gravely.

Udin had always seemed agreeable enough, and he'd been extremely hospitable when she met him at the oasis, but people often showed a different side to the rest of the world than they did to those closest to them.

"Cyrus is a wonderful husband and an excellent father. I love him. I hope that sets your mind at ease," Sashia offered softly.

"And he trusts you to choose for him?"

"He does."

"That says a lot. You will be kind to my daughter?"

"I will."

"Then I could not ask for more."

∞∞∞

Marthi's knuckles were white as she gripped her saddle horn tightly. Her foot stuck in the stirrup as she tried to dismount. Cyrus, who was there with his father to greet them, rushed forward to steady her while Viola held the horse.

"Thank you!" Marthi said breathlessly when she had both feet on the ground.

"Cyrus, let me introduce Marthi, daughter of Udin," announced Sashia.

Sashia saw the flicker of comprehension in his eyes as he remembered the reason for their previous trip to Udin's camp.

"Marthi, I am glad to meet you at last." He offered her his arm and led her to the king. "This is my father, King Kalin."

Marthi was overcome with awe, and Kalin wore an amused expression. Sashia stood staunchly by Cyrus' side as they went through the necessary introductions. Somehow, she must manage to make it through the evening without breaking down.

Udin and Baria had ridden with them, and there was a huge feast. Sashia excused herself halfway through to check on Darius. She needed to be sure he was ready to ride with them the next day.

When she reached his tent, Viola was coming out of it. She sniffled, wiped at her face, and hurried away.

Sashia entered the tent and found Darius sitting on the edge of his cot angrily punching the canvas wall.

"It looks like the tent is winning."

Darius looked at her sheepishly. "Please don't tell Cyrus. He will lecture me."

"About battling the canvas or about the girl?"

"Viola. She's leaving anyway. Quitting the army and going home."

"She is? Why?" Sashia was surprised.

Darius shrugged. "Her brother has arranged a marriage for her, so she no longer has to be a soldier. I did nothing to stop her."

Sashia sat on the cot next to him. "Did you want to?"

"No. I didn't want her to go, but I'm not ready to give her what she wants. I may never be ready."

"You may feel differently when you meet the right woman."

"I am not like Cyrus. I like fighting," he declared fiercely.

"Well, let me look you over and see if you are fit to return to it."

Darius meekly let her examine him.

"You won't tell Cyrus or Father?" he repeated when she was done.

"I bet your father already knows, and she wasn't in your unit, so you broke none of the new military regulations, though in a way, you have broken faith with her brother. He could ask you for a bride price if he finds out," Sashia remonstrated with a raised eyebrow. "But I have never kept anything from Cyrus, and neither should you."

"Cyrus still thinks I am ten years old."

"He's just being a protective elder brother. Besides, you should know by now the problems that can arise if you are indiscrete."

"I know," he grumbled.

Sashia patted his shoulder. Then she stiffened her spine and prepared to return to the feast. When she reached the ring of light surrounding the party, she found she couldn't bear to go back. An invisible barrier prevented her.

Instead, she made her way to her tent and tried to meditate. It had been a long time, too long since she had set aside time for personal reflection. Trying to focus was nearly impossible. Her emotions were too intense to examine. Breathing was about all she could manage.

She had no idea how much time had passed before Cyrus entered the tent.

"You are here," he said in relief. "I was worried about you. Why are you hiding? "

"What do you think of Marthi?"

"Why are you avoiding answering me? Do not shut me out, Sashia!"

"I am fine, Cyrus. I just wanted a moment alone."

Cyrus sat next to her and pulled her into his lap. She relented and nestled into his embrace. The comfort was something she needed desperately, though she hated to admit it. Part of her still wanted to be mad at him for the massacre of Hanin's family, but her anger was overshadowed by fears for the future.

He nuzzled her hair and kissed her temple. "Tell me what is on your mind. The only way this is going to work is if we are open and honest with each other."

"There will be some things we cannot or should not discuss, Cyrus. Marthi will need some privacy and a part of you reserved for her alone. We can never be as close as we were. You were right. Everything will change."

"Things will not change between us. I won't let them," he argued obstinately, and for the rest of the night, they pretended they wouldn't.

CHAPTER TWENTY-FIVE

After Udin and Baria left the next morning, Kalin and Cyrus' men began to break camp. Sashia went to check on Effan and found him playing in the sand.

"How are you feeling?"

"I am well enough, my lady."

"I have ordered a cart for you. It wouldn't be good for you to ride yet."

"Thank you. That is very kind." He filled up a pouch with sand, tied it tightly, and hung it around his neck.

"It may not be a good idea to keep a memento of what happened here," Sashia cautioned.

"Sand is created by the breaking down of rocks, my lady. Ice cracks it, water moves it, wind blows it, and yet the sand was here long before my people were here, and it will remain long after we are gone. I am Berushese, and when they burn my body, I will go to the earth and become part of the sand. That's what my mother taught me." He closed his eyes and clutched the pouch. "This sand will remind me to overlook our differences because in the end, we are all the same."

Sashia was amazed at his insight. "How very wise.

Perhaps I will carry some sand around myself." She smiled at him.

"Sashia!"

She turned around to see Marthi waving at her and leading a horse behind her. Marthi was considerably taller than Sashia, though still shorter than Cyrus, and it suddenly struck Sashia as humorous the girl looked up to her as a role-model.

"May I ride with you?" Marthi asked.

"Certainly."

A soldier brought Sashia her mare, and the women mounted and waited while the rest of the column formed.

"I've never been away from home before. Will you help me know what I should do and how I should behave?"

"You have good instincts, Marthi. Trust yourself. Being confident and content will take you farther than constantly trying to please or live up to others' expectations. But I won't let you misstep, never fear."

Cyrus was with Kalin and Darius at the head of the column directing the troops. Everyone came to him for orders and obeyed him instantly. Sashia was filled with pride as she observed him—tall, handsome, and regal.

"Did Cyrus say anything about me?" Marthi asked shyly.

Cyrus obviously affects her the way he does everyone else, Sashia thought wryly. "Marthi, I will never ask you to tell me what you and Cyrus discuss when you are together, and I will ask you to respect my privacy in the same manner."

"Oh, I am sorry, I didn't think!"

"I'm not angry, it's just one of many things we will have to agree on and work through."

"My father's wives hardly speak to one another at

all, and when they do, it's not pleasant. I don't wish to be like that."

"Nor do I. Nor does Cyrus." She paused. "I'm not always the easiest person to get along with, Marthi. I hope you will forgive me if I am short with you."

"I owe you everything, Lady Sashia. I could've died from my injuries without your treatment. Now, thanks to you, I have a chance to bear my own children when no one else would give it to me. I will always be grateful to you."

"Call me Sashia. You are going to be just as much a lady as I am."

"I will try, Sashia." She tilted her head as if listening to see how it sounded. "It doesn't seem right."

"It will. There is something else you should know." Sashia told Marthi about the attempts on her life. "I am telling you now because the mastermind and the motive are still unknown, and we don't know what will happen when Cyrus takes another wife. I want you to have all the facts ahead of time in case you want to change your mind."

"I'm not afraid. I would risk anything to have a child. I cannot go through much worse than I have already endured."

Sashia nodded. "Good. I hoped you would feel that way."

They rode the rest of the day together pleasantly. Sashia described to Marthi each of her children and their foibles. Marthi showed sincere interest and asked several perceptive questions. She sympathized with Sashia's difficulty finding a reliable wet nurse.

Sashia found she genuinely *liked* Marthi. The girl was insecure about her appearance and her lack of education, but Sashia felt that would be overcome in the right environment, with the right encouragement.

She just had to prevent her mind from picturing Marthi with Cyrus.

"We need to discuss which rooms Marthi should have," Sashia told Cyrus that evening. Her mouth was dry, and she struggled to form the words.

Cyrus sat solemnly and considered. He swallowed hard before he spoke. "I want all the children, all of my children, to be raised together. They should play together, eat together, study together. There should be no difference between them. To facilitate that, would it be best for her to have the apartment next to ours?"

"There are two things glaringly wrong with that, Cyrus. First, 'our' apartment should no longer be 'ours.' It should be mine. You will have to have your own."

"Why should I have my own? We've never slept separately."

Cyrus sounded hurt. Sashia gazed at him lovingly and put her hand on his knee.

"I cannot be your default. It wouldn't be fair."

"Are you saying I must spend equal time with her? I don't feel that is necessary at all," he protested. "If she knows from the start how I feel and knows I will only spend a certain amount of time with her, then I would think she could accept that without being disappointed."

"Your feelings may change."

"My feelings for you will never change!"

"There may also be times when you wish to be alone."

"There have been none yet," he scoffed.

"The second objection I have to Marthi being next door to me, which also supports the idea of you having your own room, is that whenever you are not with me, I will know you are with her. I don't know if

I can stand to see you go into her room." She shook her head. "I cannot see it."

Cyrus caught his breath. He cupped her face with his hands and kissed away the tears that started to fall. "Say the word, Sashia, and I will take you and the children and build a new life somewhere else, forget all of this, and just be responsible for ourselves."

"You mean run away? Leave this mess for your father and Darius to deal with? You would never be content to leave the life you were destined for, and you know it, though I love you for offering."

"I cannot bear the thought of hurting you."

"We've already talked about this. We know it has to happen. If we think it through, there are things we can do to make it easier."

"I know of no family with multiple wives where the women were happy and the children harmonious. We have no good examples to follow."

"Then we will be the first."

Cyrus let his hands glide slowly down her neck and followed them with his lips. "So where do you want me?"

Sashia gave a low laugh as the air left her lungs. "You know where I want you," she said as his hands continued to travel downward, "but as to room assignments, how about you take the apartment next to mine, and we move Marthi into the one in the adjoining passage? We can use your suite as a common area."

"Fine. As long as you understand I plan never to sleep there."

"Understood."

∞∞∞∞

At Sashia's request, Cyrus sent a rider ahead to ask

the servants to prepare Marthi's rooms. Kalin had had only one wife and three children, so there were several rooms in the palace that had gone unused for many years.

"Tell them to make the apartment beautiful," she instructed.

The second day of travel passed the same as the first. When they arrived in the city, Marthi exclaimed over everything.

"I have never seen so many buildings! How large they are! Look at the water! The lake is so big! I had no idea there was so much water in one place!"

"Wait until you see the ocean!" Sashia had been to the sea with Beyorn and Dorthi and to the port with Cyrus the first year they were married.

Marthi cried when she saw her rooms.

"Whatever am I to do with so much space?"

"Hopefully, you will fill it with children."

They gave Marthi a few days to settle in and get used to the palace. Her father had sent along a maidservant for her. Sashia wasn't sure if it was a good idea for another member of Udin's camp to be along. After her own experience with servants, she didn't trust easily.

"I never had a servant at home," Marthi confided. "It seems so strange to have one now."

Sashia had just finished giving Marthi an examination, discussing her cycle, and charting it out. "Do you like her?"

"I suppose so."

"Don't be afraid to make changes if you want to. Just because your father sent her doesn't mean you have to keep her on. Or if you want to change anything in the room, you can do it."

"The room is lovely," she asserted, fingering the embroidered cover on the bed.

Fashima burst through the door.

"You need to knock, dear," Sashia chided.

"But I wanted to show Marthi my lesson!"

Marthi had quickly become a favorite with the girl and had asked Fashima to teach her to read. It gave Fashima an added incentive to attend to her lessons.

"Go back and practice entering properly, and then you may," Sashia instructed.

The child meekly complied, and Marthi allowed her to enter after knocking. The two sat on the bed sounding out the neatly printed words from a slate. Sashia went to fetch Varus, who had woken up from his nap, and returned to Marthi's room followed by Tarin and Onia. Marthi soon had the children happily playing a game while Sashia fed Varus from a bottle.

"Is this a bad time for a family meeting?" asked Cyrus from the open doorway. His wavy hair had a little extra curl to it, and his smile made Sashia's knees weak.

"No, now is fine."

They corralled the children and made a circle of cushions on the floor.

"Everyone in this room is part of our family," began Cyrus. "Family helps each other, and family loves each other."

"What about Father and Darius?" asked Fashima.

"Yes, they are family too, even though they are not here right now."

King Kalin had returned with Darius to visit the Pasturas and the rest of the Augers. He would be back for the wedding at the end of the month.

Onia sucked her thumb and climbed into Fashima's lap. She was too little to understand what was going on, but the precedent they were setting would affect all of them from here on. Tarin sat on his own cushion next to Cyrus and bounced up and down on it, and his father affectionately ruffled his hair.

"Whenever possible, I would like us to eat dinner together. No matter how our family grows, I want us to have this unity. It will never be Sashia's children and Marthi's children, it will be my children, or *our* children."

"And sister," piped in Fashima.

"Yes, and sister."

"As the parents," he focused on Sashia and Marthi in turn, "we will have to be examples to the children on how to get along and work out our problems. Don't come to me with a problem with each other if you have not already discussed the issue between you. Then come to me together. I will not take sides. There is only one side here, our side. Does everyone agree?"

"I agree," said Sashia. Cyrus had discussed with her ahead of time what he was going to say.

"I've never heard anything more wonderful," declared Marthi, her dark eyes glowing. "I agree and will do my best to do as you say."

"As first wife, and due to her training as a healer, Sashia is to have the final word in matters of daily discipline, health, tutoring, and so on, but that doesn't mean you are not to have an opinion, Marthi. Sashia should listen to your ideas and concerns and make sure they are addressed. Do you have any concerns right now?"

Marthi appeared taken off guard by the question. She put her hands on her knees and rocked back on the cushion.

"I have a question," interjected Fashima.

"Not right now, Fashima," remonstrated Cyrus. "It's not your turn."

He looked back at Marthi expectantly, and she blushed.

"I would like to speak to you privately after the meeting, if I may."

Cyrus nodded. "You may. I would like to speak to you also. Fashima, what is your question?"

"Can Marthi join me in my lessons? It's so boring to go by myself."

"Would you like to do that, Marthi, at least for now?"

"Yes, I would, thank you."

"Is there anything else?"

Everyone shook their heads.

"Then this meeting is adjourned."

"Does that mean we can go?" asked Fashima.

"Yes," Cyrus chuckled. "You may go."

Tarin got up with a whoop and resumed playing.

"Come with me, children," called Sashia. "We are going back to the other room so Marthi and Father can talk."

The children trooped dutifully after her and pounced on Lang, who had brought their lunch. Sashia ate distractedly, trying unsuccessfully to think of anything other than Cyrus and Marthi alone together.

When she and Cyrus retired for the night, she was tense with the continued attempt to push it from her mind, but she swore to herself she would keep her promise to Marthi, and she would not bring it up.

"You chose well," Cyrus said softly. "Other than the fact she bows at the throne of your feminine perfection, I cannot imagine anyone more suitable to what we are trying to do."

Sashia laughed in surprise. "I am far from perfect, as you well know. I am afraid I will become even less so as time goes on."

"You are perfect for me. I cannot blame Marthi for idealizing you, because I bow at your throne also."

CHAPTER TWENTY-SIX

The days until the wedding passed quickly. Javan discovered one of the servants had been listening outside the door when Kassius had given the king his initial examination. Kalin had the servant executed. It was over before Sashia heard anything about it, so there was nothing she could do. Kassius avoided the palace until the king's wrath abated. Though he was not at fault, he was still a reminder of the ignominy.

Sashia knew Cyrus was concerned for her well-being. Lang followed her around constantly without letting her have a moment to herself. Several times, she caught the two of them whispering together in the passage. Finally, she dragged Cyrus aside and tasked him with it.

"What is going on? We said we would talk to each other if there is a problem."

"I know you believe your malaise was related to Varus' birth, and not to any deep-rooted issue that remains unaddressed, but I am not convinced. I'm afraid. I'm afraid undue stress or unhappiness may bring it on again. How can I leave you alone considering . . . what is going on?"

Sashia's first instinct was to dismiss his fears, or

compare his own bout of illness with hers, but her Magi training was too strong, and she forced herself to pause and reflect before speaking. "I understand what caused me to temporarily lose my sanity. I believe I will recognize the signs if I start down that path again. If I do, I will ask you for help right away."

"Promise me."

"I promise."

"And you will keep someone with you at all times."

"I couldn't get rid of Lang if I tried."

"What about the nights when—when I'm not with you?"

"I'm not going with you to Marthi's room, so don't suggest it."

Cyrus' face registered shock, and then turned sly. "The thought had not entered my mind, but now that you mention it . . ."

Sashia rolled her eyes, but she had achieved her aim; the mood had lightened.

"Lang can sleep outside my door if he likes. Or I can keep Fashima with me." Varus slept in a cradle near the bed, but Tarin and Onia now slept in a separate room in the apartment with Gaia. Fashima had her own room, but Sashia let her sleep with her occasionally when Cyrus was at the port.

"How about both?"

"If it will ease your mind."

"It will."

∞∞∞

On the day of the wedding, Sashia stood watching Baria and the maid assist Marthi with her hair and clothing. Marthi's parents had arrived the day before, along with several other representatives from the Auger tribe, to witness the event. Baria talked to her daughter about what to expect on her wedding night and provided her with an array of oils and other helpful items. Sashia was grateful Baria was there so she didn't have to explain it herself. She tried to imagine Marthi was just a friend and the groom was a stranger instead of her own husband.

"You are luckier than I was," Baria told her daughter. "Although Iona was unhappy with her marriage to your father, she still resented me and made my life miserable. You are joining a family that is working together for a greater good, the future of our country. This marriage is taking place for political reasons, but I believe you have as fair a chance for happiness as anyone. May you have many children and bring honor to our tribe." Baria kissed both of Marthi's cheeks and squeezed her shoulders. "You look beautiful."

"Thank you, Mother."

Marthi did look lovely. Sashia envied her height. She was wearing a high-necked dress with a sash across her chest hiding the damage done to her figure.

A servant knocked on the door to tell them it was time.

Sashia attended Marthi to the dais and stood next to Cyrus. Although her approval wasn't legally required for a Bridge Bride, she and Cyrus wanted to appear unified in their desire for peace between the tribes. If she didn't accept the marriage, it could be said the Granum were snubbing the Augers.

Cyrus gave Marthi a quick smile of reassurance, shot a swift glance at Sashia, and assumed a grave and reverent expression.

A benevolent smile was plastered to Sashia's face the entire time. Since she'd been the one to choose the bride, the story heard by those in Sherish was that the marriage was her idea from the beginning. Kassius had brought her this report during a recent visit, and she was still deciding what to do about it.

Somehow, Sashia made it through the ceremony, but the succeeding wedding feast felt interminable. King Kalin made a speech about reconciling the tribes and making peace with the Augers. Udin made a speech about the magnanimity of the king. Cyrus made a speech about the future of Berush. Sashia thought they should be glad she wasn't making a speech. It would have been something along the lines of the benefits of a matriarchal society. Amusing herself with these thoughts was the only thing that kept her sane during the dinner.

Finally, Cyrus and Marthi were led away with great fanfare, and Sashia was able to sneak out a side door.

"Are you alright, my lady?" asked Lang, concerned, as he followed her back to the family wing.

"Yes, Lang, I am fine," she assured him as she opened the door to her room. Only *her* room now, not *theirs*. She could hear the noise of the bridal party arriving in the adjoining passage from the opposite direction.

"I will be right outside, my lady, if you need anything."

"Thank you, Lang."

Of course, she wasn't fine. Far from it. She was as fragile as a soap bubble, ready to break with the slightest puff of air. Sashia shut the door and leaned against it with a sigh.

"Tarin and Onia are already asleep in their room with Gaia," whispered Fashima as she rocked Varus' cradle. The girl put her finger to her lips and tiptoed to the bed.

Sashia quickly changed into her nightclothes and

blew out the candles. Fashima fell swiftly into slumber, but Sashia stared into the darkness. A knock at the door startled her. She threw back the covers and rushed to open it before Varus woke. It was Cyrus.

"What are you doing here?" she hissed. "What is wrong with you?"

Cyrus pulled her into the hallway. Lang was nowhere to be seen.

"You are what is wrong with me. I don't think I can do this. All I can think about is you."

Sashia wanted to scream at him. How did he think this was going to help? "Cyrus, this is Marthi's wedding night. You have to be with *her*. We shouldn't be having this conversation! How do you think she's feeling right now?"

"Marthi knows I am here. She is worried about you too. She understands."

This was a nightmare. There was no way she could reason her way out of this mess. Cyrus had no idea how difficult he was making this night for her.

Before she burst into hysterics, she grabbed his collar, pulled his head down to within reach of hers and kissed him with all the passion she could muster. He responded to her, slowly at first, but was soon devouring her lips fiercely. Just before they reached the point where they would lose control, she pushed him away.

"Go. Go now."

Cyrus stared at her with wild eyes. He was teetering between giving in and doing his duty and going mad. Finally, he turned on his heel and lurched toward Marthi's room. Sashia hoped Marthi could forgive her for returning him in such a state, but it was that or nothing.

Sashia wanted to cry, but the tears wouldn't come.

She couldn't possibly return to her room now, so instead she wandered down the passage. Around the corner, she ran into Lang, who trotted after her. Eventually she found her way to the king's study. A light shone through the open doorway.

"There you are. I was expecting you," said Kalin when she entered.

"You were? Why?"

"Because you are not the kind of woman to go peacefully to sleep while her husband beds someone else."

"Is there such a woman?" she scoffed.

"I doubt it. Sit down."

Sashia sat numbly. Kalin threw a woven rug at her. She noticed she hadn't grabbed a robe, and her feet were bare. She must be cold, but she couldn't feel it. For decency's sake, she wrapped the rug around her thin nightgown.

Kalin poured a goblet of wine and handed it to her. She drank a large gulp of the fiery liquid.

"Finish it."

Sashia obeyed.

"Have you thought any more of my suggestion to go away for a while?"

"Yes, I want to leave as soon as possible."

Kalin nodded. "I will arrange it."

They sat in silence. The numbness in her body began to spread to her brain.

"I am sorry."

The king's words surprised Sashia, and it took her a moment to process what he'd said.

"I didn't know when I sent Cyrus to rescue his brother this would be the outcome," he continued.

"Would you have done anything differently if you had known?"

"No, but I want you to know it was not my intent

to make life tougher for you or my son. You have been quite heroic through this ordeal."

"Thank you," mumbled Sashia, unsure how to respond. "The people of Sherish seem to think the whole thing was my idea. Do I need to clarify my role for the sake of the Augers?"

"No, the right people know why it is happening. What everyone else thinks doesn't matter."

Kalin refilled her goblet, and she sipped it more slowly this time.

"I think I will go to Rakhlain."

"That is good."

Sashia rubbed the rim of the glass against her lower lip. "I am worried to leave Cyrus."

"Well, you said you wanted to make sure he could survive without you. Now is the time to find out. Give Marthi a chance to see what she can do."

"I'm not sure Cyrus will give her that chance."

"He might if you are unavailable, but I will talk with him. You will see your way through this. Go get some rest."

Sashia was beginning to feel a little fuzzy. The proposed visit to the Magi would give her something to think about, so maybe now she could sleep. "Thank you, my lord."

Lang followed her back to her room and lay on his pallet in the passage.

Sashia drifted off with a vision of peaceful Lake Shelomoh as her last conscious thought.

∞∞∞

"I need to speak to you both," Sashia told Marthi and Cyrus the next evening at their family dinner. The entire day had been painfully awkward. Marthi alternately blushed and threw Sashia supplicating looks, and Cyrus didn't know what to do with himself.

"I think it is best if I go away for a while, to give you some space."

"I need no space," protested Cyrus.

"There is no cause for that," Marthi objected.

"Yes, there is, and I go at the king's suggestion. The two of you will have time to get to know each other, and when I return, it should be easier to make this work."

"How long will you be gone?" asked Cyrus solemnly. His eyes were shuttered, and Sashia couldn't tell what he was thinking.

"Three months. I will go to Rakhlain. Marthi, will you help Gaia with the children? Lang will travel with me."

"Of course! I will do whatever you need me to do."

"Tarin will be alright with Marthi and Fashima, especially now that he's used to sleeping in a separate room, but I would like to take Onia along."

"Onia?" exclaimed Cyrus. "She's so young! She'll be a terror on the road."

"Lang will help with her, and the Magi are wonderful with children. I feel . . . I feel like she will tie me to you."

Cyrus reached out and took her hand. "Then take her, by all means. I feel jealous of Lang. His sole purpose is to serve you. I wish mine was so simple."

∞∞∞

Topec escorted Sashia to the Tull Pass where she met up with Restus, who would take her the rest of the way.

"I am glad to see you again, Lady Sashia!" Restus greeted her enthusiastically. "You remember Halem? He is now twelve years, and his father has given him

316

permission to join the army."

"Congratulations, Halem. I am sure you will make a fine soldier."

"Thank you, my lady."

Later, when Halem was riding farther behind them, Restus told her more of the story.

"Shazar presented him with a horse and a sword and gave him his blessing, but basically said that was all he should ever expect from him."

"How did Halem react?"

"He was unfazed. He wants nothing of his father's. Goat-herding is not appealing to him."

"It makes me happy to know he's going to train under you, Restus."

"Me too," he grinned.

The journey to Rakhlain took just over a month. Onia wasn't nearly as much trouble as Sashia expected. She seemed to enjoy travelling on horseback and took turns riding with Sashia and Lang. With her little fingers tangled in the horse's mane, she giggled and laughed excitedly. She napped more easily to the rhythm of the horse than she did normally. It was only toward the end of each day she began to squirm and fuss.

Hiking up the mountain was the most arduous part. Restus and his company left them in the foothills at a Magi lookout station. Onia was too heavy for Sashia to carry, and she was too little to walk far without tiring. Lang and their guide, a young Mage named Van, took turns carrying her. Van's proportions were gargantuan, and he carried Onia on his shoulders like she was nothing, in addition to the large pack slung over his back.

When they finally arrived at the shore of the lake, Sashia was surprised to see Aerick there to greet her.

"You are the boatman now, Aerick?"

"My term as Mage in Service is over. This is now my regular post. What do you seek?"

"Just a little rest, Aerick. To find my peace again."

Aerick cocked his head at her. "Are you sure that is it?"

Sashia frowned. She hadn't thought of what she would do if she was denied entry to Shelomoh. "Everything comes back to that. I have lost my peace of mind, my peace of heart. This is the only place I know to go."

"It is not the only place, but you are welcome, Lady Sashia." Aerick turned to Lang. "What do you seek?"

Sashia had to translate since Lang didn't speak Rakhli.

"Seek? Me? I seek nothing. No, nothing at all. At least, not for myself. I seek my lady's peace."

"Very good. Are you at peace, Van?"

"I am."

"Then climb into the boat."

Everyone carefully entered the rowboat.

"Why didn't he ask Onia what she seeks?" asked Lang.

"Children don't have to justify entrance to Shelomoh, Lang." There were times, even after nearly five years in her service, Sashia couldn't tell whether Lang was serious or in jest.

Sashia asked after Beyorn and Dorthi and was relieved to hear they were well. As soon as the boat was secured to the dock, she jumped out and led the way to her former quarters with the elderly couple.

"Sashia!" Dorthi cried when she saw her. She rushed forward and embraced her. "We heard you were coming, and we couldn't believe it. We were so excited! Beyorn, Sashia is here!"

Beyorn came out of the house and enveloped Sashia in a hug. He felt thinner and frailer than when

Sashia had last seen him, but he still had plenty of energy flowing through him.

"Child, we have missed you! Come inside and tell us everything."

Sashia introduced Onia and Lang. Van set down their packs and returned to his duties.

"She is a beautiful girl, Sashia," gushed Dorthi.

"Say hello to Dorthi, Onia."

"Hewo Dorfi!" Onia was unsure about the strangers, but she didn't hide behind her mother or Lang. The journey had presented many new things to her, and she was more curious than anything.

"Do you like to draw, Onia?"

The child nodded and Dorthi gave her some paper and a charcoal pencil. Lang sat at the table with her in his lap to make sure she didn't unwind the string and completely blacken her hands.

Dorthi brought out food, and they ate while they talked. Her back was bent with age and her knees stiff with rheumatism, but she didn't let it stop her.

"Now tell us why you are really here," said Beyorn.

Sashia told them everything that had happened in the years she'd been away. Onia became restless after finishing her meal, and Lang took her to play on the floor. Sashia switched from Berushese to Rakhli and poured her heart out to her former mentors.

"So," said Beyorn when she was finished, "you left Shelomoh to accept the calling of a healer. Then you also took on the calling of a wife. The second does not negate the first, it only takes precedence over it. Your husband's second marriage negates neither calling. Your mission is the same."

"But how do I know when I am actually fulfilling it? Why do I feel so unhappy?"

"Well, your mother is right," affirmed Dorthi. "It is normal for women to be emotionally unstable after

319

childbirth. I have not experienced it myself, but I have observed it many times." She paused and drummed her fingers on her chin. "The Magi do not allow plural marriages, and though, as Beyorn said, your purpose is unchanged, I have to imagine it will be more difficult to accomplish it now that you have to share it with someone else."

"The mission of the Magi, and truly the mission of every human being, is to promote peace through knowledge and understanding. We want to tear down and prevent the walls people build between themselves that cause enmity. You will have to be careful Marthi does not become a wall."

"How?"

"That is what you are here to find out. It sounds like you are starting out with a good foundation. We will help you all we can, but ultimately it is a question only you can answer. You and Cyrus."

∞∞∞

The next few days, Sashia tried to relax and meditate and be at peace with herself. She and Onia stayed in her old room in Beyorn and Dorthi's house, while Lang stayed in the single men's dormitory. Lang took Onia to play with the Magi children during the day so Sashia could have time alone.

For the first week, she struggled merely to keep from thinking about Cyrus and Marthi and focused instead on the beauty of the mountains surrounding the little community. Eventually the quiet and stillness of the woods and the serenity of the lake began to seep into her mind, and she felt her tension and anxiety begin to recede.

She had grown up spending most of her time outdoors, and the last few years confined primarily to the palace had made her retreat inside herself. By the second week, she felt relaxed enough to turn her mind inward again without fear of getting lost. Listing truths seemed the best place to start. Some things were constant no matter what happened.

One, she still loved Cyrus. More now than ever. Wildly, madly loved him. Being without him for this short amount of time made it painfully clear, and she missed him terribly. Knowing everything she knew now, she would marry him over again.

Two, she remained passionate about healing. However, she hadn't been able to train new healers and share her ideas to the extent she'd expected. She hadn't been able to study and continue her own learning. Somehow she had to find the time and means to do it.

Perhaps, now that she had Marthi to help, she could leave the children in her care more often. That would give Marthi purpose as well. Her happiness would have to be considered because her attitude and disposition would affect the rest of them from now on. This seemed like an impossible thing, and she wasn't sure how to go about it.

"You cannot be responsible for anyone else's happiness, Sashia. All you can do is ensure you are not deliberately contributing to her *un*happiness," exhorted Dorthi when Sashia approached her with the problem.

Sashia frowned. "I'm not sure I understand."

"Happiness is a choice. You can allow yourself to be mired down by circumstances, or you can focus on the things over which you have control. You cannot control Marthi's response to her situation, but you can, to a certain extent, control the situation."

"What steps should I take?"

Dorthi smiled. "This is not like a skin condition

you can see and treat by applying the proper salve or removing the source of irritation. It's more like a healthy diet. Provide good food and the body will flourish, but you cannot force anyone to eat."

"So the best thing I can do is choose to be happy myself."

"That is the most important step, yes."

Like Father had chosen to love Mother in spite of her failings. It hadn't guaranteed she would love him back, but she had. Sashia hadn't felt like forgiving Mother, but she had done it anyway, and their relationship had improved.

Sashia sat back and reflected on Dorthi's words. Could she choose to be happy even if she didn't feel like it? Her emotions weren't always based on facts or circumstances anyway. During the worst of her malaise, her feelings had been completely unreasonable. Maybe if she chose to behave as if she was happy, her inner state would align itself with her actions. After all, the Magi emphasized peace of body as prerequisite to peace of mind and heart.

"Here," Dorthi handed her a bowl. "Knead this dough for me. Sometimes work is the best medicine."

Sashia smiled, and this time she felt it in her heart.

CHAPTER TWENTY-SEVEN

"You look happy, my lady. Not just happy, but the happiest of happies," Lang remarked after three weeks in Shelomoh.

"I am, Lang. And it's not because I'm in Shelomoh that I'm happy. It's because I have resolved something in my own mind. Now, I am ready to go home. I'm excited to go home."

Beyorn and Dorthi expressed sorrow at her departure but were extremely grateful for the time they had. "We are especially happy we got to see your daughter. Children are a blessing and a legacy. You must write to us and let us know how she and your sons grow."

"And know we love you, too!" chimed in Dorthi.

"Thank you both, so much!"

"I enjoy your letters also," said Farouk, who had come to see her off. He'd grown nearly two feet but seemed as prone to mischief as ever.

"Make sure you attend to your handwriting as well as you do to speaking the languages you learn."

"I will. Pa'tryk will be sorry to have missed you. He asks to read all your letters."

"Hmm. I will keep that in mind."

"Did you find what you sought?" asked Aerick when they arrived at the dock.

"I did, and you were right. The answer was not what I thought it was."

"I am glad," said Aerick with his eyes twinkling. "Sometimes you just have to ask the right question."

"And I did too, find it. Not looking for anything is easy," put in Lang, guessing what Aerick would ask him before it was translated.

Onia held up a shiny pebble she had picked up on the way to the dock. "Find it!" she exclaimed, beaming.

Aerick laughed. "So you did."

Lang got into the boat and Sashia handed Onia down to him. Before getting in herself, she turned to Aerick.

"Is there anything else you can tell me about the attempts to kill me? How did the Magi know about the rock slide? Do you know who planned it or why?"

Aerick put his hand on her shoulder. "Our people are sent out for specific tasks to add to our pool of knowledge. They learn many things. Right now, we know no more than you about this issue. A Mage in Sherish happened to overhear one man warn another not to be on the road along the eastern mountains when Lady Sashia was passing by and took it upon himself to pass on the warning to you rather than follow the man. I am glad he did."

"And he felt Tarin and Mother were safe?"

"Yes. His sources were sure the threat was not from within the palace. After that, I will admit, I sent an extra Mage to keep an eye on things in Sherish, and she found out the nurse was sneaking out of the palace for secret meetings. Unfortunately, Sherish is the only place where we have anyone right now, so we are unable to trace the threat to its origin."

Sashia frowned. "What sources knew the threat was not from the palace?"

"I cannot tell you at this time. You will have to trust us."

"I do. Thank you, Aerick. Tell me, can I trust the king's advisors, Yarin and Javan?"

Aerick's eyebrow twitched. "I have no reason to say you cannot."

"Good enough," she grinned, and he handed her into the boat.

∞∞∞

Sashia watched the city of Sherish rise out of the desert heat waves with nearly uncontainable anticipation. She was so excited to share her joy with Cyrus. When they rode through the palace gates, she slid off Favor almost before the mare came to a stop.

"Where is Cyrus?" she asked Javan, the first person she encountered. At least he would know where Cyrus was.

"Lady Sashia," he bowed. "Prince Cyrus is in Lady Marthi's apartment. You are a week early."

"I know, thank you!"

She rushed inside and up the stairs toward the living areas. Lang followed more slowly with Onia. When she turned the corner to Marthi's apartment, the door was open, and Tarin was playing with Varus on the floor. Her heart swelled when she saw her sons together. Varus had grown so much!

Sashia looked up and saw Cyrus and Marthi standing by the window. Locked in an embrace. They were kissing.

Her reaction was nothing like it would have been three months ago. She was shocked at her own response. She was *happy*.

"Mama!" cried Tarin as he saw her and rushed to tackle her knees.

Cyrus and Marthi turned, startled, and quickly stepped apart.

Sashia picked up Tarin and kissed him. "Hello, darling! You are getting so big!" she exclaimed and set him down.

"Sashia!" Cyrus stepped forward.

Sashia ran to him and threw her arms around him. "Oh, my love, how I have missed you!"

"Sashia, you are back! I am so glad! So glad!" he hugged her savagely, as if he was afraid she would evaporate if he didn't hold her together. "Let me explain—"

She laughed giddily. "I will let you if you feel you must, but not right now." She turned to Marthi who was looking both radiant and guilty at the same time. "You are pregnant, I can tell! You are absolutely glowing! I am so excited for you!" She crushed Marthi in a hug as well. "How far along? Two months?"

"Y-yes, I think so," stammered Marthi with reddened cheeks.

Lang entered the room with Onia and was immediately pounced on by Tarin. Sashia scooped up Varus so he wouldn't get stepped on or tripped over in the chaos. Cyrus threw Onia in the air and made her giggle and squeal, and the focus switched to the children.

Soon it was time for dinner, and the family gathered in Cyrus' rooms to eat together. Fashima joined them for the meal, having just finished her lessons. She exclaimed and hugged Onia and Sashia when she saw them.

"Lang, come and sit with us. Allow someone else to serve. You are as much a part of this family as anyone," Cyrus said graciously.

Lang's chin started to quiver, and he froze with a tray in his hands. Cyrus silently rose, took the tray from him, and set a cushion on the floor at his feet.

"Sit, my friend. With all we have been through, I am grateful to have someone I can trust to help look after my wife and children. Thank you."

Lang sat before his legs gave out beneath him. Onia immediately climbed into his lap.

Sashia's eyes were shining as she gazed at Cyrus, and he smiled back at her.

∞∞∞

Once the children were safely in bed, Cyrus retired with Sashia for the night. As soon as she set Varus down in his cradle, his arms were around her, and he was kissing her ardently. It wasn't until much later in the evening they were ready to do any talking.

The candle on the side table had burned out, and soft moonlight filtering through the window reflected in Cyrus' eyes. "You seem different. You seem happy now."

"I am happy. Very happy."

"What changed?"

"I realized I can choose to be joyful in spite of my circumstances. I can control how I feel through my actions. My emotions will eventually conform to my behavior, not the other way around. Does that make sense?"

"I—," he looked at her and gave a little laugh. "No, I don't understand, but whatever the reason, I am glad of it." He brushed a lock of tousled, black hair out of her face and twirled it around his finger. "I was so scared, Sashia."

"Why?"

"I was scared out of my mind you wouldn't love

me anymore, that you would hate me now."

"I could never hate you, Cyrus! Especially for something not of your making."

"People hate each other for things that are out of their control all the time. You could have hated me for not resenting Marthi."

"I suppose that's true." She propped herself up on one elbow and placed her other hand on his chest. "I love you, Cyrus. I will love you as long as I have breath. Longer, because one can live for a few moments without air."

Cyrus chuckled softly. "You have thrown me off balance since the first time I saw you. All that fire and passion for life and justice made more intense by being compacted into such a small and lovely frame. I feel like I can never love you enough."

"I have so much love it is overflowing, and I hardly know what to do with it. I cannot imagine being more loved than I am in this moment." Sashia rested her head on his shoulder. "So, now I will listen to anything you want to explain."

Cyrus drew her closer and held her tightly. "Are you sure you are equal to it? I want to tell you, but only if you want to hear it."

"Tell me."

Cyrus ran his fingers absently along her arm. "Something has happened that I didn't believe possible. At first, I loved Marthi because it was obligatory, and I had compassion for her scars and the suffering she has experienced. Then I came to appreciate her unselfish care for the boys, even though they are not her children. She is kind and patient, but sensible and firm. Before I knew it, I began to have warm and tender feelings for her. It is a quiet, gentle sort of affection, very different from what I feel for you, but I do care for her. Is that terrible?"

"Of course not! You should care for her. I am glad. I knew you would." Sashia craned her neck and kissed his cheek. "And loving her does not mean you love me any less. You don't have a finite amount of love requiring you to take from me in order to give to her."

"I am relieved to hear you say that." Cyrus closed his eyes. "But what about when I'm not with you? My presence is certainly finite."

"You don't stop loving me when you are with her, any more than you would if you went to the port or any other mission. The situation is not ideal, but we will survive it."

"And someday, maybe we can change the law so none of our children will be faced with such a dilemma."

"I hope so."

CHAPTER TWENTY-EIGHT

The Twentieth Year of the Reign of King Kalin of Berush

"You have a perfect baby boy!" Sashia exclaimed as she held up the infant for Marthi to see.

"My baby," whispered Marthi with tears in her eyes.

"Just a moment and you can hold him."

Sashia handed the baby off to a midwife as she prepared to help Marthi with the afterbirth. As soon as that was over, and she and the child were clean, Sashia carefully placed the precious bundle in Marthi's waiting arms.

Marthi gazed at the baby in wonder. "I thought it would never happen and look at him!" She could do nothing but stare.

"Try to nurse him. It's important to start right away, though your milk will not fully come in for a day or so."

"If it comes in."

"It will. Your breasts are heavy. I will call Cyrus."

Cyrus entered the room reverently and knelt beside Marthi. His eyes filled with warmth as he placed his hand gently on his son's head.

"What are you going to name him?" asked Sashia.

Marthi glanced at Cyrus, and he nodded at her. "His name is Ashin, after the first king of Berush."

"The king who united all the tribes," Sashia bobbed her head. "That is very apt. I will leave you alone now," she said, smiling, as she slipped quietly out the door.

Once outside, she pressed her hand to her heart and let out a long breath. She was overjoyed for Marthi, and she'd been completely focused on the delivery, but it still hurt to see her husband have a child with someone else. Would the pain lessen with time, or would it return whenever the child was in her presence?

Father had never viewed *her* with pain, Sashia reminded herself, or at least he'd never allowed her to see it. He was stern, but she realized, looking back, he'd treated her kindly and fairly. She would do the same. She would choose to love this child like her father had loved her.

CHAPTER TWENTY-NINE

The Twenty-first Year of the Reign of King Kalin of Berush

"Are you certain you're alright?" asked Cyrus for the fifth time.

"I am fine," Sashia assured him. "Marthi being able to nurse for me has made all the difference in the world." She sat up in bed and gestured toward Marthi who was feeding the tiny infant. "We were unsure if she would be able to breastfeed at all, but despite her scars, she has enough to care for little Fashima while weaning Ashin."

Marthi wore an expression of complete contentment. "I am happy to be able to help."

"Thank you, Marthi." Cyrus and Marthi shared a look of mutual gratitude. Then he turned back to Sashia. "Rest as much as you need to," he admonished.

"There is no reason for you to hover over me. It might actually do me good to get straight back to work."

Sashia had helped Madia establish travelling training schools for midwives as well as begin educating captains and select soldiers in basic wound treatment. Already they had seen an increase in infant and mother survival rates within the city.

"If that's what you want. Just try to ease back into it, not jump in all at once."

"Where is my niece?" cried Fashima the First as she bounded through the door.

Sashia sighed. With all her positive traits, Cyrus' sister continued to resist slowing down and learning to knock.

"Here she is, darling," smiled Marthi, holding out the tiny girl. "She has finished her breakfast and needs to be burped."

Fashima collected her namesake gingerly and laid her over her shoulder with the utmost care.

"How is your father?" asked Sashia softly.

Cyrus glanced at Fashima out of the corner of his eye and shook his head. "Not good. He's asleep most of the time, and he's not eating. Kassius says it is only a matter of days, maybe hours." He looked at Sashia. "He's been asking for you."

"I must go and see him."

Sashia threw off her covers and grabbed for her robe.

"You shouldn't tire yourself," worried Cyrus.

"It's around the corner and up a short flight of stairs. I can manage it." She stood on her tiptoes and gave him a quick kiss. On her way out the door, she paused and returned to grab her leather purse.

When she arrived at the king's chambers, she found Darius sitting next to his father while Yarin scribbled away at a desk. Cyrus had summoned Darius a week earlier at Kassius' recommendation.

"Sashia." The prince's voice was anguished. "Is there nothing to be done for him?"

"I am sorry, Darius. He has a cancer. Even the Magi have found nothing to combat this." Some success had been seen with special diets, but the king's cancer was too vigorous, and his tumors had spread.

"Leave us, son," rasped Kalin.

Darius rose reluctantly. "I will wait right outside." Yarin followed him out the door.

Sashia took his place at the bedside. The king looked pale, almost blue. His lips were dry and chapped. Sashia scanned the array of ointments and salves on the table nearby, found some coconut oil, and dabbed it gently around his mouth.

Kalin grasped her hand weakly. "You are well?"

"I am very well, thank you, my lord."

"You can stop that nonsense now." His breaths were few and far between, and his words were barely a whisper. Sashia had to lean close to hear him. "Where I am going, there are no lords."

Sashia wrapped her fingers around his in sympathy, but he waved her hand away.

"It's not I who needs you. It's Cyrus. When I am gone, he will need you more than ever."

"You have prepared Cyrus well. He will be a good king."

"Of course he will," snapped Kalin. Even in his weakened state, he still had the energy to be cranky. "But that boy," his voice softened, "that man, is fueled by love. Love for his country, his family, and . . . for you. He will need to draw strength from you when the demands of any one of those are too great. He has to be more important than all this other running around you are doing."

Normally Sashia's hackles would rise when the king spoke to her this way, but today all she felt was compassion. "You are right. Cyrus wants me to slow down too. I will limit myself to working inside the city."

Kalin smiled wanly. "You have now acknowledged me to be right a total of two times. Whoever would have thought we could find so much to agree on?"

"We agree on Cyrus." Sashia reached into her purse and brought out a worn and folded piece of paper. "I have something for you." She pressed it into the king's hand.

He brought his hand up to his chest and peered at the paper. "Is this what I think it is?"

"You are the one in need of safe passage now, my lord," Sashia said in a low voice as she blinked back tears.

"Right, give it to me now, when it is close to being invalidated," he scoffed lightheartedly. "You know it was not I who was trying to kill you?"

"I know."

"I am sorry I could not find out who it was."

"There have been no additional attempts since you sanctioned the Pasturas. I believe the danger has passed."

"Javan has been vetting new members of the household staff personally."

"Thank you."

Kalin closed his eyes. The conversation was tiring him.

"Do not become complacent. That is when enemies attack."

"We will get through any trouble that comes our way. Don't worry."

"Anyone going against you will find no greater adversary."

Kassius entered the room. "Glad to see you up, Lady Sashia." He turned to the king. "Here are some herbs for the pain, my lord."

"Bah."

"I will let you rest now." Sashia withdrew, and Darius reentered.

Cyrus was gone when she returned to her room, but Marthi and Gaia were there with the children. The family went about their routine, but the mood was somber and apprehensive.

∞∞∞

"Sashia, can you read this letter to me?" Marthi asked a few evenings later. "It just arrived and I cannot find Astra."

The maid normally read Marthi's correspondence to her. No matter how hard she tried, Marthi was unable to read without great difficulty. She had acquired a vast deal of knowledge since her arrival in the palace, and could even do simple calculations with numbers, but letters made absolutely no sense to her. She said they 'swam'.

"Surely. It's from your mother," Sashia announced as she broke the seal and perused the document.

She glanced through the open door to Gaia's room and observed the children playing contentedly before reading aloud Baria's news. It was full of anecdotes about Marthi's younger siblings, the marriage of one of her friends, and other simple but important life events. When she reached the end, she frowned slightly.

"There is a postscript in a different hand but no additional signature. Does your father usually add to your mother's letters?"

"No, Father never writes anything," declared Marthi, surprised, and she came to look over Sashia's shoulder, though she couldn't read the words.

"It says, 'Continue to write us your news. All is satisfactory'."

"How strange."

"Do you send letters back?"

"I do. I dictate to Astra, and she writes them for me."

"Do you have your other letters from your mother?"

"Yes, they are in a box in my room."

Marthi went and retrieved them. Sashia took the box from her and looked at the letters. She opened one after the other and found an unusual commonality. They all appeared to have a strip cut off the bottom. The papers were slightly shorter than the sheet Marthi had just received.

"What does it mean?" asked Marthi.

"I don't know," mused Sashia. She made a mental note to speak to Javan about it.

Darius burst into the room. "Kassius says to bring Fashima and come right away. He thinks this is the end!" He paused a moment to catch his breath. "I have to find Cyrus," he said and ran off again.

Fashima heard her name and peeped through the doorway in alarm. Sashia put down the box and reached for her hand. "Come, Fashima. Mind Gaia," she instructed the others as she wrapped her free arm in Marthi's and hurried toward the king's chambers.

Outside Kalin's door, Sashia stopped and looked at Fashima. The girl was crying and on the verge of hysteria.

"Fashima, listen to me. You have to be strong. You are a big girl. It's alright to cry but try to be calm. Breathe. That's it. Take another deep breath."

Fashima breathed in and out shakily.

"Your father will want to see you, even if he cannot speak right now. Ready?"

Sashia put her arm around Fashima, who would surpass her in height within the next year, and led her toward the king's bed with Marthi following. Kassius and Yarin stepped back to make room for them. At first, Sashia feared they were too late, as he did not appear to be breathing, but then his chest moved slightly, and he took a shallow breath.

"Is there anything you want to say, darling?" prompted Sashia.

Fashima timidly approached her father's figure. "Goodbye Father! I love you!" she cried. Then she turned away and covered her face with her hands.

Sashia gathered Fashima into her arms and tried to comfort her. Cyrus strode through the door with Darius right behind him, and the little crowd parted to let them pass.

Cyrus knelt beside the bed. "Father? Father, can you hear me? It's me, Cyrus."

The king's eyelids rose slowly like they were too heavy to lift. "Csssyrussss."

"Father!" Cyrus gripped Kalin's arm.

"I wish . . ."

"It's alright, Father, whatever it is."

Kalin's eyes closed again.

"Talk to him," encouraged Kassius. "I believe he can still hear you."

Sashia was glad Kassius was there because her throat was too tight to speak.

"You have a great legacy, Father. You have three children who love you, you have five grandchildren so far. Our people are safe. We have vanquished all our enemies. You can be at peace."

"Valanai."

"Yes, you will go to Mother," Cyrus choked out.

A sob escaped from Darius.

Kalin mumbled something that sounded like "Breakers."

"The Breakers have left the Crescent. They are far away. We don't have to worry about them."

Kalin mumbled again, and Cyrus tried to reassure him. "We will be on the lookout. Darius and Restus are patrolling the borders. I am increasing the number of soldiers we maintain. We won't be surprised by anyone again, don't worry, Father."

"Taaarin."

"You want to see Tarin?" Cyrus looked around for Sashia.

"I will fetch him," offered Marthi. Sashia's arms were still around Fashima.

It seemed like forever until she returned, but Sashia knew it was only a few moments. Tarin entered wide-eyed and open-mouthed. Marthi led him over to stand next to Cyrus.

"Here is Tarin." Cyrus placed his son's hand over the dying man's.

"I . . . am . . . proud."

"Thank you, Father."

Kalin exhaled a long, slow breath, shuddered slightly, and was still. Kassius bent over and checked his pulse. He waited several moments to be sure and shook his head. "He is gone."

Tarin turned and put his little arms around Cyrus' neck. Cyrus bowed his head, and Darius let out a cry of anguish. Fashima started to sob.

Cyrus set his shoulders and stood up, picking Tarin up at the same time. "Darius, come here." He held his son with one arm and reached out to his brother with the other. "Our family is one less, so each of us will have to be that much more. For each other, and for Berush. We have responsibilities, but we will get through this together."

Sashia put one arm around Cyrus and pulled Fashima into the circle. Marthi squeezed in on Sashia's other side.

"My lord," interjected Yarin softly, "we must make arrangements for a funeral and a confirmation ceremony as soon as possible."

"Yes, of course. Darius, will you stand vigil with Father?"

Darius nodded mutely.

"I should stay too," sobbed Fashima.

Cyrus wavered.

"She's old enough to stay if she wants to," encouraged Sashia. "I can stay with her."

"The only thing you are doing is going back to bed."

"But—"

"Marthi, help Sashia with the children and make sure she goes to sleep."

He put Tarin down, and Marthi took the boy's hand.

"Sashia," Marthi's other hand was extended toward her.

Sashia took it and found she was completely exhausted. She followed Marthi back to her room without further protest. Gaia and Lang had their hands full with the remaining four children, and by the time they had the room cleaned up and everyone in bed, Sashia was too tired to even think. It wasn't until she was lying down with her eyes closed that she realized the box of Marthi's letters was gone.

CHAPTER THIRTY

The First Year of the Reign of King Cyrus of Berush

"Lang, did anyone enter my room last night before I returned?"

"Varus and Ashin were extremely fussy, and I hardly remember anything else, but Lady Marthi came to get Tarin."

"Yes, anyone else?"

"Captain Topec stuck his head in looking for Cyrus. One of the kitchen staff came to collect the dinner trays. Oh, and Astra, Lady Marthi's maid."

"Thank you." Sashia frowned. Perhaps Astra simply noticed Marthi's box and put it away for her. She debated whether or not to pursue the problem of the letters or find Cyrus and see if he needed her help. He hadn't come to her room last night, so she hadn't spoken to him yet that morning.

Deciding the funeral and confirmation proceedings were the most urgent, she picked up baby Fashima and headed down the passage, leaving Lang to assist Gaia.

First, she stopped at Marthi's room. Cyrus was not there either.

"Marthi, if you can take Fashima and feed her, I will take Ashin for a while."

"I can watch them both if you have something you need to do."

"That would be wonderful. I am going to see if I can do anything to help Cyrus."

Sashia found her husband in the study with Yarin. Several scribes scribbled furiously on parchment.

"Here are copies of a few previous announcements to use as examples." Yarin took a box of papers off a shelf and set it on the table. Cyrus took one out and poured over it. Sashia walked around the room and stood next to him.

"Did you get enough sleep?" Cyrus asked her.

"I did, but you look like you've been up all night."

Cyrus' eyes had dark circles, and he looked haggard.

"There is much to do."

"You will do it better if you are rested. Can I help? Let me take over while you go lie down."

Cyrus sighed. "That might be best. We are working on sending out announcements to the tribal leaders and our allies across the peninsula. You can read these and decide on the best format to follow." He handed her the sheaf of papers. "The funeral will take place tonight. The body is being prepared. I can take a couple hours of rest."

"How are Darius and Fashima?"

"Fashima fell asleep on the floor, and I had her taken to her room. That Auger, Effan, is with Darius. He seems to have a steadying influence on him. I think he will be alright for now."

Sashia squeezed Cyrus' hand, and he threw her a grateful glance as he headed out the door.

When he was gone, Sashia perused the papers. "I like this one the best." She handed the scribes a copy of the announcement of the annunciation of King Solius. "What else needs to be done, Yarin?"

They worked steadily for the next three hours deciding every detail of the confirmation including the date, the food they would serve, seating arrangements, and what Cyrus would wear.

"We have to schedule it at least two months out to allow time for Verda and Rakhlain to send delegations," explained Yarin.

"Do they usually send representatives? There were none for either wedding."

"Other countries typically only attend marriages when the bride is one of their own. Kings are another matter."

"Foreign nobility must be seated higher than a Berushese tribal leader, but a chief sits higher than a mere delegate," added Javan, who had joined them halfway through the planning. "If King Ilytan of Artylia attends, do not seat him next to the Verdans. They are currently at odds over a trade agreement with Cerecia."

"Which of them has made an agreement with Cerecia?" asked Sashia, surprised.

"Verda. They share no border with Cerecia and do not view them as a threat."

"Perhaps if we seat a Mage between them a truce might be achieved?"

"It's not a good idea to risk offending an ally the day you assume the throne, but that's my opinion," Javan shrugged.

"We can leave it for Cyrus to decide."

Finally, they had accomplished as much as they could without Cyrus' input and everyone went their separate ways to prepare to attend the funeral. Sashia returned to her rooms to check on her children and then peeked into Cyrus' chamber. He had kept his word never to sleep there, but the curtains on his bed were closed for the first time. She pulled them back just enough to slip through and crawled over next to him.

He was not asleep. She leaned over and placed her hand against his cheek.

"How are you?"

Cyrus didn't answer immediately. When he did, his voice sounded far away. "I've known all my life this day would come. I should be ready for it, but I'm not."

"You are as ready as anyone could be. You are a good man, and you will be a wise king. But today— today all you need to be is a son who has lost his father. Let's take one day at a time."

Cyrus folded her into his arms and wept.

∞∞∞

King Kalin's funeral pyre was the largest Sashia had ever seen. Was there a warehouse in Sherish devoted to storing wood for such an event? That was the only solution for having so much readily available.

There was a sacred hill on the east side of the city with space devoted to the care of the dead, and the earth there was blackened with centuries of ashes. The entire population of Sherish followed the royal family up the hillside in a solemn procession.

As soon as the last rays of the sun disappeared over the western plains, the pyre was lit. Cyrus, Darius, and Fashima each threw a torch. The flames greedily licked up the oil poured on the dry kindling while Cyrus began the traditional chant.

346

Once the ceremony was well under way, Cyrus whispered to Sashia, "No one will mind if you slip away. You shouldn't be up all night."

"I'll sit down, but I'm staying with you," she insisted. "Gaia is watching the baby, and Marthi will have to leave soon to nurse her. One of us should be here."

Cyrus gave her a half-smile. "I don't want you to wear yourself out, but I appreciate it."

They stayed until nearly dawn. Most of the townspeople remained and mourned with the family to show their support. Many spoke of how meeting the king had impacted them and recited anecdotes from his public life.

Lang and Cyrus each cradled one child, and Tarin was curled up in Sashia's lap. Cyrus' sister was determined to stand as long as her brothers, but when it was time to go home, she stumbled forward in exhaustion, so Darius carried her. It would take the family a week to return to their normal schedule after this, but the respect for the dead and the show of strength and solidarity were important to the Berushese.

Somehow, they all made it back to the palace with red eyes and tired feet, but their heavy hearts were eased by the sound of chanting as the citizens of Sherish dispersed across the city.

∞∞∞

Sashia sat with Marthi the next afternoon while she nursed the two-week old infant. At first, Ashin had been jealous when his mother nursed the new baby and stood next to her and wailed, but Sashia brought Varus in with an array of toys to distract him, and they played contentedly on the floor.

"Are the others still sleeping?" asked Marthi.

"Tarin has not even moved. Onia woke up long enough to eat something and went back to sleep. Not even Lang is awake. Gaia is the only one up."

"How about Fashima? I am worried about her, poor girl, losing so many family members so young."

"She really seems to enjoy helping with the children. That should prevent her from withdrawing too much. She will probably sleep all day today."

"It was a good idea to name your daughter after her."

Sashia nodded, her eyes half-closed.

"How is Cyrus?" asked Marthi shyly.

"Tired. Scared. He slept in his own room again today so he wouldn't disturb the children." Sashia hesitated before continuing. "I think you should go to him tonight if he returns there. It's still too early for me after Fashima." It was difficult for her to be so direct about it, but she managed to keep her voice even.

Marthi's eyes widened. "You want me to seek him out? I've never done that."

"It's time. He needs to know you care for him too."

Sashia had carefully worked out a schedule corresponding to their monthly cycles where Cyrus saw Marthi about one week out of each month. Making the visits objective and predictable seemed the best way to avoid jealousy and made it easier on everyone, but though he cared for Marthi, Cyrus insisted he be with Sashia the majority of the time. Sashia preferred that also, even if it didn't seem fair, but nothing about the situation was fair.

Marthi had raised no objections to the arrangement and seemed to be perfectly content to give her affection to her son and the other children, but Sashia assumed she must wish for more. It was something they had never spoken about.

Anxiously Marthi fiddled with the corner of the baby's blanket. "But . . . what if he doesn't want me?"

"Just let him know you are available and follow his lead. I doubt he will send you away. He needs us right now."

"What about Ashin?"

"Astra can stay with him. Where is she, by the way?" Sashia was glad for a change of subject.

"She took a tray back to the kitchen."

"Did she bring your box of letters back? It was not in my room when I returned the other day."

"If she did, it will be in the bottom of the wardrobe. You may check if you like."

Sashia got up and opened the wardrobe. The box was there. She wasn't sure if she was surprised or not. She removed the top paper.

"Is my most recent letter there also?"

"Yes, it is." Sashia stared at it.

"Is something wrong?"

"The postscript has been removed." She replaced the letter and returned the box to the wardrobe.

"Do you think Astra did it?"

Sashia sat down in the chair and tapped her fingers against the wooden arms. Marthi waited silently for her to respond and didn't pester her. As she had been on many occasions over the last two years, she was grateful for Marthi's patience.

"I think I need to speak to Javan. Say nothing to Astra in the meantime."

Marthi's face displayed concern, but she nodded in agreement as Sashia left in search of the spymaster. Cyrus would appoint some of his own men to his council eventually, but for the sake of consistency, any changes would have to be gradual.

"Do you have a moment?"

Javan was sitting frowning at his desk. "Certainly, Lady Sashia." He waved at a chair.

Sashia took a seat across from him. "King Kalin said you were vetting every new member of the household."

"Yes."

"What do you know about Marthi's servant, Astra?"

Javan leaned back in his chair. "What do you know about her?"

"I asked you first." Sashia folded her arms.

Javan snorted. "She is the illegitimate daughter of Udin, chief of the Augers."

Sashia gaped at him. She could think of nothing to say, and Javan smirked at her.

"I have surprised you."

"Why haven't you told us this?"

"To what end? Will you throw her out because her father abused a servant?"

"No, of course not."

"That's why I chose to keep it to myself. My job is to gather information and sort out what is useful and not useful, what is dangerous and not dangerous."

"What else have you found out?"

Javan opened a drawer, took out a paper, and handed it to her. Sashia scanned it quickly, but didn't understand what she was reading. It seemed a random series of disconnected sentences.

"What is this?"

"Those are the postscripts added to the bottom of Lady Marthi's letters, both going and coming."

"You read her letters? Did the king know this? Does Cyrus?" Sashia was shocked at the disregard for privacy. "Do you read mine?" she asked sternly.

"As I said, it is my job to know everything that is going on. I have kept that job because I have the ability to keep my mouth shut."

He was also an expert at opening sealed letters. The seal on Marthi's letter had fooled her. "Why are you telling me now?"

"I don't know if Cyrus will keep me on once he has established his reign, but even if he does, he doesn't strike me as someone who is able to sit on information. He prefers to act immediately. You, on the other hand, are more of a plotter, despite your upbringing. Look at the way you manage your husband."

Sashia's indignation was rising, but she couldn't think of an appropriate response before Javan continued.

"You already have connections all over the west, you have an army of informants in the guise of midwives and healers you have trained, and you have connections to the Magi of Rakhlain. I think it would be beneficial for us to work together."

"You're just trying to ensure your position in the palace by making yourself necessary to me," Sashia scoffed.

"Good," nodded Javan. "Yes, that is exactly what I am doing."

Sashia deferred answering by rereading the paper he had given her. She could see why he hadn't passed it on. There was nothing incriminating in it. The writers had been extremely cautious in their word choice.

Position established.

Be patient. Good things will result.

Conditions are favorable. The wind is coming from the east.

"Is it a code of some kind?"

Javan shrugged. "If it is, they are using a pre-arranged set of words and meanings that will be tough to decipher without more information."

"May I have a copy of this list?"

"It would not be wise. Without knowledge of the writers' intentions, you should not assume any unnecessary danger. Memorize it."

Sashia studied the list until she had a fairly good grasp of its contents. Then she handed it back. "So, what do we do now?"

"I will continue to monitor the situation. It may just be Udin's way of taking care of Astra by securing her employment. He makes her feel special by adding little notes for her."

"You think that is all it is?"

"No, but there is no proof of anything else."

"Should we talk to Astra?"

He shook his head. "That would only result in a cessation of communication. If anything is going on, it is best they don't suspect we know about it."

"Could Udin be behind the attacks on my life?" The end result of all the machinations the last few years was that the Augers had a vast deal more land, taken from the Pasturas, and Udin had a grandson in the palace. When he couldn't get rid of one wife, he found a way to add another. Maybe he hadn't really even wanted to get rid of her, but merely to cause the Pasturas to lose favor. But how could he have manipulated events on that magnitude?

"He could have had people cause the rock slide. I don't believe Sorin was in on it. He took the path he normally took through the mountains. He was an irascible old cuss who stood for no argument. Udin could have hired Coria and had his own messenger killed to cover his tracks. Coria was a member of the Pastura tribe though. I have verified that. If Udin had a hold over her, I haven't discovered it."

Sashia was struck with a thought and stood up suddenly. "Thank you, Javan. Keep me apprised of any new developments."

She left before he could reply. Her feet flew across the palace and back to the family wing. When she reentered Marthi's room, Astra was there.

"Hoo, I am hungry! I just realized I have not eaten any lunch. Astra, can you go and fetch me something to eat?"

"Yes, my lady," Astra bowed politely.

When she was gone, Sashia turned to Marthi. "Marthi, after your injury, when you cared for your younger siblings, did you ever care for anyone else's children? An orphaned child, or the child of someone who was ill or on a journey?"

"Yes, there was a six month old whose mother had died. She hadn't been weaned, so I had to feed her goat milk."

"When was this?" Sashia asked urgently.

Marthi frowned in concentration. "About a year after my injury?"

It was what she'd guessed, but Sashia was still shocked she was right. Coria's daughter had not died. She'd been held hostage! From what she had heard from Javan, Udin may well have been the father. Sashia turned to walk out of the room. She needed to think.

"I thought you were hungry?" Marthi called after her.

"Not anymore. I will eat later."

353

The clues were beginning to come together. The only thing Sashia didn't know was how Udin could have talked Hanin into kidnapping Darius. There was no one left who could tell them. Except Effan!

Sashia ran toward Darius' room. The door was closed, so she banged on it with her fist. It hurt her hand, but she ignored it.

Darius opened the door groggily. "What is it?"

"I need to speak to Effan. Is he with you, or in the barracks?"

"The barracks are crowded today, so he and several of my men are sacked out in here. Effan!"

Effan came to the door blinking the sleep from his eyes.

"Effan, I know it may be hard for you to speak of it, but I need you to tell me everything you know about the events leading up to the meeting at the spring."

"Er, I went about my duties like I normally did," he said slowly.

"Which were?" Sashia looked up and down the corridor to make sure no one was within earshot.

"My clan was one of the few Auger clans that herded goats. Our clan and Faban's provided the meat for the entire tribe since the rest of the clans work in the mines. I grazed my animals each day and brought them back to the camp in the evening. We had a well, but the water was drying up. That's why we needed access to the spring, but Faban wouldn't allow it without payment."

"Was it your father's idea to meet Faban and Darius at the spring?"

"I thought so."

"Did he have any visitors before he sent the message to Darius?"

"His cousin Udin came. I think it was the day before."

Again, Sashia was stunned to discover her assumptions were correct. "Thank you, Effan. That's all I needed to know."

Now she had to find Cyrus. Despite what Javan said, she could keep nothing from her husband. She did not *manage* Cyrus. He would want to act, would most definitely act, but maybe that's what needed to happen. This had to end, and Cyrus would end it. She was sure of that.

∞ ∞ ∞

Cyrus sat with balled fists and a clenched jaw as Sashia related all she had learned. Marthi looked sick and held her hand to her stomach. Sashia had debated including Marthi in the initial telling, but they'd decided they would make important decisions together, and this concerned her as much as anyone.

"Are you sure?"

Sashia nodded sadly. She knew Cyrus didn't doubt her. He was just having as hard a time believing it as she had.

"Is it possible of your father?" Cyrus turned to Marthi.

"He is not a kind man. He and Hanin were cousins and visited frequently. I was to marry his oldest son before the lion attacked me. The child was there at the time you say. I cannot say it is impossible," she replied tearfully.

"What should we do?"

Cyrus' face was formidable. "I cannot depose another leader of the Augers. We only just stabilized the region. If I remove Udin, especially on circumstantial evidence, we will lose everything we have achieved the last two years."

"He was behind Faban's murder and Darius' kidnapping."

"We think. Even if Udin suggested it, Hanin carried it out. He was still culpable."

"But Udin cannot get away with this!"

Marthi was frowning.

"What are you thinking, Marthi?" Cyrus asked her.

"Astra has been with our family for as long as I can remember. Her mother was one of our servants, and I don't know who her father was, but I think it is impossible for her to have added anything to my letters."

"How can you be certain?"

"I cannot read well, but I can write my name. I dictate to Astra, she hands me the letter, I sign it, and I seal it myself. Usually I hand it to a guard to post. Astra doesn't deliver it. If she'd added something after my signature, I would have seen her."

"She could have included it in the body of the letter without you noticing."

"But my mother would have noticed it." She paused for a moment before continuing, "Except for the letter the other day, which you opened for me, I normally open the letters myself and hand them to Astra. She wouldn't be able to cut anything off without my seeing either," she added. "I am pretty sure there was nothing under my mother's signature when I opened them."

Everyone was silent as they considered the implications of Marthi's information.

"Then . . ." Sashia frowned.

"Who else had access to the letters?" Cyrus prompted.

"Javan! He admitted he read them!"

"He's Udin's contact, not Astra."

"Then why did he allow a letter to be delivered with the postscript intact?" The answer came to Sashia immediately. "To get us to trust him!"

"Or to cast suspicion on someone else. He has been misleading us this whole time. He must have been the one to tell Sorin to take the route along the mountains. He could also have murdered the messenger Coria met with."

"He was the one who investigated it!"

Cyrus stood up. "Udin will require careful handling, but Javan is another matter." He grabbed his sword and pulled it out of the scabbard, not bothering to strap it on. "Darius is in his room?"

"Yes. At least, he was right before I came to find you."

"Good. Is Gaia with the other children?"

"Yes, and I put Lang on guard outside." Sashia held Fashima, and Ashin was asleep in Marthi's arms.

"Stay here," Cyrus ordered and marched out the door.

The women sat without speaking. Tears streamed down Marthi's cheeks. Sashia knew she must feel terrible but didn't know how to comfort her. Sashia was still trying to figure out how Javan had escaped detection all these years. Kalin hadn't known about him. Even the Magi didn't know he was in on the plots against her. What better person to escape scrutiny than someone who was constantly scrutinizing others? That was why the string of postscripts made no sense. He hadn't shown her the real ones.

Marthi bent down and kissed her son's head and held him tighter. Sashia scooted over to her and put her arm around her.

"It's not your fault."

Marthi cried harder.

Cyrus' boots thumped down the passage. Sashia stood up.

"There is no blood on your sword," she observed when he returned.

"The sword was merely a precaution."

"You're not going to kill him?"

"Oh, we are going to kill him. Darius and Effan are taking him to Udin. They will execute Javan in front of him, and they are happy to do it."

"Both of them have suffered from Udin's scheming," murmured Sashia. "Did Javan admit his complicity?"

"In a manner of speaking. He tried to convince me he was too valuable to execute, but I offered him no clemency. He took too much of a gamble when he tried to fool you."

"Was there any proof of Udin's involvement?"

"I have men searching Javan's rooms, but I doubt we will find anything. Javan is too careful."

"He's too careful *not* to have something against Udin."

"Perhaps. Whether we find anything or not, we know where we are." Cyrus looked at Marthi who had her eyes closed and her head bowed. "Marthi," he called softly.

He knelt down next to her, and she met his eyes uncertainly. He put his hand under her elbow and steadied Ashin as he helped her to her feet.

"You are my wife, Marthi. Nothing is going to change that." He kissed her forehead and let her sob into his shoulder. Over her head, he looked at Sashia with pained resolve. She nodded back at him. Cyrus would be with Marthi that night. She wouldn't have to seek him out after all.

CHAPTER THIRTY-ONE

When Darius and Effan returned, Cyrus called a council.

"I should not attend," Marthi stated firmly despite her trembling hands.

"You must! Udin is the subject of our meeting, and your absence would be conspicuous," Cyrus insisted.

"That is exactly why I cannot go. Your advisors may not speak freely if I am there. My father arranged our marriage, and my fate is tied to his. I will be a distraction."

"Your fate is *not* tied to his. I keep my word. You are my wife, and that is the end of it."

"But she may be right, Cyrus, that she shouldn't sit with us in the council. If anything, she can be called as a witness," suggested Sashia.

Cyrus shook his head. "We must present a united front from the beginning. I want everyone to be clear where I stand." He turned to Marthi and put his hand on her shoulder. "Unless you would rather not hear things said against your father. I will understand if you decline for that reason."

Marthi nodded her head but was too agitated to speak. Ashin was asleep in Astra's arms. Marthi kissed his forehead, and Astra took him to Cyrus' room with Gaia and the rest of the children.

Silently, Marthi padded behind Sashia and Cyrus like one being led to the block. Cyrus glanced at her and took her hand as they paused outside the door of the study. When they entered, Darius, Effan, Restus, Topec, and Yarin were waiting for them. The room felt crowded with so many people, but the hall was under repair and unable to be used. A marble pillar had warped and cracked along the grain and needed to be replaced.

There was only one empty chair. Cyrus moved toward it, still holding Marthi's hand. Darius, who was sitting to the right of it, jumped up and took a place against the wall. Yarin started to rise also, but Sashia waved him down and stood behind Cyrus where she could put a hand on both his shoulder and Marthi's. Topec was already standing and pacing restlessly.

"By now, you are all acquainted with the facts as we know them," began Cyrus. "Javan may have given Sorin orders to ride along the mountain path that led to his death and a score of others. It was Sorin's normal route and wouldn't have seemed unusual to him. The snake may have been a coincidence.

"Javan killed Nerod, who had relayed orders to Lotus, with the explanation that Nerod was attempting to kill Sashia, but we have no evidence other than Javan's word and the fact Nerod held a dagger as he ran down the hallway. He may have been trying to escape from Javan.

"Javan arranged for Coria to be installed as a wet-nurse and then most likely killed her contact when we tracked him down rather than let him be interrogated. Then he attempted to ingratiate himself with Sashia and cast suspicion on Marthi's maid

Astra, but we discovered inconsistencies in his story leading us to the conclusion he had been Udin's contact, not the maid.

"Against Udin, we have only circumstantial evidence." Cyrus ticked off the points on his fingers. "He ensured the king was informed Sashia had been at the oasis. Someone had a hold over Coria. Possibly Udin kept her daughter as a hostage. He's reputed to be a less than ideal husband and the father of at least one illegitimate child, but we cannot take Javan's word about that. He went to visit Hanin before the events at Silver Spur, managed to be appointed chief of the Augers, and proposed the idea of a marriage alliance.

"That is all we have to go on. Darius, let us hear your report."

Darius cleared his throat and stood up straighter. At twenty-one years of age, he had grown quite handsome, but he didn't have the same presence as Cyrus. The beginnings of a beard covered his chin and jawline, and his uncombed hair stuck out in every direction giving him a wild appearance.

"Javan refused to speak the entire trip. I tried several methods to make him talk, but all I could get out of him was 'Sand soaks up blood, but it wears away the hardest rock'. When we arrived at Udin's camp, I gave him your message: 'This is the fate of all who commit treason'. Then I executed the spymaster in front of him, as directed."

"How did Udin react?" Cyrus asked.

"He gave me a cold, hard stare, but he kept his mouth shut. We rode away without incident."

Cyrus nodded thoughtfully. "So, now the question is what to do about Udin." He looked at his advisors for their input.

Topec crossed his arms. "It seems clear enough to

me Udin is behind it all. We cannot let this pass," he said sternly.

"Why would Javan have helped Udin? What was his motivation?" wondered Restus.

"Both of Javan's parents are dead, but his mother was Udin's half-sister," explained Yarin with a note of sadness.

He had worked with Javan for many years, and Sashia wondered what he was feeling.

"I would be happier than anyone to shift some of my father's guilt to Udin, but if he was the mastermind, why did he let Sashia go at the oasis?" asked Effan timidly. "He could easily have killed her there."

Sashia started to answer, but Darius spoke first. "Someone else at the oasis might have recognized her. Plus, there is nowhere convenient to hide a body. It would have been found, and questions would be asked."

"And I had Lang," added Sashia.

"Udin should suffer the same fate as Hanin. Though he was careful to commit no crimes with his own hand, conspiracy to commit murder or treason is punishable by death," Topec argued.

"In Hanin's case, Darius was held prisoner in his camp. There was irrefutable evidence against him. We have nothing solid to tie Udin to any of this," countered Cyrus.

"Perhaps Hanin's death has put fear into him," suggested Yarin. "Nothing has happened these last two years."

"Except he has a grandson in the palace," snorted Topec.

"Be careful, Topec. You are talking about my son," warned Cyrus with a hardness in his voice Sashia had never heard before.

"But my lord, Udin planned it all. He got what he wanted, and who knows how he will use the boy in the future."

"What exactly are you suggesting, Topec?"

"You won't like it, my lord, but I have to say it. You could send them both back. Divorce her and disown the boy. Eliminate his foothold in the royal family." Topec clenched his fists and braced himself for Cyrus's reply.

Marthi inhaled sharply through her nose and froze. Sashia felt her muscles tense, and she squeezed her shoulder. Everyone turned to Cyrus to see how he would respond.

"Out of respect for your faithful service, and since I know you speak out of loyalty to me, I am going to answer you once, and I expect never to have it brought up again," Cyrus said icily. "Doing what you suggest would affect not only Udin. It would be an insult to the entire Auger tribe, and they comprise nearly a quarter of our population. Even if circumstances were deliberately manipulated and lives lost to bring the marriage about, my word is immutable. Marthi will remain my wife, and my son is my son. Nothing will change that."

Marthi's shoulders relaxed slightly. Topec stared grimly at the floor.

Cyrus continued more softly, "I appreciate that you will speak honestly to me, regardless of the consequences to yourself. I hope you will continue to do so."

Topec raised his head. "Yes, my lord."

Everyone shifted their weight and let out a collective breath.

"What other options do we have?" prompted Cyrus.

No one offered any other suggestions.

"What if," mused Sashia aloud, "what if we send a representative to Udin's camp to keep an eye on him? We could call him an official liaison, or ambassador of sorts, from the palace to the Augers. Udin would know why he was really there and that he can no longer get anything by us."

Cyrus sat up. "Yes! And Darius' patrol can stop by frequently to check in. Would you be willing to take on the job, Restus?"

Sashia remembered Restus coming around the corner as Javan stood over Nerod's body. Javan's sword had been raised, and she realized he could have killed her and Lang and blamed it on Nerod if Restus hadn't arrived at that moment.

Restus stood and bowed formally. "I am more than willing, my lord, for Deppan's sake. I will cling to him like a leech." Restus grinned. "He will hate it."

"Excellent. We will tell him after the confirmation ceremony. I will also restore the Pastura's land. He won't like that either."

After briefly discussing who would replace Restus on the western border, the meeting adjourned. Yarin lingered after Darius and the other men had left.

"Yes, Yarin? What is it?"

"First, my lord, I would like to offer my apologies for not realizing what Javan was up to. All that time, he operated under my very nose, and I was unaware of the threat."

"He fooled us all, Yarin. You are not to blame."

"Thank you, my lord. Now that Kalin is gone, I must share with you something only the king is allowed to know."

Marthi stood up, and Sashia moved toward the door.

"Stay," directed Cyrus. "Whatever you have to say, my wives can hear," he stated firmly.

Yarin hesitated, then forged ahead. "My home is a designated safe-house for the Magi. They send and receive messages and visitors there, and I relay pertinent information to the king of Berush."

"You were the one who sent me the message about Coria!" Sashia gasped. She'd withheld the Magi's role from the king needlessly.

"At the request of the Mage who was staying with me at the time, yes. After the rock slide, the Magi were given more leeway for communication. The first I learned about that incident was from you, Lady Sashia. The Mage who spoke to you at the gate overstepped his authority by revealing himself."

"So my father knew about the safe house?"

"He did. He wrote the writ for Beyorn and Dorthi at my request, since they were frequent travelers between here and Rakhlain and carried much of our correspondence. I must now ask you for another, my lord, in your name, for our next courier."

Cyrus laughed and reached for Sashia's hand. "How can I refuse when I gained so much from the last one? Have it drawn up, and I will sign it."

∞∞∞

Outside Sashia's door a few moments later, Cyrus turned to Marthi. "I will join you in your room in a moment."

She nodded to him with a shy blush, but before she went, she gave Sashia a huge hug. "Thank you for supporting me and standing up for me. And for everything else. You are more than a friend to me. I love you like a sister."

Sashia hugged her back, speechless, and Marthi went to retrieve Ashin while wiping the tears from her eyes. Both Sashia and Cyrus gazed after her when she left.

"Udin didn't get everything he wanted," remarked Cyrus. "He wanted me to marry Iesha. Thanks to you, we have Marthi instead."

Sashia turned to Cyrus and saw his hazel eyes full of emotion. He drew her into an embrace, and she leaned her head against his chest. When at last she looked up at him, he bent down and kissed her. It was not an amorous kiss, but one so full of love she felt like she was dissolving into him. It made her dizzy.

Finally, he let her go, while looking at her longingly. "You are both dear to me, in different ways, and I hate to leave you alone tonight."

"I will be alright, Cyrus," she whispered. She could live on that kiss for days. "Marthi needs you more right now."

"I want you both to be safe and happy, but I love you, Sashia, with all my heart. I don't understand how. Perhaps I have grown more than one heart, but even if I had two, I would love you with both of them, and still love Marthi and the children."

"I know." And she really did know. He loved her, and she was content. More than content. She felt immeasurable joy. "I love you, too."

∞∞∞∞

"You seem at peace, daughter," observed Haban when they arrived at the palace for the confirmation. Rolind was representing the Granum tribe, as all the tribal chieftains had a part in the formal ceremony, but many others flocked to the capital to be a part of the momentous event. Haban and Yania, as in-laws to the king, were guests of honor.

"I have learned the lesson you set for me, to love greatly and be loved in return." Sashia grinned as

Cyrus put his arm around her. "And your example helped me to understand it is something I choose as much as something I feel."

Udin and Baria arrived shortly after Sashia's parents, and the men followed Cyrus to the hall where the final preparations for the celebration were being made. Sashia was glad to see the back of the Auger chieftain. Darius and Restus made their presence felt on either side of him. Sashia put Udin from her mind knowing the situation was in good hands.

"Where are my grandchildren?" demanded Yania.

Marthi and Sashia led the way to Cyrus' apartment which now looked more like a nursery.

Rather than meet with their mothers privately in separate rooms, Sashia and Marthi took everyone to play in the pool in the family courtyard. Sashia felt it was important for both women to see Marthi was accepted and included, especially after the discovery of Udin's guilt. Not everyone knew the details, but Baria would know more than most.

Part of the river was diverted through a small channel that spilled into the pool and ran out the other side, keeping the water fresh. Sashia sat in the shade of an awning next to her mother who rocked little Fashima, while Varus napped on a pillow.

"So," began Yania in a sarcastic tone, "King Kalin's wife was referred to as 'Queen'. Will you and Marthi share the same title?"

Sashia's eyes wandered to where Marthi was splashing in the shallow end of the pool with Ashin and Baria. The pleasant sound of running water gave a measure of privacy to their conversation. "Yes. Yes, we will."

"You share everything else, so I guess that's no surprise."

Sashia ignored her mother's caustic remark. She was no longer riled by her negativity. Growing up, she'd felt like nothing she did was good enough, but she knew better now.

Tarin slipped on the edge of the pool and hit his knee. Sashia stood up to check on him, but Marthi was closer and he ran to her instead. He stood at the edge of the pool and pointed to his injury. Marthi waded over, bent down and kissed his knee, and then let him jump to her. She hugged him and soothed the scrape with the cool water.

Sashia lowered herself slowly back into her chair.

"That must bother you," hissed Mother.

"This is the way we want it to be," replied Sashia softly. "This is the way it has to be to work."

"But he is *your* son!"

"And I should be upset someone loves my son other than his natural parents?" she asked pointedly.

Mother looked abashed and settled into her chair, staring vacantly. "Your natural father was dead."

"But Father still chose to treat me as his own, for which I am grateful. Marthi treats all the children as if they were hers. Few people can do that.

"We entered into the marriage for political reasons, but she has become invaluable to me. It's not a situation I would've wished for, but it has turned out far better than I could've imagined. I am free to use my healing skills and pass them on to others without worrying about leaving the children for a day. You know the trouble I had with wet-nurses. I have plenty of time left in my life for regrets, but I have none yet."

Sashia didn't add that Marthi's cycle was as predictable as the moon, and hers was as flighty as a butterfly. Between that and Marthi's apparent ability to nurse indefinitely, Sashia expected to be able to

368

plan their pregnancies at alternate intervals. She smiled as she recalled Cyrus' protest that he ought to have some say in the matter. She had smiled then, too. There was a little room for negotiation, but he had put her in charge of the daily routine, after all.

Mother looked at her curiously. "Well, as long as you are happy."

"I am happy, Mother," declared Sashia with utter sincerity. "I have a loving husband, a good friend and partner in Marthi, wonderful children, and opportunities to share my knowledge, but it's not those things alone that make me happy. It is my choice."

"You mean you're making the best of it."

"No, I mean I am the one who decides whether I'm happy or not. Some days are easier than others. Some days, I may decide to be sad, and that's alright. Today I am determined to be happy, and so I shall be."

"Watch me, Mama!" called Tarin as Marthi tossed him into the air, and he entered the water with a tremendous splash. "Woo!" he raised his arms in triumph when he surfaced.

Onia squealed as the water splashed her. Marthi grinned, Baria clapped, Yania chuckled, and happiness bubbled up in Sashia's heart without any effort at all.

A WORD FROM DR. TATE-CASANOVA

Peripartum Depression has been called many things throughout history: malaise (as in *A Crack in the Rock*), hysteria, 'baby blues,' post-natal depression, and postpartum depression. Sashia's pregnancy with Varus was difficult, and she did not bond well with him after delivery. Her symptoms were fatigue, frustration, anxiety, being in a trance, loss of interest in normal activities, feeling the need to escape, brain fog, lack of appetite, feeling empty and emotionless, and unreasonable sadness.

Her mother tells her that many women experience these things after childbirth. Women commonly experience some symptoms during the adjustment after delivery. This is called baby blues because it requires no medical or psychological intervention. Sashia suffered from postpartum depression not baby blues.

Peripartum depression is characterized in the Diagnostic and Statistical Manual of Mental Disorders (DSM-5) as a major depressive disorder with onset during pregnancy and/or up to four weeks after delivery. Symptoms associated with this disorder may onset up to six months postpartum, therefore, any woman presenting with symptoms within twelve months may receive this diagnosis. Although the actual symptoms, severity, and duration vary woman to woman, the criteria for this diagnosis DSM-5 (APA, 2013) are:

1.   Presence of five of the following symptoms for at least two weeks for most of nearly every day: depressed mood, diminished interest or pleasure in most activities, insomnia or hypersomnia, slowing in thoughts and physical movements, fatigue, feelings of worthlessness or excessive/inappropriate guilt, brain fog, suicidal ideation.

2.   Symptoms must cause significant distress or dysfunction in social, occupational, and other areas of life.

3.   Symptoms are not related or caused by a substance or medical condition and not better explained by another disorder.

4.   With the peripartum onset, depression and mood changes happen during pregnancy or in the four weeks after delivery.

Currently, women are screened for these indicators at well-baby checkups to bring awareness to peripartum depression as well as help those that have symptoms. Some women work their way through the symptoms on their own or with their support systems. Others may need medication and therapy to overcome this challenge.

If you suspect someone is suffering from peripartum depression, please encourage them to seek help from their primary care doctor, obstetrician/gynecologist (OBGYN), midwife, therapist, family, and trusted friends. Check to see if she has a support network to help manage her responsibilities as she gets well. Here are a few resources to point her to:

www.postpartum.net

www.postpartumstress.com

Postpartum support international: 1-800-944-4773 or text 503-894-9453 (English) or 971-420-0294 (Español)

SAMHSA National Helpline 1-800-662-4357

APPENDIX OF BERUSHESE MILITARY TERMINOLOGY

Units in the Berushese military are defined primarily by function rather than size. Here are the most commonly used terms:

Company—twenty or more soldiers with one captain

Patrol—a company assigned to a particular geographic region

Squad—a group of less than twenty soldiers with a specific mission objective

Army—two or more companies under command of a general

DISCUSSION QUESTIONS

1.   Kari, Baria, Marthi, and Sashia were all involved in polygamous relationships for different reasons. What were they? Are these arguments valid in the modern world?

2.   International Law states equality in marriage is a human right. Is it possible to have equality in a polygamous relationship?

3.   How does Sashia deal with stressful situations?

4.   How did Sashia's relationship with her mother improve and why?

5.   In what ways was Sashia's father, Haban, an example to her?

6.   How do you think the title relates to the story?

7.   Do you agree happiness is a choice? Would that mindset work for everyone or in every situation?

8.   Who was your favorite character and why?

ABOUT THE AUTHOR

Ever since I was a little girl, I have loved to read. One of the first books I remember reading was a Wonder Book version of *Cinderella*. It was in the reading station in my kindergarten class, and I loved the illustrations. I would pick that book out every time, so my teacher finally removed it from the shelf to force me to expand my horizons. Now I have my own copy.

Another book that influenced me very early on was Richard Scarry's *Busy, Busy World*. It told a story of two creative painters who painted a mural of a large sun inside someone's house. I thought the idea was genius, so I drew a large sunshine on my wall with crayon. It was scrubbed off, but I continued to have a desire to express myself artistically.

In middle school, I enjoyed writing, and my English teacher told me I would write a book someday. I still loved to read, sometimes reading late into the night. When I was not reading, I was making up stories in my head for my own amusement, but I never wrote them down. I was more interested in drawing and painting than writing. I have since painted numerous works of art, including some very large outdoor murals.

Over the years, I have had a lot of trouble with insomnia. I had heard that if you write down your ideas, it will help you to be able to go to sleep. That didn't help, but I did end up writing some complete novels. Finally, I was diagnosed with narcolepsy, and understanding my sleep patterns, along with scheduling at least one nap during the day, has greatly improved my quality of life.

The line between dreaming and wakefulness for me is sometimes blurred, and some of my ideas come straight from my dreams. Others are worked out while I'm lying in bed unable to sleep. It was fun to type them out, and I am planning to continue writing. I hope you enjoy my stories and characters as much as I do.

Visit me online at facebook.com/ambergabrielauthor

Made in the USA
Columbia, SC
15 November 2020